Mor

Charlotte Smith

Contents

Volume 1

Chapter I
Chapter II
Chapter III
Chapter IV
Chapter V
Chapter VI
Chapter VII
Chapter VIII
Chapter IX
Chapter X
Chapter XI
Chapter XII

Volume 2

Chapter XIII
Chapter XIV
Chapter XV
Chapter XVI
Chapter XVII
Chapter XVIII
Chapter XIX
Chapter XX
Chapter XXI
Chapter XXII
Chapter XXIII
Chapter XXIV

Volume 3

Chapter XXV
Chapter XXVI
Chapter XXVII
Chapter XXVIII
Chapter XXIX
Chapter XXX
Chapter XXXI
Chapter XXXII
Chapter XXXIII
Chapter XXXIV
Chapter XXXV
Chapter XXXVI
Chapter XXXVII
Chapter XXXVIII

Charlotte Turner Smith (4 May 1749 – 28 October 1806) was an English Romantic poet and novelist. She initiated a revival of the English sonnet, helped establish the conventions of Gothic fiction, and wrote political novels of sensibility. A successful writer, she published ten novels, three books of poetry, four children's books, and other assorted works, over the course of her career. She saw herself as a poet first and foremost, poetry at that period being considered the most exalted form of literature. Scholars now credit her with transforming the sonnet into an expression of woeful sentiment. During adulthood, Charlotte Smith eventually left husband Benjamin Smith and began writing to support their children. Smith's struggle to provide for her children and her frustrated attempts to gain legal protection as a woman provided themes for her poetry and novels; she included portraits of herself and her family in her novels as well as details about her life in her prefaces. Her early novels are exercises in aesthetic development, particularly of the Gothic and sentimentality. "The theme of her many sentimental and didactic novels was that of a badly married wife helped by a thoughtful sensible lover" (Smith's entry in British Authors Before 1800: A Biographical Dictionary Ed. Stanley Kunitz and Howard Haycraft. New York: H.W. Wilson, 1952. pg. 478.) Her later novels, including The Old Manor House, often considered her best, supported the ideals of the French Revolution. After 1798, however, Smith's popularity waned and by 1803 she was destitute and ill—she could barely hold a pen, and sold her books to pay off her debts. In 1806, Smith died. Largely forgotten by the middle of the 19th century, her works have now been republished and she is recognized as an important Romantic writer.

Montalbert

Volume 1

Chapter I

IN one of those villages, immediately under the ridge of chalky hills, called the South Downs; where the soil changing suddenly to a strong clay, renders the country deep, and the roads bad; there dwelt, a few years since, the rector of a neighbouring parish, of the name of Lessington. In the village where he lived he was only the curate; choosing his residence there, because the house was larger and more commodious, than that which belonged to his own living three miles distant. His family consisted of a wife, two sons, and four daughters.

One of the sons had a fellowship at Oxford; the other, was a younger partner in a respectable tradesman's house in London.

The daughters were reckoned handsome; the two eldest had been for some years the toasts at the convivial meetings in the next market towns; the third was now a candidate for an equal share of rustic admiration, and her claims were generally allowed; but the youngest, who was about eighteen, when this narrative commences, though she was still considered as a child by her sisters, and treated as such by her mother; was thought by some of the few persons who happened to see her, to be much the handsomest of the four, though her beauty was of a very different character from that of her sisters.

Perhaps in these days of refinement, the imagination might be in some degree assisted, by the romantic singularity of her name; she was called Rosalie at the request of a lady of the Catholic religion, the wife of a man of very large fortune, who sometimes inhabited an old family seat, about three miles farther from the hills: Mrs. Lessington had been for some years her most intimate friend, and accepted with pleasure her offer of answering for, and giving her name, to the youngest of her girls. Mrs. Vyvian, the daughter of an illustrious Catholic family, being born at Naples, had received the name of the female saint so highly venerated in the two Sicilies; and before her marriage, had lived a good deal alone with an infirm father at Holmwood House, which having descended to her mother from noble ancestors, became hers, and was part of the great fortune she brought to Mr. Vyvian.

During the solitary years when she attended the couch of a parent, the victim of complicated diseases, the society of Mrs. Lessington had been her greatest consolation. It continued so till her marriage—a marriage which she was compelled to consent to, by her father's peremptory commands. Mrs. Vyvian afterwards passed some years on the continent with her husband, and returned to England mother of three children, a son and two daughters. And whenever this family inhabited the old mansion-house of Holmwood, Rosalie passed all her time with them. When young Vyvian was about thirteen, his sisters twelve and eleven, the young ladies were so much attached to their companion, that Mrs. Vyvian, to indulge them, took her with them to London, and afterwards to their estate in the North. Young Vyvian, the only son of the family, being sent abroad, Rosalie remained with his mother and sisters above two years, making only short visits at home. At the end of that period, Mr. Vyvian thought proper to have his daughters introduced into the world, and in a stile of life to which Rosalie could have no pretensions; she therefore returned to the parsonage, and though she could not but be sensible of the great change in her situation; her good sense, and the peculiar mildness of her disposition, enabled her, if not to conquer her regret, at least so far to conceal it, that though generally pensive, she was neither sullen nor melancholy, and entered with placid resignation into a way of life, so different from that to which she had (she now thought unfortunately) been accustomed.—Her mother, who probably remembered that she had been sensible of something like the same uneasy sensation when she bade adieu to the society of her friend, then Miss Montalbert, to marry Mr. Lessington, seemed to pity, though she forbore to notice, the dejection which was occasionally visible in her youngest daughter, in despite of her endeavours to hide it. As to her father, he treated her as he did the rest, with general kindness, but no marked affection. Her sisters were not unkind to her so long as she affected no superiority, but seemed better pleased to be considered as too young to be admitted of their parties, than to make one, where she knew she should find no enjoyment, and they were on their parts content to leave out, as long as they could, a person who would be at least a formidable competitor for the prize of beauty. The eldest was courted by a gentleman farmer of considerable property in the county, the second by an attorney in a neighbouring town, and as these lovers were accepted, parties of pleasure were continually made for the Miss Lessingtons. Sometimes to the sea-coast, or to races or cricket matches; Mr. Lessington attended his daughters on these expeditions, till the eldest was married. The care of Miss Catharine and Miss Maria, was then left to her, and the Vicar of Mayfield returned to the duties of his parishes, and his farm.

    On these occasions, Mrs. Lessington and her youngest daughter being left alone, their conversation sometimes turned on the family of Vyvian. It was a subject of which Rosalie was never weary, though it was not always that her mother would indulge her with talking upon it. Rosalie was tenderly and gratefully attached to Mrs. Vyvian, even more than to her young friends; and frequently mentioned to her mother, how much she had been hurt at remarking, during the latter part of her stay in the family, that this amiable and excellent woman was extremely unhappy. One day when they were sitting at work together, this conversation was renewed—"You hear nothing, Madam, (said Rosalie to her mother), of our neighbours at Holmwood Park, being to come down soon."—"Nothing (replied her mother, coldly); I suppose, from what Mr. Allingham said, (Mr. Allingham was the Catholic priest of the neighbouring town), that we shall not see them here this year."—Rosalie sighed.—"He told me (added Mrs. Lessington), that Mrs. Vyvian was so much indisposed when he saw her in town, that the physicians talked of ordering her to Cheltenham; it is more than two months since I have had a letter from her."—Rosalie sighed again.—"It is her mind (said she), that preys upon her frame; and will, I am afraid, destroy her."

    "I hope not (replied Mrs. Lessington), for I think her spirits have been always much the same since I knew her. Perhaps they are not mended by Mr. Vyvian's having renounced his religion, and by having her children brought up Protestants, contrary to his promise, when he himself changed; besides, you know he is a harsh and hasty man, positive, violent, and ill-natured enough to make a woman, like Mrs. Vyvian, unhappy, if there is no *other* cause."

    "Ah! that *other* (said Rosalie), I have heard a great deal about it."

    "About what?" cried Mrs. Lessington, in a tone of surprise.

    "About the—the—the lover, (replied Rosalie, blushing.) That Mrs. Vyvian was so much attached to before she was married to Mr. Vyvian."

    "I don't know (said her mother, colouring as if by sympathy), who could tell you, child, of any such foolish story."

"Nay, dear Madam, but was it not so?"

"Was it not, how? *I* really know nothing about it, and yet I believe nobody saw so much of my friend Mrs. Vyvian, as I did at that time; for though it was long after I married, I used to be almost as much with her as when we were both single."

"The gentleman is still living, Madam," said Rosalie.

"I again assure you Rose, (replied her mother, peevishly), that I know nothing of—of *any* gentleman. But I think I heard your father come into his study—Do child ask him for the key of the closet above."

Rosalie obeyed; but she well knew her father was not in his study, and saw that her mother only sent her to seek him, that she might escape from conversation, which for some reason or other, she was strangely unwilling to continue. This was not the first time Rosalie had remarked, that her mother solicitously avoided recounting any circumstance that used to happen in her girlish days, at those periods when she was connected with the family of Montalbert: and if ever she unconsciously began to speak of Miss Montalbert, now Mrs. Vyvian, she either stopped as soon as she recollected herself, and changed the conversation, or spoke in a manner particularly guarded, and only of trifling occurrences.

"What can be my mother's reason? (said Rosalie, musing to herself as she went to walk in their little garden), there is some mystery certainly; surely the marriage with the man Mrs. Vyvian was so attached to, could not have been broken off on *her* account?—Impossible! for though my mother, I believe, has been a very handsome woman, she certainly never could be compared to her friend; who even now, in ill health, and half heart-broken, as she is, is much more beautiful than either of her daughters."

Rosalie sighing when she thought of Mrs. Vyvian's illness, and regretting that she did not this year come into the country, felt all the cold and blank regret, which departed pleasure leaves. She wished now, that she had passed less time in the Vyvian family, where she had been accustomed to the conversation of Mrs. Vyvian, of which she was particularly fond; and to a manner of life, very different from that which she was now in—still more different, from what it was probable she would be expected to enter into, when her two elder sisters were both married: her father having lately said, half laughingly, and as if he supposed it would please her, that she should then go out with Maria; appear at assemblies, and try to get a husband too; for he wanted to get his girls off his hands as fast as he could.

Rosalie felt that she had an invincible aversion to this plan of dressing and going out in hopes of getting, as her father termed it, an husband. She was convinced, that to be addressed by such men as the husband of her eldest sister, or the man to whom the second was soon to be married, would render her completely miserable; for it seemed but too probable, that her father would not allow her a negative.

Youth, however, dwells not long on remote possibilities—But though no acute uneasiness assailed her, the languor and dejection of Rosalie increased as the autumn came on; solitude was infinitely preferable to the society, such as was at present within her reach; but seclusion so perfect as that she was now condemned to, depressed her spirits. In every other period of her being at home, at this season of the year, her elder brother had been there also, who being very partial to her, delighted to instruct her; but now this dear brother was gone into the North with one of his college friends, and was to be at home only for a few days before his return to Oxford. She thought every body was gone to the North, for the Vyvian family were perhaps there by this time, if Mrs. Vyvian's health allowed her to leave Cheltenham—and never had she felt so dejected and forlorn. The hill which arose immediately behind the vicarage house, afforded a view, even half way up, of a great extent of country, and Holmwood Park, the old family seat of Mr. Vyvian, though at near three miles distance, seemed to be within five minutes walk. Rosalie had now a melancholy pleasure, in viewing it from the high grounds, as the setting sun blazed on the western windows, while the characters of the inhabitants were forcibly recalled to her mind.

Mr. Vyvian, a man of very extensive possessions, and the head of an ancient Catholic family, had been rather received as an husband by Miss Montalbert, because her father commanded her to receive him, than for any other reason; for so far were they from having any sympathy, that their religion was the only thing in which they agreed, and even that tie of union between them did not long exist; for soon after the death of his wife's father, he renounced the church of Rome, and going through all ceremonies of reconciliation to that of England, entitled himself to represent a borough that belonged to him, and became a member of parliament. From that time, the tutors that had been entrusted with the education of his son, were removed; his daughters, contrary to the promise he had at first made to his wife, were no longer suffered to go to mass, or to be instructed by the old priest, who had for a great number of years resided in their mother's house. And Mrs. Vyvian, who was strongly attached to the religion of her ancestors, was from that period a solitary and insolated being in the midst of her family.

Mr. Vyvian was one of those men, who, naturally haughty and tyrannical, had never known, because he never would endure, the least contradiction. His temper resembled that of those reasonable beings one sometimes sees among the common people, who not unfrequently beat their children till they make them cry; and then beat them for crying. Just so he contrived to do exactly what he knew would make his wife completely miserable, and then quarrelled with her because she could not (though she endeavoured to do so most sincerely), always conceal her wretchedness. Till lately, she had found the estrangement of her daughters, who too much resembled their father, compensated in a great measure by the attentive gratitude of Rosalie, who used to pass much of her time at Holmwood, while Mrs. Vyvian was there alone, and her family remained in London. But lately she appeared to have lost all pleasure, even in visiting this favourite seat; and though when she did write to Mrs. Lessington, or to Rosalie, her letters expressed all her former regard, yet these letters became every day more rare; at length she hardly ever wrote to Rosalie; an air of languor and disquiet pervaded those parts of the letters addressed to her mother, that Rosalie sometimes saw; for it now and then happened, that Mrs. Lessington received letters which her daughter knew to be from Mrs. Vyvian, the contents of which she never disclosed, and did not seem pleased to be questioned upon them.—These Rosalie concluded were filled with the murmurs of an oppressed heart, that found a melancholy indulgence in pouring its hopeless sorrows into the bosom of an old and faithful friend; though she herself had never heard one repining sentence.

The venerable priest, now the only inhabitant, except servants of the solitary mansion of Holmwood, had been accustomed to walk over now and then to Barlton-Brook (the name of the parish where the Lessington family resided); and Rosalie, who honoured his character, and knew how highly Mrs. Vyvian esteemed him, was never happier than when she was allowed to make his tea for him, or to walk with him part of the way home. During the present summer, however, these visits had become less frequent, and at length entirely ceased; a terrible deprivation to Rosalie, though none of the rest of the family seemed conscious that it had happened. Rosalie at length remarked it to her mother, who answered drily, that Mr. Hayward was probably ill. "May I not walk over some day to Holmwood, Mamma, and see how he does?"

"I do not know when I can spare you, my dear," was the reply and the conversation dropped.

Another, and another week passed, and Mr. Hayward did not appear. Rosalie then enquired news of him, of one of those itinerant fishmongers who travel round the country, and who constantly carried his wares to Holmwood. The man assured her that he had that day seen Mr. Hayward in good health. Rosalie soon afterwards discovered, but with extreme vexation, that her old friend forbore to visit her, because it had been hinted to him, that the suspicion of his influencing her on religious subjects was likely to be very injurious to her future prospects in the world: Mr. Grierson, who had married her elder sister, and Mr. Blagham, the intended husband of the second, having declared their apprehensions of her becoming a Papist; in which opinion two young men who had very much admired her, also agreed. The sisters of one of them protesting that *she was sure Miss Rose Lessington was disposed to that religion, which made her give into such mopish ways, and always to affect solitude, like nuns, and such sort of people.* Thus deprived of the innocent pleasure of conversing with a man, who from her infancy she had considered almost as a second father; a cypher at home; and rather suffered as one of the family, than seeming to make a part of it, necessary to the happiness of the rest, Rosalie had no other resource than in her own mind against the unvarying medium of life. Her mother, though not more ignorant than the generality of women in middling life, had received no better education than a country boarding school afforded, which five and thirty years ago were much less celebrated for the *accomplishments* they communicated, than they are at present. Since that period, she had studied the utile, rather than the dulci. Having before her marriage lived very much in the family of Montalbert, though by no means in the stile of an humble companion (for she had a small independent fortune), she had accustomed herself to undertake many little domestic duties for the friend she loved, and after her marriage, she had a family, which kept her constantly occupied; so that never having had her curiosity raised in regard to books, and never having been accustomed to read, she had now no relish even for books of amusement; and wondered at the eagerness she sometimes heard her acquaintance express for them. It may easily be believed, that thus disposed, she had no collection of books likely to amuse her daughter; who had long since exhausted all the information or entertainment afforded, by an odd volume of the Tatler—Robinson Crusoe—Nelson's Feasts and Fasts—Harvey's Meditations — a volume of Echard's Gazetteer—Mrs. Glass's Cookery—and Every Lady her own Housekeeper.

The library of Mr. Lessington, though more extensive and occupying a room dignified with the name of a study, was not better adapted to beguile the solitary hours of a very young woman. It consisted solely of sermons—Polemic's—such publications as related to Questions on Infant Baptism, and Elaborate Defences of the Thirty-nine Articles—Clarendon's History—Rapin, and bad Translations of Mezerai and Froissart—an old History of Rome, in black letter—Josephus—Thomas à Kempis—Elucidations of difficult Parts of Scripture—and Treatises on the Nature of the Soul. Among all these it was the history only that could attract Rosalie; and during this solitary summer, she became a tolerable historian: though she did not find it either contributed to enlarge her philanthropy, or furnish her with rules for the conduct of her life; since she flattered herself, that beings so dishonest and despicable as modern history represents, are found only in those elevated regions of human existence where it was never likely to be her lot to move.

During her frequent visits to the family of Vyvian, where that language was generally spoken, Rosalie had learned to speak French fluently; could read well, and speak a little Italian, which Mr. Hayward had taken great pleasure in teaching her. The little acquirements were, she knew not for what reason, more the objects of her sisters' envy than any other of the advantages her being with the Miss Vyvians might have given her over them. She saw with surprise and concern, that though her sisters were as little, as she now was herself, in company where to speak foreign languages could be of the slightest advantage, yet that *her* being qualified to do so, vexed and humbled them. She therefore concealed what indeed there was now little merit, and less difficulty in concealing; and having no books to read in either language, and no longer any opportunity of conversing with Mr. Hayward, she felt with infinite concern that this source of amusement and knowledge would very soon be lost to her.

The only pleasure she now found was in drawing; in which, though no great proficient, she was far enough advanced to find herself improve very materially, by following, and continually practicing the few rules she had learned. To seat herself on the turf of the down above the house, on the root of a thorn, or one of those beech trees which were scattered about the foot of the hill, and make sketches of detached pieces of the extensive landscape stretched before her; or of the old and fantastic trees that formed her shady canopy, was now become her only enjoyment; and very sincerely did she regret, and very reluctantly did she obey, the summons, she too frequently received to return to the house, either to make tea for some accidental visitors of her new brother-in-law's acquaintance, or to superintend a syllabub in the summer-house. These parties calling at the parsonage, now became frequent, for this new member of the family lived in the vale, a few miles from Barlton Brook; and the house of his father-in-law lay directly in the horse way to what is called in that country, "up the hills." Those hills (the South Downs), gradually decline towards the sea. On the coast, within a few years, many bathing places have been established, where the sick and the idle pass the summer or autumnal months. The variety of people thus collected, make a visit to the sea-coast, a pleasurable jaunt to the inhabitants of the neighbouring country: and Mr. Grierson, a man perfectly at ease in his circumstances, and lately married to one of the most celebrated beauties of the county, failed not to amuse his bride and her friends with many of these tours. His future brother-in-law, Blagham the attourney, who lived at Chichester, was a great promoter of what he called "a little sociability." He gratified at once two passions; the love of what he called pleasure, and the prospect of future advantage, to which he always looked forward with peculiar earnestness. While he was bustling about with Grierson and his wife, together with his "own intended," as he chose to call her, he was displaying his skill in ordering dinners, in hiring boats for water-parties, in consoling "*the ladies*," when they were sick, and "*cutting jokes upon them when they got better*. In making sure bets at Broad[1] Halfpenny, for "Egad, Sir, he always knew what he was about." And in hedging well at poney races; and while this went on, "Egad, Sir, he never lost sight of the main chance—not he: egad, Sir, he had all his eyes about him."

And it was true, that while thus entered into what he called "the enjoyments of life, *and a little sociability*," he made acquaintance among the yeomanry, or the few of that rank of men who are still *called* so: among men, however, who had money to put out at interest, and who employed him to find for them good securities, and to transact other matters for them. So that though a young man in the honourable profession of an attorney, and newly established in the already well-stocked city of Chichester, he was considered as very likely to make his fortune; and Mr. Lessington had, in the contemplation of such a prospect, granted him the hand of the fair Catharine, his second daughter; rich indeed only in herself—in very handsome wedding clothes, that were now preparing for her; and in her connections and acquaintance among the gentlemen's families of the county.

CHAP.

Notes

↑ A down in Hampshire, on the borders of Suffex, the resort of both counties for cricket matches.

IT was on a beautiful afternoon towards the end of August, when Rosalie retired to her usual seat on the hill; was again engaged in her now favourite occupation. The rays of the sun declining early in the afternoon, gilt the landscape with tints more than usually luxurious. Holmwood House, its windows always lighted up when these evening rays glanced on them, was an object which, as it continually forced itself upon her observation, she almost for the first time in her life wished to escape from. Yet insensibly it brought to her mind a train of ideas—melancholy, yet not to be repelled, her pencils, and drawing cards, were laid down on the turf, while with folded arms, and her head reclined against the tree she was sitting under, she fell into a reverie. A long row of old stone pines, stretched their grotesque heads from the eastern side of the house towards a rising ground, where this wild and irregular avenue was terminated by an octagon temple, now falling fast to ruin; where Rosalie remembered to have passed many hours when she was a child, the happy thoughtless companion of the little Vyvians, who used to call this old summer-house their house, and to carry thither their playthings, and make their sportive arrangements, while their governess, a little old French woman, was accustomed to sit on the steps knitting or netting. The steps Rosalie could distinguish from her solitary seat on the hill, but the playful group and their odd little guardian were gone.....Rosalie recollected how happy she had been there, and already she had acquired that painful experience that had made her fear she should taste of unalloyed happiness no more. Her friend and protectress, Mrs. Vyvian, who now seemed to have deserted, from some unaccountable change of taste, the habitation she was once so fond of, appeared before her in imagination more pale and dejected than usual. She fancied she saw her slowly coming out of the little conservatory, which she had caused to be built, and in which she took peculiar pleasure: she had a nosegay in her hand for each of her girls—and Rosalie was once received under that appellation—and she beckoned to them as she saw them walking in the shrubbery, and, with one of her pensive smiles, gave to every one her little present. The Abbé Hayward, that excellent and venerable man, met her: benignity and pious resignation were in his countenance, as he endeavoured to find some conversation that might cheer the depressed spirits of Mrs. Vyvian. She bade her daughters and Rosalie walk before them; and, making a short tour of the plantations, seemed to remove her languor, and enable her to meet her family at supper with some appearance of cheerfulness.

Such were the scenes Rosalie was recalling to her mind, and such the figures with which memory was busy in peopling them, when her contemplations were disturbed by figures very different, who presented themselves under all the disadvantages of contrast....Blagham, and two other young men whom she did not recollect ever to have seen before, came whooping and hallooing from the house, and ascended the hill towards her; as it soon became very steep, Blagham leaped from his horse and ran towards her, and the other two followed him.

"Why, my sweet Rose,(cried he), my Rose of the world! why do you cruelly hide yourself among thorns? Only to be looked after—eh! my pretty Rose,—Aye, 'tis the way of you all:——there's my Kate below yonder, would fain serve me the same sauce—but I'm come to drink tea with you, my dear little sister, that is to be, and to introduce two of my friends to you. (The friends by this time were come to the spot). This, Madam, is Captain Mildred of the 69th, now quartered in our town; and this, (added he, with all solemnity), this is the Rev. Philibert Hughson, a worthy clergyman, and Rector of Higgington cum Sillingbourn in this county." Rosalie had nothing to do but to curtsey to them both: her future brother-in-law, however, had not yet done with her; but, stepping back, he made a ridiculous bow, and, in a theatrical tone, exclaimed, "And now, gentlemen, give me the superlative pleasure of introducing to *your* admiration Miss Rosalie Lessington, fourth and youngest daughter of the Rev. Joseph

Lessington, Master of Arts, Vicar of Cold Hampton, and Curate of Barlton Brooks in this county: a young lady, of whose personal perfections, gentlemen, I dare not speak; but who is, I may venture to say, endowed with every qualification to render the marriage state completely happy."—Shocked and amazed at this impertinent address, Rosalie felt her cheeks glow with anger and indignation, but, recovering herself, she asked coldly if her mother had sent for her?

"She has—she has—(cried her persecutor, whom she now perceived had added to his natural impertinence all that which liquor gives when it overflows the shallow brain)—She has, fair flower of the desert, and we are the beatified ambassadors charged with the delectable commission. Come then, bright nymph!"——

He was proceeding in this style, when Rosalie, taking from him the hand he would forcibly have held, said, "I wish my mother had sent some person who was more in possession of his reason."——"Ah! Madam, (cried the young man, who was announced as the Rev. Philibert Hughson), there are moments when reason is lost in wonder and delight, and when"——"What, Sir?" interrupted Rosalie, in a tone so unexpected, that the young divine was unable to proceed, and even blushed as he attempted to finish a speech which he probably thought was in the style of the society he was with.

As they walked down the hill towards the house she turned to Captain Mildred, who, as he had hitherto been silent, had not offended her; and who, being an officer, she hoped was a gentleman, and entered with him into the common conversation, while Blagham, too drunk to make much speed, staggered after them, and Mr. Hughson went sidling down a little before her, as if still solicitous to attract her notice, yet half afraid of another rebuff, was trying to recall his consciousness of self-importance.—The Rev. Philibert Hughson was what is called a dapper, tight-made, little man: his face neither well nor ill, but with something in the expression of it that soon let an observer of faces into his character. If the Rev. Philibert Hughson had even ventured to think, in the same unrestrained manner in which he sometimes spoke, it is very certain that he thought himself a d———d clever fellow. The second son of a very rich father, he had been a buck of the first head at Cambridge, spent four times as much as he was allowed, and contrived to get some thousands in debt. He was an excellent judge of horse flesh, and a great connoisseur in carriages: he knew the dimensions and properties of every vehicle from a phaeton to a sulky; had possessed them all by turns, and had changed them oftener than his cloaths or his friends. He had made a merit of taking orders, when he knew his careful father had bought the valuable livings of Higginston cum Sillingbourn, worth together above eight hundred a year. Nor did he determine to make this sacrifice, and, from the smartest fellow at Cambridge, sink into a country parson, till he had stipulated for the payment of his debts, and a handsome sum in ready money. He then cut off his hair, turned his green coat into a gray one, and resolved to be very orthodox and very good: his father, most devoutly hoping he would keep his word, complied with all his conditions, and was delighted when he had sworn he felt an irresistible call from heaven, and was inducted to the living of Higginston cum Sillingbourn. The most pleasant circumstance attending his new situation was, that this cure of souls was undertaken in the best country possible for killing pheasants, and not half a mile from him partrides were equally plenty. A pack of the best fox hounds in England were within five miles, and he had greyhounds of his own of the true Orford breed. To take advantage of all these pleasures, he had begun by fitting up and enlarging the stables, filling them with high-prized hunters, and sending to Newmarket for boys to attend them: he stored his cellars—furnished his house for his brother sportsmen who had promised to visit him—bought a new phaeton; changed it for a curricle; then imagined a new whisky of his own composing, calculated for the Suffex roads; and, in short, during the eight months that he had been in possession of the living, had felt so many irresistible impulses, besides that which had given so valuable a member to the church, that he had already received from the friendship of his dear friend Blagham a trifling accommodation of 'the needful'—for to apply to the old gentleman so soon was hardly discreet; parental patience, like some other virtues, being sometimes apt to wear out, if too frequently called into use.

  Mr. Blagham had not been many days introduced to the Rev. Philibert Hughson, before he discovered that something very advantageous might arise from cultivating his acquaintance. He perfectly understood the way to recommend himself, and set about it with so much zeal, that he became very soon the dearest friend he had in the world......Blagham thought he could not do better than endeavour to recommend one of the sisters of his intended wife, and he had already tried to persuade his friend that he was in love with Maria, in which he would probably have succeeded, if, at a convivial meeting where the beauty of the neighbouring damsels was canvassed, some young man, who had accidentally seen Rosalie, had not warmly assured him, that she was the prettiest girl in the county; and when another spoke of the celebrity of her sisters, agreed that they were fine women, but assured Mr. Hughson, to whom he sat near, in half a whisper, that there was no more comparison between light and darkness. This had greatly raised the curiosity of Hughson, who has since pressed his friend Blagham to carry him to the house of his intended father-in-law; a request which was heard with pleasure, and immediately granted.

  Equally rash and headstrong in whatever he undertook, Hughson was passionately in love at first sight, and as immediately determined to pursue the object that had thus struck him, nothing doubting her ready and even joyful acceptance of a man so unexceptionable in point of fortune, and so very clever a fellow. Under this impression he took no pains to conceal his admiration, but persecuted the distressed and reluctant Rosalie with speeches to which it was impossible for her to reply. She looked timidly towards her father for protection, but she saw, that far from being willing to afford it to her, he seemed delighted with the attention Mr. Hughson paid her, and smiled and rubbed his hands, as who should say, "Oh! oh! here comes another chapman for another of my girls."—Mrs. Lessington appeared to be impressed with the same idea, and overwhelmed the little man with civility, while Maria, to whom he had before shown a great preference, and who seemed to have been much better pleased with it, was piqued at his now addressing himself entirely to her sister, and showed that she severely felt the mortification, but endeavoured to conceal her vexation, by laughing and talking with Captain Mildred, who, being one of those military heroes whose talents are greater in the field than in the cabinet, she found it rather difficult to keep up the gaiety she affected; for Captain Mildred, besides that his head was very scantily stocked with ideas, was too fine a man to give himself the trouble to produce the few he had to amuse a country parson's daughter. He only came with Blagham and Hughson because he had nothing better to do with himself, and had besides an inclination to buy one of Hughson's horses, which he was in hopes of getting a bargain, and which he had therefore been depreciating, and trying to put the little divine out of conceit with it; telling him that the horse, in the first place, had been strained behind, and would never stand sound; "And besides, (said he), my dear Doctor, it grieves all your friends to see you upon such a tall, long-legged animal. By Heavens! Jack Norton of our regiment called to me the other day, as you rode through East Street, and asked me who that little fellow upon the tall horse was? 'For damme, (says he), he puts me in mind of Tom Thumb upon an elephant."—Such was Captain Mildred, on whom neither beauty nor wit could make the slightest impression, and who, equally stupid and selfish, had every qualification for a rogue, except talents. But he had a tolerable person, a red coat, and was said to be a man of fortune; so that he had been reckoned among the misses a very charming man, and their mamas had invited him to their concerts and their card parties. Before the tea was finished, at which Rosalie so reluctantly assisted, Mr. Hughson received from both her father and mother the most pressing invitation to renew his visits as often as he could. "And I hope, my good Sir, (cried Mr. Lessington), I hope you will not let the beginning of the shooting season deprive us of the happiness of seeing you, for, I assure you, we shall have excellent sport round about this village. I myself know of a great number of birds: I expect my son too; my eldest son, will be here shortly, and I am sure he will be greatly flattered by the honour of your acquaintance."

"I am sure he will not, (sighed Rosalie to herself); for never can a man be imagined whom William would like so little: but, alas! my father knows he is not coming."

Plans were now talked of for the next week, which Hughson spoke of as dedicated to the gun, with childish eagerness. He gave to Mr. Lessington a very long and elaborate description of a new gun he had bought, which had cost him five and twenty guineas: not indeed that he wanted any such thing, for he was an admirable shot—killed nineteen out of twenty, and was reckoned as sure as any man in Norfolk. "I remember about two years ago, (said he), I went out, only I and my father's gamekeeper, and we killed, that is, I killed, about forty brace in about five hours, for he hardly ever fired."

"Birds were remarkably plenty I suppose," said Mr. Lessington.

"Why no, really not so very remarkably plenty—I have seen them as much so: but, my dear Sir, Norfolk is the county for game....why, I have seen, Sir, of a morning, when the birds were at feed, the very ground covered with them, so that you could not have thrown a pebble without touching them—as close, Sir—as close."——

Lessington, who by a glance from Rosalie's eye, saw that Hughson was doing himself disservice with her by this sort of rhodomontading, saved him the trouble of finding the comparison he was seeking for, by saying, "Yes, yes——I have been in Norfolk——I know there is a prodigious quantity of game in that county." But Hughson, elevated with wine and inspired by love, could no longer check the violent inclination he always felt to relate some very marvellous story; and to make himself the hero of it, he thought it was impossible to find any audience better disposed to listen and believe, with the exception only of Captain Mildred, whose coldness he imputed to envy. He began, therefore, and told some of the most extraordinary adventures that ever were heard:—how he once, with his single arm, defended several officers of dragoons from the insults of an enraged populace, whom some of them had offended, just for throwing an old woman over a bridge into the river in a frolic...."The old woman, (said he), swam like a cork, and was taken out not a bit the worse. My friend, Ned Whatley, as honest a fellow as ever lived, gave her a crown, and bid her not make such a d——d yelling, since there was no harm done; but there came up a parcel of fishwoman and washwoman, and the devil knows who, and presently all the town, tag rag and bob tail, were under arms, and my friends were forced to retreat to the Red Lion, and there they shut themselves up in a room, Sir——so, presently up comes the mob, and begins to batter the door, Sir....Oh! oh!—thinks I—are you there, my good friends? I shall have a little conversation with you, gentlemen, in a minute....So, Sir, out I went among them all, and began to reason with them. The hissed, however, and began to be very troublesome, but that I did not mind: I seized one of the foremost by the collar; damme—(says I. I was not in the orders then you know)—Damme—(says I)—*I'll* make an example of some of you. So, Sir, up comes a fellow, six feet high, and as strong as Sampson; but I seized him with the other hand, and was going to drag both him and the first rascal into the room, when up comes a great strapping wench with a red hot poker in her hand; she gave me a blow, Sir, upon my head, which cut through a thick hunting hat, Sir, and stunned me sure enough."

"And pray, Hughson, (said the Captain, with an air of incredulity), what were your friends the officers of horse doing all this while?"——"Doing?"—(answered he)——Doing?—Why—why they were—they were shut up in the room; what *could* they do, you know."

The evident fallacy and folly of such a story would not have been tolerated in any other company; but Mildred was too heavy and too indolent to confute or ridicule it; and the rest were the very humble servants of the relator, except Rosalie, who, disgusted more and more every word he spoke, was extremely glad to be relieved from hearing either his compliments or his stories; when it was proposed they should all take a walk to the top of the hill, and that the gentlemen should walk thither with them, and have their horses led. In the bustle of their departure, Rosalie left the room as if to get her hat; but having done so, she glided away, and passing as quickly as she could through a small orchard that lay on the other side of the house, she went into a copse that adjoined to it, and was presently out of hearing the inquiries that she supposed would be made for her. Perhaps her father and mother might chide her on her return to the house; but she had so invincible a dislike to being exposed to the impertinence of Blagham, or the ridiculous speeches of his new friend, that there was nothing she had not rather submit to that temporary ill-humour could inflict, than to be exposed to such teasing and disgusting conversation.

CHAP.

THE copse into which Rosalie had thrown herself, like an affrighted bird, was very extensive, stretching along the edge of the hill, and making a curve as if to let in the few houses that composed the village; it spread beyond into a very extensive wood, and there assumed the name of the Hunacres, probably a corruption of hundred acres. It was as wild and almost as unfrequented as when the ancient Anderidæ sought their food amidst the same entangled woods, then overshadowing the whole country under the hills.

Now, however, there were some winding paths through it made to solitary farms around, and a nobleman, to whom the greater part of it belonged, had cut ridings from the Downs towards his own house in two or three directions, to facilitate the way of the sportsman. The path along which Rosalie went was so intricate, that she forgot how far or whither it carried her, till she found it became dusk, and was stopped by arriving at one of these ridings or cuts through the wood. She then recollected how far she had wandered from home, and was turning to go back, when three gentlemen on horseback, followed by two servants, came galloping so fast from a turn in this green lane a little beyond her, that they were near her almost before she perceived them. The foremost of them checking his horse, and looking at her with some surprise, said to his companions, "Here is a young lady, who, if we are not right, I am sure will be so obliging as to direct us."

Rather wondering than alarmed, Rosalie stopped, and the gentlemen who had first spoken, said, politely taking off his hat—"We are going, Madam, to Holmwood Park, which we plainly distinguished from the hill, and to which my friend here, *who ought to know*, thought he could lead us by a nearer way than that which we were directed to take; but he now thinks he has taken the wrong turning, and that we are too much to the left. Can you inform us how we can best make our way out of the wood? for if we could see the house again, we could easily reach it."

Rosalie was about to answer, that the way they were in led directly to a common, which adjoined the Park at Holmwood, when the young man, of whom the inquirer had spoken, as one who *ought* to know the way to it, jumped from his horse, and exclaimed, "I cannot have forgotten you, whatever else I have forgotten during two-years absence. It is Rosalie, my dear playfellow and companion."

"It is indeed, (answered she); but, Heavens! Mr. Charles Vyvian, how tall you are grown? Upon my word, I should hardly have recollected you. How is my dear Mrs. Vyvian?—How are your sisters?"

The other two gentlemen, seeing the dialogue was not likely immediately to end, dismounted, and were introduced to Rosalie; the one as the nephew of Mrs. Vyvian, Mr. Montalbert, who, after a long residence abroad, was come to England for a few months only, on a visit to the Vyvian family: the other as the Count de Toriani, an Italian nobleman, to whom also the Vyvians were the more distantly related. So many and so rapid were the questions that Mr. Charles Vyvian now had to make, that he wholly engrossed the conversation, and as they slowly walked down the green avenue before them, he seemed totally to have forgotten whither he was going, or that he had any other business in the world than to converse with Rosalie as long as he could. It was now, however, so nearly dark, that she thought it would be wrong to proceed any farther.—"I must wish you a good night, (said she) and make the best of my way through the wood home."

"Indeed, but you must not think of returning by yourself," answered Vyvian.—"Harry, (added he, speaking to Montalbert) let us go home with Miss Lessington.—Shall we not, Harry?"

Harry answered, "With great pleasure," and the opposition of Rosalie was in vain.

"But we need not go down this way, surely, (said Vyvian); we may go along the path I saw you in, and so through your father's orchard or garden, or something—I am sure I remember such a way."

Rosalie answered, that it was certainly a much shorter road, but it was only a footpath, and that there was a stile to pass.

"Never mind a stile, (cried the young man) we will leap our horses over."

He then led the way into the path, which only allowed two persons to walk abreast—Mr. Montalbert and the Count de Torriani followed; the former murmuring loudly against Vyvian's monopoly, and the narrowness of the path.

Rosalie expected to have found her father and mother returned from their walk, and in no very pleasant humour, because she had left them; but, on entering the house through the garden, the noise she heard in her father's book-room convinced her that the party whom she so earnestly wished to avoid were not gone, but were, on the contrary, set in to drinking; an alteration of plan which did not at all surprise her, when Mr. Blagham and Mr. Hughson were of the party.

Young Vyvian, whose sole meaning was to see her safe, was however now compelled in common civility to inquire for her mother and her sisters. Mrs. Lessington, amazed at his sudden appearance, received him with a mixture of civility and confusion, for which Rosalie knew not how to account: mingled with this extraordinary expression, there was also some anger towards her, and something that seemed like a disposition to reproach her for having introduced visitors so unexpected.

Mrs. Lessington expressing her surprise at seeing him, when she imagined he was at Cheltenham, or in the North with the rest of the family, he said, "The Count de Torriani and my consin Harry, having an inclination to see Holmwood, we agreed to make a tour round the Coast, to pass about ten days at Brighthelmstone, and to make Holmwood in our way back. The Abbé Hayward had notice of our intentions yesterday, and expects us this evening. We lost our way some how by a blunder of mine, and got down into Hunacre wood, where we had the singular good fortune to meet Miss Rosalie."

To Mrs. Lessington's inquiry after his mother's health, he said, that his last letters spoke of her as being rather better. "But it is (said he) more than six weeks since I have seen her, for so long have we been rambling about; and her impatience to have me return is now so great, that I shall only stay one day at Holmwood.—Yet (added he, evidently addressing himself to Rosalie) I am at this moment more disposed than ever I was in my life to make a longer abode at our old enchanted, but not enchanting castle." Rosalie did not seem to think any answer necessary to this, and Mrs. Lessington put on a look of great gravity and reserve, but said nothing; and as at that moment Mr. Montalbert did not seem to find any thing to say, a profound silence ensued for a minute, which was interrupted by the noisy entrance of Mr. Lessington and his friends. The former being apprised of the arrival of young Vyvian, came to pay him his compliments; and the others were about to depart, or at least to attempt it, though the whole party, without excepting even the master of the house, seemed to have taken such large potations, that they appeared to be but little in possession of their senses. Mr. Lessington, however, bustled up to young Vyvian, expressing the greatest delight in meeting him, and, amidst the confusion, Mr. Montalbert approached Rosalie, to whom he had yet hardly had an opportunity of speaking, though his eyes had declared how much he wished it. "Do you not recollect me, Miss Lessington? (said he, speaking low)—I perfectly remember you, and the days I once passed with you at Holmwood made an impression on me that never will be effaced. It has ever appeared to me since the very happiest period of the happy hours of my childhood; for I was then but a boy. It is more, (added he), than eight years ago, and you were then very young."

"You do me too much honour, (answered Rosalie); I was, indeed, very young—but (an involuntary sigh forced its way as she spoke) those were my days of unalloyed felicity; it was my golden age, and every scene has imprinted itself deeply on my memory...Yes! I well remember your coming to Holmwood—with your father, was it not?"

"Yes; and an Italian tutor I recollect, but I dare say you do not: that then I could speak very little English."

"Why, you can't speak much now, Sir, (interrupted a voice from behind Rosalie's chair). I suppose by your accent, Sir, that you are a foreigner?"

"*You* suppose, Sir, (said Mr. Montalbert angrily); and pray, Sir, who are you?"

"Me, Sir! (answered the Rev. Mr. Hughson)——Me, Sir!——Why, Sir, my name is Hughson."

"Well, Sir, (said Montalbert haughtily), whatever name you bear, I suppose it is not necessary for you to make a third in my conversation with this lady." The stout, the brave, the magnanimous Hughson, he who had kept at bay an enraged populace, and protected, with his single arm, a whole corps of officers of dragoons, was, for some reason or other, appalled by the decided and contemptuous tone taken up by Mr. Montalbert. The effects of liquor vary on different constitutions. Some cowards it renders brave, and may, perhaps, render some brave men cowards. However that might be, Hughson attempted no reply; but still, unwilling that this stranger should engross the attention of Rosalie, he determined at least to keep as close to her as he could, and therefore squatted down in the window seat near her, being in truth not very well able to stand.

Montalbert, shocked at his vulgarity and impertinence, and having no idea that much ceremony was necessary towards a man, whom he supposed to be a little, dirty, drunken curate, spoke in a still lower tone to Rosalie, and what was yet more mortifying, he spoke in Italian, while, with open mouth and watery eyes, her unfortunate admirer sat gasping and staring behind her totally disregarded.

Montalbert, as well as Rosalie, had forgotten not only that he was in the room, but that any other persons were in it but themselves. From an oblivion so pleasing, however, they were soon roused by Vyvian who, disengaging himself with great difficulty from the maudling civilities of Mr. Lessington, who was very drunk and very tedious, came hastily to Montalbert and told him they must go. Vyvian then took Rosalie's hand, and sighing said, "Alas! how little I have seen you, and *that* only by chance; can I not come to-morrow to take leave of you, Rosalie? for you know I am going abroad again almost immediately, and who knows when we shall meet once more. Tell me, Rosalie, do you think I may call here again to-morrow?" Mrs. Lessington had by this time sidled up near her daughter, to whom she did not allow time to reply, but, with an air most repulsively grave and formal, she said, "I am very sorry, Mr. Vyvian, it happens so, as your time is so short; but my daughter is particularly engaged to-morrow. We are all particularly engaged. It is extremely unfortunate indeed; another time I hope we shall be more lucky."

This rebuff seemed particularly mortifying to Vyvian. He bowed coldly to the mother, and then, gently pressing the hand of Rosalie, which he still held, he said in a whisper, "I *must* see you again; where are you going to?"—"I do not know, indeed, (answered Rosalie), for this is the first I have heard of any engagement. I am afraid it is on some party with these men." She could add no more, for a servant informed Mr. Vyvian and the other gentlemen that their horses were brought round. Lessington again came up, persecuting them with his civilities; and Mrs.

Lessington very evidently wished them gone. It became impossible for either Vyvian or Montalbert to speak to Rosalie apart, though they appeared equally to desire it, and with reluctance, that neither could conceal, they left the house.

Blagham was no longer in a situation to be troublesome, and Miss Catharine, somewhat ashamed of the figure he made, had prevailed upon him to leave the room.....Hughson, however, to whom the departure of the strangers seemed to have restored his consequence, failed not to listen eagerly to the remarks Mrs. Lessington and Miss Catharine made upon them. "I should not have known Mr. Charles Vyvian, (said the latter). How very tall he is."

"He is tall, indeed, (replied the mother); but you may see he is a mere boy. That young man, would you believe it, Mr. Hughson, is hardly seventeen? He is the son of Mr. Vyvian, you know, of Holmwood, with whose lady I used to be so intimate. My daughter Rose used to live there a good deal when she was a child, and this young man looks upon her as one of the family."——Hughson, checking a hickup which had nearly broken the sentence, cried, "Indeed!—really!—nothing to be sure can be more natural."

"Pray, Ma'am, (said Miss Catharine), who is that other gentleman; I don't mean the foreign Count, but the other English gentleman? He is remarkable handsome man."

"I am surprised dear Miss Kitty should think so, (sputtered Hughson). To my fancy now, he does not look at all like an Englishman—not the least."

"Why, certainly, (replied Mrs. Lessington), he can hardly be called an Englishman; for, in the first place, his mother was a foreign lady, and, though his father is an Englishman, he has lived chiefly abroad, and this gentleman has never been in England above half a year at a time, though they have a very fine seat in the North of England, and a great fortune in the family."

"He seems to be a very proud man, (said Hughson). I believe I half affronted him, though I am sure I don't know what I said."

"I believe, indeed, that you did not, (said Rosalie), and you will pardon me, Mr. Hughson, if I say that you seemed to intend to affront him."

Hughson, who had no clear idea of what he *had* said, would have taken her hand, but she snatched it away and hastened out of the room. Soon after she had the satisfaction of hearing the whole party leave the house, and scamper away with a degree of rashness which she thought must make her sister uneasy for the safety of her lover.

Rosalie, whose spirits were fatigued by the events of the afternoon, could not, however, compose herself to sleep. The sight of Charles Vyvian had recalled all those scenes which she had vainly been trying to forget, and to think of with less concern: and his manners, but still more those of his relation, Mr. Montalbert, formed so decided a contrast to those of the persons with whom it was now her lot to be associated, that she found she should, by continually making the comparison, be rendered more uneasy than ever. She saw too, by her mother's manner, that she would yet have to undergo some severe reproofs for having brought Charles Vyvian and his two companions home with her; and though it was easy to account for their appearance, which it must be known was merely in consequence of accidentally meeting her, yet she knew that the circumstance of her so abruptly quitting company, in which it was her father's wish that she should remain, would bring upon her reproaches that she should not soon or easily appease.

The next day verified her apprehensions. Her father ordered her to attend him in his study at an early hour of the morning, as he was going out. She entered dejectedly. Her mother was there, and both looked coolly upon her, as they bade her shut the door and sit down. Mr. Lessington thus began:

"Rose, it is fit and right that you should know that you have extremely displeased me."

"I am extremely sorry for it, Sir. It was by no means my intention."

"You think then, perhaps, that it is not improper to slight my friends, and show that you despise them—gentlemen whose notice does you so much honour, and whose good opinion perhaps may be so material to you. Do you consider, girl, that you have no fortune? That a clergyman's income dies with him? That it is your business to endeavour to procure an establishment, instead of affecting these fine romantic airs?"

"I affected no airs, Sir—I obeyed your commands, and made tea for the gentlemen—I did not know you wished me to remain with them afterwards, especially as you must have perceived that they were not in a situation in which they could be pleasant company for women."

"Prudish airs!—Were not your mother and you sisters with you? and do you think I would have asked either them or you to stay in improper company?—Let me hear no more of all this, but listen to what I have to say to you:—Mr. Hughson is a young man of fortune; he is, in his family, his situation, and prospects, every way unexceptionable: he seemed to take particular notice of you, notwithstanding your rudeness to him. I expect, if this partiality on his part should go any farther, that you will dispose yourself to receive him as a man to whom it would be agreeable to me, and highly honourable and advantageous to you, to be allied."

Rosalie was about to answer, but her father, rising and leaving the room, said, with yet more sternness, "I will have no answer, unless it be an answer of compliance." Then, turning to Mrs. Lessington, he added, "you will not fail to enforce what I have said, and to impress on the mind of this young woman, that, though she has hitherto found me an indulgent father, I know how to make myself be obeyed."——He then left the room, and Mrs. Lessington said, "You see, Rose, that your father is peremptory. If Mr. Hughson......."

"Dear Madam, (said Rosalie), what occasion can there be for all these menaces of anger, if I do not listen to Mr. Hughson, when it is not even known whether Mr. Hughson will ever think of me again?"

"Perhaps your father has reasons, with which he may not think proper to acquaint you, why he knows Mr. Hughson means to address you."

"Very certainly, Madam, Mr. Hughson could not communicate to my father what he could not know himself last night; for so far from being capable of thinking what he intended for the future, he knew not what he was about then: but, admitting it to be so, why must I be compelled to listen to him? Indeed, my dear Mama, this Mr. Hughson is a man it is utterly impossible for me to like."

"It would be something new, Rose, and altogether unlike the heroines whose adventures you have studied, if you should happen to like the man recommended to you by your friends, and in every respect eligible. Do not think of doing a thing so entirely out of rule, but contrive to take a liking not only to some other man, but, if possible, to the *very man* to whom of all others it is him possible you can ever be united."

Rosalie blushed deeply, without exactly knowing why. "Dear Madam, (said she), what a strange thing that is to say?"

"As strange as true, (replied Mrs. Lessington). Its truth, I am much afraid, will be too soon verified; but have a care, I promise you not only that nobody will defend you in this *dangerous absurdity*, but that it will be the certain means of estranging from you those friends who love you best.......I won't be interrupted, (added she, seeing her daughter was going to speak), I won't be interrupted—hear me, and tell me afterwards, whether you who have nothing, you who must go into some humble business, or even, perhaps, to service, if your father should die, have any sort of pretensions to pleasing yourself, even if *the people you fancy you prefer* were indeed so foolishly inconsistent as to think for a moment of committing such a folly as taking you out of the rank you are in, which, you may be assured, child, never entered *their heads*, whatever your vanity and your ignorance of the world may have put into yours."

"For God's sake, my dear mother! (said Rosalie, with tears in her eyes), what do you mean? This is the first time you ever talked to me in this manner! How I have deserved it now I am entirely ignorant. Did

I ever say I like any particular person?—or——"

"Pho! pho! (cried Mrs. Lessington, interrupting her), you cannot deceive *me*; but let me earnestly exhort you, Rosalie, never to think of the persons to whom you know I allude, but to determine to follow, like a reasonable woman, the advice of those who know better what is fit for you than you do yourself."

Rosalie remained silent. Her soul abhorred the idea of receiving Hughson as a lover, nor could she endure that her mother should for a moment believe her capable of hesitating about him. The conversation she had held, however, was so new, and so strange, that she had not courage to defend herself; and, after a short pause, Mrs. Lessington thus went on:—

"Did you ever know any woman who married just according to their own romantic whims in setting out in life?——Did I do it, do you think?——Did Mrs. Vyvian?"

"Of you, Madam, (said Rosalie), I cannot pretend to speak. Mrs. Vyvian certainly did *not* marry Mr. Vyvian from choice; but has she been happy?—has not her whole life been embittered by the sacrifice she made, as I have heard, to her father's commands?"

"That was very different, (said Mrs. Lessington). My friend was—————" She stopped, as she had often done before when their conversation had been led to the same topic, and then immediately changing it, said, "But you now know my opinion, and your father's commands. We are going to-day where you will again be in company with Mr. Hughson, and it is expected of you, that you will behave to him as to a friend of your father's, and a gentleman whose partiality does you honour."

"Whither am I to go, Madam?" said Rosalie in a dejected tone.

"To Chichester, (replied her mother dryly).....We dine with Mr. Blagham; his uncle is to be there with some other friends; your sister Catharine's settlement is to be signed; afterwards a party of friends dine with him on venison, and we shall remain there all night, perhaps go to the assembly the night after: you will, therefore, put up a small packet of clothes, and act accordingly."

From the manner in which this was said, Rosalie knew that no remonstrance against an expedition so very irksome to her would be listened to; and that, however hateful to her, she must obey. She retired, therefore, with an heavy heart to her own room, and began to dress and to prepare for the party.

But her mother's oblique reproaches had made a great impression on her mind: she imagined they must allude to Mr. Charles Vyvian, or Mr. Montalbert; but probably the former, as her mother could hardly suspect her of a partiality for a man she had not seen since she was ten or eleven years old. In regard to Mr. Vyvian her heart acquitted her; but she was at the same time conscious that nothing could do so great a disservice to Hughson, in *her* opinion, as putting him a moment in comparison with such a man as Montalbert.

CHAP.

ROSALIE was soon ready to proceed on an expedition, from which she found no pretence would excuse her. She mounted her sister Catharine's with reluctance; her father, mother, and Miss Lessington, were in the post chaise; the other sister was also on horseback; and it did not add much to Rosalie's prospect for the day, that this was her sister Maria who had been put out of humour the preceding evening by the unfortunate and undesired preference Hughson had shown Rosalie; and who, now sullen and pouting, endeavoured to show her sister that she had not forgotten the mortification.

They had ascended and were riding along the hill, but the morning being hot and sultry, Rosalie turned her horse towards its edge, where began a wood that shaded one side of it, and the ash and beech afforded a temporary skreen; several roads wound up the hill from the villages below, and as Rosalie was crossing one of these she saw Montalbert suddenly appear, who, approaching her with the common salutation of the morning, rode along by her side without noticing the rest of the party.

Rosalie, conscious that this would give great offense to her father and mother, and unwilling to increase the dislike they seemed already to have taken to him from the little attention he showed to them the preceding evening, inquired if he would not speak to them?

"Bye and bye, (said he coldly); but, good God, is it never possible to have a moment's conversation with you?—I have a great respect for Mr. and Mrs. Lessington, because they are so nearly related to you, but you know that I have not the pleasure of being acquainted with them."

There was something of peculiar dejection in the manner of Montalbert as he spoke.

"You are not well?" said Rosalie.

"Not very well, (replied he); but the hot weather of England never agrees with me. There is something strangely oppressive in it. I don't know whether it is that which has affected poor Charles; but, I assure you, he is seriously ill—so ill, that we do not think of going to-morrow. The Count, being obliged to be in London, left us this morning, as it was uncertain when Charles would be well enough."

"I am very sorry, (said Rosalie with quickness), it will so distress my dear Mrs. Vyvian!—Has he sent for any advice?"

"It were well worth while to be ill, (said Montalbert), were one sure of exciting interest so tender."—"But you do not answer me, (said Rosalie, affecting not to hear him). Has Mr. Vyvian sent for Mr. Harrison, the apothecary?"

"I believe Mr. Hayward intended it, (replied Montalbert), for the poor old man was frightened out of his wits. Charles, however, opposed it. Perhaps it will be nothing. But you know that his mother has nursed him to death; and that Hayward is as timid as an old woman about him."

"I am very uneasy, (said Rosalie, pausing a moment). I think I had better tell my mother; she would surely see Mr. Vyvian, as she knows how very wretched her friend would be should her son be ill at a distance from her." Thus saying, and without waiting for an answer, she rode towards the chaise and bade the driver stop. Montalbert did not go with her, but followed the chaise at some distance.

"Well?—(said Mrs. Lessington sharply, as the chaise stopped)—and what now?"

"Dear Madam, (answered Rosalie in visible consternation), here is Mr. Montalbert, whom I have met by accident, who tells me that Mr. Charles Vyvian is taken very ill?"

"Well?—(cried Mrs. Lessington impatiently)—and what would you have us do?"

"I thought, Madam, (said Rosalie, deeply blushing and speaking quick), I thought you might be alarmed on account of your friend Mrs. Vyvian, and might—might——"

"I don't see what *we* can do, my dear, (said Mr. Lessington). Probably Mr. Hayward has taken proper care of the young gentleman.—I suppose, (added he, addressing himself to Rosalie), since Mr. Montalbert came hither by *accident*, that Mr. Charles has not sent any message expressing a wish to see your mother?"

"No, Sir," answered Rosalie.

"Well then, child, there is *no call* for our interference: I wish him better with all my heart. Rose, you keep up with the chaise—Andrew, drive on, we shall be late."

Andrew obeyed, and Montalbert, who had very slowly rode on while this conversation lasted, stopped, as the chaise passed, and made a formal bow to the persons in it, but without showing any intention to speak to them. He then rejoined Rosalie, and continued to ride the pace she did forty or fifty yards behind the chaise, complaining of the perverseness of his fate, in her being to stay perhaps several days at Chichester; while she, in her turn, expressed very great uneasiness about Mr. Vyvian, and seemed to attend very little to the unequivocal expressions Montalbert used to impress her with an idea of his own attachment to her. At length they came into the turnpike road. Rosalie saw her father look out repeatedly, as if inquiring with angry countenance, whether Montalbert had left her, which she now entreated him to do. He sighed deeply, and said, in a mournful tone, "And so you are going to that town, and do not return perhaps these two or three days, and before that time we shall have left the country, and I shall see you no more."

This idea, which seemed so distressing to him, was by no means the pleasantest that could be presented to the imagination of Rosalie. Her heart seemed to re-echo, "I shall see him no more!" but she attempted to smile, and to answer cheerfully, "O yes—I am persuaded we shall meet again."—"But when? or where? (cried Montalbert, fixing his eyes earnestly on her face). Alas! Miss Lessington, *I* shall soon leave England; and this, perhaps, is the last time we shall meet!"

"I should be *so* sorry to believe that, (answered she, hesitating and blushing), that I will not stay to hear it repeated.....Adieu, Sir; fail not to assure your friend of my sincere wishes for his recovery; and tell my dear venerable friend, the Abbé Hayward, how much I lament that we never meet as we used to do."

Mr. Lessington, now putting his head once more out of the window, waved his hand impatiently for his daughter to keep up with them. Rosalie understood the signal but too well, and though reluctantly, put her horse into a gallop, while Montalbert checked his more reluctantly still; but, as he was on a rising ground, he remained in the same place, following with he eyes the object from which he was so unwilling to part, till a wood, into which the road turned, concealed her from his sight.

Rosalie, in the mean time, proceeded with an heavier heart than she knew how to account for. The illness of Charles Vyvian, which alarmed her not only on his own account, but on that of his mother, and the certainty that she should be compelled to pass two or three days among persons so extremely disagreeable to her, were indeed reasons enough for chagrin; but the concern she felt was something deeper than belonged to either of these. That she had seen Montalbert for the last time, she could not think of without the most acute uneasiness; and so much did that idea dwell on her mind, that she arrived at the end of her journey hardly knowing how she got there: nor was she roused from the indulgence of these painful reflections, till the troublesome assiduities of Hughson restored her to herself, by imposing on her the necessity of repressing his impertinence; which she did, however, with an asperity so unusual to her, that her mother severely reproved her the moment they were alone. "Dear Madam, (said Rosalie), that man is so utterly disagreeable to me: he is so forward, so ignorant——"

"It is a misfortune to you, child, (answered her mother gravely), that you have lived in a style, and among people who have given you a distaste for those of your own rank. However that may be, (added she, with still greater solemnity), I repeat to you, Rosalie, that you are expected by your father to behave to Mr. Hughson not only as to his particular friend, but as one to whom, if you should be lucky enough to procure him for an husband, would establish you in possession of a fortune much greater than you ever can have the least right to expect."—"I had rather dedicate my whole life to the most humiliating poverty, Madam, (answered Rosalie with spirit); I had rather not only go to service, but submit to the most laborious offices, even to work in the fields, than condemn myself to become the wife of Mr. Hughson."

"Very fine, indeed, (said Mrs. Lessington), very romantic, and very sublime. But hear me, Miss Rose: if you are weak, wicked, and vain enough to think, for a moment, of that simple young man Charles Vyvian, which I fear, I greatly fear, that proud coxcomb Montalbert has been putting in your head, know that the most remote hint given of any such——such an absurd and——and ridiculous idea, sent to my friend Mrs. Vyvian, would not only put an eternal bar between you, but would for ever ruin you in her good opinion."

"I think of Mr. Charles Vyvian, Madam, (said Rosalie), no otherwise than as the son of my dear benefactress!—No, indeed, my dear Mama, I never was quite so absurd as to have any other idea!"

"Take care you never *are* then, (replied her mother), and be not so blind to your own interest, or so deaf to the dictates of common sense, as to throw away, by refusing Mr. Hughson, an opportunity that may never offer again." Then, perceiving her daughter was about to answer her, she added, "Let us have no more romance, Rosalie, it will answer no purpose, but to irritate your father without changing his resolution. You will dress for dinner. To-morrow there is to be an assembly; it is already settled that we are to go; and, as it is the first time you have been seen there, I desire you will look as well as you can."

"Gracious Heaven! (exclaimed Rosalie, as soon as her mother had left her), I am thus to be dressed up, and offered like an animal to sale; and my mother seems to think it a matter of course......Oh! Montalbert, how different are your manners from those of the people I am condemned to live among!—Dear and amiable patroness of my happy infancy, little did you imagine, when you were so tenderly kind to your unfortunate Rosalie, that you were laying up for her future years insupportable mortification!—Had I never been blessed in your society, had I never known those who are related to you, I should not now be perpetually making comparisons so much to the disadvantage of persons among whom it is my lot to live, and I should then have been as happy as my sisters."

Very heavily for Rosalie passed the day. Mr. Hughson was sometimes extremely troublesome; but finding her still cold and repulsive, he now and then tried what could be affected by changing his battery, and affecting to neglect her for her sister, who, in her turn, put on a disdainful air, in evident resentment of the preference he had lately shown Rosalie, who so little desired it.

It was not, however, in the eyes of Hughson that she appeared the fairest of the rural nymphs from 'under the hills.' Others of Mr. Blagham's acquaintance, who were of their dinner party, made the same discovery, and two of them attempted, during the afternoon, to engage her for the ball of the ensuing evening. She refused them both civilly, but positively.

"Aye, (said one of them, in a whisper), I see how it is—Hughson is the happy man; is it not so, Miss Rose?"

"If you mean, Sir, (answered she coldly), that Mr. Hughson's happiness is to arise from dancing with me to-morrow, I assure you, you are mistaken."

"What, you are not engaged to him then?"

"No, Sir; nor shall I engage myself to any body."

"Hey!—(cried Hughson, rising and skipping across the room)—Hey!—what's all that?—who talks of engagements?—Hey!—why, I hope, Miss Rosalie, nobody has been pretending to take away my partner; surely you understand, Ma'am, that you are engaged to me?"

"Indeed, Sir, I do not, (replied Rosalie), and I should be sorry you understood it."

"There!—(cried one of the young men who came from a provincial town in another country),—there! I have still a chance. Sir, (added he, addressing himself very solemnly to Hughson), I'll tell you what is a rule with us—that is with our ladies—and you know what excellent, genteel, fashionable meetings we have at——. Sir, it is a rule among the ladies of—— never to engage themselves to a gentleman in a black coat, while they have a chance of being asked by any other, and damme if I don't think they're in the right."

"*You* think, Sir, (said Hughson, colouring violently and trembling with passion); and pray, Sir—I say—Sir, that is—was there any question asked as to what you, Sir, think, Sir?"

"I beg, (said Rosalie, who had no inclination to have a quarrel begin between these two coats of different colours on her account), I beg that the conversation may drop; I have no intention, Mr. Hughson, of dancing at all."

"Oh! (cried the young man, his opponent), the whole room will rise, by G—, against such an inhuman resolution.....No, no, that will never be allowed.—Here, Blagham, before you sit down to cards, you dog you, come and set this matter to rights for us."

"I beg leave to retire from the discussion then, Sir, (said Rosalie rising), though I cannot imagine how either you, or Mr. Blagham, can be interested in a matter so immaterial to you both."

"Eh! (cried Blagham)—why, my Rose of beauty, you have all your thorns about you to-night. Aye! aye! Sir, thus it is—thus it is—thus do these imperious little divinities treat us till they are married...Why now, there's my Kitty as great a tyrant as that little lioness her sister; but you see she begins to look tame and demure already. Come, come, Miss Rose, frowns do not become the fair, child."—He was proceeding in the same style, when, her patience being entirely exhausted, she snatched away her hand, which Blagham endeavoured to hold, and left the room.

Before she retuned the card tables were adjusted, and Mr. and Mrs. Lessington, who dearly loved a game at whist, were settled with Blagham, who really had, and Hughson who fancied he had, great skill in the game. Rosalie, therefore, seeing her two persecutors employed, and her father and mother deeply engaged, took out her work and sat down behind Mrs. Lessington, as much out of sight as possible: but this peaceful state she was not long suffered to enjoy. The idle man who remained insisted on making a party for a round table, and with whatever reluctance Rosalie was compelled to join them, and to be listening for three mortal hours to the sad attempts at wit which a commerce table never fails to produce.

At length, however, the evening ended; and for Rosalie the following arrived too soon.

Dragged to a scene, where she considered herself exposed as an animal in a market to the remarks and purchase of the best bidder, it was with extreme reluctance that Rosalie entered the ball-room; nor had she by any means taken that pains to add to the attractions of her person which her mother had insisted upon. The simplest and neatest muslin dress, without feathers, flowers, or ribbands, was all she put on; while her sister Maria came down as showy and blooming as ribbands and rouge could make her.

Mrs. Lessington would have reproved her youngest daughter for having thus neglected her admonitions; but, when she saw the three together, she could not help being sensible that Rosalie looked like a girl of fashion, while Catharine and Maria had the appearance of people dressed for the performance of strolling plays, with all the finery the property man could furnish. Without any remonstrance, therefore, she was suffered to go with the rest; but not so easily did she escape from the renewed importunities of Mr. Hughson to dance with him, who having engaged her father to interfere in his favour, she received so peremptory an order to accept him, accompanied by looks so angry and menacing, that she was compelled, though with extreme reluctance, to submit. Her sister on the point of being married was of course taken out by her lover, but by some mortifying fatality Miss Maria was unasked; and the first dance was nearly ended, when, to the extreme surprise of Rosalie, who with her skipping partner was arrived at the bottom, she saw (almost doubting the information of her eyes) her sister Maria standing up with Montalbert.

The change of her countenance, when it was her turn to take hands with him, expressed more forcibly than words could have done her astonishment. Montalbert perceived it. "You rather wonder to see me here?" said he.—"Wonder! (cried she)—Good Heavens!—and your friend, how does he do?—He is certainly better since you could leave him." The figure of the dance obliged them to separate; but in a few moments declining to do down the dance, which was soon after over, Montalbert seated himself by her, taking without any scruple the place of her partner, whom she sent away for some negus. "You inquire after my friend, (said Montalbert), with an interest so tender, that, however I may envy his happiness in exciting that interest, it becomes me to satisfy your inquiries: yet you might, perhaps, obtain more satisfactory information from himself."

"From himself! (cried Rosalie eagerly); is he here then?"

"Alas! (answered Montalbert, again deeply sighing), he seems insensible of the good fortune which *I* would purchase with worlds, if I possessed them, for there he is conversing with Lady——, and Lady Anne——, at the other end of the room. Shall I go and tell him, Madam, (added he coolly), that you desire to see him?"

"By no means, (replied Rosalie), by no means—not for the world!"

"Insensible fellow! (cried Montalbert) whom rank can a moment detain from Miss Rosalie Lessington. Ah! if he saw with my eyes—if his heart felt as mine does!"——

"I am very glad, however, (said she, affecting not to understand this), I am extremely glad to find Mr. Charles Vyvian so much recovered; I was quite alarmed at his threatened illness on account of his mother."

"On account of his mother!" repeated Montalbert.

"Yes, Sir, (said Rosalie gravely), certainly on the account of his mother."

At this moment two persons of very different description approached them....Hughson came smirking and prancing with a glass of negus, and began telling how he had mixed it after a manner peculiar to himself; but seeing that Rosalie gave no attention to him, and that Montalbert made no offer to resign the place he had usurped, he remained looking even less wise than ordinary, till his dismay was increased by the appearance of Vyvian, who, putting him on one side with very little ceremony, entered into conversation with Rosalie, who expressed as warmly as she felt it the pleasure his recovery gave her. She loved Charles Vyvian exactly as she loved her brothers: brought up with him from her childhood, she had never considered him for a moment in any other light, nor did she suppose it possible, notwithstanding what her mother had said, that any other person could entertain an idea of his having for her any other attachment than that which might subsist between a brother and a sister. Vyvian was fourteen months younger than she was, and nothing could, in her apprehension, be more absurd than to suppose Vyvian, not yet eighteen, would see her in any other light than she thought of him. This gave to her manner towards him an ease which she was far from feeling when she conversed with Montalbert; and now, without any hesitation, or indeed any apprehension of impropriety, she rose from her seat, and walked with him to the end of the room, Montalbert taking his place in silence on the other side, while the luckless Hughson drank up himself what he had fetched for his partner, and then went with a rueful countenance to find at the sideboard below something more powerful to dissipate the chagrin he felt, as well as the awkward sensations of conscious inferiority. Rosalie, in the mean time, not thinking about him, was inquiring of Charles Vyvian why he prolonged his stay in the country, when he was well enough to go? "I thought, (said she), I thought you told me, that Mrs. Vyvian did not even know of your intentions of being at Holmwood. If she should hear of your remaining there on account of illness, 'tis so far from advice, I cannot imagine why you stay."

"What would you think, (replied he in a low whisper, as if he was solicitous that his cousin might not hear him)—what would you think, Rosalie, if I were to tell you, that I went thither in the hope of seeing you; that I linger here for no other reason than because I cannot prevail upon myself to quit the country where you are?"

"I should think, (said Rosalie hesitating), and I should say, that I was very sorry Mr. Charles Vyvian should talk so wildly and improperly——————." She was proceeding, though she hesitated, blushed, and was evidently disconcerted, when she was interrupted by her mother, who, coming towards her, said, with more appearance of anger than she had ever yet shown, "Why is it, Rose, that you thus quit Mr. Hughson!—I am astonished at your rudeness, child, and *must insist* upon having no more of such behaviour."—Mrs. Lessington then seized her hand, and giving it into that of Hughson, said, with a sort of convulsive laugh, "Here, Sir—I am sure Rose will be happy—he! he! he!—to go down the dance with you—I am sure she does not wish to be left out of this dance."

Hughson then, endeavouring to smile and smirk in order to conceal the extreme vexation he felt, advanced to take her hand; but, from some unusual courage which at that moment she felt, some sudden impulse for which she could hardly account, and which she afterwards thought blameable, she snatched away the hand Hughson would have taken, and telling him disdainfully that she did not know that she should dance any more, she turned to the seat she had before occupied, whither Vyvian, wholly regardless of the evident anger of Mrs. Lessington, followed her.

Hughson, swelling with rage and resentment, which he had, however, no means of satisfying, now seemed to give up the point in absolute despair; but, accustomed as he had been to fancy that so clever a little fellow, with his fortune and expectations, might have his choice among the young women of the whole county, he could not repress the mortification he felt. The plan that Montalbert had adopted of dancing with Maria Lessington, in order to obtain the opportunity of conversing with her sister, had been so far from answering, that it had entirely baffled his purpose......He now saw himself engaged for the evening, and prevented from enjoying a moment's conversation with Rosalie, while his more fortunate cousin was happy enough wholly to engross her attention.

Montalbert, however, who had seen too much of the world to be easily diverted from his design, made a false step as he was going down the dance that was now begun, and protesting he had hurt himself so as to make his going on impossible, was limping to a seat; but seizing on poor Hughson in his way, he cried, "My good Sir, I perceive your fair partner declines dancing any more; I am, most unfortunately for myself, disabled—It will be happy for you, for you will have the pleasure of taking one lovely sister instead of the other."

Hughson, clever fellow as he thought himself, was so over awed by the easy manners and conscious superiority of Montalbert, that he had nothing to say, but advancing towards Miss Maria, as if this was an arrangement to which he was under the necessity of submitting, they sullenly finished the dance together; while Montalbert, availing himself of the success of his stratagem, seated himself on the other side of Rosalie, who, however unwilling to disoblige her mother, forgot in a few moments that she was likely to do so, while she attended sometimes to Vyvian as to a brother whom she loved, or as to a very young man whose wild sallies were pardonable; but to Montalbert she listened with sensations very different: she knew far less how to repress the oblique declarations he made to her—declarations which she trembled to listen to, while she felt conscious, though not daring to own it to herself, that all the future happiness of her days depended on their sincerity.

Mrs. Lessington had retired to cards after her last sharp remonstrance to her daughter, and the eagerness with which she always pursued her game, kept her in another room for some time. At length, however, she was either put out of the game by rotation, or some evil-disposed persons had whispered to her what was passing among the dancers; for about an hour and an half after her last rebuke she returned to the ball-room, and, in a voice and manner more angry than before, told Rosalie that she was going home, and should take her thither at the same time. "As to your sisters, (added she, laying great emphasis on her words), as *they* know better how to behave, I need not interrupt their amusement——*they* shall stay as long as they please."

Rejoiced to be released on any terms from a repetition of reproaches in a public room, she assured her mother that she was quite ready to attend her. "Very well, Miss, (replied Mrs. Lessington)—it is mighty well.......Come, Sir, (continued she, turning to Charles Vyvian), as we are old acquaintance, you know, you shall favour me with your arm——but stop——I must beg that you will first be so good as to accompany me to the top of the room, I must speak to Catharine and Maria."—Without waiting for an answer from Vyvian, she took his arm, and led him away.

"My blessings on your dear Mama! (said Montalbert, smiling half maliciously)—how kind she is to me—but the moments are precious—tell me, I do beseech you, Rosalie, is it impossible for me to see you again before I leave this country—before I leave England—for years!"

"How is it possible?" answered Rosalie, hardly knowing what she said.

"It would be possible, (replied he), if you would only try to oblige me."

"O no! no! (cried she with quickness), pray do not think of it; it would be utterly improper if it were not impossible."

"Do you rise early? (said Montalbert, disregarding this faint repulse)—Do you never walk before breakfast?"

"Why will you ask?" answered Rosalie.

"Because, as I shall certainly quit Holmwood House after to-morrow—as I cannot again importune you—as I shall probably—ah! too probably—never see you again, let me entreat you only to see me for one half hour before I go?"

"I cannot indeed, Sir! (answered she). To what end would you ask, what I am sure you would think it very wrong were I to grant?"

"But if I am in the neighbourhood of your house, early on the morning after to-morrow, I might have a chance of saying adieu for the last time?"

Rosalie did not reply, for her mother was by this time returned, and sharply bidding her follow, went hastily to the hired chaise that waited for them.

CHAP.

VERY bitter were the reproaches which Rosalie was compelled to hear during their way home. She bore them with patience and silence, conscious perhaps that they were not wholly unmerited; she was, indeed, willing enough to acknowledge that she should not so rudely have repulsed Hughson in positive disobedience of her father's commands; but why her mother should make her conversation with Charles Vyvian so great a crime, she could not imagine, since in fact she had shown a much greater disposition to converse with his cousin than with him, and was perfectly conscious that she gave him no other preference than what arose from the long intimacy, that being so much together in childhood, had created between them.....

On this conversation, however, it was that Mrs. Lessington dwelt with acrimonious repetition—protesting to her daughter, that if Mrs. Vyvian were acquainted with the impropriety, folly, and disobedience she had been guilty of, that her favour would be forfeited for ever.

After listening to such sharp reproaches, intermingled with many assurances of the anger and resentment of both her parents, unless she behaved in a very different manner to Mr. Hughson, Rosalie obtained with some difficulty leave to retire, when, the image of Montalbert was the only one that she found rested forcibly on her mind: his conversation made a deeper impression the more she reflected on it. Montalbert was not only the most elegant and agreeable man she had ever conversed with, but he appeared to her to be the most unlikely man in the world to amuse himself with the cruel, yet too frequent folly of making professions that mean nothing. Montalbert therefore loved her. An idea so soothing acquired new power to charm her in proportion as she reflected on all he had said, and the manner in which he said it. How fortunate would be her destiny, should she become the wife of such a man, and how was it possible that her mother, who must see the marked preference he gave her, could hesitate a moment between him and such a man as Hughson. It was true Mr. Montalbert was a Catholic, but of what consequence was that?—Was not her mother's earliest and best friend of the same persuasion?—Such were some of the contemplations which engrossed the thoughts of Rosalie, and, fatigued as she was, kept her from repose till she heard the whole party return. Loud mirth, which echoed throughout the house, declared the joyous hearts of the company. Rosalie particularly distinguished the boisterous laugh and horse-play of Blagham, and the ideot-like chuckle of Hughson. Rosalie delighted to have escaped this conclusion to the evening, and fearing that her sister, who shared her bed for that night, might either be elated with the amusements of the latter part of the evening, or not yet have recovered of the ill-humour she had felt at the beginning of it as to enter into conversation with her, either to testify her pleasure or vent her ill-humour, Rosalie affected to be asleep. The next morning was fixed for their return home.

At breakfast every body affected to resent to Rosalie what had passed the evening before; and while Mr. Lessington regarded her with evident marks of displeasure, and would not speak to her, while her mother, still more angry, talked at her, and encouraged Blagham, in his strictures on the company who were to assembly, to ridicule the two travelled men, who were, he said, the greatest coxcombs he ever recollected to have seen——to which Hughson very warmly assented, casting at the same time a look of resentment at Rosalie, as if to say, "Yet you, Miss, preferred these men to me?"

"For my part, (said Blagham), by the Lord, if I had a sister who preferred such Frenchified chaps to honest Heart of Oak Englishmen, why I send her off to be a Signora or Mademoiselle among them—I should think such a bad taste a disgrace to my family. To be sure, in regard to these two fine gentlemen, they being Papists is reason enough for *their* being educated among your Seniors and Monseers; but what the use is of sending our young nobility and gentry to learn a parcel of useless coxcombry amongst them, I never could discover; and I own, Sir, (addressing himself to Mr. Lessington), that when I consider this matter, I cannot but think that the Legislature of our three kingdoms ought to interfere."

Before Mr. Lessington, who never spoke without due consideration and emphasis, could return an answer, Miss Maria said, "Oh! there they go!"

"Who go?" inquired her mother.

"My sister Rose's great and fine friends, (answered Maria), Mr. Vyvian and Mr.——, I forget his name, that very finest of all fine men."

Rosalie, who had seen them as well as her sister, could not help but blushing. Montalbert had looked earnestly in as he passed, and checked his horse a moment when he perceived he had caught her eye.

"I hope, (said Mrs. Lessington austerely), that Mr. Vyvian is returning immediately to his mother, who is extremely ill, who knows nothing of his being here, and who would be extremely unhappy were she to be informed of it. It was but the day before yesterday he was ill in bed, (added she, casting a significant glance at her youngest daughter), and last night he was at a ball."

"He did not dance, however, Madam, (said Rosalie), and I understood came hither only to consult a physician."

"Who informed *you* of all this, Ma'am, (answered her mother), and why do *you* take upon you to answer for him?"

Rosalie, whose conscience was perfectly clear in regard to Vyvian, answered calmly, "He told me himself, Madam, and I answered, because I thought your conversation addressed particularly to me."

"Humph—(said Mrs. Lessington contemptuously)—silence, child, would often become you much better."

The other young ladies had a great deal to do in the town, for Miss Catharine was now to be married in three days. Mantuamakers and milliners were therefore to be hurried, and, as soon as breakfast was over, they went out together for that purpose, attended by Blagham and Hughson, while Rosalie remained where she was, having no ambition to accompany them; her preparations for her sister's wedding were confined, (as it was intended that Maria only should accompany the bride), and about these she was by no means solicitous.

Disagreeable and uneasy to her as the remonstrances and reproaches were that she was still obliged to hear, she flattered herself that one good effect would arise from the circumstances of the preceding evening—that Hughson, convinced of its inefficacy, would carry his suit no farther, and that his pride would prevent her being teazed with addresses, which her sister seemed disposed to receive favourably.

But in this hope she was disappointed. The admiration Rosalie had so universally excited, while her sister had been hardly noticed, the whispers of approbation that he had heard from the most fashionable set in the room, for whose opinion the whole country around had the most implicit deference, as well as the impression she seemed to have made on Vyvian and Montalbert, were altogether circumstances so far from deterring Hughson from pursuing her, that they served only to inflame his ambition; and, though he affected to direct his attention towards Miss Maria for a while, in hopes of piqueing Rosalie, he soon renewed those expressions of affection and protestations of unwearied perseverance, from which Rosalie foresaw so much persecution and trouble.

As Hughson was to perform the marriage ceremony between his friend Blagham and

Miss Kitty Lessington, he went back with the family, and by his troublesome assiduities, and ridiculous attempts at gaiety and wit, deprived her of the satisfaction she would have derived from having left a place so very disagreeable to her as the provincial town where they had passed the last three days.......At home she as least hoped to enjoy the solitude of her own room, but she dared not ask herself, whether she ought to venture the meeting Montalbert had so earnestly solicited....She felt all its impropriety; then endeavoured to reconcile herself to a step from which she thought no evil consequence could possibly arise. "My mother, (said she, arguing this point with herself), my mother will never forgive me, should she know it—but how will she know it?— and what real harm is there in it?—It would certainly have a bad appearance, were a young woman known to have private meetings with any one—but what *meetings* can I have?—Is not Mr. Montalbert immediately going back to Italy, and is there any probability of my ever seeing him again?—Ah! no."—The argument concluded with a deep sigh, but it had not helped to determine her from an almost intuitive sense of propriety, for she had received but little instruction on such matters; she was conscious that she ought not to go out with a view of meeting Montalbert: yet to think that she had seen him for the last time, to let him go with impressions of her having a predilection in favour of such a man as Hughson, of her being happy among such society as she was condemned to, it was impossible to determine on it. Sleep the ensuing night was driven from the pillow of Rosalie by these debates; but it was at this season, long before day appeared with its first dawn, however, she left her bed, for it would very soon be necessary to determine whether she would venture to commit such an impropriety as meeting Montalbert, or suffer him to depart under the impressions he would carry with him, if she saw him no more.

His dejection when he spoke of immediately leaving England, his respectful manners, the warm and lively affection he seemed to have for her, the advantageous light in which his honourable addresses appeared to her, all contributed to dispose her to meet him; against it there was only that internal sense of prudence, (which, like the voice of conscience, could not be entirely stifled), and the fear of offending her mother. Yet why should her mother be offended?—Considered in every way, whether as to fortune, rank of life, family, or prospects, there could, she thought, be no comparison between Montalbert and Hughson; and if to have her married well was the wish of her parents, why should they be angry at her not declining an acquaintance which seemed likely to end in an establishment above their hopes. There was some truth, but more sophistry, in the arguments she used with herself to conquer her remaining apprehensions; when, having determined to venture, since it could be but for once, she left the house, and, trembling and looking behind her at every step, hastened through the heavy dews and gray fogs of a late October morning to the copse where she had first unexpectedly met Vyvian and Montalbert, and where he had told her he should be very early on this morning, the last of his stay in the country, in hopes of her giving him an opportunity of taking a long leave of her.

As she had usually been a very early riser, and frequently walked to some neighbouring village, or farm-house, before the rest of the family were risen, the servants and labourers, who saw her pass, took no notice of it, and she had crossed the orchard, and traversed the first copse with the swiftness of an affrighted fawn, before she gave herself time to breathe. The gloomy quiet of every object around her, the heavy gray mists that hung on the half-stripped trees, their sallow leaves slowly falling in her path, had something particularly aweful and oppressive: she could hardly draw her breath, and her heart beat so violently that she leaned against the style that in one place divided the wood. "Whither am I going? (said she); to meet a man, who till a week since was a stranger to me! How am I sure that he will not despise me for this early compliance;

perhaps I shall forfeit his good opinion—perhaps—surely it were better to retreat." There was, however, no longer time to hesitate, for at the end of the path before her Montalbert appeared. He sprang forward eagerly the moment he saw her—"This is very good, dearest Miss Lessington, (cried he); how infinitely I am obliged to you!"

"And now, (said Rosalie, collecting all her resolution), let me not risk my mother's displeasure by staying long; but receive, Sir—receive my sincere good wishes for your health and happiness, and suffer me to bid you adieu!"

"Good Heavens! (replied he), and will you already leave me?—No, Rosalie, our time is precious, and I will not throw it away in a profusion of words: I love you, and am sensible that on you alone depends the happiness of my future life. I will not, however, deceive you: I am a younger brother; and though the fortune of my family is very considerable, much of my expectations depend on my mother, who is a native of another country, who has hardly ever been in England, and who dislikes the customs, the manners, and, above all, the religion of this; with a great number of prejudices, which contribute but little to the happiness of her family, nor, I fear, to her own; she has, however, always been to me an affectionate, if not a tender mother, and it would be equally ungrateful and impolitic, were I to act in absolute defiance of her known wishes. Yet, surely, a medium may be found—without incurring her displeasure, I may escape the misery of resigning the only woman I ever saw, with whom I wish to pass my whole life."

"I do not see how, (answered Rosalie, trembling and faltering). No, Sir; however flattered I may be by your good opinion, I entreat you to think of me no more, otherwise than as a friend. The obstacles between us are insurmountable, and————"

"Not if you do not make them so, Rosalie, (interrupted he). Hear me with patience: Though you may think my mother's known aversion to my marrying an English woman and a Protestant, together with the state of my fortune, sufficient reasons for refusing immediately to unite your destiny with mine—yet surely you need not therefore refuse to remove the fear, the tormenting fear, of losing you, by promising that you will not give yourself to another, at least till I have attempted to conquer the obstacles that oppose my happiness. O Rosalie! if you had any idea of the agonies I feel, when I think that while I return to Italy in the hope of finding a remedy against the perverseness of my destiny, the object of my affections may be the wife of another—even of this Hughson, on whom it seems to be the resolution of your family to throw you away."

"If it be any satisfaction to you, Sir, (said Rosalie in a low voice), to know that Mr. Hughson can never be more to me than a common acquaintance, I most positively assure you of it."

"I am persuaded you think so now, (answered Montalbert with vivacity); but who shall assure me, Rosalie, that you can always resist the importunities, the commands of your father; family convenience, and what is called the voice of prudence, and all those motives that may be urged to enforce your obedience? Besides, if you should have resolution enough to dismiss this man, how many others are there who may have the same pretensions? No, nothing can give me a moment's peace, unless you promise me, loveliest of creatures, that you will await my return from Italy—that you will then be mine, if the obstacles now between us can be removed."

"On so short an acquaintance, can I, ought I, to promise this?" replied Rosalie with increased emotion. She then, though in broken sentences, and in a faint and low voice, urged all the reasons there were against her forming such an engagement; but Montalbert found means to convince her of their fallacy one by one, till at length he extorted from her the promise he demanded. He insisted on being allowed to cut off a lock of her hair, and on her taking a miniature of himself which he drew from his pocket, and which he owned had been drawn in London for his mother. He then told her that he should write to her, and that she must find some means of their securely corresponding. This Rosalie declared was quite impossible; but while he was pressing her to reflect farther, a loud voice was heard in the part of the wood adjoining the orchard calling on Rosalie. Terror now seized her. "It is my father, (said she). If he finds you with me, what shall I not suffer!—leave me—leave, me for Heaven's sake!"

"You terrify yourself needlessly; it may only be a servant sent to seek you."

"And why to seek me, (replied she), if there was no suspicion of my being improperly absent? It is not usual for them to inquire or call after me."

Montalbert now saw her so affected with apprehension, that he would not longer detain her; but kissing her hand, and pressing it a moment to his bosom, he told her he would find the means of writing to her, and disappeared, while Rosalie, endeavouring to recollect and compose herself, took the path that led towards home.

CHAP.

HAD it indeed been Mr. Lessington himself, who had thus loudly summoned his daughter to return home, it would have been difficult for her to have concealed from him the agitation of her mind, notwithstanding her utmost endeavours to compose herself; but it was only Abraham, a servant who was occasionally bailiff, coachman, footman, groom, or whatever was wanted in the family, who, approaching her out of breath, cried, "Lord, Miss, I've been ever so long looking a'ter you....Why, here a been all on em looking for your coming; for what d'ye think?"

"Indeed, I don't know," replied Rosalie, breathless, and terrified at this preamble.

"Ah! Miss—Miss!—you can't guess whose come?"

"No! no! Abraham—do pray tell me?"

"I've got a good mind not, for your giving me such a dance after you. (Abraham had seen her grow up from infancy, and was no observer of forms). However, I'll tell you for once: 'tis both our young masters; 'tis Mr. William from Oxford, and Mr. Francis from London—both—both on um be comed to be present at the wedding, and a rare time we shall all on us have on't I warrant too."

"I am very glad, indeed, (said Rosalie, relieved from a thousand apprehensions of she knew not what). I thought my brother William would not be here till to-morrow, and as for Frank, I did not know he was expected." She then hastened into the house, and in meeting her brothers, particularly the eldest, to whom she was much attached, the embarrassment of her manner was not remarked, nor was any inquiry made where she had been.

It was not till she retired to dress for dinner that she was at liberty to reflect on all that had passed with Montalbert. The promise she had given seemed to be a relief to her spirits, when she remembered that it should make her consider herself as betrothed to the only man in the world whom she preferred to all others; that she had now the best reasons in the world to strengthen her resolution, never to listen to Hughson; reasons, which if she dared plead them, her father himself could not disapprove. She ran over in her mind every look, every sentence of Montalbert, and sincerity and tenderness seemed to dwell upon his tongue. What but real affection could induce him to speak, to act as he had done? and what could be so fortunate as her inspiring such a man with a passion such as he professed to feel for her. A consciousness of attractions, which till very lately she had never suspected that she possessed, gave her a momentary pleasure; but she felt that those attractions would have been without value, had they not secured for her the heart of Montalbert.

Soon dressed for the day, she sat in the window of her bed chamber, pensively looking towards the quarter where Holmwood House was situated, though she could not distinguish it. "He is gone! (said she). Already he is on his way to London; in a few days after he arrives there he will leave it—will leave England—the sea will be between us!" She took out the picture he had given her, and, for the third time since it had been in her possession, fixed her eyes earnestly upon it. The candour and integrity of the countenance struck her particularly. "Never, (sighed she), can the heart that belongs to these features be otherwise than generous, tender, and sincere." She was thus feeding the infant passion which had taken entire possession of her mind, and was lost in thought, holding the picture still in her hand, when her elder brother opened the door. "Are you dressed, Rosalie? (said he), and may I come in?"—"O yes! yes! brother, (answered she, hurrying the picture into her pocket), pray come in."

"I have a great deal to say to you, my dear Rose, (said he); come, give me a place in the window by you. You are very much improved, my love, since I saw you last; I don't wonder at the havoc you make; but my mother complains of you, Rose."

"On what account, my brother? I am sure I never intentionally offended my mother."

"But she tells me that you have now an opportunity of marrying extremely well, but that from some unaccountable perverseness, or unreasonable prejudice, or perhaps, (added he, fixing his eyes earnestly on hers), perhaps through some unhappy predilection, you drive from you, with contempt and disdain, a man every way unexceptionable."

"You have seen him, brother, (answered Rosalie), and can tell whether you think him all that my mother has represented."

"I have only seen him for a moment, and have hardly exchanged ten words with him. His person is neither good nor bad, but surely my sister has too much sense to refuse a man merely because he is not an Adonis."

"But indeed, brother, it is not that. Mr. Hughson is a man, whom it is impossible I can ever like: he is silly , noisy, and conceited; a boaster, and a sort of man whom I know will displease you when you see more of him. I dare say his fortune is greater than I have a right to expect; but I never saw a man more likely to spend a fortune than he is, and I cannot think there is much worldly wisdom in marrying a man with whom I might enjoy a short affluence, that would only make me feel more severely the indigence he might reduce me to."

"All that is very well, (said William Lessington); but tell me, Rosalie, what do you say as to this prepossession in favour of another, of which my mother accuses you?"

"I can say nothing, (replied she), because I—because I know that—indeed I do not know who she means."

"Is there no such predilection existing then, Rosalie?"

"Not for the person my mother thinks of," answered she, colouring still higher.

"You allow there is for some other then?"

"Not at all—I am sure I did not say any thing like that; but if there were, why, my dear brother, should it of necessity be in favour of a person who would disgrace my family?"

"There may be very improper attachments, Rosalie, (replied he very gravely), which may not be disgraceful in the usual acceptation of the word: as, for example, if a young woman should be flattered into a partiality for a *boy* of a *different* religion, and in whose power it could never be to fulfill any promise which a childish passion might induce him to make. (The complection of Rosalie changed to a deeper scarlet). I see how it is, my sister, (added he), and will now distress you no farther; but I trust to your own sweetness and candour to give me an opportunity of discussing this matter when we are both more at leisure.......I believe dinner is now ready."

"Before you go, my dear William, (cried Rosalie, recovering herself a little), let me assure you, that my mother has no grounds whatever for her suspicions, but because Mr. Charles Vyvian has appeared particularly pleased at our meeting, and what was more natural? We were brought up together from children. As to myself, I certainly did the other night find more pleasure in talking to my old friend, whose mother I love so much, and am so much obliged to, than in dancing with Hughson, who is the most disagreeable man in the world to me—perhaps I might be rude to him—I am afraid I was; but why would my mother compel me to dance with him?"

"And is *that* all, Rosalie?"

"That is all, upon my honour, (replied she), in regard to Mr. Vyvian."

Young Lessington, who did not know Montalbert even by name, appeared satisfied, and they went down together; when, from the beginning of the dinner, conversation, and the quantity of wine that Hughson soon swallowed, Rosalie flattered herself that long before the close of the evening he would do or say something that would thoroughly disgust her elder brother, and, by convincing him that she was right in refusing him, procure for her a defense against the irksome importunity of his future addresses.

In this she was not mistaken; before young Lessington had been two hours in company with Hughson, he was compelled to own that Rosalie could not be blamed for having kept at a distance a man whose manners were so unpleasing. The other brother, however, who had seen very different company, and whose ideas had taken quite another turn, thought of him as he did of himself, that he was "a clever, sprightly, little fellow."

Dinner was hardly over, and the bottle going as briskly about as it could do before the ladies retired, when Abraham came stumbling into the room, and muttered something which nobody understood, and, before there was time for inquiry, Mr. Charles Vyvian and Mr. Montalbert entered, to the displeasure of some of the company, and to the astonishment of Rosalie, who, on meeting her brother's eyes, looked so confused, that all the suspicion Mrs. Lessington had hinted to him in the morning seemed to be confirmed. The reception they received was cold and formal, particularly from Mrs. Lessington, who gravely expressed her surprise, after what Mr. Vyvian had told her, at his making so long a stay in the country.

"Oh! (answered he), I was so unwell yesterday, that my good old doctor would not hear of my setting out to-day; and, as my mother thinks we are still upon the ramble, and will not be uneasy, I have persuaded my worthy old Abbé to say nothing about it: however, we intend to be good boys, and to go off to-morrow; and, upon my honour, (continued he, rising and taking her hands), my dear Mrs. Lessington, I only cam to know if you could not give me some little commission to my mother, to put her in good humour with her truant boy........Come—come—I know you will oblige me with a letter—or—you, Madam, perhaps, (turning to one of the other sisters)—if not, I am sure Miss Rosalie will."

The repulsive gravity with which Mrs. Lessington answered him, was but ill seconded by the increasing confusion of her daughter, who hesitated, blushed, and stammered out a few incoherent words; symptoms which did not escape her brother, who narrowly watched her, and who failed not to impute it all to a very different motive than the real one.

Montalbert, in the mean time, was on thorns; surrounded as she was, there was no possibility of speaking to her, and he could not bear to leave her without having fixed on some means by which they might hear from each other. He recollected that none of her family understood Italian: he looked round to see if it was likely any one in the room did, and being soon convinced he had nothing to apprehend, unless it was from the Oxford man, and even with him he thought the chances were much in his favour, he told Rosalie, addressing her with great gravity, that since he had the pleasure of seeing her, he had recollected the words of the Italian song she had mentioned, and that, if she would favour him with a pen and ink in the next room, he would write them out.

At this moment the mistress of the house, receiving an hint from her husband to depart, said, as she rose from the table, "We will send you one down, Sir."—"O no! (replied he), rather let me write it, dear Madam, in your apartment; and, Vyvian, as we must immediately return home, we will now wish Mr. Lessington and his friends good night." This short ceremony passed with great formality on all sides, and Vyvian and Montalbert following the woman of the family into another room, the latter sat himself down with great solemnity to write out his song, which having done in the plainest Italian he could imagine, but written as if it was in measure, he gave it to Rosalie; and Vyvian, who had been talking earnestly to her the whole time, reluctantly took his leave also, and they both departed.

They were hardly out of the room before Mrs. Lessington, whose anger and suspicion were roused anew, demanded to see the paper Montalbert had given her. Rosalie, not without fear and trembling, delivered it to her. She looked at it a moment, and believing from the manner in which it was written it was really a song, gave it back to her again, not without evident marks of displeasure, and many hints of her resolution to inform Mrs. Vyvian where her son was, and of the impropriety of his conduct, if he did not leave the country the next day. Of all this, as Rosalie was not obliged to think it addressed to her, she took no notice.

The next day the wedding of her second sister and Mr. Blagham was celebrated. The party were more noisy and disagreeable than is even usual on such occasions. Hughson was the most drunk, and consequently the most impertinent; and never was an hour so welcome to Rosalie as that which took them all away, by the favour of a full moon, and left her alone with her mother.

Till now the tumult, with which she had been surrounded, had not allowed her a moment, except those allotted to repose, to indulge reflections on what had passed. The sullen calm that succeeded was calculated to restore her dissipated and bewildered thoughts. Her mother, busied in arranging her house, left her to herself; her father had accompanied the bride and bridegroom to their house, and was afterwards to go on a tour with them into the eastern part of the county. It was at once a matter of pleasure and surprise to Rosalie, that he had never once proposed to her being of the party, and she remarked that he now appeared much less anxious than her mother to promote with her the suit of Mr. Hughson; it seemed as if he would have been as well contented that his daughter Maria should ensure this important conquest.

Mr. Lessington was one of those men who have just as much understanding as enable them to fill, with tolerable decency, their part on the theatre of the world. He loved the conveniences of life, and indulged rather too much in the pleasures of the table. His less fortunate acquaintances (a race of people to whom he was not particularly attached) knew that Mr. Lessington was not a man to whom the distressed could apply with any hope of receiving any thing but good advice. Those who were more fortunate had for the most part a very good opinion of Mr. Lessington. If he was exact and somewhat strict in enacting his dues, he was also very regular in the duties of his office; and if he did not feel much for the distresses of the poor, he never offended, as some country curates have done, the ears of the rich, by complaints which those who *overlook* the labourers in the vineyard are always so unwilling to hear. He had brought up a large family respectably, and every body concluded he had some private fortune, besides the two or three thousand pounds he was known to have received with his wife. He kept a post-chaise; not, indeed, a very superb and fashionable equipage, but very well for that country: his cart horses drew it, but they were sleek and well trimmed, and Abraham, trussed up in a tight blue jacket, and his broad cheeks set off by a jockey cap, made a very respectable appearance as conductor of a vehicle which gave no inconsiderable degree of consequence to its owners in a country thinly inhabited by gentlemen. Mr. Lessington was the most punctual man imaginable at all meetings of the clergy, where he did equal honour to the sublunary good things that were to be eaten, and the spiritual good things that were to be listened on. He had an high idea of his consequence in the church, and was a violent opposer of all innovations; against which he had drawn his pen with more internal satisfaction to himself than with visible profit to his bookseller. His works, though he read them with extreme complacency, by having, though want of orthodox taste in the modern world, the misfortune to be, according to a term most painful to the ears of an author, *shelfed*.

This, however, affected Mr. Lessington less than it would have done many authors: for he wrote less for literary fame, or literary profit, than to recommend himself to certain persons who so greatly dreaded any of those impertinent people that dare to think some odd old customs might be altered *a little* for the better; that nothing would, he knew, be so effectual a recommendation to the favour of these dignitaries as zeal, in stopping even with rushes the gaps threatened by such innovators, even before they were visible to any but the jealous eyes that saw, or fancied they saw, the whole fence levelled. The prosperity of his family might be considered as being in some degree the effect of his thus keeping always on the right side, for he was reckoned a rising man, and one who would at no very remote period be promoted to higher dignities. Mr. Blagham had not been entirely without considerations of this sort, when he married a wife with no other portion than her wedding clothes; but Mr. Lessington had promised her something handsome at his death, and there was no doubt in the mind of the lawyer of his ability to fulfill his promise.

    Mrs. Lessington and Rosalie had now been at home alone for three days. The former had settled her house, and was quietly enjoying the order she had restored after all the bustle they had lately been in; while Rosalie, with mingled emotions of fear, anxiety, and doubt, waited for intelligence from Montalbert.

    It was in the evening of the third day, that as she was walking in a sort of court, that was before the house next a road, an horseman stopped, and inquired if this was not the parsonage? On Rosalie's answering in the affirmative, he produced a letter, which he said he had been sent with from Lewes.

    The predominant idea in the head of Rosalie being Montalbert, she trembled like a leaf when the man gave her the letter, and, without considering whether it was likely her lover should send it thus openly, or how it should come from Lewes, she hastened breathless into the house to obtain a light to read it by, for it was now nearly dark. In her way to the kitchen she was met by her mother, who seeing her extreme agitation, and a letter in her hand, for she had not had presence of mind to conceal it, immediately fancied it came from Charles Vyvian, who was always haunting her imagination. In this persuasion she took if from her daughter, and carrying it immediately to a candle, found—not a billet-deux to Rosalie, but intelligence of a very different nature—it was a letter from Mr. Blagham, informing her, after a short preface, that Mr. Lessington died that morning in an apoplectic fit.

    Though nothing was more likely than such an event, from the form and manner of life of her husband, it had never once occurred to her as possible. The shock, therefore, was great, and the widow's grief not a little increased by the reflection, that their income arising from church preferment was at an end.

    Rosalie felt as she ought on the loss of a parent; but as it was more to the purpose to endeavour to assuage her mother's sorrow than to indulge her own, she gave her whole attention to that purpose. Mrs. Lessington was too reasonable to be a very inconsolable widow, and in a few hours was in a condition to consider what ought to be done, which Rosalie set about executing, by writing to Mr. Blagham, and giving such orders as her mother thought necessary.

CHAP.

IT is not necessary to relate all that passed in the Lessington family, till the period when all its members were assembled to hear his will read. It was then found that he had given his widow, for her life, a third of all he possessed, which amounted in the whole to about eight thousand pounds, and divided the rest among his children, to each of whom he allotted a certain portion to be paid at a certain time, except Rosalie, whose name was not even mentioned in the will.

All expressed their surprise at this except Mrs. Lessington, who said nothing in answer to their exclamations of wonder. Rosalie, indifferent as to fortune, of which she knew not the want or the value, was no otherwise grieved at this strange omission, than as it proved her father's total want of affection for her—a conviction that cost her many tears; nor were those tears dried by the remark she made on the behaviour of her sisters and her younger brother, who all seemed pleased, though they affected concern. The behaviour of her elder brother, however, would have given her comfort, could she have conquered the painful idea, that her father had thrown her off as a stranger to his blood. As soon as the funeral was over, her brother William took occasion to talk to her alone. "Be not so dejected, my dear Rosalie, (said he); unpromising as your prospects appear, you have at least the consolation of knowing that you have always a friend in me, who will never forsake you."

"You are too good, dearest William, (replied the weeping mourner); but do not imagine that it is the want of my share of my father's little property that grieves me—no; if he had but *named* me with kindness, I should not have been so unhappy; but when I think that he must certainly have died in anger with me, that either from my seeming to refuse Mr. Hughson, or some other cause, he was irritated against me."

"If you reflect a moment, my sweet sister, on the date of the will, you will see that this could not be. The will is dated above three years since, when the very existence of such a man as Hughson was unknown to him, when you were only between fourteen and fifteen years of age, when you had been more with Mrs. Vyvian than at home, and when it was every way impossible that you could have given him the least offence; I rather think that this strange circumstance arose from the opinion he entertained, that Mrs. Vyvian would provide for you."

"How could my father think that, (said Rosalie), when he must have known that Mrs. Vyvian, notwithstanding the large fortune she brought, has not even the power to hire or discharge a servant, and is hardly allowed enough yearly to appear as her rank requires, least, as her cross tyrant of an husband says, she should squander his fortune on begging friars and mummers of her own religion? She had, indeed, a settlement of her own, but I heard him reproach her with having disposed of it in some such way; but, however that may be, my father must know that it was not in her power to do any thing for me. Of late too, he must have thought that it was not her wish, for she has appeared almost entirely to have forgotten me."

"There is, however, no other way of accounting for the circumstance, and the more I reflect on it the more I am persuaded that this is the truth."

Rosalie, though far from being convinced by the reasoning of her brother, was consoled by his tenderness, and by degrees regained her serenity, which was, however, again disturbed by a letter from Montalbert, in which he renewed all the professions he had made on their parting; told her he had continued to postpone his journey to Italy for some time longer, and had done so only in the hope of seeing her again.

He did not seem to have heard of her father's death. She knew that her being left destitute of fortune would make no alteration whatever in his affections; the little she would in any case have possessed could never indeed have been any object to him, even if fortune had ever once been in his thoughts. She wrote to him, therefore, of what had happened; and without affecting to deny the partiality she felt for him, and lamenting the little probability of their meeting properly, submitted it to him, whether it would not be more prudent to forbear a meeting at all till there was less danger of offending her mother. She told him, that of the future destination of the family she knew nothing; but that, from what she could learn, her mother had some thought of taking a small house in or near London, when the period came on which she must quit their present habitation.

Rosalie now found herself for a while relieved from the irksome importunities of Hughson, who was obliged to be absent. Her mother too seemed to have relaxed a good deal in the earnestness she had formerly shown on this subject, and had not her extreme uncertainty, in regard to Montalbert, been a constant source of anxiety, she would at this period have tasted of more tranquility than had long fallen to her share.

Sometimes when her brother William, who continued at home, was either instructing her as the kindest tutor, or amusing her as the tenderest friend, her heart reproached her for her insincerity towards such a brother, and she was half tempted to relate to him her engagement with Montalbert; but when she had nearly argued herself into a resolution of doing this, her natural timidity checked her: she recollected how material it was to her lover that their engagements should remain a secret; and she was besides deterred by the fear that her brother would, from education and principle, in all probability, strenuously oppose her becoming the wife of a Catholic.

But naturally ingenuous and candid, it was impossible for her so well to dissimulate, but that Mr. Lessington saw there was something more on her mind than she ever ventured to express. The impression that his mother had given him of some attachment between her and young Vyvian frequently returned to his recollection, though he thought it could be only a childish passion on the part of Vyvian, who would think no more of it after he left England, he dreaded least the spirits and health of Rosalie might suffer, as he had seen so often happen to young women, who had been incautiously led into listening to vows and promises that were meant by the men that made them only as the amusement of an idle hour.

In his frequent conversations with his sister, therefore, and intermingled with the lessons he sometimes gave her, he found opportunities continually to hint at the weakness and danger of attending to such sort of professions; while, at other times, he took notice to say, how generally unfortunate marriages turned out to be where the parties were of different religions, giving Mr. and Mrs. Vyvian as an example immediately within their own knowledge. On these occasions he fixed his eyes on those of Rosalie, and, sure that he meant more than he expressed, her countenance betrayed her consciousness; for whatever her brother said, when he remotely alluded to Vyvian, was equally applicable to Montalbert, and whatever resolutions she sometimes made, when she was alone, to avow ingenuously the truth, these hints entirely deprived her of the courage she had been thus trying to obtain.

Montalbert, who by means of a servant at Holmwood House, on whose fidelity he could depend, continued to write to her and to receive her letters, became now impatient to learn where was to be her future residence. As this seemed still uncertain, he implored leave to come down incog. to the neighbourhood of Holmwood; than which, he said, nothing was more easy, as he could be concealed in the house of a farmer, a tenant of Mr. Vyvian's, who, being a Catholic, was entirely devoted to his service, and of an integrity on which he could rely. Rosalie, however, extremely alarmed at such a proposal, urged so many reasons why it should not be executed, and assured him it would make her so extremely miserable, that he, for that time, consented to relinquish it, which he consented to with less reluctance, when she informed him, that within a few days her mother had talked in more positive terms of their immediate removal to London, or to its nieghbourhood; that her brother was gone to look for a house for them, and she thought it extremely probable, from the impatience her mother expressed, that they should there begin the new year. Rosalie was at a loss to comprehend by what means Montalbert prolonged his stay in England so much beyond the time, when he had told her, his mother expected his return to Naples, where she generally resided; this surprised her still more, when she found by part of a letter from Mrs. Vyvian, which Mrs. Lessington read to her, that Charles Vyvian was already gone. The sentences of the letter which her mother chose to communicate ran thus:—

"I have determined, in order to be near Dr. W——, without residing immediately in London, to take an house at Hampstead, and my upholsterer informs me he has found one that answers my description. Mr. Vyvian has, in his cold way, assented to my engaging it, taking care, however, to let me understand, at the same time, that he thought my not being well or able to live in London was a mere whim, and that the air of Hampstead was not at all better than at his house in Park Lane, or even so good. Till now I did not know he had taken an house in Park Lane, instead of that in Brook Street; but, alas! my dear old friend, there are many other reasons, besides the difference of the air, that will make me adhere to my intention of going to Hampstead. It is an unpleasant circumstance surely to be a cypher in one's own house, and such I am become; now that my son, my dear Charles, is gone, I feel that there is nobody here that is at all attentive to me. The Miss Vyvians, young as they are, are introduced into the world by their father, or their father's friends: the countenance of a mother seems not necessary to them; they are fumed, I believe, with spirits to enjoy all the pleasures of gay life, and seem to fear, from me, that interruption which certainly it is not my intention to give them. The eldest, though not yet sixteen, her father thinks of marrying to a man of high rank, with whom she got acquainted while she was with her father's sister in Yorkshire. He has not, however, the title to which he is to succeed; but his uncle, whose heir he is, is old and without children, and having some political connection, I know not what, with Mr. Vyvian, it is by them that this union is proposed, while the mother of the young man, who had an immense fortune in her own disposal, has hitherto shown a disinclination to the match, in the persuasion that my daughter is still a Catholic. I have learned these particulars from persons who are in their confidence, which I am not, and I easily comprehend that his intended connection adds a strong reason to many others why the father and the daughter would be quite as well pleased if we saw no more of each other, during the winter, than we have done for these two last summers. Do not, however, grieve for me, my dear Catharine; you know my sufferings, and you know how I am enabled to bear them. From Mr. Vyvian why should I expect kindness? I am thankful that my lot is not yet more bitter than it is. It would be a great pleasure to me, should your affairs allow you to settle in the neigh bourhood where I have determined, for the present, to fix my residence. I am, as you well know, no great judge of such matters; but, I believe, from all the inquiries I have been able to make, that you would not, in point of economy, find the difference so great between living near London and in a country town as you may perhaps imagine; at least not to a family, which would not, I imagine, enter much into the card-playing societies of the village, but would live a good deal retired, though, considering your two unmarried daughters, you could not, perhaps, be quite such a recluse as I shall be, who, except my nephew Montalbert, whose stay, however, in England will not be long, shall probably live for weeks together without seeing any body but my confessor."

"The rest of the letter, (said Mrs. Lessington, as she put it into her pocket), is of condolence, and so forth, on Mr. Lessington's death."

"And is there no other mention of me in it?" said Rosalie.

"No, not any other, (answered her mother coldly); but what, does that make you sigh?"

"Indeed it does, Ma'am, (answered she); for how can I help lamenting that Mrs. Vyvian, who used to love me so, seems, and indeed has long seemed, entirely to forget me."

"O, when she sees you again, she will recollect her former partiality for you. You know that my friend is so wrapped up in a particular set of notions, and such an enthusiast in her religion, that she thinks it a very wrong thing to be much attached to any body, and endeavours to wean herself from all affections that may prevent her giving up her whole heart to God; and really, considering the way in which her family treat her, I really think it is extremely fortunate that her tender heart and weak spirits have taken that turn; otherwise to be treated, poor dear woman, as she is, to have such a husband, and such children, would certainly break her heart."

"Though her daughters, (said Rosalie gravely), are certainly very unlike what she could with them, I believe her son is dutiful and affectionate—I never saw any thing wrong in him."

"*You* never saw, (repeated her mother)—I dare say—it is very becoming in *you*, to be sure, Rosalie, to enter on his defense. I wish I may be mistaken, but I am much afraid that her son will no more contribute to her happiness than her daughters: however, the boy is gone now, thank God, and at least will not give her the *sort* of uneasiness she would have felt, could she have known of his behaviour while he was here."

"What behaviour, dear Madam?" said Rosalie, who wished to know the extent of her mother's suspicions.

"What behaviour—why, did he not talk a great deal of nonsense to you?—

Did he not pretend to make love to you?"

"No, upon my word, (answered she); he said a great many civil things, and foolish things, if you please to call them so, but nothing that was at all like making love to me."

Mrs. Lessington then put an end to the conversation, by saying, that as he was now gone abroad for some years, it did not much signify what boyish nonsense he had talked, since it had gone no further; and Rosalie left her, well pleased to find from what she had said that her intention of removing her family to Hampstead was confirmed by this letter from her old friend, and that she meant almost immediately to put it in execution.

In a fortnight afterwards, all their arrangements being made, they departed for ever from a part of the country where Mrs. Lessington had resided about seven and twenty years, or rather from her native country, for she was born not far from Holmwood House. She left it, however, with much less regret than people usually feel on quitting a spot to which they have long been habituated. Miss Maria—or, to speak more properly, Miss Lessington, for she was now the eldest unmarried sister, was pleased with a change which offered her a prospect of seeing London, where she had never been for more than two or three days.

The Abbé Hayward, dismissed by Mr. Vyvian from Holmwood, had now left that venerable edifice to servants. The way of the Lessington family to the next post-town lay through the park; as Rosalie passed this scene of her former happiness, a thousand mournful thoughts crowded on her recollection, but she consoled herself with the thoughts of being soon near Mrs. Vyvian, and that she was going where, since Charles Vyvian would no longer be there to alarm the vigilance of her mother, she hoped to be allowed the innocent pleasure of conversing with Montalbert, without the necessity of contrivances that she felt to be unworthy of both.

CHAP.

MRS. Vyvian arrived at the house she had taken at Hampstead a few days after the family of Mrs. Lessington had become inhabitants of that village. The description of the first meeting between her and her old friend may be given best in Rosalie's own words to Montalbert; whom, it was agreed, should not appear immediately on their arrival. "At length I have seen her, my friend—this dear Mrs. Vyvian—so nearly related to you, and therefore dear to me—the first and best friend of my childhood; for I never recollect having received so many proofs of affection from my mother as from her......Ah! Montalbert, how is she changed since I saw her last; yet it is but a little while, not yet two years; but trouble, as she said with a melancholy yet sweet smile, makes greater havoc in the constitution than time. I do not know, Montalbert, whether it is her being so nearly related to you, or the memory of her past kindness, or both, but to me there is an attraction about Mrs. Vyvian that I never was conscious of in any other person. The eminent beauty she once possessed is gone, and its ruins only remain, but the delicacy, the faded loveliness of her whole form, is, perhaps, more interesting than the most animated bloom of youth and health. She had not spirits for the first two days after her arrival to receive us all. My mother only was admitted to see her. Yesterday, however, my sister and I were allowed to attend her at an early hour of the afternoon. Maria was going to the play with a family who live here, who are distantly related to the husband of one of my sisters, and who imagined, and perhaps not without reason, that to make parties for us to visit public places is the first kindness they can show to some of the family. Only Maria, however, accepted this invitation, for I had hopes of passing the evening with Mrs. Vyvian; a pleasure I would not have exchanged for the most brilliant spectacle that London offers.

"How can Mr. Vyvian treat this charming woman with coldness, even with cruelty, as I am afraid he does, though my mother says she never complains?—How is it possible that her daughters can neglect her?—Were I her daughter, I think it would be the greatest happiness of my life to watch her very wishes before she could express them, and to relieve that languor which always seems to hang over her spirits, and cloud the brilliancy of an understanding naturally so good. But I have heard, Montalbert, she was compelled to resign the man to whom she was attached, and to marry Mr. Vyvian, who, though he knew her reluctance, was determined to persevere. Strange that there can be found a human being so selfish as to act thus, and then treat with cruelty the victim whom he has thus forced into his power. I hope I shall never again see this man, for I feel such an antipathy to him that it would really be painful to me. As to the young ladies, I find they are frequently to visit their mother, but I shall avoid them as much as possible, for they are so much changed since we played together as children of the same family, that there is no longer any affection probably between us—I shall be despised as the daughter of a country curate; and though, I hope, I am not proud, I do not love to be despised......Ah! Montalbert, it is your partiality that has, perhaps, taught me to feel this sensation more than I ought to do. The little rustic thinks that she is preferred by Montalbert, and forgets her humility.

"I thank you, most sincerely thank you, for your forbearance. Believe me, a little self-denial now will greatly accelerate the security with which we may see each other hereafter. My mother has so little idea of your having any partiality to me, that she seems quite easy now Charles Vyvian is gone, and, except that she still thinks I have done extremely wrong in refusing to encourage the addresses of Hughson, she seldom dwells on what is passed. From present appearances, my dear friend, it seems as if we should be fortunate enough to pass a few tranquil and pleasant hours in the society of each other before you go to Italy; alas! they will be but transient—for yesterday, Mrs. Vyvian, in speaking of my drawing, and recommending to my mother to procure me a good master, she said, 'When my nephew, Montalbert, goes back, as he must now do very soon, since I find his mother is become very impatient at his long stay, he shall send over some chalks and crayons, for Rosalie, much better than can be found in London.'—If either of them had looked at me, at that moment, they would have remarked, that I did not hear with indifference the name of Montalbert, but fortunately I escaped observation, and soon recovered myself.

"It is long, very long, since any circumstance has given me such pleasure as being restored to my beloved benefactress, yet she says little to me; she makes no professions of that kindness towards me, which, I believe, has not been lessened even by our long separation; but there is an affection in her manner which I cannot describe. She is civiller to my sister than to me; but she addresses her as Miss Lessington, while she calls me Rosalie. I recollect that it is *her* name, and it seems in *her* mouth to have peculiar charms.

"I have passed, perhaps, too much time since I left her in reflecting how happy I might be, could I be related to this dear woman without opposition from the more near relations of Montalbert. You have often told me, that you love her as a mother, though only the half sister of your father. The sweetness of her manners, even that weak health, and that air of pensive sorrow, which her own children, at least her daughters, seem to consider as the effect of bigotry or unsociable humour, make her to me an object of tenderer attention. O Montalbert! what delight it would be to me to soothe the hours which are embittered by matrimonial discord, and, I fear, by filial neglect.

"Yet, while I think thus, perhaps I am continuing a correspondence with you, that may be displeasing to her, that may add to her solicitude, and deprive her of the satisfaction of seeing her nephew married to a woman of equal rank and of his own church. This reflection is extremely bitter to me, and it occurs the oftener, because I see with what alarm she thinks of her son's making any other alliance than what his father would choose for him; though it is very certain that ambition only will govern him, and that, in regard to religion, she cannot, if Mr. Vyvian dictates, be gratified.

"I shall hardly hear from you, Montalbert, again, before you will be here. As now I expect you, I shall not, I think, betray myself when we meet.—Till then, my dear friend, farewell!"

That she was totally destitute of fortune gave not a moment's concern to Rosalie; dependent wholly on her mother, and likely, in case of her death, to be left wholly destitute on the world, since the share she had of Mr. Lessington's fortune was to go to her other children at her decease, she felt not the least uneasiness as to pecuniary circumstances, but, with easy faith of youth, trusted that the attachment of her lover would save her from every distress, and that before she should be deprived of her surviving parent, whose life was apparently a very good one, she should be the wife of Montalbert.

He now saw her almost every day, for as he had always been attentive to Mrs. Vyvian, there was nothing remarkable in his frequent visits to her; nor was it strange that he should renew his slight acquaintance with her friends.

Miss Lessington, whose acquaintance increased every day, had continual invitations to stay at the houses of some of them for several nights together. Rosalie failed not sometimes to receive the same kind of complements, but she generally declined them, saying, that she could not leave her mother alone: but, in fact, she had no wish to mix in those societies, or to enter into those public amusements, which gave so much pleasure to her sister. While Maria, apprehensive of the superior elegance of Rosalie, showed a visible disinclination to her joining the these parties, and gradually discouraged her friends from giving these invitations, by observing, that her sister was of a very reserved turn; that she had formed connections in a very different sphere of life from the rest of her family; and that it was merely giving her the trouble to find excuses, to invite her to scenes or society for which she had a decided repugnance.

In a very short time, therefore, the attornies and brokers wives, to whom Mr. Blagham had introduced the family, forbore to attempt engaging a young woman who they imagined gave herself airs, and was extremely proud and reserved.——Miss Lessington was left in undisturbed possession of all the admiration the set of men that belonged to these "worshipful societies" had to bestow, and Rosalie at liberty to pass her time in company much more agreeable to her.

Her mother, less refined, and loving cards rather too much, was not equally difficult as to her companions; though she had really as much affection for Mrs. Vyvian as she was capable of feeling for any body, she could not help being sometimes sensible of a want of variety. Her friend's piety and estrangement from the world made her, as good Mrs. Lessington sometimes thought, rather respectable than amusing, and instead of such long visits from her confessor, Mrs. Lessington secretly wished for another, that they might *make up a rubber*. Insensibly she became acquainted with some "mighty agreeable people" in the village, who never played high, but were happy to make a little snug party just to pass away the long evenings. One of these parties introduced a second, a second a third, till Mrs. Lessington could hardly spare one in a week to pass with her friend Mrs. Vyvian, who, when Rosalie was with her, seemed, however, to be scarce sensible of the absence of her mother.

But from that unfortunate prepossession received early in life, that to deny herself the most innocent gratifications were sacrifices acceptable to Heaven, Mrs. Vyvian frequently abstained from indulging herself with the cheerful conversation of Rosalie, who then, as her mother was so frequently out, and now went occasionally to London for two or three days among her own and her eldest daughter's friends, was left at home, and the visits of Montalbert were uninterrupted, and without inquiry. To be continually in presence of a beloved object, to see or suppose that his attachment every moment becomes stronger, to listen to arguments to which the heart yields but too ready an assent, was a situation of all others the most dangerous for a young woman who had not seen her nineteenth year. Montalbert, besides the advantages of a very handsome person, had the most insinuating manners and the most interesting address: he was naturally eloquent—love rendered his eloquence doubly formidable; and Rosalie had nothing to oppose to his earnest entreaties for a secret marriage, but the arms with which he had himself furnished her—the fear of discovery on the part of his mother, which he owned would injure, indeed ruin, his future prospects in life. This he still acknowledged, but averred that it was impossible his mother, who resided in Naples, should know that he was married in England. Rosalie represented, that if Mrs. Vyvian knew it, it must inevitably be known to her. Montalbert insisted that there was no necessity of Mrs. Vyvian's knowing any thing about it. Rosalie entreated that he would first go to Italy, without risking the displeasure of a parent on whom he depended. Montalbert declared, he should be wretched to leave her; that he did not know how to acquire resolution enough to absent himself, leaving her, perhaps, exposed to the persecution of other lovers, which it distracted him only to think of, while he passed the miserable hours in which he should be absent from her, in anxiety, in torture, which, if she was once securely his, would be infinitely less insupportable.

But notwithstanding the frequent opportunities they now had of meeting, and even of passing whole hours alone together, how was it possible that a private marriage could be effected?—Rosalie knew that to escape to Scotland, and return without being missed, and without avowedly eloping, was impossible. Montalbert allowed it to be so, but he had another expedient ready—they might be married by a Catholic priest. Rosalie had heard, but in a vague way, that such marriages were not valid, but Montalbert reasoned her out of this persuasion. "Admitting, (said he), my dearest love, that it were as you have heard, would not such a marriage be binding to me? Might it not at any time be renewed according to the laws of any country where we may reside, when I shall be wholly at liberty? and is it material to you what restrictions are laid upon such marriages in England, if your husband looks upon other laws binding to him?—Even if we were to have the ceremony performed in your church, I should think it necessary to have it gone over a second time by a priest of ours." By such arguments he sometimes shook the wavering resolution of Rosalie, who, except the single circumstance of his mother's known aversion to his marrying an English protestant, which her reason told her was unjust and unreasonable, saw nothing that ought to prevent her giving her person where she had already given her heart. In point of family and fortune, Montalbert was infinitely her superior. Her mother therefore, however she might reproach her with having married clandestinely, could not accuse her with having debased herself or degraded her family. She had no other person to whom she was accountable, unless it was her elder brother, whom she loved too much to be quite easy as to his sentiments; but, on the other hand, it was impossible he could make any objections, unless it was the difference of religion; yet she dared not venture to tell him, least that single circumstance should appear to him of consequence enough to prevent entirely a union otherwise so desirable.

    Every opportunity that occurred, Montalbert pressed his suit with redoubled ardour: he urged, with all the vehemence of passion, the necessity of his immediate return to Italy, as he had already, on various pretences, prolonged his stay two months beyond the time he intended.— There was now a danger that his mother might suspect that some of those connections, she was so averse to, were the occasion of his prolonged absence, and might engage some of her friends in England in an inquiry that would be the cause of discovering what nobody now seemed to suspect. This and numberless other reasons Montalbert always had ready to offer why there was no time to deliberate: he had already conquered one obstacle—the difficulty of finding a Catholic priest who would venture to perform the ceremony.

    Besides the consequence, both in England and in Italy, of his family and his connections, the ease with which a dispensation might be obtained whenever his mother withdrew her opposition, and the pecuniary advantage Montalbert promised the priest, with whom he had at length succeeded; knew that Rosalie was the daughter of a country clergyman, and had no relations who were at all likely to be displeased at her marrying a man so greatly her superior, and of course not likely to proceed against one who had committed a breach of law so much to their advantage: he rather wished to detach Montalbert from his pursuit, by representing the great distance between him and Rosalie in temporal concerns, as well as the difference in spiritual affairs, which appeared to him so momentous. Finding it, however, very bootless to argue with a man of three and twenty, madly in love, he consented to do as Montalbert required, and reconciled his conscience by that accommodating reflection at hand on so many occasions, "If I do not do it, some other will." He stipulated with Montalbert, however, that if there should be any probability of his incurring the heavy penalty for marrying a minor, that he should be immediately sent to Rome at the expence of Montalbert; an expedient which Montalbert immediately agreed to, as indeed he would have done so to any demands the father thought proper to have made, however unreasonable they might have been.

    The longer Rosalie reflected on the proposals of her lover, the fainter became her opposition; yet still conscious that it could not be right to dispose of herself without the consent of her mother and her brother, she more than once intreated Montalbert to allow her to consult them; but he heard this request always with impatience, declaring, that if she determined to tear herself from him, to abandon him to all the horrors of that despair which her loss would inflict, she could find no way more certain than what she proposed. His vehemence, and the conviction of his sincerity, which that vehemence brought with it, once more conquered her scruples. Montalbert extorted once more a reluctant and trembling acquiescence, and then eagerly insisting on finding some immediate opportunity for them to meet, where the priest might attend, Rosalie, terrified at the step she was about to take, again recoiled, and intreated to be released from her inconsiderate promise.

Though the attachment between these young people seemed not even to be suspected either by Mrs. Vyvian or Mrs. Lessington, yet the conflict in the mind of Rosalie had such an effect on her frame, that the former one day observed it to her as they were sitting together alone. "Surely, my dear, (said she, laying down her work, and looking very earnestly at Rosalie), surely you are not well."

"Dear Ma'am, (answered Rosalie), why do you suppose so?"

"You are pale, (said Mrs. Vyvian); your eyes are heavy and languid, I am afraid, my love,—————————-" She hesitated, and the conscience of Rosalie at that moment accusing her, a faint blush overspread her countenance as she eagerly cried, "Afraid, my dear Madam, of what?"

"Nay, of nothing, Rosalie, that need alarm you: I will tell you my fears—either you have some affection that makes you uneasy, or the almost total seclusion in which you live is too much for your spirits."

"Indeed, Madam, my spirits would be very ill bear the dissipation in which my sister lives. The seclusion that gives me an opportunity of passing some of my hours with you, is the greatest gratification I can enjoy."

"But to the other article, Rosalie, what do you say?"

"To what article, Madam?"

"Oh! you have forgot already—to what I told you I feared as one cause of the alteration I have observed."

"Indeed, my dear Mrs. Vyvian, I am sensible of no alteration. You know how few people I see, and that with fewer still I have much acquaintance, or with it."

Mrs. Vyvian shook her head with an air of incredulity, and as Rosalie fancied of concern; but she suffered the discourse to drop, and Rosalie left her, trembling lest the truth was suspected, and dreading, yet feeling it necessary, to give an account of this dialogue to Montalbert.

CHAP.

WHAT had passed the preceding evening between Mrs. Vyvian and Rosalie was no sooner repeated to Montalbert, than it served as an additional argument to enforce the consent he had been so long soliciting. Montalbert was of a warm and impetuous temper: though he had never yet been emancipated from the government of an high-spirited and imperious mother, he was not the less bent on pleasing himself, than are those who have never been contradicted. It seemed, indeed, as if the severe restraint he had so long habitually been under, disposed him to be more earnest in a circumstance on which the whole happiness of his life depended; and when Rosalie asked him how he could hope ever to reconcile his mother to a marriage to which he himself owned she would have unconquerable objections, he inquired, in his turn, what amends she could make him for opposing the only connection which could make him happy, only from prejudice and difference of opinion in matters wherein he could not think as she did, and wherein he thought it unreasonable that her prepossessions should interfere with his choice. "I will certainly not make my mother uneasy, (said he); I will so far pay a compliment to her unfortunate prejudices, as to conceal from her what would make her so: but to relinquish the only woman I could ever love, is surely a greater sacrifice than she ought to demand of me. If, indeed, I were about to disgrace her, Rosalie, by uniting myself with a woman without reputation, or of a very mean and unworthy origin, I should feel that I ought not to be forgiven; but why, because our modes of worshipping God are different—why, because my mother was born in Italy, and you in England, should an imaginary barrier be raised, which must shut me out from happiness for ever? What has reason and common sense to do with all this?"—Rosalie was compelled to acknowledge that it had very little: still, however, the idea of a clandestine marriage shocked her; she solicited most earnestly that her mother might be made acquainted with it. This he strenuously opposed; representing, that if Mrs. Lessington knew it, it would not be a secret from Mrs. Vyvian, "Who, however, she may love you, (said he), would make it a point of conscience to prevent my marrying a Protestant, and ruining myself, as she would conclude I should, in the affections of my mother for ever. You know, Rosalie, how much I love my aunt. There is a pensive resignation to a very unhappy fate, a sort of acquiescence, which arises not from want of sensibility, but from the patience and self-government she has learned, that render her to me infinitely interesting, while her kindness and affection to me demand all my gratitude. But with great virtues, and I know hardly any one who has for so many, she is not without prejudices, which greatly add to her own unhappiness. It is unnecessary to point out to you what these are; nor need I tell you, Rosalie, that they are exactly such as would induce her to think it her indispensible duty to inform my mother of our attachment. Then all the evils, I apprehend, would follow. I must either hazard offending her beyond all hope of forgiveness, or I must lose you for ever."—Let no fastidious critic, on the characters of a novel, declaim against the heroine of this, as being too forward or too imprudent. There are only two ways of drawing such characters: they must either be represented as——

"Such faultless monsters as the world ne'er saw"——

Or with the faults and imperfections which occur in real life. Of these, many are such as would, were they described as existing in a character for which the reader is to be interested, entirely destroy that interest. There are other errors, which, in an imaginary heroine, we may at once blame and pity, without finding the interst we take in her story weakened. This is the sentiment that Rosalie may excite; who being tenderly attached to a man, not only amiable in his person, but of the most insinuating manners, believing his declarations of love, and persuaded that her friends could not disapprove of the step he so earnestly urged her to take; fearing, on the other hand, to lose him; that he would be convinced he was indifferent to her, would return to

Italy, and make an effort to forget her; found her objections giving way before so many motives, and at length, though with trembling reluctance, agreed to the expedient Montalbert proposed—of their being married by the priest whom he had engaged for that purpose. Rosalie neither knew the danger this man incurred, nor that her marriage would not be binding. She knew, however, enough, from such information as she had casually picked up, to express her doubts to Montalbert as to its legality, who found the means of satisfying her scruples. "It is binding to me, (said he), since the ceremony is performed after the laws of our own church; and where then, my Rosalie, can be the foundation of your doubts?—In a few, a very few days after that fortunate hour, which shall give me a right to call you mine, I must leave you; but I shall know myself to be your husband; I shall feel no disquiet, lest the persuasion of your family, or any other circumstance, should throw you into the arms of another, and the hope of returning soon to England to claim you for my wife, will give me patience not only to endure this enforced absence, but will animate me to those exertions that may shorten its duration."——The calmer reason of Rosalie sometimes told her, that there was much sophistry in many of these arguments; but what young woman her age listens to reason, in opposition to the pleadings of the man she loves?—Montalbert was equally passionate and perservering: he had some plausible manner of obviating every apprehension, and it now only remained to be considered, how the marriage ceremony might pass with most secrecy.

Though Montalbert had not seemed to make more frequent visits than usual at the house of Mrs. Vyvian, nor to appear oftener at Hampstead, he had in reality hardly ever quitted it since Mrs. Vyvian had settled there; but had taken an obscure lodging in the lower part of the village, where he was sure he should not be known, and this gave him an opportunity of remaining later either with his aunt, when Rosalie happened to be there, or at the house of Mrs. Lessington, who was now more frequently than ever in London. Then it was that Rosalie passed the evenings entirely with Mrs. Vyvian, and nothing was so natural as that Montalbert, when he happened to be there, should attend her home, to which Mrs. Vyvian never seemed to make any objections on Rosalie's account, though she often expressed her apprehensions of the danger he incurred in returning so late to London.

It was strange, that suspecting as Mrs. Vyvian seemed to do, some attachment which made Rosalie unhappy, she had no notion that her nephew might be the object of this attachment; but it seemed never once to have occurred to her, and Montalbert conducted himself so cautiously before her, when Rosalie was of the party, that she had no reason to believe he regarded her otherwise than as a common acquaintance. Montalbert, young as he was, had been a great traveller: he had lived at Paris, at Vienna, at Turin, at Rome, and at Florence, and had acquired in the more early part of his life the reputation of being a young man of dissipation and intrigue. These gaieties had been exaggerated, and Mrs. Vyvian had received an impression of his libertinism, which had never been effaced. She now, therefore, could not imagine, that for such a man the simplicity fo Rosalie's beauty could have any attractions; and persuaded, as she was, that he was engaged in intrigues among many women of a very different description, she sometimes gently reproved and sometimes slightly rallied him, on these fashionable excesses. He humoured her in the answers he gave; listened as if half disposed to feel contrition, or defended himself, as if conscious of the truth of these charges—management which would have concealed his real sentiments and designs from a more penetrating observer than Mrs. Vyvian.

During the few days that Montalbert was in doubt how to procure unsuspected the admission of the priest to Rosalie, while he was with her, the family of his aunt arrived from their house in the north to settle for the winter in Park Lane. Mr. Vyvian contented himself with calling one morning on horseback, with a slight and cold inquiry. He told his wife, that he had directed his steward to attend her whenever she pleased on money matters, and that his daughters should visit her the next day: he then mentioned the marriage of the eldest, of which the preliminaries were now settled; he did not, however, tell Mrs. Vyvian of this, because he thought her approbation of any consequence, but spoke of it as a matter settled, signifying, at the same time, that it was his pleasure she should speak to her daughter of the arrangement, as being what every part of her family would not but approve. Mrs. Vyvian acquiesced, without any remonstrance on the cruelty of thus disposing of her child at so early an age, without even consulting her mother. A few tears involuntarliy fell from her eyes as soon as her unfeeling husband was gone; but she immediately went to her oratory, and found consolation in the duties of religion; to which, under all these trying circumstances, she had ever recoursed.

 But the appearance of the two Miss Vyvians had another effect on Montalbert. These ladies, young as they were, had been early initiated into the world. They were no longer diffident and unassuming, but had all the confidence of women of middle age, without their judgement; were careless of the opinion of all the world as to any thing but their beauty and air of high ton, and rather inclined to provoke censure, by their singularity, than to conciliate by civility, or engage by gentleness. They had already learned that disdain of all inferiors which belongs to people of the very first world; and the alliance the eldest was about to form, which would eventually place her in the first rank of nobility, seemed to have elevated the haughty spirits of both: an alteration which, on their very first visit, their mother saw with additional disquiet; while Montalbert, who was with Mrs. Vyvian when they came, beheld and heard them with disgust, that amounted almost to aversion.

 During the stay Montalbert made her father's seat in the north, Miss Vyvian had been piqued at the little attention he had shown her, and mortified to observe his neglect of those charms, which *she* thought, and which her maid assured her, ought to attract the homage of all the world. That Montalbert was so far from paying her this homage, that he took the privilege of his near relationship to tell her of her faults, was not to be forgiven by Miss Vyvian. She had by no means forgotten, now that she met him in London, the slights she had received in Yorkshire, and attacked him with severe sort of raillery, which he failed not to return, though with more good humour than the lady deserved. Thus passed the first visit; but, on the second, (as the young ladies affected still to retain so much consideration for their mother as to make their airings very frequently towards Hampstead), it happened, unluckily enough, that Mrs. Vyvian, not aware of their coming, had sent for Rosalie to sit with her. Montalbert soon after came in; and as Mrs. Vyvian was pleased to encourage her taste in drawing, Montalbert, who without any affectation understood it extremely well, was giving her some rules, and, leaning over her chair, was lost in pleasure of instructing his charming pupil; but he sometimes varied a little from what he undertook to teach, and, instead of giving her a sketch of the object he was describing, he wrote a line or two in Italian. Mrs. Vyvian was pensively at work, and did not regard them. The room where they sat was at a distance from the door to which the coaches drove up, and while this was going on, a footman entered, announcing the two Miss Vyvians.

 Montalbert in confusion quitted the table near which he was standing, and Rosalie, whose cheeks were dyed with blushes, was putting away her drawings; but Mrs. Vyvian, speaking mildly, bade her not disturb herself; then, welcoming her daughters, she said, "My dears, here is your playfellow and acquiantance, the youngest Miss Lessington, your old friend Rosalie."

 Miss Vyvian, towards whom her younger sister seemed to look, as if to regulate her own behaviour, turned haughtily to Rosalie, and making her a formal and cold curtsey, muttered something in so low a voice, that it could not be heard; then, without taking any further notice, began to tell her mother where she had been, and who she had seen. Miss Barbara, the youngest, took not the least notice of Rosalie, but, as if she had never seen her before, sat profoundly silent.

Montalbert, who remarked with indignation this insolent behaviour, and who saw a faint blush of grief and regret wavering on the pale cheek of Mrs. Vyvian, was tempted to express some part of what he felt, but he checked himself, and had determined to go, when Miss Vyvian, casting a malicious look at the drawing-table, and then at Rosalie, who sat by it unoccupied, said, "Oh! I see now, Mr. Montalbert, from whence it happens, that your friends in town complain that they never see you——you have found employment here in teaching some of the fine arts."

"If I were capable of teaching them, (replied Montalbert, who could not so command his countenance, but that it expressed his resentment), if I were capable, Miss Vyvian, of instructing, I should think myself highly honoured were that young lady to become my scholar; but, I assure you, she is already so great a proficient, that it would not be in my power to improve the elegance of her execution."

"Oh! I dare say, (replied Miss Vyvian); and now I recollect, Miss Lessington, I think you used to be fond of drawing, and had some lessons *when you lived with* us. But, Mr. Montalbert, since this lady has no occasion for your instructions, do tell me what it is you do with yourself? Do you know, that out of the few people I have seen, at least a dozen have asked me, what is become of my gay and gallant cousin? Some have affected, (added she, with a very significant look), that you are married, and others, that you are become melancholy mad for the love of some *rural* beauty; but all agree that you are a lost creature."

Mrs. Vyvian, however, hurt at such a wild and improper speech, had not time to express, as much as she dared do, her sense of its indecorum, before she was struck with the pale countenance of Rosalie, who seemed ready to faint. Montalbert was about to reply, when Mrs. Vyvian, as if unable to check herself, rose from her seat, and taking Rosalie's hand, said, in a tremulous voice, "I am sorry, my dear Miss Lessington, that you are so shocked at the unkindness and rudeness of Miss Vyvian; I will take care that you shall not again be subject to it. My woman shall wait on you home, and I beg you and your mother will accept my apology, thus hastily made, till I can renew it in person."

Rosalie, who had never seen Mrs. Vyvian exert so much spirit before, but who was more terrified than ever, least the retort of her daughter should bring on a quarrel of which she would be the cause; alarmed too at the hint given about Montalbert, and almost sinking under her apprehensions of every kind, was glad to quit the room, which she did immediately; but, disabled by the violence of her emotions to go farther than the next, she sat down and burst into tears.

While she was, however, reasoning herself into some degree of composure, Mrs. Vyvian, whose languid spirits were roused by the ill-behaviour of her daughter, was reproving her in very bitter terms, such indeed as she had never used before; but far from feeling the severity of a remonstrance she so well deserved, she affected to turn off her impertinence with a laugh. "Dear Madam, (cried she), I had no notion of making you so angry. Upon my honour I meant nothing in the way of affronting your fair protogée; and as to behaving as if I had forgotten her, dear, you know one really forgets every body in a year or two."

"You have at least forgotten *yourself*, Miss Vyvian," said her mother.

Miss Barbara now fancied it necessary for her to enter into a defence of her sister. "I am sure, Madam, my sister meant nothing; but one must really feel it grating to find that Miss, that country parson's daughter, preferred to us. People have often said, indeed, a great while ago, that the Lessington family had as much of your favour as your nearest relations. I am sure neither of us, neither my sister or me, had a thought of offending you—but it *does* seem hard to your own children, to see people, who are comparatively strangers, so much more taken notice of."

"It is you and your sister Barbara, (said the unhappy mother, while sobs stifled her voice), who have estranged yourselves from me; it is you and your sister————-" She could not go on. Montalbert, shocked by the sight of her distress, approached her, and, tenderly taking her hand, said, "Dearest Madam, do not, I implore you, distress yourself thus. These ladies are young and inconsequent; they *may* learn, and, I heartily hope, will, to know the value of such a mother." The agony of Mrs. Vyvian redoubled. "Nay, but I intreat you, (continued he), to be calm. Allow me to send your woman to you."

"O no! (cried she with a deep sigh), do not leave me, Montalbert. I have in you all the consolation which is left me, now that my son is sent far from me."

"Since you oblige me to speak plainer, Madam, (said Miss Vyvian, who seemed wholly unmoved at her mother's distress), since you compel me to say disagreeable things, I must tell you that it was quite time my brother *was* sent, as my Papa sent him; for *he* too was in danger of becoming too much attached to the same people that have weaned your affections from us. I should never have mentioned it, though, I assure you, if I had not seen *that girl here*, and been so found fault with for not worshipping her enough; for now my brother is gone, it is a matter of indifference to me who her heart attracts; *other* people are old enough to take care of themselves—but come, sister, our company does not seem just now to give Mama any pleasure; another time, perhaps, we may be more fortunate."

"Before you go, (said Mrs. Vyvian, endeavouring to stifle her convulsive sighs, and to speak distinctly), I conjure you to tell me what you mean about my son."

"It is a very unwelcome task, Ma'am, (replied her eldest daughter), and I might not be believed; but if you ask the Abbé Hayward, he, perhaps, may obtain credit, even when he tells you so unwelcome a truth, as that your son, when you thought him engaged in quite another tour, was at Holmwood with one or two of his friends, (she cast a malicious look at Montalbert as she said this), and there was reason to apprehend that this Miss, or some of the Misses her sisters, were the occasion of his paying much more frequent visits at the parsonage house, than even you yourself, perhaps, would have approved of, since, I can hardly think, your friendship would induce you to overlook the shocking disparity between the only son of Mr. Vyvian and *such people as those*."

It seemed as if the unfortunate mother was uttery incapable of answering. She repeated in a faint voice, "The Abbé Hayward!—My son—My son at Holmwood!"—Her daughters, who appeared thus to have plunged a dagger in her heart, left her without any attempt to mitigate the pain they had inflicted, and she remained alone with Montalbert, who, during this conversation, had exhibited symptoms of anger and disquiet, which Mrs. Vyvian was too much affected to observe. It was some moments before she had recovered herself enough to command her voice. "Tell me, dear Montablert, (cried she at length), what does Miss Vyvian mean?—Tell me, when was my Charles at Holmwood?—When did he thus visit Mr. Lessington's famliy?"

"Never, Madam, I can venture to assure you, with the least improper design.....It is true, that when we were upon our tour this summer round the coast, the Count and I expressed a wish to see Holmwood. He, as having heard it spoken of as a fine old place; I, because I used to be fond of it when I was a boy, and passed there the most pleasant of my hours during my occasional visits to England. As Vyvian was fond of the scheme as we were, we went thither for four or five days. Charles fatigued himself too much, and was taken ill; but he recovered perfectly the next day: for some reason or other, he did not seem to wish you and his father should know he had visited Holmwood. This I only know by his enjoining the Count to secrecy, when, he being obliged to return to London, left us there."

"You stayed there then some time?"

"I cannot be correct, (answered Montalbert hesitating; our stay whether there or elsewhere, seemed to me to be a matter of no consequence at the time—nor could I imagine why it was necesary to keep a man's visit to the seat of his father a secret. As near as I can recollect, we were there about seven or eight days."

"Seven or eight days! (repeated Mrs. Vyvian); and did Charles pass much of his time at the house of Mr. Lessington?"

"Indeed he did not. I believe I may venture to assure you, he never was there but when I accompanied him: I am sure, I may say, that he went with no design that you could disapprove, and that all Miss Vyvian has thought proper to say orginates in misrepresentation on one side, and malicious jealousy on the other. For Heaven's sake, dearest Madam, make yourself easy! I am persuaded, that, in regard at least to Charles, you have no reason to be otherwise."

A little soothed by these assurances, Mrs. Vyvian became more clam, and at that moment seeing the Abbé Hayward coming up the garden, of which he had a key to let himself in, from his morning walk, Montalbert rang for Nesbit, Mrs. Vyvian's woman, and leaving her mistress in her care, hastened away to speak to him.

Their conference was long and serious. Mr. Hayward assured Montalbert, that he would quiet the spirits of Mrs. Vyvian relative to the supposed visits of her son at Barlton Brooks, and recommended it to Montalbert very earnestly to conceal as far as was now possible the disagreeable dialogue which had passed that morning. "You know Mr. Vyvian, (said he), and how violent and unfeeling he is....There is no knowing what rudeness and reproaches he may throw on that excellent lady, if this family dispute goes to any length.......I tremble for her peace."——The council this good man gave was perfectly reasonable. Montalbert felt that it was so; yet there was something in his manner, when he spoke of the Lessington family, which gave Montalbert an idea of some mystery that he could not comprehend. He returned, however, no more to the house, but hastened to find Rosalie at that of her mother.

Mrs. Lessington had gone to London early in the morning, was to go to a play that night, and to an opera the next, a spectacle which she had not seen for many years, and about which she had expressed as much eagerness as a girl. It was in hopes of making his advantage of this absence, that Montalbert had met Rosalie at Mrs. Vyvian's in the morning. Rosalie, dreading importunity which she had no longer resolution to contend with, had taken her shelter there. Mrs. Vyvian, not at all expecting either Montalbert or her daughters, had engaged her to stay all day; when Miss Vyvian's jealousy and malice awakened by the sight of Rosalie, whom she had never thought so very handsome before, had, together with some circumstances hitherto concealed or stifled, occasioned the scene of the morning: a scene which did more to accelerate the views of Montalbert, than he could have done in another week with all the eloquence of the most passionate love.

CHAP.

There could be but little doubt but that the correspondence between Montalbert and Rosalie was suspected, if not absolutely discovered. Firmly as he thought he could rely on the fidelity of the person he had employed, it was but too evident that he was in some degree betrayed, and Rosalie, whom he found in tears, acknowledged that their situation admitted not of hesitation; that Montalbert must either return immediately to Italy, or risque every discovery in regard to his mother, which he had so many reasons to avoid.

It was vain to weary themselves with conjectures as to the source from which Miss Vyvian derived the intelligence that she detailed with so much malicious pleasure. On any other occasion Montalbert would have flown into one of those transports of passion to which he was but too subject, and have insisted on an explanation; but the tears and terrors of Rosalie, who saw the discovery likely not only to produce evey kind of mischief they dreaded, but eventually to separate them for ever, now checked every impulse of resentment, and left to Montalbert no other wish than to secure her his, and to return to Italy before the malignity of his cousin should have conveyed intelligence thither, which would embroil him for ever with his mother, and probably deprive him of that affluence to which it was now his delight to think he should raise the woman he adored.

There now seemed no alternative between resigning Montalbert for ever, depriving him of his inheritance by a discovery, or consenting to sacrifice her own scruples. It is not difficult to forsee that she chose the latter. Another whole day was to pass before the return of her mother; and it was settled that the priest, whom Montalbert had engaged, should call early in the morning on pretence of a messge from Mrs. Lessington to Rosalie; that Montalbert should soon after arive on his way to Mrs. Vyvian's, of whom he was supposed to be on the point of taking leave—and that the marriage should then be celebrated according the the Romish ritual, in the persence of a friend whom Montalbert was to bring with him. There was, in fact, neigher difficuly nor danger of detection in this arrangement. The country servants of Mrs. Lessington, a maid and a boy, took every thing that was told them for granted. The ceremony was soon over, and a testimony of its performance being given to Rosalie, the priest departed to London with the friend of Montalbert, while he himself went to Mrs. Vyvian's, where he intended to dine, and where he hoped his aunt would, without any solicitation, send for Rosalie. In this, however, he was mistaken: he found Mrs. Vyvian so much affected by the scene of the day before, that she was confined to her bed. She admitted him to her bed side, and he was shocked to see the havoc which even a few hours acute uneasiness had made in her enfeebled frame. "You see, (said she), how it is with me, Montalbert. I have no longer strength to resist that more corrosive of all miseries, the estrangement and ingratitude of my own children—of my daughters, I ought to say—for Charles, my poor boy, I believe loves me; but what I suffer from them, Montalbert, is indeed——

'*Sharper than the serpent's tooth*."

Montalbert endeavoured to sooth her agitated spirits, by representing to her, that her daughters were young and thoughtless, giddy with youth, health, and prosperity, and that a few years would, in all probability, produce a fortunate change in their volatile dispositions. "A few years? (said Mrs. Vyvian, with a melancholy smile); and do you think that a *very* few years, or more probably a very few months, will not finish all for me in a much more certain manner?—O yes! yes!"......

She paused a moment as if to recover herself, and then said, in a still lower tone, "But there is one thing, my dear Harry, that I wish to say to you, perhaps—perhaps I may never see you agan, and I would feign———"

Montalbert remained silent in anxious expectation of what she was going to say; but, as if she could not collect resolution enought, she sighed deeply, put her hand to her head, and seemed to suffer great pain there; then, becoming more languid, said, "But I hope I *shall* see you again, Harry, when I am more able to converse: yet surely you do not mean to prolong much your stay in England?"

"If my mother would grant me permission, (answered he), to stay till spring, I own it would be agreeable to me."

"I should not suppose she would, Harry, (said Mrs. Vyvian). I understood that her last letters expressed great anxiety for your return, and you know she does not very patiently bear contradiction.....But I wonder, Montalbert, what attractions England can have for you. Oh! if it were *in my* power to go to Italy, how ready would I quit this country for ever; and yet————"— Again she hesitated and sighed, and Montalbert, finding no pretence for naming Rosalie, and that it was unlikely he should pass the day with her as he had fondly hoped, assured her he would see her again several times before he left England, since he should await the arrival of his next letters before he fixed the day of his departure, and then took his leave.

It was but too certain, however, that he had that morning received the most positive commands from his mother to set out immediately, mingled with some severe reproaches for his having delayed his journey, from time to time, so much beyond that which he had originally fixed for his stay. He now thought it more than ever impossible to leave Rosalie, though he had sworn that if she were once irrevocably his, he would go without further hesitation. To invent some plausible pretence for the evasion of this promise was now his object, and so great was the reluctance with which he thought of going, that he sometimes determined rather to brave the displeasure of his mother, and boldy to combat her prejudices, than leave his wife, now more dear to him than ever: but was there no medium between these extremities? was it not possible for him to take her with him?—While he meditated on the practicability of such a project, and the arguments he should use to prevail upon her to consent to it, he found himself before the door of Mrs. Lessington's house, and was going in, when he was amazed and concerned to observe her and her daugher Maria getting out of a coach, which he had till then imagined had just stopped at the house of one of her neighbours. As he could not retreat without being seen, and his uneasy curiosity was excited by this unexpected and unwelcome return, he advanced towards Mrs. Lessington, and was beginning a speech about Mrs. Vyvian, whose name he meant to use as an exuse for his calling; but, without seeming to attend, she began to apologize for not having it in her power to ask him in, being, she said, in great alarm on account of her daughter.

"What daughter?—and oh! for Heaven's sake, what is the matter?" were words that were on the point of issuing from Montalbert's lips, who thought only of Rosalie: when this indiscretion on his part was prevented by Mrs. Lessington's proceeding to tell him, that her eldest married daughter, who was near her time, had suffered from being overturned in a chaise, and had entreated to see her mother, who had, therefore, hastened from London, where she received the letter, to pack a few necessaries, and was setting out post immediately afterwards for the house of her daughter in Suffex. Montalbert, alarmed lest Rosalie was going too, trembled so much, that he had not courage to ask; but to leave the house without knowing was impossible. Regardless, therefore, of the rules of decorum, which certainly demanded that he should absent himself, he followed Mrs. Lessington into the house, where his sudden reappearance, and the unexpected arrival of her mother, had such an affect on the countenance and manner of Rosalie, as could not have excaped observation, had not Mrs. Lessington and Maria been both much engaged with the immediate preparation for their journey; for amidst her maternal anxiety for her daughter, the elder lady was by no means indifferent to the appearance she was to make among her former country neighbors; and though she was still in deep mourning, she observed that it was not the less necessary to be "tolerably dressed."

Miss Maria was of course more solicitous on this important matter than her mother, and in the midst of their giving orders to one to run to the mantua-makers, and another to fetch home a new bonnet, &c. &c. they neither one of them seemed to recollect that it was neccsary to make some arrangement about Rosalie, or even to remember that she was in the house.

She remained, therefore, a few moments in the parlour with Montalbert, who, advancing trembling to her, inquired eagerly if she also was going? "I think not, (answered she); but my mother, in her hurry, seems totally to have forgotten me."—"I pray Heaven, (said he), that you may be left behind! If you go, I shall be distracted. When will it be decided?—How can you know?"

"I had better go up to my mother, (answered Rosalie), offer to assist her, and ask for her commands."—O hasten, (cried Montalbert), my angel, or I shall die with impatience!—I *must* stay till I know what is to be your destination, and will make some pretence for my intrusion." Rosalie then went up to her mother, who seemed to be awakened, by her presence, to some sense of recolletion as to what was to become of her youngest daughter during her absence. "I don't know, child, (said she), how to take you with us very well, as you brother Blagham is in town for two days on law business, and is desirous of going down with us in a post chaise."—Rosalie's heart beat so, that she could hardly breathe.

"I declare, (continued her mother), I know not how to manage about you. To be sure it will be but a disagreeable journey, and I suppose, my dear, you do not want to go?"

"If I could be of any use to my sister," said Rosalie hesitating.

"Oh! as to *that*, (answered Mrs. Lessington) there is no *occasion* to be sure; but it will be lonely for you at home, unless, indeed, Mrs. Vyvian would be so good as to take you."

Rosalie knew, from the scene of the preceding morning, that Mrs. Vyvian could not, without the exposing herself anew to the insults of her daughter, which it was painful even to think of.

This, however, she could not now explain to her mother, who, after a moment's hesitation, proceeded......"I have a mind to send to Mrs. Vyvian; yet I don't know—perhaps it will be inconvenient to her. There are times when I know it would be painful to her to have company;—but—let me—see—I dare say my friends the Hillmores would take you for a few days, and then you might come back; and Mrs. Vyvian would, perhaps, nay I am sure she would, have you with her as much as her spirits will allow, and by that time—most probably, you know we should be come back."

Though Rosalie knew the Hillmores were the most disagreeable people in the world, she had neither courage to object, nor presence of mind to propose any other plan. She thought she saw in her mother's manner an evident wish to get her off her hands, on the present occasion, without much solicitude as to the propriety of her situation during her absence; and at that moment she felt happy in the consciousness of being the wife of Montalbert, who would, in every event, defend and protect her.

She remained silent, however, and Mrs. Lessington, who was still busily engaged in packing, at length turned to her, and said, "Well, child! and what do you say to the plan of passing the little time we shall be away between Mrs. Vyvian and Mr. Hillmore's?"

"I know very little of Mr. Hillmore's family, (said Rosalie timidly); but I dare say, Madam, you are sure they would be kind enough to receive me."

"To be sure I am, (replied Mrs. Lessington); and as to Mrs. Vyvian, I wish I could see her myself—but—I have not time.—However—stay—do you think Mr. Montalbert is gone?—I dare say he would be so good as to carry a message for me."

"I am persuaded he would, (said Rosalie timidly), if he is not gone."

"Do go down and see: no—I will go myself." She then descended to the room where Montalbert still remained, who, when he heard the commission she gave him to his aunt, accepted it with transport he could with difficulty disguise. "I only waited here, (said he), to know if I could be of any use to you in your present hurry, and you cannot oblige me more than in employing me." He then hastened to Mrs. Vyvian, to whom he delivered a message rather suited to his own purposes than very exact as to correctness, and modulating Mrs. Vyvian's answer in the same way, he returned instantly to Mrs. Lessington, who, concluding the disposal of Rosalie settled her own way, told her she would leave a note for her friends the Hillmores, which she hastliy wrote, and then directed Rosalie to stay a few hours after her to adjust the house and put every thing away, which her present hurry did not allow her to attend to. After which an hackney-coach was to convey Rosalie to Mincing Lane, where Mr. Hillmore lived, and she was herself to deliver the note that was to secure her reception for the first three or four days of her mother's absence; after which, if that absence continued, she was to return and remain under the protection of Mrs. Vyvian.

This arrangement was so exactly calculated to answer all the wishes of Montalbert, that he now trembled with apprehension lest it should be revoked. He would not, however, venture to stay, lest Mrs. Lessington should entertain any suspicions of the cause of his extraordinary zeal; he therefore wished her a good journey, and left her. Soon after which Rosalie saw her mother and sister get into a post-chaise, which was ordered to stop to take up Mr. Blagham at the house of a friend at Islington, and then they drove away, leaving her to reflect on the extraordinary circumstances that had thus left her at liberty, and to await with a beating heart the return of Montalbert.

In less than half an hour he appeared, and telling the maid who opened the door that he brought a message from Mrs. Vyvian, he was admitted. As nothing was so easy as for Rosalie to leave the house with her clothes under the directions her mother had given her, nor less hazardous than to postpone her visit to Mr. Hillmore's family for a day or two, Montalbert vanquished every objection she made to going with him; the hackney-coach, therefore, that was to have conveyed her to Mincing Lane, and in which she did not set out till towards evening, went no further than to the suburbs of London, where Montalbert waited for her with another, from whence they got into a post-chaise, and were soon at a distance from London.

Thither, however, it was necessary that Rosalie should return in two days at the farthest, least her mother direct to her there, and her absence should be discovered. It was long before Montalbert would listen to her earnest representations of this subject: but there was no alternative; he must either tear himself from her, or suffer it to be known that she had eloped, nor could it long remain a secret with whom. Her representations were so forcible, and he felt them to be so just, that his reluctance at length gave way to the considerations of his wife's traquility, and he consented to her return to town, whither he conducted her, and putting her into a coach, followed it at a distance on foot, till it set her down at the house of her mother's friends.

But as Mrs. Vyvian had no acquaintance or communication with this family, the principal of whom was an attorney in the city, nothing was more easy than to conceal the day on which she left their house, as she had concealed the time when her mother intended her visit should begin to them. This, how ever, depended on the return of Mrs. Lessington.

Rosalie, on her arrival at the house of Mr. Hillmore, found a very cordial reception; but the manners of the whole family were so unlike those she had in the happiest part of her life been accustomed to—the old lady was so vulgarly civil, the young men so impertinently familiar, and the misses so full of flutter and fashions,—that Rosalie forsaw she would be esteemed very bad company. They had already, from the report of Miss Maria, entertained an idea that their guest was proud and reserved; and Rosalie saw by their manner, that they disliked her and wished her away. The mother, because she feared her beauty might attract one of her sons; the daughters, through jealousy of their lovers. The next day after her arrival there she received a letter from her mother, which informed her that though Mrs. Grierson was doing well, yet it would be ten days before she should return. Rosalie, therefore, armed herself with patience, to pass a few days longer where she was before she returned to Hampstead, but Montalbert could not suffer her to remain there without seeing her. As he was not known to the people of the house, he called under pretence of a message from Mrs. Vyvian, but he could only see her in a formal way in the presence of Mrs. Hillmore and her daughters, who *prodigiously* admired him as a *very elegant genteel man indeed.*—He found they were going that evening to the play, where he determined to be himself.

It was then that he saw the superior beauty of Rosalie attract all eyes, and heard inquiries around him, who that lovely girl was in mourning? The faces of the Miss Hillmores were well known, though their party would have passed wholly unnoticed, but for the brilliant star that now first appeared among them. Montalbert, from the other side of the house, enjoyed a particular kind of pleasure at the admiration excited by his wife: but one of the foibles of his temper was jealousy; when therefore he saw two or three young men, acquaintances of the Hillmores, enter their box, evidently with a design of being introduced to her; when he saw young Hillmore, who was a sort of city wit and city buck, displace one of his sisters in order to sit near Rosalie, he could remain where he was no longer; but crossing the house, went into the next box, where he sat the remainder of the evening, not near enough to speak to her, so entirely was she surrounded; but suffering inexpressible torments because she was spoken to by others.

His impetuous spirit could ill submit to a longer course of such punishment. He went out, therefore, to a tavern, a few moments before the play was over, and wrote a note to her, in which he insisted on her leaving the Hillmores the next morning. "I will send a sevant, (said he), with a chariot and a letter, as if from from Mrs. Vyvian........As the people you are with know neither her carriage nor her writing, you may very easily leave them without the least suspicion. I will take care of the rest; but remember, Rosalie, I must not be refused—I would not leave you exposed another day to the impertinence of the vulgar puppies you are surrounded by to be master of an empire."

Montalbert, having sealed this letter, waited at the door of the box for her coming out; but as she had on each side of her competitors for the honour of leading her out, it was not without difficulty he found an opportunity of giving it to her.

The next day an handsome chariot, with a servant in livery, was at the door of Mr. Hillmore by eleven o'clock; the latter brought a note apparently from Mrs. Vyvian, which Rosalie showed as a reason for leaving Mrs. Hillmore, who, while she expressed great concern that they were so soon to lose the pleasure of *her good company*, was, as well as the young ladies, heartily glad to see her depart. A short time brought her to a place where Montalbert waited for her to begin another short excursion from London. He endeavoured to appease the excessive fear she expressed, lest these journeys should be discovered, by assuring her that he had taken every possible precaution to prevent it. That Mrs. Vyvian did not expect her for two or three days, at the end of which time he promised she should go back to Hampstead, and he had engaged a person to convey to him any letters that might arrive in the mean time from Mrs. Lessington, lest, from any alteration in her plan, she should return and not find her daughter where she expected.——These measures, and Montalbert's solemn assurances, that as soon as he saw her once more safe under the protection of her mother, he would no longer delay a journey which was so necessary on account of his own, and that he would force hmself, though at the expence of his present felicity, to pusue such measures as might secure uninterrupted possession hereafter.

CHAP.

WHILE Rosalie was thus, as Mrs. Vyvian believed, passing part of the time of her mother's absence as she had directed, that excellent but unhappy woman, Mrs. Vyvian herself, was suffering under the most acute anxiety. The absence of her son, the estrangement of her two daughters, and the cold and even severe conduct of the man to whom she had been sacrificed, made together a cruel combination of evils; which, however, did not so entirely occupy her mind, but that she felt for Rosalie, to whom she had ever shown the tenderest partiality, and to whom she would with delight have granted an asylum in her own house, had she not been deterred by the envy and ill-humour which her daughters had expressed, and terrified at the hints they had given of an affection for her on the part of her son, which, if it should once reach the ears of Mr. Vyvian, would, she knew, so greatly enrage him, that he would forbid her ever receiving any of the Lessington family again. Timid and mild, and with nerves shaken and enfeebled by a long course of unhappiness, Mrs. Vyvian was unequal to contention with a violent, haughty, and unfeeling man, who disdained to listen to reason, and held all friendly attachments, every thing that did not coincide with self-interested motives, to be mere cant and pretence. He had never considered the Lessington family with an eye of favour; but while Lessington lived, he had been useful to him in electioneering matters, and therefore he, and of course his family, had been endured; but the apprehension of any attachment between young Vyvian and a person whom his father considered so infinitely beneath him, would not have been suffered a moment, and Mrs. Vyvian knew that on the slightest suspicion she should be overwhelmed with menaces and reproaches, which she found herself altogether unable to sustain. This dread alone prevented her from hazarding a repetition of the language her daughters had held, and compelled her to submit to so great a deprivation as that of often resigning Rosalie's company, whose interesting gratitude, and innocent, yet sensible, conversation, formed one of her greatest pleasures, and was best calculated to soothe her wounded heart.

Still, however, she was uneasy that so young and so pretty a woman should be consigned to the care of people of whom she had no very high opinion. She fancied they were low bred, and was persuaded that if the morals of Rosalie were in no danger among them, her delicacy of mind must suffer from the style of such company: when, therefore, she saw Montalbert, who, while Rosalie was really at Mr. Hillmore's, called upon his aunt as usual lest his absence might be remarked, she continually questioned him about these people, and he, not willing to appear to know much about them, gave her such answers as served rather to increase her solicitude for her former protegéee, and her regret that she could not give her protection in her own house.

Montalbert never loved his aunt so well as when he thus saw her interestd for Rosalie; and sometimes it seemed as if this interest was so strong, that she could not be angry at finding his sentiments so entirely agreed with hers. Half resolved to open his whole heart to her, and entreat her countenance, her protection, for his wife, he sat meditating what to say, when the entrance of Mr. Hayward, or some sentence Mrs. Vyvian uttered, again shook his resolution, and deterred him from entrusting to her a secret of so much consequence; while, if it still remained a secret to every body but to her, his Rosalie could derive no benefits from the partial information, for Mrs. Vyvian would still be deprived of the power of receiving her as Rosalie Lessington, and as the wife of Montalbert it would be still more impossible.

It was now time for her to return to Hampstead, where all Mrs. Vyvian could do was to receive her on those days when none of her own family were likely to call upon her, or if they did, to send her into another room. Montalbert, during the four or five days that were to be the last of his stay in England, passed a part of each with Mrs. Vyvian, who, while she thought it her duty to press him to begin a journey that had been so long delayed, began to be seriously uneasy about his health, which she thought was evidently declined. He was pensive and absent, spoke little, and had lost his appetite—symptoms that she fancied indicated a decline, and induced her to urge him with increased earnestness to begin his journey, in the persuasion that the winter in England was inimical to his constitution. Montalbert every day promised to fix the day of his departure; but every day brought with it some excuse:—his baggage, some things he had bespoke as presents to his Italian friends, were not ready; his own servant was taken ill; he must wait the arrival of a friend from the country, with whom he had business relative to his family's northern property—and while this went on, he lived in a miserable state of restraint, never seeing his wife but for a short time in the presence of Mrs. Vyvian, unless she happened to be there of an evening, in which case he went home with her, but attended by a servant, under pretence that his horses were at a stable not far from the house of Mrs. Lessington.

    Such a state of constraint was insupportable. More passionately attached to Rosalie than before he became her husband, the idea of leaving her for weeks and months was become more terrible than that of death: he fancied it disgraceful to submit to divide himself from all he held dear, influenced merely by pecuniary considerations, and often resolved to acknowledge his marriage and brave the consequences; but then the fear of reducing to poverty the woman he adored—of exposing to the inconveniences of indigence her whom he thought worthy of a throne, checked his resolution of making this dangerous avowal; and again he determined to leave her in the hope of returning to claim her, and place her in a situation of life which she seemed born to fill.

    Rosalie seized every opportunity that now presented itself to press his going.—She urged his former promises, his own acknowledgements of the necessity of his departure: again he promised he would go, but again found it impossible to tear himself from her. But now her mother returned, and their meeting must become more rare and more difficult; and at length, but not till after he had received another letter from his mother, Montalbert determined to go. The last interview he could obtain with his wife was short and hazardous. Neither of them could say farwel; and when he was gone, and Rosalie knew she should see him no more, she felt so depressed, that, apprehensive of the remarks that might be made, she retired to her bed under pretence of a violent head-ach, though the pain she felt was in her heart.

    This pretence could not, however, be long continued, and Rosalie returned, though reluctantly, to the common business of life, while Montalbert, scarce knowing what he did, pursued his way to the sea coast from whence he was to embark for France, meaning to pass through that country to Italy; but the greater the distance became between him and the object of his love, the less supportable it became: a thousand times he was tempted to return, and rather hazard every future consequence than subject himself to the present misery of a separation so painful. Arrived on the borders of the sea, this distracting irresoulution redoubled. It was yet in his power to return to all he held dear on earth—a few leagues of land only were between them, but soon immense worlds of water would divide them, and he was conscious, that the single circumstance of its being out of his power to return when he would, must increase all the impatience he now felt; yet his reason told him, that his temporary absence ought to be undergone, since it might secure the repose hereafter of the woman he loved.

    As it was now a time when multitudes of English, who had long been prevented by the war from visiting the continent, were hastening to France, Montalbert was not many hours waiting for a wind, before he met some of his acquaintance, from whom it was impossible for him to escape. The gaiety and vivacity of these men, fatigued without amusing the mind of Montalbert; they were, however, of some use to him in calling off his attention from the subject, on which it was painful and useless for him to dwell. One of his friends rallied his supposed melancholy, another rattled away on past adventures and future projects of his own; and, amidst this variety of conversation, the wind becoming favourable, the whole party were summoned on board, and in a few hours Montalbert found himself in Calais.

His friends, impatient to get to Paris, hastened on their way, while Montalbert was again left alone to indulge his uneasy reflections.

The traveller, who quits England with anguish of mind, has often found a transient relief in the variety and novelty offered by his arrival in a country, which, though so near his own, offers scenes so unlike those he has been accustomed to. But this change had lost its power over the mind of Montalbert, haveing travelled so often between Italy and England through France, each country was equally well known to him; and relapsing into his former despondence, he wandered along the French coast, looking with aching eyes toward England, and again tempted to return to it.—At length, however, after two days indulgence of this weakness, for such he owned it was, he once more reasoned himself into a resolution to proceed, and though with an heart which became more heavy every league, he hastened towards Naples, making no stay in Paris, or any other town through which his route lay.

While he was thus obeying the imperious dictates of duty, Rosalie, concealing the wretchedness of her heart, endeavoured to pass the time of this cruel absence in perfecting herself in those branches of knowledge most agreeable to him; but very unpleasant were the many hours she was obliged to pass among people who had no ideas in common with her, who were engaged in other pursuits, and who seemed to consider her, what indeed she really was, a being of quite another species, who, in being among them, was evidently displaced.

The only time she passed with any degree of satisfaction, was that when she was admitted to sit with Mrs. Vyvian, and to converse with the Abbé Hayward.—Miss Vyvian was now married and gone, accompanied by her father and her sister, to the seat of her husband's family in great parade. Her mother, of whom she had taken cold leave, sunk into deeper dejection than ever: not that she felt as a misfortune this more certain separation from a daughter, who had long ceased to return her maternal tenderness; but it seemed as if her form could no longer resist the sorrow inflicted upon her by the absence of a son she adored, aggravated by the ingratitude of his sisters.

Rosalie appeared to be more dear to her than ever, and there was now no impediment to their being often together; but Mrs. Vyvian, whose health visibly declined, was not always well enough to leave her bed, or to be amused with Rosalie's endeavours to relieve her long hours of solitude by reading or music. When she was able, however, to sit up, the duties of her religion, which she fulfilled with the most scrupulous exactness, alone detained her from the society of Rosalie. Whatever might be the dejection of Mrs. Vyvian's mind, her penetration was not blunted, and she saw that something unusual pressed upon the spirits of her young friend: again then she spoke to her of what she apprehended—"You are certainly not well, Rosalie, (said Mrs. Vyvian, as they were sitting alone together), *or* you are unhappy?"—"I am well, indeed, my dear Madam, (she replied); as to being unhappy, I am not particularly so—I own to you, that the continual round of company in which my mother is engaged is far from adding to the pleasantness of my life; and sometimes I languish for an abode in my native country, as solitary as our parsonage under the southern hills."

"There is more in it than that, dear girl," said Mrs. Vyvian, with a look that expressed her incredulity.

"You would not surely wonder if there were, (answered Rosalie). I have often wondered at my own inconsequence in not being more depressed, when I recollect that, whenever I lose my mother, I shall become a friendless and destitute orphan."

"Not, if I live, (said Mrs. Vyvian—then, pausing a moment, she added in a slow and solemn voice)—for, as I think, my early indulgence to my daughters, or rather to myself, in having you so much at Holmwood during your infancy, has perhaps been the means of estranging you from your family, I consider it as my duty to make you what little amends I can— much, alas! is not in my power, for the unintentional injury I have done you."

The tears rose in the eyes of Rosalie as Mrs. Vyvian concluded this sentence. "O no, dearest Madam, (answered she)—your kindness to me, never, never, injured me—so far otherwise, that I think I should, *but* for that kindness, have been the most unhappy creature in the world. At least I know that the only moments for which I would wish to live are those when you permit me to be with you."

"And therefore it is, my love, that I think I have injured you. Your mother, your sisters are happy among acquaintance and parties of their own, from which you fly with disgust: nor is this all—I am sensible that you have refused a very advantageous match from the same prepossession."

"I assure you, my dear Mrs. Vyvian, that, as far as I am able to judge, I should have refused Mr. Hughson, though I had never enjoyed the advantages of being admitted to Holmwood. Indeed, had I been in the most humble condition of life, I am sure I should have preferred remaining in it, and even embracing the hardest labour, to giving my person to a man from whom my heart recoiled."

A deep and long-drawn sigh, as if some painful recollections had arisen at that moment, half interrupted the answer of Mrs. Vyvian, who said, "You are certainly right in the sentiment, Rosalie—but it is sometimes not in the power of young women to resist parental authority. However, admitting that a man, less disagreeable than you represent this Hughson to have been, should now present himself; tell me, Rosalie—answer me ingenuously—would he not be equally rejected?"

The eyes of Mrs. Vyvian, which, though generally soft and languid, were very expressive, were fixed steadily on the countenance of Rosalie as she asked this question. Rosalie, who affected to be steadily at work, looked up, and met these penetrating eyes: a deep blush suffused her cheeks; she was conscious of it, and became more confused. Yet, making an effort to recollect herself, and to speak with composure, she said, "O nothing is so—so very unlikely, as that *any* man should have a preference for me!—I never thought whether I should refuse any other offer or no—because it is so improbable, that it is hardly worth while to suppose about it."

"Not so improbable as you affect to imagine, Rosalie—but you are not sincere. I do not wish, my dear, to distress you, and we will drop the discourse at this time; but another day, perhaps, I may talk to you further, for I have something very serious to say to you, and I think, Rosalie, you will not deceive me, since it may be very material to us both."

More and more confused, and not doubting but that by some means or other Mrs. Vyvian had discovered her marriage, she was too much agitated to allow herself to consider, whether, if this were really the case, it was likely Mrs. Vyvian should speak as she had ever done; but trembling and breathless she hastened to put her work into the work-basket, and, affecting to understand what her friend had last said as an hint to depart, she smiled, and replying that she was always happy to answer any questions from her, and that she hoped always to be ingenuous with so good a friend, she hastened away, which Mrs. Vyvian did not oppose.

CHAP.

THE night that followed this conversation was the most uneasy Rosalie had ever yet known. From what had passed she could not doubt but that Mrs. Vyvian knew of her marriage; yet it was incomprehensible if she did, that she should have expressed so little anger or diaprobation: yet what else but her knowing of the mutual attachment between her nephew and her protegee could have urged her to speak as she did?

The various conjectures that agitated the mind of Rosalie, allowed her not to sleep. She had never till now tasted, in its full bitterness, the pain that is inflicted on an ingenuous mind by concealment and dissimulation. Conscious that she merited the loss of Mrs. Vyvan's good opinion, and that the longer this mystery was continued on her part the more unpardonable it would appear, she endeavoured to reason herself into a resolution of unbosoming herself to Mrs. Vyvian, and rather enduring her reproaches for precipitancy and indiscretion, than suffer the misery of living in continual dread of being detected in a falsehood. The most probable conjecture she could form was, that Mrs. Vyvian knew the truth, and had held the conversation she had heard the preceding evening to give Rosalie an opportunity of declaring what was already known. This supposition strengthened her wavering resolves, and she arose in the morning, believing she had force of mind enough to disclose the secret that weighed upon her mind; but when a note came from Mrs. Vyvian requesting to see her as soon as she had breakfasted, her courage at once forsook her, and hardly could she find the strength to obey the summons.

On her arrival, however, at the house of Mrs. Vyvian, she found nothing remarkable in the manner or looks of her friend, who seemed as to her health to suffer less than usual. Rosalie inquired, as she had been acustomed to do, if she should fetch a book—Mrs. Vyvian answered no; and bid her take her work.

For some time the conversation ran on indifferent topics; at length contriving to bring it without abruptness to the point she wished, Mrs. Vyvian renewed the subject on which she had touched the day before. Rosalie, whose heart was beating so violently that she could hardly breathe, listened to her in silence.

"I spoke to you yesterday, my love, (said she), with a desire to hear your sentiments on a matter very important to you. You say that you sometimes accuse yourself of not having sufficient prevoyance—of looking forward with too little solicitude to a fortune, which certainly promises but little prosperity.—What, if a way was to offer of escaping from these fears?—If an establishment in most respects unexceptionable were to be found?"

"I am not my own mistress, you know, my dear Madam," said Rosalie, speaking this equivocation, for it could not be called a falsehood, in so low a voice as hardly to be heard.

"That is true, (answered Mrs. Vyvian); but I think, indeed I am *sure*, your *friends* would not dispprve the proposal in question—indeed there can be one objection to it, which I think would not have much weight; the gentleman is a Catholic."

"A Catholic!" repeated Rosalie faintly.

"You are surprised, I see; but you know, Rosalie, there *are* considerations that may influence persons to overlook this difference of opinion. Tell me now ingenuously: *should* a man of that religion offer, whose circumstances, whose character, are such as would preclude all those fears that you, or those who love you, might have as to your future fate?—Tell me, if you should hesitate to accept of his hand?—Remember I expect you to be candid——Would you receive such a man as your husband?"

The first attempt Rosalie made to answer this question failed, she was unable to articulate a syllable; collecting, however, all her resolution, she at last found courage to say, "I am very sensible, Madam, that I ought to feel extremely grateful for the notice of any man of whom you have a good opinion;—but—my dear, dear benefactress, (added she in a voice that her agitation rendered indistinct, and rising from her seat), I cannot longer conceal the truth from you—*I am already* married."

"Already married! (exclaimed Mrs. Vyvian with a tone and look of amazement);——Already married!—Merciful Heaven! and to whom?"

"Can I hope, dearest and best of women, to be forgiven, when I tell you—O no!—I dare not—you will reproach me, perhaps detest me, and cast me off for ever."

"Speak, (said Mrs. Vyvian, trembling as much as the unhappy girl)—speak"....she had her salts in her hands, and her eyes were eagerly fixed on the face of Rosalie, who was compelled to support herself by holding the table.

"Since you have just said, Madam, that a Catholic might, in your opinion, make such an alliance."———

"A Catholic!" cried Mrs. Vyvian, still more faintly.

"I might hope, perhaps, (continued Rosalie), to be forgiven for every thing, but the presumption of becoming part of you family—of marrying a very near relation of your own."

Rosalie might have continued her confession without interruption another hour, Mrs. Vyvian heard no more, but sunk back in her chair to all appearance lifeless.

In an agony of terror, to which no words can do justice, Rosalie flew towards her, then to the bell, which she rang with violence, and when her servants came, she assisted in carrying Mrs. Vyvian to her room, though she was herself in a situation but little better......"I am undone, (said she)—I shall never be forgiven.......No, I see that my more than mother cannot, will not, forgive me.—O Montalbert! why are you not here to plead with me for pardon?—What will become of your unhappy Rosalie, if her first, her best friend abandons and abhors her, while you are far far off, and unable to protect her from the insults of the rest of the world?"

While Rosalie was making this mournful monologue on one side of the bed, the applications used by Mrs. Vyvian's woman were so successful, that she opened her eyes; but, turning them on Rosalie, she seemed shocked by the sight of her, and, without speaking, waved her hand that she might leave her.

This was too much. Rosalie, regardless of the presence of the servant, threw herself upon her knees by the bed side, and attempted to take Mrs. Vyvian's hand—she snatched it from her with abhorrence, and, speaking with great difficulty, said, "Wretched, most wretched girl—if you would not see me die before your face—go—I conjure you go."

"Hear me but for one moment; let Hallam leave the room while I speak to you for the last time, if it must be so."

The maid, who understood nothing of all this, and who felt no curiosity to know what it meant, restrained by some degree of terror, retired without being bid; and Rosalie again most earnestly imploring for pity and pardon, Mrs. Vyvian, in a voice at once shrill and plaintive, said——

"It is now I feel, in all its severity, the punishment I have deserved: long has the dread of it pursued me—long had it embittered every moment of my wretched existence—but at length it overtakes, it crushes, it destroys me......Miserable girl!—the unfortunate young man, to whom you believe yourself married—is—gracious God!—do I live to tell it—is your brother!"

"My brother!—(cried Rosalie)——Heaven defend me!—My dear Madam—Mrs. Vyvian!——" Nothing occurred to her at that moment, but that the senses of her friend were gone.

"You are my daughter, (said Mrs. Vyvian), the unhappy child of an unfortunate man, whose very name I never suffer to escape my lips."

This confirmed Rosalie in the apprehensions that her mind was deranged; but, heart struck with horror, she could not speak. Mrs. Vyvian, after a short pause, proceeded———

"Destined from your birth to be an outcast—to appear a stranger even to your mother—I guiltily indulged myself with a sight of you, till Vyvian, my son, victim of *my* crimes————-"

"Vyvian! (cried Rosalie, not knowing what to believe)——it is not Vyvian, but Montalbert, who is my husband."

"Montalbert!—and am I not then the wretch I thought myself?—O Heaven! hast thou yet mercy upon me!"

"If dearest, dearest Mrs. Vyvain, you would but listen calmly to me————-" Terror, for still she apprehended that Mrs. Vyvian was become insane, again prevented her proceeding; nor was this impression weakened by the solemnity with which she now spoke.

"Yes, Rosalie, (said she), you are my child—I am not mad—I am only miserable—yet not so very miserable as I thought I was. Oh! why have so many cruel people been endeavouring to embitter the sad hours of my unhappy life, by repeating to me continually that Vyvian was so strongly attached to you, that neither reason nor absence could cure him of his passion. They knew not that in raising this idea in my mind, they poured into my heart the most fatal poison.—Alas! they knew not that the dread of this horrible crime drove from me my Rosalie—the dear, unhappy object of so many years of silent anguish and stifled solicitude."

Rosalie, more and more amazed, and doubting the evidence of her senses, could only listen in breathless wonder, while Mrs. Vyvian, whose heart seemed to be already relieved, proceeded——

"Montalbert then is your husband.....Ah! my poor girl, what a store of future misery you have laid up, it is too probable, for yourself. I am now amazed at my own blindness. Many, many hours of the most cruel anxiety would have been spared me, had not so strong a prepossession been given me of Charle's frantic passion for you: yet I now wonder I did not discover that it was Montalbert you loved — that you were attached to somebody I was sure, and when I thought it was Charles———oh! no words can do justice to the tortures that wrung my soul."

Rosalie sighed deeply; but not knowing what to say that should express the mingled emotions she felt, she remained silent, still holding the hand of Mrs. Vyvian, who seemed to be collecting some of the presence of mind her late terrors had so entirely dissipated.

The pause had something of horror in it. Rosalie watched her countenance with a fearful and anxious eye, still assailed by the idea of some temporary derangement of intellect: for how could she, whose parents were never even doubted, be the daughter of Mrs. Vyvian?—The whole scene appeared to be a dream, and, during this silence, Rosalie apprehended that she should again see her relapse into frenzy. Till these fears gradually subsided, as Mrs. Vyvian began with some degree of calmness to inquire into the particulars of the marriage; it was legally and properly celebrated according to all her ideas."

"But tell me, (added she, when this inquiry was at an end)—was Montalbert ingenuous with you?—Did he tell you that he depends for every thing, but a bare subsistence, on the bounty of his mother?—Did he tell you, that mother has prejudices the most unconquerable against the natives and the established religion of England?......Ah! my poor dear girl, the same softness of heart that destroyed *me*, has been, I fear, most dangerous to you. I cannot, (continued she, deeply sighing), I cannot now tell you the sad particulars of your birth....I have not strength either of mind or body—the horrible idea, that my unhappy, perhaps guilty, attachment would be punished by a yet more fatal one between my children, was so very terrible, that it could not be sustained.—I tremble still like a wretch, who having seen himself on the brink of a precipice into which he must inevitably fall, is snatched from it as it were by miracle, and can hardly believe his safety.......Let it suffice, my dearest love, for the present, to tell you, that there are the most material reasons why you should conceal, even from Mrs. Lessington, this unexpected explanation between us—let her not know, I conjure you, what has happened; but let her, at least for a while, suppose the secret known only to her and to me. I need not tell you, that your future welfare, and that of my nephew, depend entirely on your still keeping secret this clandestine engagement. There are events that may obviate the inconveniences I forsee.—Ah, Rosalie! from an affection cherished in secret, arose the misfortunes that have embittered my life, and fearful to my imagination is any dissimulation; but I dare not speak farther now—I am unequal to it: already there is too much reason to fear that the violence of our emotions may have given rise to conjectures, which it is so necessary for us to stifle. Let what has happened be supposed to arise from indisposition on my part, and on yours from the fears that indisposition occasioned; and try, my best love, to recover yourself as much as you can, and to resume your usual composure."

Rosalie, still in astonishment at all she had heard, and surprised at the tranquility with which Mrs. Vyvian now spoke, obeyed her as well as she could; but, as she kissed her hand, and would have bade her adieu, the new sensations she felt, while she considered as her mother the friend whom she had always so tenderly loved, quite overcame her spirits, and her tears blinded her. Mrs. Vyvian, yielding for a moment to the tenderness she had for so many years suppressed, clasped her daughter fondly to her bosom, and, for almost the first time in her life, called her by the dear name of her child. There was some danger that they would both have indulged too long in these effusions of natual affection, but a rap at the chamber door compelled them hastily to recover themselves. It was a message from the venerable Mr. Hayward, who, returning from his morning walk, had heard of Mrs. Vyvian's being greatly indisposed, and now solicited leave to inquire after her. Rosalie, therefore, who knew that for every wound of the mind Mrs. Vyvian found a resource in the spiritual consolation offered her by this excellent man, hastened to follow her wishes as to leaving her, and remaining only a few moments in another room to recover herself yet a little more, she left the house of her real, and returned to that of her supposed mother.

Nothing could be less in harmony with her feelings than the group she found assembled there. A large party from the city, some of whom were entirely unknown to her, had been on a jaunt of pleasure to a village about ten miles distant, and, on their way back to London, had been engaged by Miss Lessington, who was one of the company, to dine and pass the rest of the day at her mother's house at Hampstead.

Some of the gentlemen, who seemed to be of that rank of beings who are called "*City Bucks—Young Men of Spirit—Fine Flashy Fellows*"——were, in Rosalie's opinion, the rudest and most insupportable set she had ever yet seen: agitated almost beyond endurance, as her spirits were, she was yet under the mortifying necessity of remaining for some time in this company, which did not separate till one of the men proposed finishing their pleasurable party by a jaunt to Ranelagh: it was not early spring, and it was not without difficulty that she was at length allowed to decline going, and saw Miss Lessington and this group of good folks, so perfectly contented with themselves, depart without her.

She was then left alone with her supposed mother; but to conceal from her the perturbation of her mind was by no means difficult. Mrs. Lessington, whose new manner of life was much more pleasing to her than that she had lived in, the uniform insipidity of a country village, retained, however, so much of her original notable economy, as to use every hour to advantage which was not given to the vigils of the card table; she now, therefore, busily employed herself in domestic arrangements, that she might enjoy with higher relish the rubber of the evening; and she had, therefore, no time to make observations on the appearance of Rosalie.

    Thus left to herself, she reviewed with astonishment the strange discovery of the day; to find herself the daughter of Mrs. Vyvian, though of her father she was yet ignorant, seemed to be knowledge more flattering, more elevating than any event that could be imagined.——She was now ready to account for a thousand things which had before seemed extraordinary. The little affection Mr. Lessington had ever shown for her; his leaving her name entirely out of his will; the indifference of Mrs. Lessington, who sometimes, and particularly lately, had seemed to forget her assumed character of mother, and to express only what she felt, the cold civility of a common acquaintance; the want of even the slightest family resemblance between her and the other children of the family, and innumerable other circumstances which now crowded together upon her recollection. But if on one hand she now saw only strangers among those whom she had hitherto considered as her nearest relations, she beheld in Mrs. Vyvian a mother whom her heart bounded to acknowlege. To be her daughter, to be with her knowledge the wife of Montalbert, left her hardly any thing to wish, but that the hour was come when she might claim at least the latter title, and be received as belonging to a man, who had not disdained to give her that title when he thought her Rosalie Lessington, and knew not that she inherited a portion of the nobel blood of the Montalbert family: a family which, though now debarred from farther elevation by differing from the established religion, and estranged by foreign connections, had not formerly been inferior, either in antiquity or honour, to the most illustrious of the British nobility.

    END OF THE FIRST VOLUME

ROSALIE now saw the beloved parent, whom she yet dared not own, every day; and the discovery of her marrige with Montalbert, which she had so much dreaded, had been the means of procuring her the knoweldge of the blessing she possessed in a mother, who now secretly indulged all the tenderness of her heart. The eldest Miss Vyvian, now Mrs. Bosworth, was still at the family seat of her husband with her sister, and her father was gone into the north during the recess of parliament; no impediment, therefore, existed at present against Roslaie's passing almost all her time with Mrs. Vyvian, and so happy did this indulgence make her, that, had Montalbert been in England, she would hardly have had a wish left ungratified.

It was now indeed that such a friend was more necessary to her than ever, and it was more requisite that this dear friend should know she was a wife, since she found it was probable she should become a mother. Nothing was more immediately pressing than that Montalbert should be informed of this; but without the concurrence of Mrs. Vyvian, and indeed without her assistance, she dared not hazard a letter, which, if it fell into the hands of his mother, might be the most fatal consequence. The two letters she had received from Montalbert were but too expressive of his despondence and uneasiness; and though he seemed to stifle part of the anguish of his heart from tenderness toward his wife, she saw that the reception his mother had given him was far from having been pleasant, and that, while he yet acknowledged the necessity of his journey, he regretted that he had made it.

But Mrs. Vyvian, who had received letters from her son, knew yet more: she had learned that one reason for the impatience, expressed by the mother of Montalbert for his return to Naples, was, that she had projected a marriage for him with the daughter of a friend of her own, who had lately lost her husband, a Roman of high rank, and was now a very rich widow. Charles Vyvian related all the advantages offered by such an alliance: on the beauty of the young widow, and her predilection in favour of Montalbert, with whom she had been acquainted before her first marriage, he dwelt particularly; but added, laughingly, that he supposed Harry had left his heart in England, for at present he seemed as insensible to the charms of the lady, as deaf to the remonstrances of his mother.

Mrs. Vyvian was extremely distressed by this intelligence, which she carefully avoided communicating. Though she loved Montalbert extremely, she had many doubts whether in affairs of love he had more honour than other gay young men. She had reason formerly to believe his principles were very free, and she could not but fear, that he might consider his marriage with Rosalie, celebrated as it had been contrary to the laws of England, as an engagement so little binding, that he might break it whenever ambition or the love of variety might induce him to it.

The situation, therefore, of this beloved child, more dear than ever to her, was a dreadful weight on the spirits of Mrs. Vyvian; and she now felt renewed, in the person of Rosalie, all those cruel sensations which had corroded her own heart, when, betrayed by an unhappy passion into great and dangerous imprudence, she was compelled to undergo all the meanness of concealment, and all the terrors of detection. The similarity of their destinies hitherto endeared to her mother this lovely unfortunate young woman, who seemed too likely to be doubly a victim; yet, circumstanced as she was herself, she could not protect her openly, and even trembled every time she reflected that, with the return of the family of her husband, the indulgence of ever seeing Rosalie must be resigned; and that they must equally stifle their fears and their affections.

Every day rendered the situation of Rosalie more critical. Though Mrs. Lessington seemed, as if by a tacit agreement with Mrs. Vyvian, not to notice the preference Rosalie so evidently gave to the latter, and to suffer her to act as she pleased, others, who still supposed her a member of the Lessington family, could not be but surprised at her associating so little with them, nor help remarking, that whenever they did see her among them, there was something peculiar in her manner and appearance. The men, who had admired her beauty, but who had been repulsed at her coldness, now discovered, as they always do on such occasions, that the poor girl was in love; and while the elder ladies thought her proud, conceited, and full of airs, some of the younger entirely agreed with them, while others, more candid or more sensible, pitied her on the supposition that she had an "unhappy attachment;" or, as the damsels of lower rank would have expressed it, "that she was crossed in love."

Mrs. Vyvian was too deeply interested to have a moment's tranquility; and when the hour of Mrs. Bosworth's return approached, this anxiety became more and more insupportable: and it was certain that health so delicate could not long resist such painful solicitude.

After long deliberation and consulting with the Abbé Hayward, who had long been aware of who Roslaie really was, Mrs. Vyvian determined to write to Montalbert with the same precautions as those Rosalie used by his directions. This she executed, not without finding it the most difficlut and painful task she had ever undertaken. To avow the dissimulation of her whole life to her nephew, to explain to him circumstances of which she knew he must be entirely ignorant, words were not easily found. At length, however, the letter was written and sent off, and she returned once more to her long and pensive conferences with the object of it, with whom also a task yet remained quite as distressing to her.

This was to tell Rosalie to whom she owed her birth; to give a relation of circumstances which she knew must appear very strange to her. Mrs. Vyvian saw her often look as if she at once dreaded and expected this explanation; but never yet had she acquired courage to begin the conversation, and Rosalie was too timid to make any inquiries that led to it.

But Mrs. Bosworth and Miss Vyvian would now return in a short time, and then the mother and daughter must no longer indulge themselves with being together for whole days as they were now—a heavy presentment of future evil, to which the former was too apt to yeild, told her, that if the present time was lost, future opportunities might be wanting.—The next morning, therefore, after having made her resolution, she put it into execution.

Rosalie, whom she had desired to come early, was seated at work by her bedside, for she was too much indisposed to leave it; when Mrs. Vyvian, opening a little casket which she had previously placed near her pillow, put into the hands of Rosalie a miniature picture, and, in a trembling voice, said, "It is the likeness of—your father!"——It represented a man of two or three years and twenty: the countenance expressed understanding and vivacity of sentiment, and the whole figure was remarkably handsome. Rosalie gazed on it in silence, and with sensations that cannot be described. "Do you see no resemblance, my Rosalie, (said Mrs. Vyvian), to a face you know?—Ah! do you not trace in these features the likeness you bear to - - - - - - - - - -?—Believe me, my child, (continued she, unable to restrain her tears), this morning is the first time for many years that I have allowed myself to look at that picture, and now I resign it for ever—take it, my dear girl, and may you not resemble him in fortune as in features."

"Does my father yet live, Madam?" Rosalie would have said, but she could not articulate the sentence: her mother, however, understood her. "He does, (replied she), but not in England—I shall never see him more—nor am I guilty or wretched enough to wish it.—Never have these eyes beheld him since that fatal hour when I was compelled to give to another the hand which was his in the sight of God; but, though my hand was not at my own disposal, never has it acknowledged any sovereign but him to whom my fist vows were given: yet I very sincerely tried, when under the cruel necessity of giving myself to Mr. Vyvian, to fulfill the duties that were imposed upon me. He knew that I was compelled to marry him—he was indelicate and selfish enough to consider only the convenience of my fortune, and a person, which was then an object to a man, licentious and dissolute as he was: yet I *think* he never has had any just reason to complain of my counduct since I have borne the name of his wife. He knew I neither did nor ever could love him—for I told him so when I married him. He was contented to possess my fortune and my person—my heart he never thought worth the experiment that some men would have made to have gained it." A deep sigh and a long pause, which Rosalie did not interrupt, now followed.——

In a few moments Mrs. Vyvian seemed to have regained her resolution, and thus proceeded——"You should have an idea of what sort of a man, my father, Mr. Montalbert, was, before you can imagine how I was situated. I do not believe you know more than his name; for Mrs. Lessington was probably cautious of entering into any part of my unfortunate history.—— Mr. Montalbert then, my father, was the elder brother of a family, which, from its name, was evidently of Norman extraction—a boast that is generally deemed a sufficient ground for the pride of ancestry in England. The Montalberts, however, could carry their genealogy much farther, and were content to begin it only among the Emperors of the East. As English Peers, they adhered to the unfortunate James the Second, were banished with him, and lost their property, their title, and their rights as British subjects. My father, being much connected with nobel families more fortunate, had interest enough to obtain restitution of a small part indeed of the great fortune of his family, but sifficient to give once more a footing in England, where he was happy enough to marry one of its richest heiresses. My mother, who was the only offspring of an alliance between two noble houses, inherited all their possessions, and gave them and herself to my father, in despite of the opposition of such of her family as pretended to any right of giving their opinion; for her father and mother being dead, there were only uncles or cousins whose dissent could not prevent her following her own inclinations.

"This great property was divided between me and my brother, the father of Montalbert, your husband, but not equally; for he had of course the greatest share. The nobel castle and the estates, belonging to it in the north, are the pinicpal part of what remains to him in England; for having early formed connections upon the continent, he never loved or lived long in England: his life was not long, for he died soon after the birth of your husband; so soon, indeed, that he had neglected to make for him the provision he ought to have made, and, by a prior will, Harry Montalbert was left almost entirely dependent on his mother.

"In consequence of the long absences, and afterwards of the early death of my brother, I came to be considered by my father as an only child. Dissatisfied with a world, which he had, from personal infirmities, no longer the power of enjoying, he retired to Holmwood when I was about fifteen, and, from that time, you may imagine my life was very recluse, for then the country around it was less inhabited, and the roads less passable than they are now.

"Harsh as my father was, I loved him very tenderly, and therefore did not murmur at the confinement thus imposed upon me at a time of life when other young women enter the world and enjoy its pleasures: nor did the fatigues of constant attendance in a sick chamber, and continuing to read sometimes for half the night, for a moment deter me from doing my duty, or for a moment induce me to repine.

"I have since thought, Rosalie, that this period, with all its little hardships and inconveniences, was the happiest of my life.—My friend Mrs. Lessington, though then married, and some years older than me, was still often my companion, and shared a task which without her I could not have executed so well. Whenever I was released from the chamber of my suffering parent, I saw around me scenes of nature, which seemed to put on new beauties as if to reward me for my perseverance in painful duties; and if I tasted not the pleasures which are accounted happiness by very young women, I was at least content. Thus, without much variation, passed more than three years of my life.

"My father had a relation in Ireland, whose ancestors having suffered in the same cause as that in which the Montalberts had lost their property, had not been so fortunate in re-establishing their affairs; but their descendant was, with a numerous family, obliged to live on a very small estate, and in great obscurity in the north of Ireland.

"One of the sons, however, having been sent young to the East Indies, had done so well, that he wrote to have *two* of his three brothers follow him, informing his father, that though he could not make remittances for the purpose of fitting them out, he was sure when they arrived there of getting them into situations nearly as advantageous as his own.

"In consequence of this, their father sent his third and fourth sons to England, to solicit among their friends and their relations the means of equipping them in such a way as might enable them to avail themselves of these advantageous prospects. The eldest of the two soon found sufficient assistance in London, and departed; but the younger having been seized with a violent fit of illness in London, was under the necessity of seeing the last ship of the season sail without him, and at the invitation of my father, who had taken most of the expence of his equipment upon himself, he came down to Holmwood to recover his health, while he waited for an opportunity of following his brother, which was not likely to offer for some months.

"Ormsby was about one and twenty when he was thus received into the house of my father, who soon learned to consider him as a son; becoming so attached to him, that he was not easy in his absence.

"Even at this distance of time, I reflect with wonder on the carelessness with which my father suffered two very young people to be continually together, without appearing to think of the probability there was that they might form an attachment to each other. It is true that I have myself discovered inattention of the same sort in regard to you and Montalbert; but besides the prepossession of your predilection in favour of Vyvian, with which my mind was distracted, the character of Montalbert was so different from that of Ormsby, that it never occurred to me that there was equal hazard in your being continually in his company."——

Mrs. Vyvian now seemed to be much fatigued, and to be so little able to continue a narrative so affecting to her spirits, that Rosalie entreated her to forbear concluding it till she was less likely to suffer by dwelling on scenes which it gave her so much pain to recall; but the probability that their long and private conferences might be less frequent when they were continually liable to be broken in upon by Mrs. Bosworth and her sister, and the necessity there was that Rosalie should know the circumstances of her birth, and what were Mrs. Vyvian's wishes as to her future conduct, determined her, to exert herself to the utmost of her power, to conclude all she had to relate—the singular circumstances of her former life.

CHAP.

IN the evening Mrs. Vyvian found herself able to proceed, and thus continued her narrative:——

"My friend Mrs. Lessington, who had now a family of children, was no longer at liberty to give me so much of her time as she had hitherto done; but, at this period, the living of Mayfield, which was in my father's gift, becoming vacant, I was fortunate enough to procure it for her husband, and had the comfort of seeing her settled within four miles of Holmwood.

"Greatly, indeed, had I need of the prudence and steadiness of a friend......Imagine, my Rosalie, how I was at this time situated. Ormsby, though he lived so much with me, was yet so sensible of the distance fortune had placed between us, that for many months after he became an inmate in our house he never breathed the most distant expression of his affection; yet, young as I was, I could not mistake the meaning of his looks, and those silent attentions he incessantly paid me. He *seemed*—ah! he *was*—too artless to disguise entirely his sentiments; but the ineffectual struggle he made to do so was a spectacle infinitely more dangerous for me than the warmest professions could have been: he had even the generosity to avoid me for some time, and, as if by tacit consent, we met only in my father's room, where he now almost always supplied my place, and sat whole days, and often whole nights, with a tenderness and patience that, in my opinion, overpaid the debt of gratitude which he owed him. But sometimes, when my father's old servant was able to give that attendance for which he was often disqualified by illness, Ormsby was unexpectedly released; and it was at one of these periods that the explanation was brought on, which afterwards cost me so dear.

"My father had been extremely ill for many days. It was spring, a season that always brought on the most painful paroxysms of the gout: his old servant, harldy less a victim to this disease than himself, had been laid up, and Ormsby had been my father's attendant for ten days, almost without taking off his clothes, and certainly without having had any interval of rest.

"Barford, my father's servant, having a little recovered, came down to his relief, for no other person was suffered into the room but Ormsby, myself, and this man.

"As at this time Ormsby was so much fatigued, that he could hardly support himself, he hastened to procure what refreshment a change of clothes afforded, and then to relieve a violent head-ache, the effect of want of sleep, he wandered into the garden for the air..........

You remember, Rosalie, the temple at the end of the avenue of stone pines—thither I have often went with my work, or with a book, when I was alone; behind it is, you recollect, a copse, which at the season of the year now present, for it was the middle of May, echoed with the music of innumerable birds. Every object breathed of peace and beauty; and as my heart had long since learned to associate the idea of Ormsby with every scene that gave me pleasure, I was meditating on future possibilities of happiness, when the object of my dangerous contemplations suddenly appeared coming towards the place where I sat.

"To the lively interest he always inspired was now added, that which arose from the fatigue he had evidently undergone. He was pale and his eyes were heavy for want of rest. I saw him with a slow and languid step ascend the little turf hill on which the temple is situated: I could not have escaped from it without his seeing me, if I had wished to have done so; but, in truth, I had no desire to fly from him; and though I trembled as he approached me, it was with a sort of delightful apprehension, for I fancied he would now speak to me, if not in direct terms—yet in such as would leave me no longer in doubt as to his real sentiments: yet while I wished this, I dreaded it; and when he entered the place where I sat, I know not which of us appeared the most confused. He had long studiously avoided me, and certainly did not now expect to meet me; but as he knew I had seen him, and perhaps had not resolution enough to deny himself the unexpected opportunity of speaking to me, he came into that wing of the temple, and, after the common salutation of the morning, sat down near me.

"I inquired after my father, though it was not an hour since I had been in the room; but it gave me occasion to say, though in a faltering voice, how much I was obliged to Ormsby for his constant attendance. I had not concluded the sentence, when he said, 'Obligations, Miss Montalbert!—surely all obligations are mine; but were it otherwise, were not your father my best friend—that he *is your* father would be enough to induce me to make any sacrifices: there is happiness in being able to serve him as my benefactor; but there is something more than happiness in thinking that, in attending on the respectable parent of Miss Montalbert, I save her from one hour's fatigue, or mitigate to her on hour of anxiety.'

"I will not relate the sequel of our conversation before it ended: Ormsby, while he accused himself at once of presumption and ingratitude, professed for me the most violent, though hopeless, passion. He saw too evidently, that if it depended on me it would not be hopeless: already my heart had said to me much more than Ormsby, even in making this declaration, dared to intimate. It had whispered that my father's partiality for him might very probably conquer the objections that his total want of fortune might raise. I had fancied that it was impossible my father could leave us so much together, unless he meant to give a tacit consent to an affection which was so likely to arise between two young persons. I had imagined, that, finding us both necessary to his comfort, he intended to unite us: my fortune must be such as, I supposed, made any consideration as to that of my lover entirely needless.—Alas! how little is the inexperienced mind of youth capable of judging of those motives that influence men in advanced life. Though my father was retired from the world, he had not lost in retirement the passions that influence men of that world: on the contrary, living where he was the lord of many miles, where none, either in his house or around it, ever disputed his will, he had, like a despot, entirely forgotten that others had any will at all. Of a marriage of love he had no idea; for did it ever occur to him, as a thing possible, that a dependent relation, who was indebted to his bounty for a subsistence, could dare to lift his eyes to a daughter of the house of Montalbert, for whom, though he had never yet hinted at them, my father had very different views.

"But love, too apt to listen to the voice of hope, suffered us not to see the misery we were laying up for ourselves; and even amidst the reproaches Ormsby often made himself, for what he termed treachery and ingratitude, the flattering illusions into which we were betrayed by youthful inexperience, not only quieted these alarms of conscience, but made us listen with something bordering on resentment to the remonstrances of my friend, Mrs. Lessington, who took every occasion of representing the danger of my indulging my predilection for Ormsby. I endeavoured to persuade her, as I had persuaded myself, that I should one day become his wife, with the permission of my father. Mrs. Lessington, who undoubtedly knew the world and my father's temper much better than I did, nothing unafraid that was likely to convince me of this dangerous error: she even threatened to inform my father of the truth, unless I endeavoured to conquer this fatal prepossession; and she assured me if she did, the consequence would be the immediate disgrace and dismission of Ormsby. This menace, which I knew she would never execute, had an effect exactly opposite to that which she intended. The idea of Ormsby, driven from the house, suffering poverty and mortification, and abandoned by the world only for his attachment to me, endeared him to me infinitely more than he would have been, had I seen him surrounded with affluence and prosperity. Nothing is so dangerous as pity; and my friend, in attempting to save me, hastened my ruin by exciting it.

"I cannot, Rosalie, trace the progress of this fatal passion. My confessor, who alone might have checked its progress, was surely careless of his charge, or was possibly become indifferent to the welfare of a family he was soon on the point of quitting. He went to Rome exactly at the time when he might perhaps have saved me, and it was some time before he was replaced by Mr. Hayward.

"During that interval, as Mrs. Lessington was gone into the west on a visit to her husband's relations, Ormsby was more than ever alone with me. Every hour, indeed, in which the attendance of the one or the other was not necessary in my father's room, we passed together. From an habit of indulging myself in the illusive hope that I might one day be his wife, I insensibly learned to consider myself already so in the sight of Heaven.......Ormsby was young and passionate: he was not an artful seducer; but I had no mother, I had no friend, and those who candidly reflect on my situation will surely compassionate, though they may not perhaps acquit me.

"How soon, alas! was this deviation from rectitude and honour severly and bitterly punished. Though my father had been wilfull blind or strangely negligent, the servants, and from them the neighbours, saw enough to make them suspect more. We had little or no communication with the gentlemen's families around us, divided from them as we were by the difference of religion, habit, and connections; but in ours, as in every other neighbourhood, there were officious and impertinent people, whose greatest pleasure was to inquire into the affairs of others, and disturb as much as was in their power the peace of families. The country town adjoining to Holmwood produced at that time, as indeed it has done since, but too many of this description.—I, who hardly knew that such persons existed, was, however, marked out for the victim of their malignity; and, as if the terrors that now incessantly beset me were insufficient, for I found myself likely to become a mother, one of these officious fiends completed, or rather accelerated, the evil destiny that hung over me.

"While I waited with agonising impatience the return of Mrs. Lessington, whose counsel was so necessary in my present alarming situation, Ormsby, more wretched than I was, attempted to sooth and console me, and I was insensible of any other comfort than what I derived from weeping in his arms. Little dreaming of the storm that was ready to burst upon us, I sought him as usual one morning in the plantation, where we were accustomed, as it was yet early autumn, to meet in a morning before either the family were likely to interrupt us, and before my father demanded either his attendance or mine—I found him not; supposing it earlier than I had believed, I traversed for some time the walks of the woods without uneasiness—but at length his absence surprised then alarmed me. I returned slowly toward the house, more and more amazed that Ormsby did not appear—I met the under gardner, and, without any precise design, I asked him some trifling question—the man, instead of answering, looked at me with a countenance expressive of terror and surprise; then, without answering, hurried away; while I, dreading I knew not what, quickened my steps toward the house, and was met in the lawn that immediately surrounded it by my own maid, a young woman who had been lately sent to me from France by a friend, and who was already much attached to me. *Her* countenance startled me infinitely more than that of the man I had just passed—I hastily inquired what was the matter?—Helene attempted to utter a few words in French, but her voice failed her, and, seizing my hands, she looked at me with such an expression of terror and anguish, that the only idea it conveyed was the death of my father: before my incoherent and breathless inquiries, or her attempts to answer them succeeded, my father's old butler came out, and, though he seemed equally terrified, he had just command enough of himself to tell me that I must immediately attend his master; without having any distinct notion of the cause for which I was thus unexpectedly summoned, I obeyed in such confusion of mind that I know not how I reached the room.

"My father was not as usual at so early an hour in his bed, but sitting in a chair—I saw that something had greatly disturbed him, and my guilty conscience whispered me that our fatal secret was discovered....Trembling, so that I could not move across the room without the assistance of Helene, I at length approached the place. My father's eyes were sternly fixed on my face; his lips quivered, and his voice falterd, while he reacheh his hands toward me, and gave me a letter he held in it.

'Read that—(said he sternly)—read it—and hear me for the first and the last time I shall ever speak again of so hateful a subject. *If* I thought you capable of any part of the folly, the infamy, which this letter attaches to your conduct, I would not hold even this parley with you—but I *will* not think it; though I severly arraign myself for my inattention, yet I know that a daughter of mine would not dare to encourage any man without my approbation; still less, is it possible that Rosalie Montalbert should think of a boy, who, though distantly my relation, and therefore a gentleman, is a beggar....He is gone—you will see him no more.'

"I heard, indeed, no more—for my senses forsook me, and I escaped from the rage and reproaches of my father; nor was I awakened from this trance till I found myself on my bed, with Helene weeping by me.—'What has happened to me, Helene?' said I; for at that moment my recollection was confused, and, though I had the impression of something very dreadful on my mind, I remembered no more than that some dreadful evil had befallen Ormsby. Helene could only answer by tears and sobs——I raised myself in my bed—'Tell me, (said I), my dear friend, what did my father mean?—what is become of Ormsby?'

'Ah! dear young lady, (replied Helene), what would become of you, what would become of us all, if our master knew the truth, which he now will not allow himself only to suspect.—Oh! he is so passionate, he is so terrible, when he is angry, that I believe, upon my honour, he would destroy us all.'

'I wish he would destroy me, Helene, (said I, sighing deeply); but, unless you now intend to suffer me to die before you, tell me, I conjure you to tell me, what my father meant by saying that I should never see Ormsby more?'

'Indeed, (replied Helene), my dear mistress, I know no more of it than you do. In this great house you know that what is done at one end of it may very easily be unknown at the other.....I am as ignorant as you are how—but Mr. Ormsby is gone, or - - - - - - -'

"She stopped and hesitated.—'They have killed him, (exclaimed I)—I know they have destroyed him—do not deceive me—I will not be deceived——but let not my father, my inhuman father, imagine that I will survive—no, I will instantly go, I will avow the truth, and follow my husband to the grave.'——The frenzy that possessed me gave me strength: I sprang from the bed, and, in a state of desperation, was rushing towards my father's room, when Helene, terrified at my attmept, threw herself before me, and shutting the door, locked it, and secured the key. This presence of mind alone saved me from the destruction on which I was throwing myself; for I believe, that had I at that moment appeared before my father, acknowledged my situation and my attachement to Ormsby, that he would without hesitation, have stabbed me to the heart.

"Such was the distracted state of my mind, that it was only when my strength was entirely exhausted that Helene could prevail upon me to listen to her arguments. At length I sunk into silent despair, because I had no longer the power of speaking, and then Helene ventured to leave me, carefully locking the door of my chamber after her, as well as that of the anti-room, and hasten away to procure not only some medicine for me, which she hoped would quiet my agitated spirits, but the benefit of the counsel she knew she should recieve from the Abbé Hayward, who, though he had not been more than a week in the house, had gained the confidence and good opinion of every one in the family.

"When she was gone, I endeavoured to recall to my mind the words, the looks, and gestures of my father.....I shuddered as they passed in my memory, and I dared not think steadily upon the scene I had passed. Even now, Rosalie—even at the distance of almost nineteen years, I find that I cannot dewll upon it without horror."

It was true the recollection affected Mrs. Vyvian so much, that a cold trembling seized her. Her voice failed, and Rosalie, terrified at the situation in which she saw her mother, entreated her to fobear any farther exertion till she was more able to undertake it. It was more than an hour before she was sufficiently recovered for Rosalie to leave her; at length, finding Mrs. Vyvian more composed, she retired to the house she used to call her home, having settled to be again at her mother's bedside at a very early hour the following morning.

CHAP.

ONCE more seated by the bedside of her mother, who, on this morning, was too much indisposed to be able to leave it, Rosalie listened in silence to the continuation of a narrative in which she was so deeply interested.

"While Helene was gone, (said Mrs. Vyvian), I collected strength enough to rise and go to the window of my bed chamber. It was now night, but there was light enough to enable me to discern every object on the lawn round the house. I gazed, however, without knowing why, or on what:—the thought of Ormsby gone—lost to me for ever—perhaps destroyed—filled me with such undescribable horror, that my power of reflection seemed to be annihilated. Impressed with that one idea, my heart seemed petrified; the certainty of instant death would have been received as a matter of indifference. All that I wished was, to be assured of the fate of Ormsby——I thought that if I knew what was become of him, I could brave the severest anger of my father, and die content, since I believed my death inevitable.....How dismal every object that I surveyed from my window appeared!—not a human being appeared round the house: the woods that you may recollect terminate the lawn on one side were almost half stripped of their leaves; but they looked black, dreary, and fit for deeds of horror.——Yet do not, my dear Rosalie, believe, that however cruel I at that moment thought my father, I could suppose him capable of so dreadful a crime as that of directing the death of Ormsby; but I figured to myself, that, rendered desperate by the force that had been used to tear him away, he had resisted, and sunk under the numbers of unfeeling men who were ready at every hazard to obey my father's orders—no otherwise could I account, in the present confused state of my mind, for his having disappeared without sending me one line—one last adieu!——or having made any attempt to give me notice of the scene that awaited me, or to arm me with the courage it required to pass through it.

"I cannot discriminate the various emotions that agitated my mind during the absence of Helene, who, on her return in about an hour, found me still sitting at the window, as if I expected to see Ormsby pass, as he sometimes used to do under it of an evening, when he used to tell me he had peculiar delight in watching the light in my room, and seeing me pass across it, long before he dared to tell me he loved me.

"But now, alas! he was to appear there no more—and when Helene returned and came into my apartment, carefully locking the door after her, the expression of fear and dismay which her countenance wore renewed all my terrors......I flew towards her, and, though unable to speak, she saw that I anticipated the worst news she could relate to me.

"She tried to command herself, that she might prevail upon me to be tranquil enough to attend to my own safety. It was, however, some time before I was in a condition to listen to her.

"Helene at length related to me that the house was now apparently quiet, but that an air of amazement and consternation was perceivable on the faces of all its inhabitants; all of whom seemed afraid to speak or even to look at each other.—The Abbé Hayward, she said had been alone with my father the whole day, and none of the servants had been permitted to wait but the old butler; that, on her applying to him for intelligence, he said he had orders to tell her, when she came down from her young lady, that Mr. Montalbert ordered her attendance.

'Ah, Madam, (said Helene in French), how I trembled when I heard this......I went, however, and my master ordering me to approach the place where he sat, said—Helene, it is my express orders, as well to you as to every other servant in my house, that no gossiping, no conversation, not even a word, shall be uttered as to any circumstance that has happened, or that you may suppose has happened in this family. The slightest failure in this respect will be attended with ill consequences—the least of which will be the loss of your place.....I ask you no questions as to your *past* discretion——As to your lady, tell her from me that I expect she will to-morrow appear before me as my daughter ought to appear; on which condition only, the folly, or the affectation of this day, for I know not which to call it, shall be forgotten. You will tell her, as I have already caused it to be intimated to my people, that from this hour the name of Ormsby is never to be mentioned within these walls——go—and remember what I say to you——Your father, Madam, (continued Helene), looked more stern than ever, as he said this; and indeed I trembled so, that I thought I must have fallen down as you did. That dear good man, the Abbé Hayward, looked at me as if he wished, but dared not, say any thing to comfort me. I got out of the room as well as I could, and went, looking I believe more white than a ghost, into the servants' hall, where I saw no person but the coachman and the gardener; neither of them spoke to me—they seem even afraid of speaking to each other. I passed into the housekeeper's room, under the pretence of asking for something for you: Mrs. Nelson was there, with the two house-maids and the laundry-maid; but instead of asking me any questions about you, as Mrs. Nelson almost always does if you are at any time the least ill, she never inquired after you, though she knew you had been confined to your room ill the whole day; as to the maids, they seemed like statues, and while I stayed on one pretence or other, in hopes of gaining some intelligence, Mrs. Nelson would have sent one of them to the store-room, but she turned as pale as death, and said it was impossible to go unless one of the other maids went with her. Mrs. Nelson gave her a strange look, but said nothing, and they went away together.'

"All of this, so strangely obscure and unaccountable, redoubled my inquietude.—Something very unusual then had happened in the house, which had impressed terror on the minds of its inhabitants—What could this be but some violence that had been offered to Ormsby, which was known to all the servants, but which none of them dared to speak of?—There were few events, the certainty of which could be so dreadful as the state of horrible suspence I was now it. I think that my intellects, unable to sustain, sunk under it, and that the artificial calm that followed was the effect of the agonies in which I passed this melancholy day, and the night that followed it.

"Still placed in the window, with my eyes fixed on the lawn and woods that surrounded it, I heard the incoherent narrative of Helene, and continued to torment myself with every terrific idea that my sickening brain could raise....Hideous shadows seemed to flit before me—I almost imagined that, in the murmurs of the wind, I heard the dying groans of Ormsby—that I heard him call upon me, and bid me adieu.—From the indulgence of waking dreams so horrible, I was startled by the rapping at the door of the anteroom that led from the staircase to my bedchamber. Helene, fearing she knew not what, hesitated, and dared not open it; she asked me what she should do, but I was utterly incapable of answering, and we were at length relieved from our terrors by hearing the voice of Mr. Hayward, who desired to be admitted.

"He spoke to me with so much soothing kindness, and reasoned so properly with me, that tears, which had been for so many hours denied me, flowed from my eyes: I dared not, however, ask—for I yet knew but very little of Mr. Hayward—I dared not ask what was become of the unfortunate Ormsby; but, as if this worthy man had read the thoughts, I had not courage to express—he gradually managed his conversation so as to bring it to the point he wanted to speak upon.—'I was extremely concerned, (said he), that the precipitancy of Mr. Montalbert's manner alarmed you as it did....Indeed I have told him, that I greatly blame his needless harshness, produced only by an anonymous letter, and certainly unfounded. I can easily imagine how the abrupt manner in which he spoke to you might have the effect it had, and I have at length persuaded him to believe, that without any improper attachment to Mr. Ormsby, you might be affected in the manner you were. He is become more reasonable since his passion has subsided, which was raised to a degree of frenzy by that infamous letter, and he seems concerned for the terror he inflicted upon you, and willing to forget it upon one positive condition.'

"Having no courage to ask what that condition was, I remained silent. Mr. Hayward thus proceeded——

'As Mr. Montalbert cannot subdue his displeasure, when he thinks it possible that Mr. Ormsby had or could be supposed to have been guilty of the presumption of pretending to you, he has thought it proper to remove him from hence immediately, and, to put an end at once to the very recollection of such a report, he insists upon it that the name of Ormsby is not mentioned in the house.'

"I sighed, but dared not ask what was the fate of this unfortunate Ormsby....I felt, however, considerable relief from the manner in which Mr. Hayward spoke of him; for I was persuaded, that had my father taken any very cruel measures in regard to him, such a man as Mr. Hayward would neither have tolerated such conduct, or, if he could not have checked it, would have spoken of it so calmly.

"Still, however, the sad uncertainty of what was become of him seemed so heavily to press on my heart, that it was ready to burst......I could not speak; but Mr. Hayward, who appeared to be well acquainted with the painful sensations which were probably pictured on my countenance, went on, in the most soothing manner, to tell me what was, he thought, the best part I could take for my peace of mind, and for the general tranquility of the family.

'What I wish you to consider of, my dear Miss Montalbert, (said he), is, whether it would not contribute much to your future ease and comfort, could you determine, in compliance with your father's commands, not only to mention no more of this unfortunate young man, but to resolve on appearing before your father tomorrow, at the hour he has appointed, to hear mass, with a calm and even cheerful countenace. Let him not suppose that the observance of his commands is a greater sacrifice than it ought to be—appear to think, that whatever is his pleasure ought not to be disputed, and, I think, I can venture to say, that whatever uneasiness this wicked letter has raised in the breast of your father will be at an end, as your behaviour will prove to him that the charges in it were entirely unfounded:—you will be restored to *his* confidence and to your own peace.'

"I was still incapable of answering; but, as I remained quiet, and shed not a tear, Mr. Hayward thought he might venture to proceed.

'I am convinced, (continued he), that you feel the force of all I have urged; but, I believe, it is better to state to you what are my apprehensions of the consequences, if you fail of acquiring this command over yourself........It will, I fear, make your father suspect, that this malicious informer had some ground for the assertions he or she had dared to make. It is much to apprehended, that Mr. Ormsby, who is wholly, I *believe*, in his power, will suffer if such an imagination predominats in your father's mind; and I should doubt whether the extreme indignation which he suffers himself to feel might not so far annihilate his tenderness for you, as to urge him even to so harsh a measure as that of sending you to a convent in Italy, and compelling you to take the veil.'

"Mr. Hayward stopped, expecting that I might by this time have so far recovered my spirits, as to be able to promise that I would attempt at least to regulate my behaviour by his advice—but I remained silent....Rendered desperate by what I had heard, I became incapable of attending to the consequences of the step I was about to take: the moment, however, I could find voice and words, I related in a slow and solemn tone, the dreadful truth; but before I had entirely finished my melancholy narrative, the room turned round with me, my eyes became dim, and my senses forsook me.

"When I recovered, Helene was chafing my temples, and taking other means to bring me to myself; the Abbé Hayward was traversing the room in the agitated manner of a person who had received some alarming intelligence, and knows not how to act. When he saw that I was a little restored, he approached me, and, in a voice hardly inarticulate, said, 'Most unhappy young woman, this is no time to flatter—destruction hangs over you, and it is only in your own power to escape it; for without your own efforts, nobody can save you. I will not decieve you, Miss Montalbert—I will tell you what I really believe, that if your father was assured of what you have now entrusted me with, the life of Mr. Ormsby would be insufficient to satisfy his vengeance—though he would be the *first* victim......Heaven direct me for the best! (cried the good man). Heaven direct me!—What can I do?'

"He again traversed the room in silent anguish; but what were his feelings compared to mine!

"At length he recovered himself enough to speak again with composure.

'Something must be done, (said he); but till I have more time to consider what, let me once more ask you, if you cannot, my dear Miss Montalbert, command resolution enough to appear before your father to-morrow with some degree of serenity?—Relfect a moment how much depends on this exertion on your part:—no otherwise than by this necessary dissimulation can you hope to avert the impending danger—danger that may so fatally affect more lives than one.'

"I now acquired steadiness of voice enought to say, 'Let Ormsby live—let *him* but escape the vengeance which ought not to fall on him, and let *me*, who alone am to blame, perish under the indignation of my incensed father......One victim will perhaps satisfy him——I desire to die—and when I am dead, the resentment raised by injured honour may surely be appeased.'

"That I spoke at all, and spoke calmly, though it was with the sudden sadness of despair, seemed to Mr. Hayward to be a favourable symptom. He pursued his argument, therefore, and endeavoured to convince me whatever hope remained of concealing this fatal secret, must rest entirely upon my own resolution and discretion.

"The life of Ormsby, he said, was in my hands:—he recalled to my mind the temper of my father—the fierceness of his anger—the steadiness of his resentment....I listened and shuddered.

'If, (said he), the mere information that the suspicion of such an affection between you and Mr. Ormsby was entertained in a neighbourhood, where he cares nothing about the people, has so enraged Mr. Montalbert as to induce him to act as he has done in regard to Mr. Ormsby—what would there not be to dread from the fury of his resentment, were he to know what you have to-night related to me - - - - - - -'

"I took advantage of a pause Mr. Hayward made to repeat some of the words he had used.—'Acted as he had done, (cried I, in regard to Ormsby); tell me then—I conjure you to tell me—how has my father acted?—By what stratagem, or force, could he tear away that unhappy young man, even before he knew that there was the least ground for the charge that was made against him?—Oh, Mr. Hayward!—if you are capable of mercy—if you really pity the agonies that rend my heart, tell me, I conjure you tell me, what is become of Ormsby?—I think, that if I once knew, I should become calm—I think I could summon resolution enough to consult my own safety; but, indeed, the misery of this uncertainty is such.....All my thoughts are so full of horror, that the death with which I am threatened would be a welcome release from such intolerable torture.'

'I solemnly assure you, (replied Mr. Hayward), that I do not know what is become of our unfortunate friend, nor, perhaps, shall I ever know......I dare not make any inquiry; and all I have been able to learn is, that, on receiveing the infamous scrawl last night, your father ordered every body out of his room, and remained alone, or only with Ormsby, for some time. He then directed two of the grooms to be sent to him, and that the steward might also attend.....Mr. Ormsby appeared no more. These two men, the grooms, have never been seen since; but there is no track of a carriage around the house, nor has any body been seen to leave it. The steward observes the most profound silence, and all that is known in the house is, that something has happened which has obliged Mr. Ormsby suddenly to leave it; that he has deeply offended Mr. Montalbert; and that it is required of all who would not enrage their master, and be dismissed from the family, never to mention the name of Ormsby even to each other.'

'My father *did* see him? (inquired I)—had they any conversation which urged on this precipitate violence?'

'I believe they had, but I know nothing certainly—any attempt on my part to draw from Mr. Montalbert more than he chooses to entrust me with, would not only be abortive, but would, in all probability, deprive me of every future opportunity of softening the asperity of his resentment. Let me conjure you, my dearest Madam, if you would not hearafter reproach youself with the fatal effects of this resentment, to exert your utmost resolution—endeavour to command yourself so as to appear to-morrow before your father....The second attempt will be more easy, and I trust, in a day or two, your spirits wil be so much calmed, that you will be able to consider of taking the measures so necesary to be thought of for the preservation of your reputation, perhaps of your life.'

'You believe then, (said I), that the life of poor Ormsby is safe?'

'Believe it!—(exclaimed Mr. Hayward)—surely I believe it.....To whatever extremities the unhappy prejudices or violent passions of Mr. Montalbert may drive him, and none can have greater apprehensions on that subject than I have, hitherto I hope and believe that Mr. Montalbert has taken no unjustifiable measures in regard to this luckless young man.—(Then deeply sighing, Mr. Hayward added)—In my opinion his future fate depends entirely upon you——it is in your power to save or to destroy him.'

'Gracious Heaven!—(exclaimed I)—what right has my fahter over this ill-starred young man?—*My* life may be in his power—he gave it me, and most willingly would I resign it; but Ormsby surely ought not to suffer.'

'Mr. Montalbert, (interrupted Mr. Hayward), will consider but little what he *ought* to do, or what he has a *right* to do, when vengeance is in question; but surley I need urge this subject no further—you are perfectly acquainted with his temper—you know that he is master of the country around for some miles. His servants, his dependents, his tenants, are in such habits of obeying him, that he is in some measure capable of exercising a sort of despotism, which, though frequent enough in other countries, is seldom seen in this......I will now leave you, my dear Miss Montalbert—again beseeching you to consider what I have said, and to command yourself as much as possible to-morrow.'

"Mr. Hayward then left me, and sent to my faithful Helene to attend me, who had been absent during our conversation; but my senses were yet stunned by the violence of the shock I had received—I could not shed a tear, and sat like a statue repeating almost unconciously to myself——'Ormsby is gone!—he is lost for ever—he is condemned to ignominy and disgrace, and it is *I* who have undone him, who may perhaps occasion his death!'

"I know not now by what arguments Helene at length prevailed upon me to take some refreshement, and to undress myself......I believe that by the contrivance of Mr. Hayward, who, as I afterwards found, kept a small dispensary of medicines in his own room, Helene gave me some remedy that assisted in quieting my spirits—for after passing some time in a state of mind which I cannot even at this distance of time reflect upon without horror, I sank into insensibility, from which I was suddenly startled by a fancied noise, and awoke only to recollect all the bitterness of my destiny."

    The narrative of Mrs. Vyvian, which became every moment more interesting to Rosalie, was now interrupted by a letter which announced the arrival of Mr. Vyvian, Mrs. Bosworth, and her sister, in London. Her spirits were already agitated by recollecting scenes in which she had formerly suffered so much, and this intelligence contributed to overwhelm them. The visit from her family was not to be made till the second or third day after the present; there was yet, therefore, time enough for her to relate the sequel of her story; which, at the request of Rosalie, who sacrificed her own impatience to consideration for her mother's health, was postponed to the following morning.

CHAP.

MRS. Vyvian on the following day thus proceeded——

"When I look back on the situation I was now in, I am astonished that I ever supported it—description at this distance of time could but do little justice to the state of my mind, even if I were capable of discriminating now the variety of miseries I then suffered under. It seems, on retrospection, the most extraordinary circumstance in the world, that in such a state of mind as I was in, I should have acquired resolution enough to appear before my father, as Mr. Hayward recommended, on the following day; but this I did do; and though I cannot but suppose that my figure and countenance bore full testimony to the state of my heart, he seemed determined not to notice the deadly paleness of my countenance, or the feeble and uncertain step with which I approached him: yet, when he supposed I did not remark him, he cast toward me looks of indignation and resentment, the meaning of which I could not mistake. I shuddered when I observed them, but in my turn affected to be as tranquil as before this storm that had wrecked for ever my happiness and my peace.

"It was highly probable that the violent agitation I had undergone, as well as the dreadful uneasiness that preyed on my mind, for the fate of my unfortunate lover, would finish my inquietudes for the future, and bury in oblivion the fatal secret of this hapless affection; but this did not happen, and now every hour as it passed added such insupportable dread of what was to happen in future to the miseries of the present moment, that to exist long in such a state seemed impossible—yet were my sufferings but begun.

"Nothing could be more dreary and desolate than every object appeared round the house. It was the dark and melancholy month of November, and nature seemed to be in unison with my feeling. I looked now on the same scenes as I had so lately beheld luxuriant in foliage, and illuminated with the summer sun—the same scenes in which Ormsby had so long been a principal object.....Now—as the leaves fell slowly from the sallow trees, they seemed to strew his grave—the wind, as murmured hollow though the perennial foliage of the pines and furs, sounded to my ears as if it were loaded with his dying groans——I heard him sigh among the thick shrubs that bordered the wood walks; he seemed to reproach my calmness—yet it was not the tranquility of indifference, it was the torpor of despair.

"I went out alone, that I might weep at liberty; yet, when I found myself in the silent solitude of the woods, I was unable to shed a tear, but sat down on one of the benches, and gazed on vacancy with fixed eyes, and without having any distinct idea of the object I beheld. In these dismal rambles rain and tempest, and once or twice night, overtook me. I was careless or insensible of outward circumstances; and certainly if my father had not determined to shut his eyes to the truth, as if the only alternative were between extreme severity and total ignorance, he must have discovered from my conduct that all his suspicions did not go beyond the reality.

"Some very fatal catastrophe would have followed the state of mind I was in, had not the pious and friendly councils of the Abbé Hayward, and the assiduous care of Helene, saved me from myself: the one exhorted me to patience, and a reliance on the mercy of Heaven; the other soothed and flattered my sickening soul with the hope of better days, and enabled me to endure the present by encouraging me to look forward to the return of Mrs. Lessington, who alone seemed to be likley to advise and succour me in a situation which every hour and every day rendered more perilous.

"Mr. Hayward frequently followed me into the depth of the woods, argued, remonstrated, and then soothed and endeavoured to console me. I heard his arguments, and even his reproofs, with submission and calmness; but when he told me that I ought to be cheerful, to be resigned, to endeavour to conquer my affection for Ormsby, and to attempt, by every means in my power, to conceal that it had ever existed to so fatal an excess—I lost my patience, and my respect for this good man did not prevent my flying from him with something like resentment and disgust.

"So passed a month—a wretched month, during which time the name of Ormsby had never reached my ears, save only when Mr. Hayward, in the conversation which he thought it necessary to hold with me, reluctantly named him, or when I could so far command the agonies with which my heart was torn as to name him to Helene, and listen to the conjectures with which she attempted to relieve me as to what was become of him.

"Of this, however, she knew no more than I did; yet, from the looks and manners of the servants with whom she conversed at the times when they were necessarily altogether, a thousand vague ideas floated in her mind, to which she sometimes gave utterance with more zeal than prudence. From her I learned, that the two men who had disappeared when Ormsby was so suddenly sent away had never since returned, and that the places they filled were now occupied by others. I heard too, that though the name of Ormsby was never mentioned whenever the steward, my father's old servant, or the housekeeper were present; yet that the inferior servants were continually whispering strange things, and that the people in the neighbourhood talked of nothing else; some of them going so far as to say, that inquiry ought to be made by people authorised, for that Mr. Ormsby had certainly been spirited away; while others gave dark hints, that, considering the revengeful temper of Mr. Montalbert, it would be well if something worse than being spirited away had not befallen the poor young man.

"All this I heard with alternate anguish and depression, of which it would be difficlut to convey with any idea to another. The fatal predilection that I had for Ormsby was then known, for no other reason could be given for such conduct towards him as was imputed to my father. I now saw none of the neighbours, for of the very few who had been accustomed to visit at the house, not one at this time approached it, and as I believed curiosity would have prompted them to come if they had no other motive, I thought it certain that my father had taken measures to prevent their visits. This I was not displeased at, for *their* looks would have been more uneasy to me than were those of the servants; whenever I saw any of *them* I was covered with confusion, and fancied they would remark and account for the sad change in my face and figure, of which I could not fail to be myself conscious.

"But if I fled thus from the observation of servants, what was my fear when compelled to appear before the severe and scrutinising eyes of my father?——I had always an awe approaching to dread of him, even in those comparatively happy days when no reproaches of conscience assailed me......Now I endeavoured to attend on him with the same assiduity as I used to do before Ormsby became a sharer in the task, or rather undertook it entirely; but whether it was that my timidity made me awkward, and that, therefore, I was incapable of acquitting myself as I formerly did, or whether my father, more really angry than he chose to avow, took these occasions to vent in peevishness some part of the resentment and indignation he felt. Certain it is, that his harshness and asperity were almost insupportable, and the unkind expressions he sometimes used, the looks of rage and disdain he cast upon me, were not unfrequently such as affected my spirits so much as to throw me into fainting fits, from which I reproached my poor Helene for recalling me....Death, which alone seemed likely to end my miseries, I continually invoked, and I know not what would have been the consequence of such a series of present suffering, added to the dread of the future, had they continued much longer.

"Yet before the return of Mrs. Lessington, to which only I looked forward with the least hope of mitigating my woes, I had some trial of fortitude to encounter more difficult to sustain than any I had yet experienced.

"At the end of a long row of elms, of which now a few single trees only remain, you recollect a high mount now planted with firs, poplar, and larches, into which, as it is railed round, nobody now enters; you perhaps remember too, the very large yew tree that shadows a great space of ground near it, and which is also railed round. That mound covers the ruins of a small parish church, and that yew tree was in the church yard.

"An avenue of ancient trees was terminated by this church, at the distance of something more than a quarter of a mile from the house. It was merely the chancel of a larger edifice which had belonged to a monastery, some of the ruins of which remained scattered over the ground, and when I and my brother were children, we had been told by the servants many of those legends that almost always belong to such places. It was said too among them, that beneath these vestiges of buildings, which were not considerable above the ground, there were arched vaults, and subterraneous passages, which formerly served as burial places for the religious persons of this monastery. Their coffins, placed in niches along the walls, had been formerly seen by several persons, who had given a very terrific account of the skeletons in these dismal recesses; accounts which were now traditional in the neighbouring villages, and were of course greatly exaggerated.—The mournful relics that had been seen under the earth were imagined to visit its surface, and the place was universally believed to be haunted. The style of the building that remained, where light was admitted through long windows obscured by pieces of coloured glass, and now darkened by the ivy that mantled almost the whole edifice; the walls of great thickness, in some places green with the damps that continually streamed from the roof, in others marked with the remains of Latin sentences, surrounding the half-effaced representations of the crucifixion, all contributed to give an air of wildness and horror to this almost-deserted building; where, though at the Reformation, as it is called, under Henry the Eighth, it became a parish church, yet service was performed in it only once a year, as a mere matter of form, for the parish contained only the house of Holmwood, and three cottages belonging to my father, and since pulled down. So that when it was his pleasure to destroy this small church entirely, and unite the parish it belonged to with another, there were none to oppose the act of parliament he solicited and obtained for that purpose. At the time, however, of which I am speaking, this desolate spot inspired all that melancholy sort of horror which naturally gives rise to the reports of supernatural appearances; there was not a servant who would on any account have gone thither of a night, and even the gardeners and workmen, who were at any time occupied near it, related strange stories of uncommon noises, as of mourning and complaint, and more than once have run in terror to their fellow labourers, declaring that some obscure figures had issued from the vaults beneath, and then melted into air.

"Such as was the stern spirit of my father, and he so little knew how to make allowances for any weakness which he had never felt, that had any domestic betrayed fears of this sort before him, they would have been dismissed with disgrace; nor did my brother and I, while children, though *we* knew all the legends of the country, ever dare to speak to him of the stories we had been taught. Thus compelled to stifle our infantine fears, they were gradually subdued as our reason became stronger; and we were accustomed not only to find our way in the dark all over the extensive old buildings of Holmwood, but to traverse without fear the avenue that led to, and even the area that surrounded, the ruined church, though we credited the probable account that in the vaults beneath rested the remains of the former inhabitants of the decayed monastery.

"At the time I am now speaking of, I mean about six weeks after the departure of Ormsby, such was the gloomy temper of my soul, that I was pleased only with the horrors, and it was through the avenue of elms, and toward the ruins that I now frequently directed my solitary walk. I observed, however, that when, in compliance with Helene's earnest entreaty, I told her which way I was going, she shuddered and turned pale; and if I seemed disposed to go thither, when she was with me, she would find every possible excuse, such as that it was dewy from the high grass, or dirty, or the wind was in our faces, or any other objection she could raise against our taking that path; but none seemed to suit *me* so well......I found a melancholy sort of satisfaction in indulging the sad thoughts that incessantly pressed on my mind, in a place where I was sure none would interrupt my sorrow: even the labourer, fatigued with the toils of the day, or the benighted traveller from one village to another would not, to save a longer journey, cross my father's grounds near this place. An adventurous sportsman, perhaps, might violate the gloomy shade with his gun; but, at the season of which I now speak, the end of December, even the hostile sounds of field sports were seldom heard—a dreary and mournful silence reigned around Holmwood, for it was long since the voice of hospitality or gaiety had been heard. The rooks returning in the evening to the high elm trees that led to the church-yard, and the owls that inhabited the ivies that half mantled it, seemed to be the only living creatures that could endure the melancholy solitude.

"My father, who had at this time an interval of ease, though the asperities of his temper were now seldom mitigated, sometimes released me from my attendance after dinner early enough to allow me to take my solitary walk before it was too dark.

"The intelligence I had received on this particular evening from Mr. Hayward, that he had heard Mrs. Lessington would be at home in two or three days, had given some relief to my spirits, and, rather less oppressed than usual, I strolled almost mechanically up the avenues. It was a calm and still evening—so still, indeed, that every bird was heard whose slender feet perched on the leafless boughs, or flitted among them, and the bells of the sheep folding in the distant fields, and the remoter sound of a mill and mill stream, were brought in low murmurs to the ear.

"The well-known objects around me were becoming indistinct, but I continued to walk slowly on—I even sat down for a few moments on the remains of a rustic tomb, and listened to the dull sighing of the wind as it sang round the buttresses, and waved the black boughs of the old yew tree. As I sat musing, I recollected the stories I had often heard of spectres being seen, and strange noises being heard round these receptacles of the dead.——So little pleasure had I in looking forward to any thing that life could now afford me, so long had my thoughts been accustomed to consider death as the only end of all my miseries, that I felt no horror in the idea of seeing, or, if it were possible, of conversing with departed spirits. A sort of chilly and shuddering sensation, however, warned me to return before it was quite dark to the house. I arose from the mass of broken stone on which I had been sitting, and, advancing a few paces to return into the elm avenue, I fancied I saw a form glide before me among the trunks of the trees; but beneath the trees it was so dark, that I could not distinguish what it was. I continued, however, to gaze steadily on the place where I fancied this shape had appeared: the illusion was over—I saw nothing. Without any emotion of fear I proceeded, therefore, exactly to that spot, for it was my direct path to the house; I entered it, and, looking down the avenue, again fancied I saw an object moving at a distance about fifty yards beyond me; but almost immediately my attention was attracted by something white that lay just before me in the path. It seemed to be a book, a letter, or a folded handkerchief: I stooped and took it up—it was a sheet of paper, folded like a large letter, and tied with a bit of black ribbon. The circumstance rather surprised than alarmed me: I wondered what it could be, because I knew that the path was never frequented, or at least by persons who were likely to drop a paper. I put it into my pocket, and went hastily towards the house; when I got thither, I found my father had been inquiring for me, and I soon discovered that his temper was much disturbed......For more than two hours I was compelled to stay with him, and listen to reproaches and sarcasms uttered with the utmost ill-humour. Alas! I should have borne these more calmly, had I not felt that I deserved his indignation; but now they pierced my very soul.—At length, however, I was dismissed to my own room, where the vision, or fancied vision, of the evening, immediately recurring to me, I hastliy drew the paper from my pocket. Ah, Rosalie! imagine the sensations with which I read these lines——

'Vivo oh Dio!—ma più non ti vedrò—Prima di scriverti in questo modo, pensa quante pene, e quanti martiri bisogna aver sofferti, o più tosto che il tuo bel cor non fa rislessione sopra la nostra forte tiranna Abbia cura della tua preziosa salute; ora non si puo far 'altro per il sventurato O.'

'I exist—but we never meet again!—Think what I must have endured before I could write thus, or rather do not reflect on our inevitable miseries, but take care of your health—it is all you can now do for the unhappy O.'

"The writing appeared to be Ormsby's; but the lines were crooked, and the letters ill-formed, as if they had been traced by a weak and uncertain hand. As I gazed on the paper, that, and every object round me, swam before my eyes——again I read the words, again attempted to recall what I had seen, or supposed I had seen, in the elm walk, and it seemed possible that it was Ormsby himself—for who else could have appeared there?—Yet, from whence did he come?—Where had he so long been confined, or how could he now escape?—If it were indeed himself, why did he not approach?—if it had been but to have spoken one word to me, with the assurance that he lived.....Ah! it could not be Ormsby!—Ormsby would never have seen me so near him, and have left me to tears, conjectures, and terrors; but if it were not himself, who could have written the billet I found there, in a language only a scholar, no other person in the house, except my father and the Abbé Hayward, knew a syllable?—Who was likely to write a hand resembling Ormsby's?—Who, indeed, except my father, whose fingers being entirely disabled by the gout, had almost always employed Ormsby to write, knew his hand well enough to attempt an immitation of it?—Any conjecture that led to a supposition of its being a forgery, seemed even more probable than that it should be Ormsby himself—if any thing could be more improbable than that he was so greatly changed as to be so near me, and yet fly from me. This uncertainty, and my own conjectures, equally endless and uncertain, soon became so insupportable, that my reason once more threatened to forsake me, and I believe I should have lost it, had I not communicated to Helene what had happened, and explained to her the purport of the letter. As I did this, I observed her countenance change; she grew pale and trembled—then, in an hurried way, said in her own language, that I should recollect how often she had entreated me not to go into the elm walk—not to frequent the ruins about the chapel.

"I eagerly inquired what those precautions had to do with what I was now talking of. Helene, trembling and weeping, at length told me, it was the opinion in the family, that Mr. Ormsby had been killed in attempting to resist the force that was used to remove him from the house; that he was buried in the vaults under the old church and ruined monastery; and that his spirit had been frequently seen since. This at once accounted for the apprehensions I had seen Helene so often express, and renewed all the terrors for the life of Ormsby, which the assurances of Mr. Hayward had a little appeased.....My heart sank within me, and again I seemed to be on the point of losing my misery and my existence together. The horrible idea thus conveyed, could not be a moment sustained without forcing the mind to an effort for its own relief. The moment I had recovered myself enough to reflect, my reason returned to dissipate this hideous fantasy. I might have believed that I had seen the shade of Ormsby lingering about the place of his interment—for to what weakness might not such sufferings as I underwent subject the understanding? but I knew that the spirit of the dead write no letters, and by whom but Ormsby could the lines I held have been written? Who, but either himself, or some agent he had employed, could have dropped the unsealed paper I had found? As soon as the tumult of my spirits were a little calmed by these reflections, I took courage to question Helene farther on the reports that had passed on this subject in the family.

"She told me that ever since the sudden disappearance of my unhappy lover, strange stories had been whispered in the family at every opportunity, when the inferior domestics had an oportunity of escaping from the observation of the steward and housekeeper; that the most frightful reports had got abroad in the country; and that it was every where believed that Mr. Ormsby had fallen the victim of my father's violence, and had been buried in the vaults: a report which was the more strongly credited, as the two men who disappeared with him had never returned. To this account, which was nearly the same in substance as that which she had at first related, she added many wild stories of noises heard, and sights seen, every one of which some person might be brought to attest. Nothing could be more dreadful than to reflect on these impressions among the neighbours, which, from the account given by Helene, seemed to be gaining ground, and might not improbably bring on some inquiry that might irritate to frenzy such a temper as my father's, and overwhelm me with shame and disgrace."

The recollection of this part of her life, added to the fatigue of having spoken so long, was more than Mrs. Vyvian could now sustain; and Rosalie once more prevailed upon her to delay the rest of her strange and melancholy narrative till the next day, which was likely to be the last they should uninterruptedly pass together.

CHAP.

THE narrative of Mrs. Vyvian thus went on——

"I had not yet recovered any degree of composure after the strange circumstance of finding the letter, which I continually read and studied, when some of the apprehensions, to which the intelligence I had got from Helene had given rise, were but too fatally realized. Such, indeed, were the various tortures in which I had been kept for some time, that it is astonishing, in the situation I was in, how I survived it. I might well, in the words of a favourite air which I should have sung, had not my heart been too heavy to find relief even in music——

Lasciami[1], o Ciel! peitoso,
Si non ti vuoi placar,
Lasciami respirar,
Qualche momento!

Rendasi col riposo,
Almeno il mio pensiar,
Abile a sostenar,
Nuovo tormento.——

"I know not whether my mind dwelt most continually on the circumstance of the letter, or on the dread of the inquiry that might be made from the reports that had been spread in the country. In regard to this last, however, I endeavoured to persuade myself, that Helene, understanding English imperfectly, might misconcieve or exaggerate the expressions made use of by the rest of the servants; and while I attempted to mitigate part of my anxiety by this persuasion, I endeavoured to acquire courage to investigate the ground of the other; and for this purpose I took again and again the walk alone, for not even Helene's sincere attachment to me would, I knew, have engaged her to have accompanied me without great reluctance. I thought too, that if by any strange means which I could not comprehend, nor hardly think possible, Ormsby yet lingered round Holmwood, he would be prevented by the presence of a third person from speaking to me. Life was now in my eyes of so little value, that to fear, unless it were fear of my father, I was insensible; and I believe that I should have met with indifferece, or rather torpor, the most terrific figures that imagination has ever dressed out to deter from crimes, or to enforce repentance. In my solitary and gloomy walks, however, I saw no more any object like that which had before alarmed me, nor did I hear any noise but such as I could easily account for. Every evening, without any regard to the weather, or to any thing but the precautions necessary in regard to my father, I took the same lonely walk, and for many evenings returned more astonished and depressed; for the longer this mystery remained unexplained, the more I became the prey of wild conjectures and tormenting solicitude.

"But imagine, my Rosalie, if it be possible, imagine what I suffered, when, about five days after the circumstance of my finding the letter, I was alarmed by the sudden entrance of Helene into my room, who, breathless with some new terror, endeavoured to explain something, which it was long before I understood. At length I made out that a neighbouring gentleman in the commission was come, as the servants believed, to apprehend my father with peace officers, for that a regular complaint had been laid, it was not known by whom, of the sudden disappearance of Ormsby; and at length, the accusation of having murdered him had been so often repeated, and the clamours of the country, where certainly my father had many enemies, had become so loud, that the gentleman in question could act no otherwise than he did.

"Endeavour to imagine what I endured while such a conference as this lasted, which it did for upwards of two hours; at the end of that time, the magistrates and his myrmidons departed together. Helene, who had watched them, came to tell me so: they had been out for some time with the steward and the old butler, and she was sure, she said, they had been up to the church; then they returned to the house, and, after a few moments of farther conversation with my father, quitted Holmwood apparently satisfied.

"So confused, so mingled with horror and amazement, were all my ideas, that I recollect nothing of what passed in my mind, till I saw myself seated at table as usual to help my father, who sat opposite in his great chair; when I falteringly made the usual inquiry of the day, he did not answer me. I began, however, to carve as usual for him, but he fixed his eyes on my face, with a look so menacing and stern, that it was with the utmost difficulty I supported myself....I looked in vain for comfort in the faces around me; the old butler looked as if he pitied, but could not assist me; and the footman seemed to be under such terror, that having made two or three awkward blunders, he received a very severe reprimand, and was ordered to leave the room. Our silent and melancholy meal was soon over, for my father ate little, and I in vain attempt to swallow. The table cloth was removed, and I collected voice enough to ask him, as nearly as I could in my usual manner, whether I should read to him?—He answered loudly and angrily—No——

"Then, after a pause, a dreadful pause, during which I was afraid I should have sunk upon the floor, my father spoke thus——

'If I thought only for one moment, that the infamous reports, which have gone forth in the country, had originated in your folly, or rather wickedness, I should not hesitate what to do. As for the ungrateful villian, who might, perhaps, have had the insolence to attempt, as a return for my receiving him into my house, to steal my daughter and my property from it, you will never see him or hear of him more, nor can a matter of self-defence be again tortured into what the laws might *here* call a crime; but for yourself, know that it is my pleasure that you immediately prepare to receive, as your husband, a friend of mine, whose estate is such as you have no pretensions to expect, unless it be as my daughter—I will not suffer myself to suppose you have forfeited that title—on your part you will be pleased to make up your mind, and to divest yourself of a manner and behaviour which I will suffer no longer: I should have forborne to have given you my commands in regard to Mr. Vyvian, till his arrival, if I had not remarked your perserverance in a sort of conduct which *I will not understand*, lest the most terrible vengeance should follow......I have said enough—go to your own room, and learn to obey.'

"This terrible sentence, which ended in so loud a tone as almost to stun me, deprived me for a moment of my recollection; as soon, however, as I was able, I arose from my chair, and with difficulty reached the door, my father's eyes following me with a look so scrutinizing and angry, that I wished at that moment the earth might open beneath my feet and swallow me for ever. I found Helene near the door; for, alarmed by the transactions of the morning, and probably by the report of the footman, she waited there for me—without her aid I should never have got to my own room. I sat down in a state of torpid despair, which it is impossible to describe. Helene spoke to me in vain. The words I had heard, the dreadful command I had received, still vibrated in my ears, and the horrors of my fate were so forcibly presented to my mind, that the few distinct thoughts that passed through it pointed to suicide as the only way to escape from a destiny I was utterly unable to support. At length the tears and prayers of my faithful Helene restored to me some degree of recollection; she knelt at my feet, imploring me to have mercy on myself, if it were only to save my father from the crimes to which his furious revenge might excite him. She endeavoured to persuade me, that what he had said of Mr. Vyvian might be only a finesse; or, that if there was such a marriage in agitation, I might delay or escape it by the interposition of Mrs. Lessington, who was probably by this time, or would be in a few days, within four miles, and from whose prudence, as well as influence over the mind of my father, much might be hoped.

"Though I knew great part of this reasoning was fallacious, I affected to be more calm, that Helene, who would not be dismissed, might talk to me no longer; but what a night did I pass! and when I obtained by opiate half an hour of unquiet slumber, with what anguish did I recollect, the moment I awoke, all that had passed the preceding day, with what dread look forward to what might befall me in that which was begun.

"One consolatory circumstance happened in the morning, which enabled me to go through it; I received a letter from Mrs. Lessington, to inform me she was arrived at home, and would see me the next day. This prospect of alleviating my sufferings gave me the power of going down to dinner with some degree of resolution—I even took courage to meet the piercing eye of my severe, my sometimes cruel father, and to repeat, when dinner was over, my question, whether I should read to him?—He again answered, No—though with less harshness than the evening before: he felt himself indisposed, and said he should endeavour to sleep.

"I no sooner had left him, than in despite of the earnest entreaty of Helene, who incessantly besought me to have more regard to my own safety, I went into the avenue, though it was nearly dark; an early moon, however, lit up, with faint but cheering radiance, the winter sky, and her rays glancing through the leafless trees, and falling on the gray trunks of a few arbeals and birches that were scattered among the more gloomy elms towards the middle of the line, I could have indulged my shuddering fancy in supposing them, indistinctly seen as they were, to be spectres beckoning me to the only sure asylum of all sorrows in the cemetary beyond.

"Why should those fear who have nothing to hope?—Of beings of this world I had no dread, for I was so miserable that religion only arrested my feeble hands, or they would have been lifted against a life which might have been called a living death; supernatural beings I had never learned to fear—if such were ever permitted to appear. Thus arguing and reflecting, I had reached the top of the avenue, and stood a moment looking at the half-ruined church, and meditating on the horrible idea taken up by the people of the country, that Ormsby was destroyed and buried in this place.......What an opinion must they have of the violence and ferocity of my father's spirit! What an idea of the provocation he had received, before they could have supposed him likely to be driven to extremities so dangerous and dreadful!—It was impossible but what the cause for such vengeance must be suspected. The secret of our attachment, my disgrace and shame, then were known, or, what was nearly the same thing, guessed at, though I no longer supposed it possible that my father could for a moment harbour a thought so contrary to humanity as the destruction of the unhappy Ormsby; yet there were a thousand daggers for my heart in the reflection that such a history was the conversation of the surrounding country, and that the real or imaginary crimes of our family were discussed by the ignorant, and enjoyed by the malicious.

"But even these reflections were ease compared to those that assailed me when I remembered the conversation of the evening before and repeated to myself the dreadful name of Vyvian.—There is a kind and a degree of grief that annihilates the feeling from its violent pressure, as the extremities of bodily pain are said to deprive the sufferer of sensation. This was the effect which the commands of my father had on my mind, now that alone, and amidst the silence of the night, I reflected on them—lost in the terible contemplation of the future,I forgot the present, and was unconsious of the dreary scene around me, till I was startled from my reverie by the sight of a man, who, coming from among the ruins, slowly approached. Rivetted to the spot by fear, mingled with a strange desire to know whether this was a being of another world, or whether it brought me intelligence of Ormsby, I had no power to stir. The figure approached, and, as if encouraged by my remaining where I was, spoke to me in a low voice, and said something as if entreating me not to be alarmed; but I heard only the beginning of the sentence; the voice was, I thought, Ormsby's, and a thousand sensations, which I could neither discriminate then, nor can describe now, contributed to deprive me of my senses. The predominant idea, however, was, the hazard Ormsby was in, in thus returning round the house, for of any supernatural appearance I had none.

"On recovering some degree of recollection, I found myself on the ground, and a man kneeling by me, whom I still believed to be Ormsby, till he explained himself in these words——

'I have long waited for an opportunity of speaking to you, Miss Montalbert—recover your recollection—your presence of mind——the life of Ormsby depends on you.'

'Of Ormsby?' cried I faintly.

'Of Ormsby! (answered he)—my unfortunate brother.....It is you who must either release him; or must either restore him to life and liberty, or condemn him to end his miserable days in poverty and imprisonment.'—I have not strength, Rosalie, to relate every word as it passed; suffice it therefore to tell you, that it was one of the brothers of poor, unhappy Ormsby, who related, that he had come from Ireland on finding that my father had imprisoned Ormsby for debt; and that he had declared to the elder Mr. Ormsby by letter, that he never would release him, unless, under the most positive promise, that he would go immediately to India—never again to see or correspond with me, and renounce, in the most solemn manner, every claim that I might have given him to my person or my affections. This Ormsby had positively refused to do.

My father, irritated to frenzy by a circumstance that renewed all his suspicions, declared, in terms of the greatest violence, that Ormsby should perish in prison. His father could do nothing for him; but sent over his second son, only two years older than Ormsby, to endeavour to appease the anger of Mr. Montalbert, by engaging his brother to make the concessions that were required of him.

'I have now (said the young man) lingered about the place more than a fortnight, in hopes of having an opportunity of speaking with you. At the risk of my life I have attempted to make my way into the house, and probably have owed my preservation to the notion impressed upon your father's servants, that the restless spirit of my brother, whom they supposed to have been murdered, haunted the house and gardens.....Now, dearest Madam, (continued George Ormsby), if you have, indeed, honoured my brother with your regard, resolve to save him—resolve to restore to my poor, unhappy parents the peace this fatal circumstance has robbed them of.'——I asked faintly what I could do?—He answered, that by consenting to marry the man proposed to me by my father, I should end at once the persecution of Ormsby, and secure my own peace—I shuddered, and was on the point of declaring why it was impossible for me to do this, when the noise of voices at a distance compelled him hastily to quit me. He retired again among the ruins, and I, without knowing how I found strength, walked towards the house. I met Helene and one of the men servants coming in search of me: Helene, in accosting me, trembled so she could hardly speak—I leaned on her arm and reached the house, where I had again to encounter the angry looks and fierce interrogatories of my father. I know not how I answered; overwhelmed by the scene I had just passed I sunk once more under the violent agitation of my mind, and could hardly be said to be sensible till the soothing voice of Mrs. Lessington, at my bedside the next morning, restored me in some measure to my reason. But notwithstanding the perfect reliance I had on her friendship, I should never have had courage to relate to this dear friend the extent of my imprudence and its consequences; but Helene had already told her so much, that she entered at once upon the subject as soon as I appeared in a state to attend to her; by transferring the blame from me to my father, she reconciled me in some measure to myself, and, with some degree of composure, I suffered her to speak of what could be done in circumstances so dreadful and distressing.

"Nothing, however, could be immediately determined upon. I agreed with her, that it was necessary her husband should know my cruel embarrassment, for without his assistance and participation she could do nothing. She gave me in the mean time every consolation in her power; but I thought I perceived, not withstanding she evaded the conversation that she thought I ought to relinquish every idea of ever again seeing Ormsby, and that if I could escape from the perils of my present melancholy situation, I should dispose myself to act in compliance with my father's commands.

"Many were the conferences we now had; but probably it would have been impossible to have saved me from that death, which my father might have thought could alone wipe away the dishonour I had brought upon his family, had not Providence interfered in my favour.

"Mrs. Lessington now met and conversed with George Ormsby: they agreed that the only means of saving his brother was to procure his renunciation of every pretension to me in whatever form my father should dictate. This I alone could engage him to do, and this at length Mrs. Lessington extorted from me in a few lines, by which I *asked* this of him—with a trembling hand, and eyes overflowing with tears, I signed the fatal paper. Mrs. Lessington assured me George Ormsby went immediately with it to London.—In about ten days afterwards, Mrs. Lessington, who remaind at Holmwood, informed me she had heard from him; that his brother Charles was released, and on his voyage to India. There was something in all this that I could not comprehend; but I dared not trust myself either with inquiries or with conjectures—Ormsby was lost to me for ever, and I, sometime in the bitterness of my soul, accused him of having abandoned me, though, in more reasonable moments, I was compelled to acknowledge that his stay would have been destructive to us both...My father, who, as it appeared from his conduct, knew much of the truth, though this loss of my honour was yet unknown to him, became somewhat less severe toward me; yet I shrunk more than ever from his eye, and my timidity and terror must have betrayed me, if the change in my person, now every day more evident, could have escaped observation; but, whether it was that the violence of temper, which my father had yielded to in regard to Ormsby, had aggravated his arthritic complaints, or whether his constitution was breaking entirely up, he became at this period so ill, that a physician, who had always successfully attended him, was sent for from London; he gave him some relief, but declared, that unless he went to town, where constant attendance could be given him, the consequence would be greatly to be apprehended.

"The result of his advice was, that we removed to London. Thither also my friends Mr. and Mrs. Lessington removed; and Mrs. Lessington being then near her time, it was so managed, that when the hour arrived when you, my beloved child, came into the world, you were concealed by Mrs. Lessington for three weeks, and then produced as twin with the daughter of which she was delivered, who is since dead.

"You may imagine, my Rosalie, how very difficult it was to conceal the fatal secret of your birth—you may imagine, for I cannot describe, what were the terrors I had to encounter—the anguish of heart with which, when I had once beheld you, once pressed you to my heart, I saw you torn from me, and knew that I should never dare to call you mine, or again to shed over you the tears excited by the resemblance your infant features bore to those of your father.

"But, on calmer reflections, I agreed with Mrs. Lessington, who represented to me incessantly, how thankful I ought to be for the good fortune with which I had saved my reputation, if not my life. The suspicions that had been entertained, in consequence of my father's violent conduct towards Ormsby, were now, she said, blown over and forgotten. His own family had reported, that so far from his having undergone any persecution from Mr. Montalbert, it was to him he was obliged for the advantageous situation in which he was gone to India; that the circumstances which had given rise to such strange reports in the neighbourhood of Holmwood originated in error and misrepresentation; and, in a word, that the Ormsbys, instead of showing any resentment toward my father, every where made his eulogium as the benefactor of the whole family. I was not, however, the less miserable, though I owned the truth of all Mrs. Lessington urged; and whenever I was alone, I gave way to that anquish of heart, which, while I was with her, I endeavoured to repress or conceal, because I would not be thought ungrateful, or insensible of the obligations I owed to her friendship.

"During my father's very severe illness, I heard no more of Mr. Vyvian—Indeed I seldom saw my father, and when it was unavoidable, only for a few minutes. Mrs. Lessington, in whom he had great confidence, and expressed a regard unusual for him to feel, had contrived to obtain his leave for me to stay with her while she was very ill and unable to come to me, and by this management only it was that I escaped observation at the period when I could so little bear it. As my father recovered, however, my more constant attendance was again necessary. He now sometimes ordered me to read to him, and, when he was still more at ease, to play at chess with him. I was, indeed, but a poor substitute for Ormsby or Mr. Hayward; but I fancied that the latter sometimes got out of the way, as if on purpose to make me more necessary to my father, and to leave us together.

"It was in one of these tête-à-tête parties, that my father, without much ceremony or much preface, asked me, whether I had reflected on what he had determined upon in regard to Mr. Vyvian, who would now in a few days be in England, whither he came on purpose to receive my hand?

"The violent effect of this intelligence was evident on my countenance—I tried in vain to speak; my lips refused to articulate a syllable. Not only disregarding, but enraged at the pain I seemed to feel, he declared, in a voice that made me tremble like a leaf, that if I did not determine to obey without remonstrance, or hesitation, he knew how to punish, and *would* punish me as I deserved. He added, that *I* had already been the occasion of his undergoing uneasiness, which had brought on his late illness; of scenes the most disgraceful to his character, never sullied till he found a curse instead of a blessing in his daughter; and that not content with having once been nearly the cause of his death, I now was disposed to complete my work, and destroy him who had given me life.——Figure to yourself, if it be possible, what I endured at this moment, and, if it be possible to carry your imagination farther, suppose what I must have suffered before I was compelled to give my hand to Mr. Vyvian, while my heart was devoted to Ormsby; while I would most willingly have shared with him the most obscure destiny; while I would have followed him to India, or to Nova Zembla, and have exposed myself to endure any hardships in any region of the world, rather than have been mistress of the world on condition of being the wife of Mr. Vyvian.

"My friend Mrs. Lessington, however, and the Abbé Hayward, joined in this cruel persecution. The former removed you from my sight entirely, and sent you into the country; the latter seemed to have lost his usual humanity and tenderness, and to think that duty, which I had once violated, had now stronger claims upon me than before the fatal indiscretion I had been guilty of. From your father I heard nothing. His family reported every where that he was married to a woman of fortune, with whom he became aquainted on her voyage to India, whither she was sent for by an uncle, whose heiress she was. This I believed, as I had done many other stories that were among the artifices that were used to force me into this marriage. They succeeded but too well, or rather the extreme terror I had of my father left me no means of escape. I became then the wife of Mr. Vyvian. I have been ever since the most miserabe of women; my son only, and the consolation of having sacrificed myself to duty, alone supported me. Before, however, I was driven into this miserable union, I executed, as I was then of age, a deed of gift, in which I made over, during my life, to Mr. and Mrs. Lessington, the interest of four thousand pounds, which was the gift of a relation, and which I possessed independent of my father, but without the power of alienating the principal. This is part of the money which Mr. Vyvian has so often reproached me with *wasting*, as he terms it, on begging monks and chanting hypocrites; though, had I really bestowed it on my necessitous fellow creatures, I should have thought myself well justified in such a disposal of it.

"I had not been married above fifteen months when my father died, and left Mr. Vyvian in possession of that fortune, which was undoubtedly his chief motive for overlooking my reluctance which I repeatedly avowed to him, and which he well knew accompanied me to the altar. After my father's death, he no longer affected to treat me with the least degree of regard. We went abroad for some years, which served in some measure to relieve and dissipate the heaviness of my heart. I had often the consolation of hearing from Mrs. Lessington, and in her letters, with the acount she gave me of her family, my Rosalie, as one of that family, was always mentioned. When I returned to England, I found you, child of my fond affections, all that my fancy could form of loveliness and perfection. So many tears had my fatal error cost me, and so much I hoped had been expiated by the subsequent sacrifice I made, that I trusted it was not criminal to indulge myself with a sight of you: you know how easily I enjoyed that happiness, but *I* only knew what exquisite happiness it was till you grew up, and till Charles, returning from abroad, showed so much partiality for you, as made me tremble for the consequence. This fear, which a thousand circumstances contributed to irritate, rendered my life miserable—I thought, that as the heaviest punishment it could inflict, Heaven might permit a fatal passion to take place between you. This was the cause not only of the deep melancholy into which I fell, but of conduct which you then thought and I felt to be unkind and cruel."

Mrs. Vyvian here ended her long narrative, and, kissing the tears from the cheeks of her daugher, she dismissed her for that day, referring till the next day any farther conversation in regard to Montalbert.

CHAP.

Notes

↑ Metastasio

AT home and alone Rosalie had time to reflect on the story she had heard; and though she knew very little of the world, and Mrs. Vyvian had failed to be very minute in many parts of her story, it seemed certain that the family of Mr. Ormsby had been the principal instruments in terrifying her into a marriage, which would have rendered her life miserable even if her heart and her person had not belonged to another. The Italian letter, which was probably written in that language lest it should fall into other hands, and might have been read had it been in English; the improbability that George Ormsby should venture to appear about Holmwood, unless with the connivance of some of the family, if not of Mr. Montalbert; and the eagerness with which Mrs. Lessington and Mr. Hayward had adopted the views of Mr. Montalbert, though they knew her situation, were a combination of circumstances which seemed to leave no doubt in the mind of Rosalie but that her mother had been betrayed by some or all of those whom she considered as her best friends. Their motives were probably good; but Rosalie could not help reflecting, that had not such been their conduct, she might now have been the acknowledged daughter of her most tender and affectionate of mothers; she might have known and been blessed by the fondness and protection of her father; and they might in a happy union have effaced the remembrance of their early indescretion, for the death of Mr. Montalbert would soon have left his daughter at liberty, and her life would not have been passed in the miseries of such a marriage, nor her spirits have been overwhelmed with the consciousness of being the wife of one man while her whole heart was another's.

"I should not then, (said Rosalie, as she considered these events), I should not then have been despicable in the eyes of Montalbert's relations—I might have been received by *his* mother with pride and pleasure, from the hands of my own; but now I am an outcast, and have no right to claim the protection of any human being, unless it be thine, Montalbert, and thou art far, far from me!—Heaven knows whether we shall ever meet again!"

A shower of tears fell from her eyes while she indulged these melancholy thoughts; but, from longer meditation, she was roused by a short note from Mrs. Vyvian, who informed her, that her daughters had just been with her; that they should now seldom be at liberty to meet, for that Miss Vyvian, who, for some reason or other, did not seem happy and satisfied with her sister, was to come to her mother during an excursion Mr. and Mrs. Bosworth were about to make to Scarborough.—"She is my daughter, (said Mrs. Vyvian), and I cannot refuse her my protection—alas! I will fulfill to the end of my life the duties that have been imposed upon me. Hitherto the consciousness of having acquitted myself of a very arduous task, to the utmost of my power, has sustained me in many an hour of anguish; it will smooth the bed of death, and no inconvenience I can sustain, no ingratitude with which I may be repaid, shall for a moment weaken the resolution I have made to acquit myself to my own conscience......Come to me, however, my Rosalie, to-morrow, as Bab will not be here till evening; Mr. Vyvian stayed only a day in London. He is now gone into the west to visit the borough for which he is representative, and is afterwards to make I know not what tour, with I know not whom, which is likely to detain him all the summer. Alas! I dare not hope that the monotonous life I lead can be pleasant to Barbara, who probably comes with reluctance that will render us both equally miserable. How differently, my Rosalie, *could* I indulge myself with having you always with me, would our hours pass; but I will not add a word more on this subject."

Rosalie saw that, from this unlucky arrangement, she should be deprived of the consolation she might derive from the advice and conversation of her best friend, when she most wanted such comforts. The aversion that Barbara Vyvian seemed to have to her was even greater than that of Mrs. Bosworth; and on recollecting several circumstances that had happened since the estrangement the sisters had shown towards her, Rosalie could not but imagine that they knew, or suspected, her near relationship to their mother......Ingenuous and liberal as her own heart was, she imagined not that it was possible for envy only, malignant hatred of superior excellence and beauty, to call forth the ill-humour and provoke the ill-offices of these young women, though she had already had a specimen of the effect of those odious passions in the behaviour of the Miss Lessingtons, whom she once thought her sisters.

In this family she now seemed to be almost a stranger. The character of Mrs. Lessington, since the death of her husband, seemed totally changed; and her passion for cards, and for the society of the set of people among whom she now lived, absorbed almost every other feeling but her passion for money. To Rosalie she was not only become perfectly indifferent, but seemed wary of the task of affecting sentiments she did not feel; from the present situation of Mrs. Vyvian, it was probable she would never be able to increase the annual gift she had made as a consideration for adopting her daughter, and her former and long attachment to her, seemed, if not entirely forgotten, at least insufficient now to urge her to any exertions of friendship and attention. She seldom saw Mrs. Vyvian, and, when she did, her conversation related entirely to the people with whom the latter held no intercourse, and her visit appeared to be always a matter of ceremony rather than of choice. Though the solicitude in which Rosalie was left was infinitely the most pleasing circumstance of her present residence, yet she could not but imagine that the style in which she was treated in the family must occasion suspicions of the truth: the difficulties of concealing for a series of years such a secret, appeared the more wonderful the longer she thought of it; but, from these meditations on the extraordinary events Mrs. Vyvian had related to her, she recovered herself only to reflect on what was to be her future fate. Her mother had been abandoned by the man to whom she had sacrificed her honour and her peace; and though probably it was to preserve her life and his own that this separation had been submitted to, though it was certain that compulsion had at first been used to bring about this cruel separation, and that reason and a respect for the object of his unfortunate love had afterward prevented Mr. Ormsby from making any attempt to write to her, Rosalie could not think, without extreme pain, that even *such* an attachment was not proof against time and absence. Mrs. Vyvian had said, that she believed that though Mr. Ormsby still lived, he had forgotten her entirely; she added, that she most sincerely *hoped he had*; but, as she said this, her tears fell more abundantly, and her heart seemed to feel all the bitterness that attends the conviction of being forgotten by those we have fondly loved. Rosalie thought that nothing could ever induce her to even *say*, that she wished to be forgotten by Montalbert.

It was now some weeks since she had heard from him. There had even been time for an answer to Mrs. Vyvian's letter. Should he long delay answering it, what agonies of mind should she not be exposed to; she trembled to look forward to such a possiblitiy, and felt that it would be difficult for her to exist long under doubts of Montalbert's affection.

When she saw her mother in the morning, it was with increased concern she observed the deep dejection into which Mrs. Vyvian had sunk; the little strength which she had collected to enable her to relate to Rosalie what it was necessary she should know, was now exhausted, and, pale and languid, she appeared to sustain with difficulty the fatigue of leaving her bed to receive her daughters, who were to be with her at noon: the one to take leave of her again for some time, the other to become a resident in a house which offered scenes so different from those to which she had long been accustomed.

As the sight of Rosalie seemed rather more deeply to affect than to relieve her mother, she shortened her visit, and returned to her usual home, where she passed the day entirely alone;

Mrs. Lessington and her daughter being both in town, and not likely to return till the following morning.

In the evening she sat down to write to Montalbert, and had nearly finished her letter, when a maid (for there were only two female servants in the house) came to tell her, that there was a person at the gate who desired to speak to her; who, upon her asking his business, answered that he could communicate it only to herself.

As Rosalie had no acquaitance likely to make such a visit, nor any business to transact, and as so near London there is always danger of admitting strangers, she bid the servant tell him, she could speak to no person with whose name and purpose she was unacquainted. The girl stayed for some time, and then returned with a piece of paper, on which was written with a pencil, "Be not alarmed—it is Montalbert, who, compelled to return in secret, has been to Mrs. Vyvian's, and finds persons with her before whom it is impossible for him to appear."

The mingled joy and surprise, not without some alloy of fear, with which Rosalie read this, may be easily imagined; but it would be more difficult to describe, in adequate terms, the transports of Montalbert on meeting after so long an absence, or with what tenderness and gratitude Rosalie learned the purpose of his journey. As soon as they were calm enough to converse upon it, he told her that as soon as he had received Mrs. Vyvian's letter, he determined to come over himself to England at every hazard.—"It was not very easy, (said he), to prevail on my mother, who has, unluckily for me, projects in her head for establishing my fortune, which made her more unwilling to allow for my absence; but a young Sicilian nobleman, with whom I was brought up, and who is distantly related to my mother, was exactly at that period returning to Sicliy for a few months. I communicated my distress to him, and he managed the difficulty so well, that I obtained a short leave of absence, and am now supposed to be with him in Sicily. A thousand circumstances may happen to betray me; but I trust much to the friendship and prevoyance of my friend to guard against detection at present; and, for the future, I know my Rosalie will not shrink from any trial of that affection which makes the happiness of my existence—even though a greater sacrifice were required of her than to quit her present abode."

The answer that Rosalie gave to this was, that with him every place and every country would be equally pleasant to her. He then explained to her his views.—"Unable to live without you, (said he), I have never ceased, since I have been in Italy, to meditate on the means of conciliating my happiness, and the deference I owe my mother. That friend, of whom I have just been speaking, is now master of his fortune; he has offered me a small, but beautiful villa in Sicily, about seven miles from Messina, and not more than two and a half from the sea. There you may live, my Rosalie, unremarked and unquestioned; and there I can pass months with you, without incurring, on the part of my mother, any suspicion, or any other remonstrance, than must in every event arise from my refusal of the match she wishes to make for me: when, however, she finds I am determined, and loses her apprehensions to an English woman and a Protestant, I shall be left at liberty to wander about Italy occasionally as I used to do; and we may be happy at the present with each other, without risking the loss of that prosperity hereafter, in which it is the first wish of my heart to place you."

This plan appeared to Rosalie not only practicable, but delightful. The unfeigned pleasure with which she embraced it seemed to redouble the satisfaction with which Montalbert expatiated on their future prospects: he appeared, indeed, to have thought of every thing, and settled what should be said to persons in England, to account for her departure. It was to be given out, that Mrs. Vyvian had procured for her a situation in a foreign family of distinction, who were desirous of having a young Englishwoman as instructress to their daughters; an establishment, which, as Rosalie Lessington was left entirely without fortune, was extremely advantageous and desirable.—However improbable such an arrangement might appear to those who were acquainted with Italian customs and manners, Rosalie and Montalbert agreed, that there were none of that description among those who were likely to inquire of the Lessington family; she had appeared, indeed, so little in their societies, that it was probable she would soon be wholly forgotten.

Mrs. Bosworth and Miss Vyvian were certainly more likely to inquire after her with more active malignity, and doubting any story that was at all unlikely to form conjectures to her disadvantage; but, as the journey of Montalbert, at this period, was unknown to them, as they had no communication with the Lessington famliy, and were both too proud to annex any consequence to Rosalie, except what she had derived from their fears of their brother's or their mother's too great affection for her, it was probable that when they saw her, and heard of her no more, they would cease to think about her.

It was, however, a very inconvenient circumstance to them, that the presence of Barbara Vyvian prevented Montalbert's seeing her mother, with whom it was so necessary for him to consult. As he could not stay more than a week in England, there was not a moment to lose. Many purchases were to be made for Rosalie, as well as many precautions to be taken; and it was proper that Mrs. Vyvian and Mrs. Lessington should meet to adjust several points relative to a person in whom both were interested.

After some debate how to obtain admittance to Mrs. Vyvian, it was agreed that this could be done only by the means of Mr. Hayward. To him, therefore, Montalbert immediately wrote, engaging him to meet him at a tavern early the followig morning; then reluctantly, and not without her repeating her remonstrances on the impropriety of his staying any longer, he took leave of Rosalie, and retired for the night to the house, where, in pursuance of his appointment, Mr. Hayward came to him the next day at six o'clock.

They together contrived so well, that Mrs. Lessington was admitted to the apartment of her friend without any suspicion on the part of Miss Vyvian; and in a few days every necessary arrangement was made, and Rosalie ready to depart.

There were in England only two persons, of whom to take leave for so long a time, perhaps for ever, gave her severe pain. These were her real mother, for whom her affection seemed to be greater than if she had been accustomed always to consider her in that endearing relationship, and the eldest Mr. Lessington, from whom she had for so many years received instruction, and towards whom she had been used to look for future protection and regard. To him, however, she could have no opportunity of saying farewell, as he was gone into Wales with a young man of fortune, from whom he had expectations of preferment. Rosalie dared not even write to him, as Mrs. Lessington, for some reason or other, objected to it; she was compelled, therefore, to go without bidding him adieu.

Her parting with her mother was attended with many tears on both sides; but each wished to shorten a painful scene, which it was not safe long to continue, as Rosalie and Montalbert were introduced into the house by stealth. This sad farewell being over, they got into a hackney coach with their baggage, and being set down at an inn in Holborn, a quarter of the town where Montalbert was little likely to be observed by any of his acquaintance, they there found his servant waiting with a post chaise according to his orders, and immediately proceeded on their way to Dover.

CHAP.

THE fatigue of travelling, and the sufferings from sea-sickness, were rendered supportable to Rosalie by every care and attention which vigilant love could dictate. Having recovered from the latter, and wondered at the novelty which a French town presents to one who never before crossed the channel, the travellers proceeded, after a few days rest, to Paris, and from thence to Lyons. Rosalie, though delighted with her journey, and acquiring new ideas at every step, was impatient to proceed, because she dreaded nothing so much as that the mother of Montalbert should discover, by his protracted stay, that he had been to England; while he, more solicitous for the health of his lovely wife, than influenced by any other motive, regulated his journey rather by her convenience, than by the necessity of appearing in proper time for his supposed Sicilian voyage, leaving his friend, the Prince of ——, the care of keeping up appearances for him as well as he could.

Had not apprehensions of what might happen to embitter his future felicity a little derogated from the enjoyment of the present, it would have been difficult to have found a happier being than Montalbert. While he pointed out to Rosalie the beauty of the country through which they were passing, every scene, every view, seemed to acquire new charms: the pleasure which the varied prospects of nature gave to her young and unadultrated heart, the desire of information she expressed, and the sense and solidity of her remarks, communicated to him delight more exquisite than that which he felt in contemplating the beauty of her form and face, which, he could not but observe, attracted universal admiration wherever she appeared, even in the haste of a journey, and under the few advantages of a travelling dress.

In France, superior or even common beauty is generally much noticed, and almost at every post town Montalbert heard some observation on the loveliness of *la jeune Anglias*; or, if they remained in any city more than a day, had an attempt made by some gay young man or other to be introduced to his notice.

From these sort of acquaintance, however, Montalbert shrank, with a sensibility unusual on such occasions to his natural character, which was open, unsuspicious, and sociable. He not unfrequently was sensible of something like jealousy, for which he failed not to reason with himself; but still his dislike of the adulation which he saw likely to be offered to his wife, wherever she appeared, conquered the sense he had of the absurdity of feeling such a sentiment in regard to her, who was all innocence and simplicity; who certainly lived but to please him, and was so unconscious of her personal attractions as not to have the least idea of the reasons which made him avoid every sort of society on the road. She imputed his shunning it, to the fear he had, lest he should be met by some of his former acquaintence, who might betray to his mother his present expedition.—There was, however, in this reserve of Montalbert's less of personal jealousy than of another sentiment. The mind of Rosalie, unadultrated by the false refinements of modern education, and yet anew to the world, seemed, to her husband, capable of being adorned with all that lends grace to beauty, and gives perfection to genius. She had seen so little of society since her short residence near London, that the bloom of the mind (if such an expression may be allowed) had not been tarnished by any commerce with inferior society, or the common studies of a circulating library. Her natural understanding was excellent, and she had more judgement than generally attends on so much genius as she possessed; but hitherto this judgement had been unexercised, and this genius dormant.

The little she had read was but ill-calculated to form the first, and the society she had been usually among, had allowed her little scope for the latter: but, at a very early period of her life she became conscious, that such sort of people as she was usually thrown among, people who only escape from dullness by flying to defamation, were extremely tiresome to her, though she saw that nobody else thought so, and suspected herself of being fastidious and perverse. The cold, and sometimes contemptuous treatment she had met with from her supposed sisters, the little real afection she had ever found from the persons whom she believed to be her parents, had rendered her timid and dissident.—As nobody but Mrs. Vyvian seemed to love her, she supposed that to none but Mrs. Vyvian she seemed worthy of affection. Since the explanation that had been given all the passages of her former life appeared in a new light, and she accounted for the indifference of her supposed, and the tenderness of her real, parent.

This extraordinary discovery was a frequent topic of conversation between her and Montalbert as they pursued on their journey; and they often canvassed the circumstancs that would, if the narrative of Mrs. Vyvian had been less authenticated, have given rise to incredulity.—Montalbert, when he first heard it from Rosalie, had remarked these circumstances—"It is strange (said he) that the account you have of your father's present situation is so vague, so indistinct, that you have no clue to guide you even to the certainty of his existnece, none by which you can identify yourself to him. I can make every allowance for the singular circumstances in which Mrs. Vyvian was placed; for the timidity of her temper, and for the violence of my grandfather, whom I have always heard represented as a tyrant, who was not to be, would not be, contradicted. Still it appears equally unfortunate and strange, that she omitted to tell you whether he knew of your birth? whether the family of Ormsby were apprised of it?"

In answer to these remarks, the justice of which she however acknowledged, Rosalie bade him recollect, how much of all the circumstances most interesting to her might be unknown, even to Mrs. Vyvian herself.

"When I remember (said she) the countenance and manner of my mother, when she recalled those scenes in which she suffered so cruelly; when I think how little capable she was, even at this distance of time, of dwelling on those parts of her story, where she had occasion to name my unfortunate father, and the awe she had of her own, as well as the tyranny she has since experienced from Mr. Vyvian, and the necessity there has ever been for secrecy as to a part of her former life, which would undoubtedly have aggravated her actual sorrows, I cannot wonder, though, perhaps, I may have occasion to lament, the incomplete information this dear unhappy parent has given me......I have seen her lips tremble, and cold and death-like dew on her temples, while, in a languid voice, she was relating what I have repeated to you; and I know that no motives less powerful than her love and her fears for me could have engaged her to write as she did to you. Long years of sorrow have so broken her spirits, that the most gloomy ideas sometimes take possession of her mind; she trembles, lest incidents in her life, for which surely she has already been punished sufficiently, should still draw the anger of Heaven on her children, as well as hazard her future happiness. She thinks, that she should not have deceived Mr. Vyvian; though, had she not done so, there is no imagining what might have been the consequence from the furious temper of her father; and the consciousness of having done so has made her patiently submit to very unworthy treatment—offering (to use her own pathetic phrase) her sufferings as a sacrifice to the God whom she had offended, and hoping their bitterness and duration might expiate the errors of her early life.—From hence I account for many parts of my mother's conduct, (continued Rosalie), that before appeared mysterious. Her severe penances; her voluntary resignation of the world, and her patient submission to the undutiful and even cruel conduct of her daughters; and from the pains these ladies took to alarm her about their brother's attachment to me, though ignorant of all the agonies they were inflicting, I have an explanation of that forced and involuntary neglect of me, which rendered me so very wretched for some time, and of which I am persuaded nothing but this cruel idea could have induced her to assume even the appearance."

Montalbert listened silently to this natural and sensible vindication of conduct, which appeared to him more extraordinary and less accountable than it did to Rosalie. He thought it, indeed, almost impossible that Mr. Vyvian should be so ignorant of his wife's former attachment as he seemed to be; and he was sure that her father had known, if not all, yet so much of the truth, as had induced him to act in concert with Ormsby's family, or at least to compel them so to act with him as to have saved his daughter's honour at the expence of her happiness.

The conversation on this subject was frequently renewed during the progress of their journey, and the tears of Rosalie as often flowed from the recollection of the sad state of spirits and health in which she had left her mother. So great were Mrs. Vyvian's apprehensions of accident, that might discover the secret so long cherished like a serpent in her bosom, that she had desired Rosalie and Montalbert not to write to her on the way, thus depriving herself of what she owned would be one great alleviation of the restraint and misery under which she was condemned to repine. The moments of reflection, therefore, on the uneasy hours of this beloved parent, were the only moments that passed without pleasure, amounting sometimes to rapture, when, as they approached the Alps, the most sublime and magnificent views of nature were opened to her astonished view.

Accustomed of late to the flat, monotonous, and uninteresting views round London, she had frequently sighed for the more animating landscapes of her native country, and had no ideas of beauty superior to that which is formed by those green and undulating hills, in some places fringed half-way up by beech woods, in others, rearing their turfy mounds, covered with sheep on one side above the once impenetrable forests of the weald, on the other gradually declining towards the apparently boundless ocean that forms the English channel.

But when she saw the rich and luxurious country, which nature, "with all her great works about her," spreads before the astonished traveller, between Lyons and Civita Vechia, the port from whence Montalbert determined to embark for Sicily, in order to avoid both Rome and Naples, her mind was exalted by scenes so much superior to any she had ever formed an idea of either from the efforts of the pen or the pencil, she seemed transported to a world of higher rank in the universe than that she had inhabited while she was in England; and she was of an age and dispositon to forget, or at least be indifferent to those circumstances which can hardly fail to remind English travellers, that, though other countries may have more bold and attractive scenery, their own is that where life is enjoyed with the greatest comfort.

Arrived at Civita Vechia, after an abscence of ten weeks, from England, Montalbert felt some degree of uneasiness when he knew he must hear from his friend, the Count d'Alozzi, what had passed during his absence. From this he was relieved by finding a servant of the Count's waiting for him with a small vessel hired to convey him and Rosalie to Messina, where the Count waited his arrival, that, after Rosalie was fixed at the habitation he had prepared for her, they might return together to Naples.

Montalbert, who now saw himself freed from the painful solicitudes that had so long perplexed him, would not, however, listen to Rosalie's entreaties to embark immediately; but, fearful of exposing her too soon to sea-sickness after the fatigue of so long a journey by land, he remained a few days at the port, while Rosalie, who had no terror so great as that of meeting the mother of Montalbert, and no idea how far she was from her, concealed herself at the inn where she lodged, and could not, without alarm, suffer Montalbert to quit her for a moment.

Montalbert, however, knew that this was not a place where it was likely he should be known, remained with great tranquility for three days. All seemed to favour their voyage, which he cosidered, not without some pain, must be twice as long as if he had sailed from the Bay of Naples. The weather, however, was mild, and the wind favourable; and a voyage begun thus propitiously was as happily concluded, though not till they had been eight days at sea. On the evening of the last, they entered, by as bright a moon that ever enlightened the swelling of the Mediterranean, the port of Messina. Never did the magnificent spectacle it afforded give more delight than Rosalie felt, as, sitting upon deck, Montalbert pointed out to her the beauty of the scene: the inconveniences and tediousness of the voyage were no longer remembered. As the vessel slowly approached the shore, every object, in the beautiful bay, was distinctly visible; the bright light of the moon fell on the long line of magnificent buildings that overlook the sea:, above which rose the mountains, whose outline was boldly marked in the deep blue æther, while Etna, no otherwise distinguished than by its towering grandeur, rose sublimely above the rest. The sea, calm as the Esculean above it, scarce broke in trembling lines as it approached the shore, but seemed to be with all nature in deep repose. At the distance of two or three miles were seen floating lights of the fishermen employed in taking the *pisca spada*, or sword-fish, which gave to the gently undulating tide the appearance of being enchanted, and of bearing fairy lights on its bosom.

 Arrived at the lodging provided for him by the active friendship of his friend, the Count d'Alozzi, Montalbert saw his beloved Rosalie in safety, and all his cares were for the present suspended; but this could not, he knew, last long. He had many acquaintances at Messina, and many people were there occasionally who knew his mother; it would, therefore, be unsafe for him to appear publicly with his wife, and, after one day of repose at his lodings, they removed in a carriage, with which they were accomodated by the Count, to the villa he had lent them, at the distance of hardly three miles from Messina, where they found every thing that could contribute to their convenience; and were, in a few days, as much settled as if they had already inhabited this enchanted spot for for many years.

CHAP.

WHILE Montalbert felt himself highly gratified and obligated by the care his friend had taken to provide every thing in their new abode that could render it convenient and agreeable to Rosalie, she was never weary with contemplating the beauty of the scenery around her. A garden, which even the false Italian taste could not spoil, arose behind the house, and its orange trees fringed the foot of a hill, which would in England have been called a mountain. Even the verdure of England was in some measure enjoyed here amid the glowing suns of Italy; for the higher lands are refreshed by dews, which prevent their being parched like the plains. Beyond the enclosure, shrubs, which are carefully cultivated in Engalnd, grew spontaneously, and formed a natural wilderness of the gayest colours and lightest foliage. From hence the most glorious view presented itself that imagination could picture: the sea, and the opposite coast of Calabria; the Lipari islands; Strombolo, marked by a black wreath of curling smoke staining the mild and clear sky; innumerable vessels scattered about the blue expanse of water; and the faro of Messina giving to the whole a new and singular feature, connecting the varieties of an extensive sea view with a port, seemed almost to unite the island to the opposite continent.

Divested of every care that related to the past, save only her solicitude for Mrs. Vyvian, Rosalie would have fancied herself in Paradise, had not Montalbert been reminded by the Count of the necessity of their immediately departing together for Naples.

This zealous friend had forborne to visit them till some days after their being settled in their new habitation. He appeared to feel for Rosalie all that respecful admiration which beauty and sweetness, like hers, naturally inspired. Her manner of speaking Italian was particularly interesting to the Count, who seemed to be delighted to instruct her: he lamented to her the cruel but necessary representations that he thought himself obliged to make to Montalbert, that he must either determine to go back to Naples, or give up the plan of concealment which had already cost him so much trouble. Rosalie, in her ingenuous and interesting manner, confessed their obligations to him, but sighed, and with difficulty restrained from tears; while acknowledging the truth of his observation, she trembled at the necessity of yielding to them.

Montalbert, with whom reason and love were at variance with each other, became every day more gloomy, pensive, and uneasy. Sometimes he determined to hazard every thing rather than leave her. "After all, (said he, as he entered into these arguments with himself)—after all, what is it that I am contending for?—for what is it that I am sacrificing those hours that will return no more?—for money which I may never enjoy—for high prosperity which is not, that I know of, conducive to real happiness. Is it not true, that a day, an hour, at this season of my life, is worth half an age toward its close?—yet I am throwing away these precious hours of youth and health, in hopes of being a very rich man hereafter."

These arguments, however, whatever might be their solidity, if tried by the maxims of Epicurean Philosophy, sometimes yielded to other considerations.—He was not devoid of amibition; but could he wholly divest himself of that sort of attachment toward his mother, which, though it had more of fear than of love in it, had become a sort of principal from habit.

His frequent fits of silence, his melacholy looks, and long solitary walks by the sea side, the evident irresolution and deep depression he laboured under gave to Rosalie the most poignant uneasiness. She sometimes was afraid of increasing these symptoms of a mind, ill at ease by appearing to notice them; at other times she ventured gently to remonstrate with him. At length, after a conference of some hours with Alozzi, he suddenly took a resolution to depart the next day; Alozzi was returning to Naples, and they were to embark together.

This resolution he seemed to have adopted in consequence of having reflected, that, if he did not soon go, he might not return time enough for the hour so dreaded, yet so desired, when

Rosalie might give birth to another being only less dear to him than herself. This was to be expected now within two months. To be absent at such a time was infinitely more formidable to his imagination than leaving her now; and, as if this had never occured to him before, he now resolutely determined to tear himself away.

Rosalie saw him depart with anguish of heart, which she endeavoured to stifle, that what he felt might not be increased; but when Alozzi had carried him off, almost by force, so dreadful did it seem to him to say adieu!—she was so much affected, that she could not remain at the window till they were out of sight; but, shutting herself in her own apartment, she gave herself up to tears.

The remonstrances, however, of her Italian woman, who was already much attached to her, and the care which under such circumstances she owed to her own health, even for his sake, whose absence she lamented, roused her at length from this indulgence of useless regret. She now sought to amuse her mind by contemplating anew the scenes around her; but their charms were in a great measure lost. Montalbert was no loger with her to point out the beauties that every where surrounded their abode, or to enjoy them with her. There was an awful sublimity in the great outline of Etna; its deep forest, and magnificent features, which afforded a kind of melacholy pleasure. Not in a situation to explore the scenes it offered more minutely, yet feeling infinite curiosity, she endeavoured to amuse her mind with the prospect of future days, Montalbert would return to her; she should be blessed in beholding his tenderness for his child; she should again listen to his animated description of a country replete with wonders, or be able, perhaps, to visit it with him. In the mean time she determined to pass the heavy, heavy hours in cultivating the talents he loved. She took up her pencils, and, strolling into the garden, placed herself on the seat where, as they often sat together, he had pointed out to her some points of view which were particularly favourable to the painter; she would have sketched them, but her efforts were faint and uncertain. In spite of all her exertions, dark presentiments of future evil hung upon her spirits. Their depression she imputed to her personal sufferings; the period, to which it was so natural for her to look forward with dread, was now near. She had heard, indeed, that in the climate of Sicily infinitely less was to be apprehended than in England; but this she only knew from the report of persons who might say it to appease her fears and reassure her spirits. Perhaps it was her destiny to be snatched from Montalbert, to realease him from his embarrassment, and to make room for the Roman lady, to whom his mother was so desirous of uniting him.—While these thoughts passed through her mind, in gloomy succession, she repeated, from the little, simple ballad of Gay——

"Thou'lt meet an happier maiden,
"But none that loves thee so!"

At length, however slowly, the tedious hours wore away. Montalbert returned; he returned apparently more enamoured than before this absence of nine weeks, and Rosalie forgot that she had ever been unhappy.

When, the first joy of their meeting being a little subdued, Rosalie spoke to her husband of his mother, she fancied that though he declined conversation on the subject, that he was in reality less anxious about the future consequences of his marriage than she had ever yet seen him. When he could not wholly evade speaking on the subject, he affected an indifference, which made Rosalie believe he was himself at ease; for, little skilled herself in dissimulation, she did not for a moment imagine that this tranquility was artificial.

At length the hour arrived when real joy succeeded to this external calm. Rosalie brought into the world a lovely boy, and her own health was so soon re-established, that, in a very few weeks, her beauty appeared more brilliant than before her confinement. More attached to her than ever, Montalbert could hardly bear to have her a moment out of his sight; yet the time was come, when, if he followed the dictate of that prudence to which he had already made so many sacrifices, he must return to Naples.

Alozzi, whose friendship for him appeared to be undiminished, failed not to remind Montalbert of the necessity of this return; but his remonstrances, however reasonable and gentle, were always received with uneasiness, and sometimes with impatience and ill-humour. The visits of Alozzi had not been more frequent than formerly; on the contrary, he had been more rarely their visitor than during his former stay at Messina; though he returned thither before Montalbert, he never appeared at the residence of Rosalie till his friend arrived there. Notwithstanding these precautions, however, the fault of Montalbert's temper found food to nourish itself in the looks of Alozzi, whom he fancied regarded Rosalie with too much admiration, and sometimes fixed on her eyes in which passion and hope were too evidently expressed. This idea having once seized the imagination of Montalbert, became a source of inexpressible torment, and when he reflected, that he must soon leave his wife in the house of this friend, who was, he persuaded himself, in love with her, neither her virtues, nor her attachment to him, neither the honour of his friend, nor the confidence he ought to have had in Rosalie, were sufficient to quiet his apprehensions, though he felt them to be alike injurious to his own peace, and to that of those whom he most loved.

Sometimes he gazed on Rosalie as she sat with his boy sleeping in her arms, and tried to persuade himself, that if once his mother could see these interesting creatures, she would not only pardon him, but receive them to her protection and tenderness. Then, recollecting what had passed during his last visit to this violent and impracticable parent, he felt that all such hopes were delusive: he became ashamed of what often appeared to him an unpardonable meanness, and resolved, at whatever pecuniary risk, to throw off a yoke which degraded him in his own eyes; to produce his wife and his child, and abide the consequences of his mother's displeasure.

While Montablert was thus deliberating, and every hour forming and abandoning projects for the future, a letter he received from Naples, compelled him to adopt the measure of immediately going thither. It was from a female relation, who usually resided with his mother; and who now informed him, that she was extremely ill, and it was absolutely necessary for him to see her as immediately as possible.

Wretched is the policy which too often puts at variance the best feelings of human nature; which sets the parent against the child, because expences either affect his ease, or are painful to his avarice; which estrange the brother from the sister, and make enemies of the amiable and lovely group, who, but a few, a very few years before, were happy associates in the innocent, thoughtless hours of childhood.—Ah! wretched is the policy which makes the son, too, often rejoice, when she who bore him and nourished him mingles with the dust; when those eyes are closed which have so often been filled with tears of tender anxiety as they gazed on him!—and yet all the contrivances, which cunning and caution have invented for the security of property, have a direct tendency to occasion all this, while mistaken views of happiness, unfortunate mistakes in the head, or deficiency of feeling in the heart, do the rest, and occasion more than half the miseries of life.

Montalbert, on receiving the letter that gave him notice of his mother's danger, felt, for a moment, that he was her son; but almost as soon as this sense of filial duty and affection was lost in an involuntary recollection of the release which her death would give him from the pain of concealing a clandestine marriage, or reducing himself and his posterity to indigence if he betrayed it.

He had no sooner felt this sentiment arise in his mind than he was shocked at and resisted it; but again it arose, and he found all his affection for his mother weak, when opposed to the idea of the advantages he might derive from her quitting the world where she alone was the barrier between him and happiness with the woman he adored.

It was not, however, a time to investigate these sentiments deeply, but to act in pursuance of the letter. He hastened, therefore, to inform his wife of its contents, who agreed with him entirely as to the urgency of his immediate departure, yet wept and hung about him as if impressed with some unusual apprehension of future sorrow; and, as she kissed her child, she almost drowned it with her tears.

Montalbert, who felt none of this violent grief at an absence, the duration of which would, as he thought, depend on himself, consoled her with views of future prosperity and uninterrupted happiness.

Alozzi had a few days before left Messina, and was gone to Agrigentum, where he intended to remain for some time. Montablert, therefore, who had no doubt but that he should return within five or six weeks, felt no uneasiness at the thoughts of leaving to frequent interviews with his wife, in his absence, a man whom all his reason did not enable him to see with her, in his presence, without pain.

The letter Montalbert had received was written in such pressing terms, that there was no time to be lost, and he determined to begin his journey on the next day.

Rosalie, far from feeling even the usual tranquility, saw the moment of his bidding her adieu arrive with agonies of sorrow, for which she knew not how to account—yet could not stifle or command. Nothing new had occurred in her situation to make this absence more dreadful than the two preceding ones; indeed it should have been otherwise, for the presence of her infant, on which she doted with all the fondness of a first maternal affection, was what was most likely to console her in this temporary parting from its father: nor had she to say, with the unhappy Dido——
"Si quis mihi parvulus aula
"Luderet Æneas, qui te tatem ore referret;
"Non equidam omnino capta aut dferta viderer."
VIRGIL'S ÆNEID.

The servants about her were the same as those with whom she had formerly reasoned to be satisfied. The situation around her offered all that the most lovely scenes of nature could do to assuage the pain inflicted by her husband's involuntary and short absence. All this she urged to appease the tumult of her spirits; she owned the justice of it all, but nothing gave her any consolation, and, when she at last allowed him to tear himself away, the resolution to see him depart was acquired by an effort so painful, that he was hardly out of sight before her senses forsook her, and it was many hours before the remonstrances of Zulietta, her Italian maid, and of an older woman who assisted in the care of her infant boy, so far roused her from the despondence into which she fell, as to engage her to attend to the care of her own health, on which depended that of the child she nourished at her breast.

By degrees, however, she became more composed; she received cheerful letters from Montalbert, sent by a vessel which passed them at sea. It mentioned, that they were becalmed, but that he was perfectly well, and had no doubt of writing to her the next day from Naples. Ashamed of fears and of despondence, which seemed, as soon as she could reason upon it, to have so little foundation, she returned once more to the the amusements which used to beguile the hours of her husband's absence, and all that were not dedicated to the care of her child, whom she attended to herself, she passed in cultivating those talents which Montalbert loved, and in which he had assisted and marked her progress with such exquisite delight.

CHAP.

IN Sicily there is no winter such as is felt in more northern countries, and now, in the month of February, spring every where appeared in the rich vales that stretch toward the sea from the base of Etna. His towering and majestic summit alone presented the image of eternal frost, and formed a singular but magnificent contrast to the vivid and luxuriant vegetation of the lower world.

Having only Italian or Sicilian servants about her, her former knowledge of the language was so much improved, that Rosalie now spoke Italian with ease, and read it with as much pleasure as English; but, since Montalbert had been gone this time, she felt the want of new English books; she read over the few she had with her, repeated frequently some pieces of poetry she was fond of, and sometimes longing to hear the sound of an English voice, and fancying, that if Montalbert's absence was lengthened, she should forget her native tongue, or pronounce it like a foreigner. From this train of thought her mind was naturally carried to England, and when she reflected how entirely she was secluded from all knowledge of what passed there, she felt her tenderness and solicitude return for Mrs. Vyvian, and would have given half a world, had she possessed it, to have known how that beloved parent bore her absence, and what was the state of her health. Even the passionate fondness she felt for her child most forcibly recalled that affection which she owed her mother....."Just so, (said she, as she studied with delight, in the features of her little boy, the resemblance of Montalbert), just so, perhaps, my poor mother, as soon as she dared indulge herself with a sight of me, endeavoured to make out, in my unfortunate lineaments, the likeness of my unhappy father—that unfortunate Ormsby, whose uncertain fate has thrown over her days the heavey gloom of anxious despondence, more difficult, perhaps, to bear than despair itself....Dear, unhappy parents!—never shall your daughter see either of you perhaps again—never shall she know the blessing of being acknowledged by a father; of being pressed to the conscious heart of a mother proud to own her!"

A flood of tears followed this soliloquy; but she remembered for how many misfortunes such a husband as Montalbert ought to console her, and tried, though in vain, to call a train of more cheerful ideas. The gloom, however, which hung over her mind, and for which she could not herself account, was neither to be reasoned with, nor dissipated entirely; and having neither books nor conversation to beguile the time, her spirits became more and more depressed. A thousand vague apprehensions beset her for the health of her child; she now never quitted him a moment, and watched him incessantly with a vigilance which fed itself with imaginary terrors.

This state of mind had continued some time, with no other relief than what the hope of Montalbert's speedy return afforded, when, sitting in a lower apartment with her infant in her arms, Rosalie was surprised by a singular motion in the floor, which seemed to rise under her feet; she started up, and saw, with horror and amazement, the walls of the room breaking in several directions, while the dust and lime threatened to choke her, and so obscured the air, that she could hardly distinguish Zulietta, who ran from another room, and seizing her by the hand, drew her with all the strength she could exert through a door which opened under an arch into the garden. Zulietta spoke not; she was, indeed, unable to speak.

Rosalie, to whom the tremendous idea of an earthquake now occurred, followed as quickly as she was able, clasping her boy to her breast[1]. They were soon about fifty yards from the house, the ground heaving and rolling beneath them like the waves of the sea, and beyond them breaking into yawning gulfs, which threatened to prevent their flight; Rosalie then looked round, and saw, instead of the house she had just left, a cloud of impenetrable smoke, which prevented her knowing whether any of it remained about the convulsed earth that had entirely swallowed part of the shattered walls. No language could describe the terror and confusion that overwhelmed this little group of fugitives; for no other fearful spectacle can impress on the human mind ideas of such complicated horrors as now surrounded them. They heard the crash of the building they had just left, as it half sunk into a deep chasm; before them, and even under their feet, the ground continued to break; the trees were torn from their roots, and falling in every direction around them; and vapours of sulphur and burning bitumen seemed to rise in pestilential clouds, which impeded the sight and the respiration.

  Rosalie called faintly, and with a sickening heart, as conscious of its inutility, on the name of Montalbert. Alas! Montalbert was far off, and could not succour her. To the mercy of Heaven, who seemed thus to summon her and her infant away, she committed him and herself; and laying herself on the ground, with her child in her arms, and Zulietta kneeling by her, she resigned herself to that fate which appeared to be inevitable.

  Flight was vain—all human help was vain, but nature still resisted dissolution, and she could not help thinking with agony of the state of Montalbert's mind, when the loss of his wife and child should be known to him. Another thought darted into her mind, and brought with it a more severe pang than any she had yet felt: Montalbert proposed about this time to return; within a few days she had begun to expect him, in consequence of his last letters. It was possible—alas! it was even probable, that he was already at Messina, and he too might have perished: he might at this moment expire amid the suffocating ruins—crushed by their weight, or stifled by subterraneous fires. The image was too horrible; she started up, as if it were possible for her feeble arms to save him; she looked wildly round her—all was ruin and desolation, but the earth no longer trembled as it had done, and a faint hope of safety arose almost insensibly in her heart. She spoke to Zulietta, who seemed petrified and motionless; she coujured her to rise and assist her—yet whither to go she knew not, nor what were her intentions, or her prospects of safety.

  While Rosalie yet spoke incoherently, almost unconscious that she spoke at all, a second shock, though less violent than the first, again deprived her of the little presence of mind she had collected—and, again prostrate on the ground, she commended her soul to Heaven!

  In a few moments, however, this new convulsion ceased, and the possibility that Montalbert might be returning, might be seeking her in distracted apprehension, restored to her the power of exertion. The hope that she might once see her husbad, served as a persuasion that she should see, and she advanced heedless of any danger she might incur by it towards the ruins of the house, where it was probable he would seek for her; but between her and those ruins was a deep and impassable chasm, which had been formed during the last shock.

  Zulietta, from her abrupt and wild manner, had conceived an idea that her mistress meant, in the despair occasioned by terror and grief to throw herself into this gulf. Impressed with this fear, she seized her by the arm, and making use of such arguments as the moment allowed, she drew her away, and they walked together, as hastily as they had strength, through the garden and up a rising ground beyond it, which was terminated by a deep wood, which had been less affected than the lower ground, though one or two of the trees were fallen and some half uprooted. Unable to go father, Rosalie sat down on one of their trunks, and Zulietta placed herself near her.

  Evening was coming on, but the deep gloom that hung over every object made the time of day imperceptible. Almost doubting of her existence, Rosalie seemed insensible to ever thing till the feeble cry of her infant boy, missing its accustomed nourishment at her breast, awakened the terrible apprehension of seeing him perish before her eyes for want of that nourishment.

  "Zulietta, (said she, in a mournful and broken voice)—Zulietta! what will become of my child?"—"Ah! what will become of us all?—(answered the half-senseless girl).—O Dio! we shall die here, or we shall be murdered by the men who frequent these woods."

"Could I but save my child! (exclaimed, Rosalie, little encouraged by her companion).—
—Could I but know whether Montalbert lives!—O Montalbert! where are you—if you exist?"—
—-

A shriek from Zulietta interrupted this soliloquy. She started from the tree where they sat, and fled to some distance; Rosalie involuntarily followed her, looking back toward the dark woods. "I saw some person move among the trees, (cried Zulietta, in answer to her lady's eager inquiries), I am sure I did—banditti are coming to murder us."

"And were that all I had to dread, (said Rosalie, collecting some portion of resolution)—were that all I had to dread, how gladly would I give up my life and that of this infant. But recollect yourself, Zulietta; who should at this time pursue us?—I have heard————————-(she paused, for her memory was confused and distracted)—I have heard, that it is among the ruins of houses that, at such times as this, the robber and the assassin throw themselves.....Oh! would we could find any nourishment; but where to look for it—I cannot see my baby die, Zulietta—ah! what are any fears I may have for myself, compared to those I feel for him!—In the woods, perhaps, we might find some fallen fruits."—Zulietta was not a mother, and the apprehensions of these banditti had taken such strong possession of her startled and dissipated senses, that every noise she either heard or fancied, she imagined to be their steps among the woods; and the reddening light of the declining day, as it faintly glimmered among the trees, was supposed to be their fires at a distance in the forest.

Had Rosalie, however, been accompanied by a person who had more fortitude, there would have been less occasion for her to exert that resolution which her superior good sense gave her, and which was now absolutely necessary for the preservation of them all. A moment's steady reflection lent her courage to attempt at least appeasing the groundless fears of Zulietta—enough of real apprehension, alas! remained.

It was not, however, without great difficulty, that she could prevail on her servant to follow her, not into the wood, for that she peremptorily refused, but round one of its extremities to a small eminence which Rosalie thought must command a view of Messina; at least it was not far from this spot, as she now remembered, that she had once been shown a prospect of the town by Montalbert. They exerted all their strength, and slowly gained a still higher ground, which commanded an extensive view of the city, the surrounding country, and the sea. The country remained, but not at all resembling what it had been only a few hours before; the sea too was visible, though heavy and dark clouds hung over it, and it seemed mingled with the threatening atmosphere above it; but Messina was distinguished only by more dismal vapours, and by the red gleam of fires that were consuming the fallen buildings.—Rosalie listened if, from among the desolate ruins, she could hear the wailings of the ruined!—but silence and death seemed to have enwrapt this miserable scene in their blackest veil, and such an image of horror presented itself to her mind, as that which since inspired the sublime and fearful description of the destruction of the army of Cambyses in the desert, ending thus——

"Then ceas'd the storm.—Night bow'd his Ethiop brow
"To the earth, and listen'd to the groans below
"Grim horror shook:—a while the living hill
"Heav'd with convulsive throws—and all was still."
DR. DARWIN'S ECONOMY OF VEGETATION.

Maternal love, the strongest passion that the female heart can feel, still sustained the timid and delicate Rosalie amidst the real miseries of which she was herself conscious, and those which the disturbed and agitated spirits of Zulietta represented.—She must struggle to sustain herself, or what would become of her child? Could she not bear any immediate evils better than the dreadful idea of leaving this lovely, helpless creature to the mercy of the elements?—Tears, hitherto denied to her, filled her eyes as she carried her mind forward to all the possibilities to which this fearful image led her; she found relief in weeping, and once more acquired voice and courage to ask Zulietta what it would be best for them to do?—Some time passed before Zulietta was capable of giving a rational answer; at length, however, they agreed, that it would be better, before it became entirely dark, to endeavour to find some house where they might be received for the night—"for surely (said Rosalie) some must remain, wide as the desolation has been."

In this hope, Rosalie and her attendant moved on as well as their strength permitted them; but it was by this time nearly dark, and round the skirts of the wood it became very difficult for them to discern their way.

Languid and desponding, Zulietta some times declared she could go no farther, and the spirits of her unhappy mistress were exhausted in vain to reanimate her courage.

A path, which they thought might lead to some habitation, had insensibly bewildered them among the trees, and the darkness, which now totally surrounded them, again raised new terrors in the mind of Zulietta, who, clinging to Rosalie, insisted upon it that she heard the footsteps of persons following them: they listened—a dreary silence ensued; but presently Rosalie was convinced that at least this time the fears of her woman were but too well grounded; the voices of two men talking together were distinctly heard, and, on turning round, they saw a light glimmer among the trees. As these persons, whoever they were, followed the path they had taken, and were advancing quickly towards them, escape or concealment became impossible; half dead with fear, and almost unconscious of what she did, Rosalie now stopped, determined to await the event.

The men approached, and, as soon as the light they held made the figures before them visible, one of them uttered an exclamation of surprise, and eagerly advanced towards Rosalie— it was Count Alozzi, who, with one of his servants, had come in search of her. Without, however, staying to tell her what circumstances had brought him thus from Agrigentum, or how he knew that she had escaped with her child from the destruction that had overwhelmed the house, he entreated her to suffer him to conduct her to place of security, which he hoped, he said, to find not far off.

The dread of perishing with her child in the woods being thus suddenly removed from her mind, hope and gratitude as rapidly succeeded.—Ah! what so comfortable to the weary wanderer, even in the common paths of life, as the soothing voice of a friend!—and such Alozzi now appeared to Rosalie. As she suffered him to lead her on, his servant preceding them with the light, she eagerly questioned him, if he knew any thing of Montalbert?—Whether it was possible that he might be arrived at Messina?—and then, trying to persuade herself he was safe, she went on to compare the probabilities there were that he had not suffered, but was either at Naples, or at sea on his passage. These inquiries Alozzi answered with great coldness: he told her, (which was true), that he had not been at Messina; that of Montalbert it was impossible any thing could yet be known, and that all they could do was to wait with patience for the next day, when, if they were not visited by a new shock, the survivors might be able to know the extent of their loss.

The mournful manner in which Alozzi uttered this, gave to Rosalie the most poignant alarm. Without reflecting how natural it was for him to speak thus, if only the general misfortune of the country was considered, of which he bore himself a share proportioned to his property, she immediately figured to herself that he knew something of Montalbert, and was willing by delay to prepare her for the intelligence he had to give her. She had not, however, power to repeat her questions; but a melancholy silence was observed on all sides till they reached a house, which, with two or three others, were situated among olive grounds, and which, Alozzi said, belonged to his estate. These buildings had received but little injury, yet the inhabitants of them, still doubting whether they might remain under the roofs, were so terrified and dejected by what had passed, and the dread of that which was to come, that the presence of Alozzi seemed to make no impression upon them. They coldy and silently acquiesced in affording the accomodation he asked, for the lady he brought with him, and set before the party such food as they happened to have. Zulietta, recovering some degree of courage, pressed Rosalie to eat, and Alozzi watched her with eager and anxious solicitude, which, when she observed, she imputed to his solicitude, or sorrow for the fate of his friend, which she still fancied he knew.

Fatigue, however, both of mind and body, and the care necessary to herself for the sake of her child, overcame for a while her excessive anxiety for Montalbert, of whom Alozzi again and again repeated he knew nothing; at length Rosalie consented to retire with Zulietta to a bed, or rather mattress, which the wife of one of the tenants of Alozzi prepared for her, where her child appearing to be in health and in present safety, sleep lent a while its friendly assistance to relieve her spirits, and recruit her strength, after such sufferings and such scenes as those of the preceding day.

Her repose was broken and disturbed, for she fancied she heard Montalbert call her, and that the buildings were about to crush her and her infant. In the morning, however, she was refreshed and relieved, even by this partial and interrupted forgetfulness, and able to receive the visit of the Count, who waited on her with inquiries after her health, and to consult with her what she should do. To this last question she was entirely ignorant what to answer, and could only, instead of a reply, put to him other questions; what he believed Montalbert would have directed, had he been present? and what he himself advised.—"It is impossible (said he gravely) to tell what Montalbert would have done, were he here; but, for myself, I own it appears to me that there is only one part to take. It is but too probable that another shock will be felt before many days are over. Here I have no longer a house to receive me, for that I inhabited at Messina is, I know, destroyed, though I was not near it yesterday when the earthquake happened, but about a mile from the town on my way home. The villa, which you did me the honour to inhabit, has shared the same fate. I approached it; I saw part of it buried in the earth, and the rest is by this time probably reduced to ashes. What then can I do but quit this devoted country, and return to Naples?—There I have a home, I have friends.—If you, Madam, will put yourself under my protection, I will defend you with my life, and consider myself highly honoured by so precious a charge."

"To go to Naples! (cried Rosalie, interrupting him);—Ah, Count! Do you recollect how many reasons I have for wishing to avoid Naples?—And is it thither, do you think, Montalbert would conduct me, were he now here?"

"Alas! (replied Alozzi), it is impossible to say whether those reasons exist which would formerly have influenced him. His mother may no longer be there, or, if she be, it is more than possible that pride and pique may be lost in general calamity, and that at such a time."

"You think then, (said Rosalie, eagerly interrupting him), I am sure you think that her son, that Montalbert, is lost—or what other calamity would reach her?"

"You exhaust your spirits in vain, my dear Madam, (replied Alozzi); to yield to vague fears can avail nothing. If any evil has befallen my friend, your destroying yourself cannot recall him—if he lives, as he probably does, you owe it to him to preserve yourself and his son."

"Oh! how coolly you talk! (exclaimed Rosalie, falling into an agony of grief). I see now that it is indeed easy to bear the misfortunes of others with calmness."

Alozzi, finding that argument only served to irritate her uneasiness, desisted, and took the wiser resolution of returning to his house, to see if any thing useful to his late guests could yet be saved; which, though improbable was not impossible. He communicated his intentions to Zulietta, who, with the true chambermaid's eagerness to find her few fineries, immediately asked leave to accompany him. Her terrors were now dissipated, or greatly weakened, for she was not of a disposition to be very solicitous about others, and thought herself not only in present security, but in the way of returning to Naples, which she had long been very desirous of doing. She tripped away, therefore, with the Count and his servant, leaving her mistress at the house where they had slept, and whither Alozzi proposed to return in a few hours.

When they were gone Rosalie went out with her baby in her arms, and seated herself on an open piece of ground, about a hundred yards from the house, which commanded from between the stems of a few straggling olive trees an extensive view of the city of Messina and the country round it. It presented a strange contrast of beauty and destruction. Those parts of the country that had not been convulsed or inverted were adorned with the blossoms of the almond, waving over fields of various coloured lupines and lentiscus; hedges of myrtles divided the enclosures, and among them the pomegranate was coming into flower; the stock doves in innumerable flocks were returning to feed among them, or fluttering amist the purple and white blossoms of the caper trees: but within half a mile of this profusion of what is most soothing to the imagination, black and hideous gulfs, from whence pestilential vapours seemed to issue, defaced the lovely landscaped. The beautiful town of Messina seemed more than half destroyed, and now Rosalie saw not far from her many groups of sufferers, who, frantic from the loss of their friends, their children, or their substance, were wandering about the fields without any hope but of passing the next night as they had done part of the preceding one, under the canopy of Heaven, gazing with tearless eyes on the melancholy spot where all their hopes were buried. From the sight of misery, which she could not relieve, her sick heart recoiled; she walked slowly back to the house, and attempted but in vain to form some resolution as to her future plans; but such was her situation, and so entirely did she feel herself dependent on the Count, that this was hardly possible......Again, in a convulsive sigh, she repeated the name of Montalbert—again implored the mercy of Heaven for him and her child, on whose little face, as it was pressd to her bosom, her tears fell in showers!

She turned her fearful eyes on the people among whom she was left. Many were now in the house whom she had not seen before, and some among them gave her but too forcibly the idea of those banditti, of whom Zulietta had expressed so many fears the evening before as they passed through the woods. Some of them were men of large stature, in a kind of uniform, and she fancied that they passed through the room where she was on purpose to observe her. A new species of terror assailed her in consequence of this remark, yet she endeavoured to reason herself out of it, and to suppose that where Count Alozzi had left her she must be in security.

The people, who appeared to belong to the house, brought her some slender meal, which she eat mechanically, and would then have questioned them as to the probability of the Count's return and the distance of his late residence; but they appeared averse to any conversation, and she thought looked as if they wished her away, but of their real motives she had not the remotest idea.

Hours passed away, and neither Alozzi nor Zulietta appeared. Many new faces entered the house, and she understood, from such conversation as she heard and put together, that they were come to obtain an asylum for the night. One of them was a lovely Sicilian girl, of sixteen or seventeen, who wept grievously, as Rosalie comprehended, for the loss of her sister and her sister's children. The beauty of the little Montalbert, as he lay sleeping in his mother's arms, seemed to interest and affect this young person; she spoke to Rosalie, and was approaching to caress the child, when an old woman who was with her said something in a sharp and severe accent, and drew her hastily out of the room.

This circumstance, and indeed every remark she now made, increased the impatience and uneasiness with which she waited for the return of Alozzi. Night was at hand; the parties in the house were contriving how to pass it most at their ease, but nobody seemed to attend to her; on the contrary, she believed that a disposition to shun her was evident in the women, while the looks of the men gave her infinitely more alarm, and she sometimes resolved, rather than pass the night among them, to set out alone, and seek the protection of Alozzi.

On this then she had almost determined, and, trembling and faint, left the house with an intention of discovering how far such an attempt might be safer than to remain where she was. She had proceeded only about a hundred yards, when a new convulsion of the earth threw her down, and her senses entirely forsook her; nor did she recover her recollection till she found herself on board a small vessel at sea, her child laying by her, and a woman, whom she had never seen before, watching her. As soon as she appeared to be sensible Alozzi came to her, endeavouring to sooth and console her. He told her, that another shock of an earthquake had compelled all who could leave Sicily to depart; that he had before engaged a bark; that they were now far on their way to Naples with a fair wind, and that they should be there in a few hours.

The shock she had received, the terror and confusion with which she was yet impressed, were such as left Rosalie little sensation but that ever predominant one of love and anxiety for her infant boy, whom she clasped with more fondness than ever to her breast, and, amidst the terrors that on every side surrounded her, found in his preservation something for which to be grateful to Heaven.

CHAP.

Notes

↑ When ruins came to be cleared away, says Sir William Hamilton, the bodies of the men who had perished were universally found in the attitude of resistance; the women in that of prayer, unless it was those who had children with them, in which case they were observed to have taken such postures as were likely to shelter and protect them.

WHEN the vessel, freighted with these wretched victims of calamity, reached the port of Naples, Rosalie was carried on shore with the rest almost insensible. The woman, whom Alozzi had placed about her during the voyage, was extremely careful of her and her child; he appeared to have suffered much less than might have been expected. The anxiety of Rosalie for his safety recalled her to life and recollection, but with these came the cruel remembrance of all she had suffered, and the dread of all she might yet have to encounter: youth, and a good constitution, were on her side. With her the soothing voice of hope had not yet been silenced by frequent disappointment; a few hours of repose, therefore, with the consciousness of present safety, gave her strength of mind to look steadily on the prospect before her, obscured as it was by uncertainty and fear.

A stranger in Naples, and without the means of inquiring of any one but Alozzi, who saw her only for a few moments every day, she continued to torment herself with vague and fruitless conjectures as to the fate of Montalbert, of whom she incessantly spoke to the Count, entreating him to make every inquiry, and, above all, to visit Signora Belcastro, his mother, as the probability of Montalbert's safety could be guessed at only by calculating the time of his departure. To these earnest and continual applications Alozzi at first answered by promising to do as she desired; after three or four days he said, he was informed by the servants that their lady was gone to Rome; that Mr. Montalbert left Naples about ten days before her, but whither he was gone they were ignorant.

This account Roslaie thought Alozzi delivered with a degree of sang-froid very unlike his usual manner, especially when so dear a friend as Montalbert was concerned. It served, therefore, only to irritate her impatience and awaken new fears. She was now entirely dependent on Count Alozzi, and though she was unconscious of that jealousy which had rendered Montalbert uneasy before their last parting, she was sensible that it was extremely improper for a woman of her age to remain under the protection of such a man as Alozzi, who was not related to her, and who had, she knew, the reputation of a libertine. Variety of apprehensions assailed her, from which she knew not how to escape. Though she was ignorant of Montalbert's particular suspicions, she had often remarked with concern that general tendency to jealousy, which was almost the only blemish she had discovered in his character; and it was but too probable, that when they met again, (for the idea of Montalbert's death her heart repelled as soon as it approached), their meeting, and perhaps their future lives, might be embittered by the uneasiness her present situation would create his mind. Nor was that all. In what a light might she not be represented to his mother, already too much prejudiced against her.

However perplexed by these considerations, Rosalie was under the cruel necessity of keeping them within her own breast; for how could she speak of them to Alozzi?—The woman, who had supplied the place of Zulietta, was not only of an inferior description, but was resolutely silent when questioned on any subject whatever; and all Rosalie could learn of her maid was, that, during the hurry and confusion of their embarkation, Zulietta was among those who had been left on shore, where the waves soon after rose so suddenly that they swept off a multitude of people in their reflux, and it was more than probable that this unfortunate girl was drowned. Of the woman, now her attendant, who was called Maddalena, she was told, that she had lost her husbnad at Messina, and that he had been Maitre d'Hotel to the Count at his house in that city; Maddalena had fled to the villa, and had arrived just as those were embarking whom the Count admitted into the vessel. This story, however probable, and however confirmed by the account Alozzi himself had given, was told by Maddalena with an air so calm and even cold, that Rosalie could not help doubting of its truth, and thought it impossible, that, had she sustained such a loss, she could have spoken of them with so little emotion.

However that might be, she was perfectly convinced that Alozzi had given this woman orders, which she seemed determined to obey. Day after day passed; on some of them the Count did not appear, on others he sat with her an hour or two, endeavouring to keep up some thing that might resemble common conversation; but the moment Rosalie spoke of Montalbert, of her increasing anguish of heart, of the awkwardness of her situation, and of the burden she must necessarily feel herself to him, Alozzi seemed impatient to put an end to his visit, still persisting to say, however, when he could not entirely evade her questions, that he believed in the safety of Montalbert. But there was something in his manner of saying this, that gave Rosalie greater pain than if he had spoken more doubtfully. There seemed to be some mystery for which she could not account, and a carelessness as to the fate of his former friend, which was quite unnatural. Alozzi, it is true, treated her with great respect: he appeared hurt at the remotest hint of any trouble she might give him, and said fine things as to the delight it afforded him to be of any use to her. These sort of speeches he had not unfrequently made while Montalbert was present and they lived together at the Sicilian villa; but now they were made in another manner, and Rosalie shrank from them with something like terror and disgust.

Anxiety, such as at this time assailed her, could not long be patiently endured. The natural strength of her understanding told her, that to remain under the protection of the Count, and concealed in an obscure lodging at Naples, must in the event be infinitely more prejudicial to her future happiness with Montalbert, if he yet lived, than even the discovery in regard to his mother, which had formerly been the source of so much uneasiness. If Montalbert was lost, how could she think of suffering his son to remain in obscurity, without claiming for him the protection of his father's family, and the fortune, small as it might be, that belonged to him?—This idea gathered strength from hour to hour as she indulged it.—She looked at her son, who visibly improved in health and beauty, and reproached herself for the injury she was doing him by the concealment of a secret, which, perhaps, there might be no danger in revealing; or, if there was, which could affect only herself.

She considred, that if Montalbert had been a moment in danger, and was restored in safety to his mother, she would hardly at such a time refuse him her pardon. If, on the contrary, his fate was uncertain, if he had sailed for Messina before the tremendous catastrophe which had happened there, and was not yet returned, the fears his mother must entertain for his life would surley prevent her driving from her the fatherless child, for whom she should implore her pity and protection; for herself she had nothing to ask, but to be received as the mother of that child. Almost convinced, by this reasoning, that she ought immediately to throw herself at the feet of Signora Belcastro, she formed plans for proceeding, and even thought that, if they succeeded, Montalbert would be made completely happy by this reconcilliation. Fully possessed by this design, she knew there was no way of executing it without the participation and even the assistance of Alozzi, to whom she took the first opportunity to explain her plans and her reasons for adopting them, desiring Alozzi to make immediate inquiries as to the probability of Signora Belcastro's return to Naples; or, if that was not likely to happen soon, she desired to be put in a way of addressing her properly at Rome.

The Count heard her with unaffected astonishment, and with anger and concern, which he in vain attempted to stifle; he observed, from her manner, that she had long thought of what she now spoke upon. He listened, however, with as much patience as he could command, and then set himself to prove to her the wildness and impossibility of what she proposed; the injury it might be to Montalbert, the risk it would be to herself. He represented Signora Belcastro as the most violent and vindictive of Italian women, and bade Rosalie consider how she could meet the eye, or endure the reproaches, of such a person? How bear to be treated with contempt and insult, if, as was very probable, Signora Belcastro protested against the legitimacy of the little Montalbert? Or how, on the contrary, support his being torn from her, which, Alozzi protested, she might expect, should the capricious passions of his grandmother take another turn?

Rosalie listened and shuddered, but still persisted in declaring, that if in two days no news arrived of Montalbert, she would adopt this expedient of claiming for his child the protection of his own family, and, conscious that in doing so had done her duty, would leave the event to Heaven.

These two days Alozzi hardly ever left her, nor did he omit any argument to dissuade her from, what he termed, a scheme of the wildest desperation. Some expressions, however, that he let fall in the warmth of this debate, served only to confirm her resolution. She told him very calmly, that many of the reasons he had given against her acting as she proposed seemd to her to be the very reasons why she should pursue her plan; that she should have been very much obliged to him would he have lent her his assistance; but added, with a degree of resolution she had never exerted before, that since he declined it, she knew there were Englishmen in Naples, and she was sure, that when her situation was known, there was not one of them but what would come forward to protect and support her.

A flood of tears followed this temporary exertion of artificial courage, for her forlorn and friendless condition pressed more forcibly than it had ever yet done on her mind; she caught her child to her bosom, and sobbed with a violence of grief which she was not longer able to command.—Alozzi, almost thrown off his guard by the mingled emotions he felt, and alarmed by the mention of her appealing to her own countrymen, now endeavoured to sooth and appease her. He besought her to give him a little more time to make inquiries after his friend, from people who were every day coming in from Sicily; represented how possible it was that he might yet be seeking her there, and gave so many plausible reasons why she ought to wait a little longer before she took a measure which she might repent, when it would be too late, that, at length, he extorted a promise from her to do nothing without his knowledge, and to wait at least another week.

This week, the third of her arrival at Naples, was rapidly passing away. No news of Montalbert arrived, and now Alozzi affected extreme concern whenever he was spoken of, and the tormenting suspense of his unfortunate wife became almost insupportable. Her former plan was again thought of: if it was followed by none of the advantages she hoped for she should at least learn what was by his own family supposed to be the fate of Montalbert, of which it was improbable they should be as ignorant as she was. Even at the moment when she was suffering all the misery of conjecture, it was possible he might be at Naples, as uncertain in regard to her fate as she was of his; and what other means but those she now thought of, had she to discover whether he yet lived?

Among the variety of thoughts that offered themselves as she considered this subject, there was one which she wondered had never occured to her before. This was, that Charles Vyvian was certainly in Itlay, and might very probably be at Naples: what a consolation it would be to see him, even though she dared not reveal how nearly they were related!—She, therefore, busied herself in contriving means to discover the names of the English who were now at Naples; but, upon examining this nearer, she found it knowledge that was very difficult for her to obtain. Of the people of the house where she lodged she knew nothing; they had never once appeared in her sight, and her cook was, as Alozzi told her, a Sicilian, who had come over in the same vessel with them, whom he had taken out of pity into his service; but when Rosalie attempted to speak to him, by way of giving him commissions, she found him to be a fellow who had orders to evade executing them, and perfectly knew his part; she even fancied she had seen him before, though she could not recollect where or when. As to the woman, she declined doing any thing, and her reasons too were plausible; she was a stranger at Naples; she did not even know her way in the streets. How was it possible for her to do what Signora Rosalia desired? And how could she go to inquire after English Signors?—and where?——"Ah, Signora! (said the artful Italian, venturing now on a liberty she had never taken before)——Ah, Signora! If you should find those rich and great Signori Inglese, do you think there is among them a finer or a nobler gentleman than Count Alozzi?"

    Rosalie to this impertinence gave a cold and haughty answer. It sunk, however, deeply into her mind; but should she resent it as it deserved, she might, perhaps, deprive her child of the cares of this woman, and it was possible another would be less attentive and less experienced: nor had she, indeed, the means of discharging her, or could she consider her as being her servant.

    The observations which every hour forced themselves upon her mind, were at length so accumulated and so painful, that some immediate relief became necessary; but where was it to be found? Stranger and depressed as she was at her first arrival, she had neither strength nor inclination to go out; nor had she then a change of clothes to appear in. Alozzi had supplied her with every article of dress in proportion; but of these she had forborne to take more than was absolutely necessary, not knowing whether Montalbert could ever repay his friend these pecuniary obligations.

    Now, indeed, the weight of them became intolerable, for Rosalie, having once had her fears awakened that the intentions of Alozzi were dishonourable, seized with trembling avidity on every circumstance that confirmed these fears; and, as generally happens in these cases, they went even beyond the truth, and she figured to herself the many imaginary evils: that Signora Belcastro had never been absent from Naples; that her son was even now there, deceived by the artifices of his treacherous friend, and perhaps lamenting as dead the wife and infant who actually existed in the same city—then a train of frightful possibilities followed. Convinced of her death by the report of Alozzi, he might determine to oblige his mother and give his hand to the Roman lady, whom she was so desirous of his marrying. He might then, perhaps, leave Naples for the neighborhood of Rome, she should lose sight of him for ever, and, with her helpless, deserted boy, become a forsaken wanderer upon earth.

    With these terrors sleep forsook the pillow of Rosalie, and peace no longer visited her for a moment during the day. The sight of her child, but yesterday a balm to her anxious heart, no longer afforded her unmixed delight; his innocent eyes and unconcious smiles seemed to reproach her for timidity, which, while it was unworthy of herself, might irreparably injure both his father and him.

    By these reflections her wavering resolution was at last so confirmed, that she determined to write to the mother of Montalbert; and as she could imagine no other safe or even possible way of conveying it, she determined, when her letter was written, to direct it in the most correct manner she could, and walking into the street give it to the first lazzerone she found; such a person could have no interest in deceiving her; and as she intended to give him a small reward when she delivered the letter, and promise one more considerable when he had executed her commission, she thought she should at all events obtain information so very material to her, as whether Signora Belcastro was now at her house at Naples.

    This plan she executed without difficulty because, among all the attempts to write that

Alozzi had guarded against, that of her giving herself the letter to the first she met of the numerous lazzeroni in the streets of Naples, was what had never occured to him as possible.

The letter was long and explanatory, and, if not written in the very purest Italian, was infinitely better than many Italian natives could themselves have penned. It contained expressions of the tenderest nature towards Montalbert; of humility and deference for his mother, on whose pity and protection she threw herself, and with whom she pleaded for her infant boy with a pathos which few hearts could have resisted.

Having then sealed and directed it, she took her child in her arms, and, her attendant being engaged in another part of the house, walked down into the street; she trembled as she looked around her, and shrunk from the eyes of the few passengers that she saw. Such a person, however, as she had occasion for was soon found. A stout boy of sixteen, half clothed, eagerly presented himself; Rosalie, in a hurried and faltering voice, gave him his commission and two carlinoes[1], promising him double that sum if he returned within an hour to the house she had left, which she pointed out to him, and gave her the information she required. The lad promised to do all she directed, and sprang out of sight in an instant. Rosalie, hardly able to support herself, returned to her apartments, from which she had not even been missed. The die was now cast. The future happiness or misery of herself and child depended on the answer to this letter: breathless with fear, she awaited the return of her messenger, who came back almost immediately; she flew to the door, the lad told her, that Signora Belcastro was at Naples, and that he had given the packet to one of her servants, who would deliver it to his lady. It was now then certain, that Alozzi had deceived her......Alas! it was certain too, that, in this attempt to emancipate herself from his power, she had been compelled to commit her whole happiness to a woman, whose proud and vindictive character she now thought upon with more terror than ever. It was, however, too late to recede, nor did she wish to do so, but armed herself with the fortitude conscious integrity ought to give, and determined to endure whatever should happen, while no wilfull imprudence or impropriety could be imputed to her.

Her own words will now be used to describe how far she was enabled to act as she proposed; when doubting of the existence of him to whom her letters were addressed, she yet found relief in relating her sufferings, and in keeping a register of the melancholy moments as they passed.

CHAP.

Notes

↑ A Carlino is 5d. in English.

A Letter from ROSALIE to MONTALBERT.

"WHEN consciousness of existence returns only to bring with it the consciousness of misery—can I feel any satisfaction in recollection?—Yet I might have been more wretched—I might have been driven quite to distraction; for my little angel Harry might have been torn from me—but he is still with me, still the innocent, unconscious companion of his mother's sufferings!

"Where art thou, Montalbert?—Alas! if thou hadst really been lost at Messina, as that treacherous Alozzi insinuated, would it be worth the pains that are now taken to persecute thy unhappy wife; to arraign the legality of thy son's birth?—Ah! no, Montalbert!—thy cruel mother would then have left me to my ignominious fate, or, if common humanity had touched the heart of Signora Belcastro with pity for an unprotected stranger, she would have sent me and my child to England, where we could never have offended her more. But, Montalbert, the husband and the father lives, and his inhuman parent knows, that in whatever country we are, his unwearied love will discover us, unless we are hidden in some hideous prison like this. Barbarous Belcastro, it is thus that your cruelty defeats itself!—for amidst these dreary scenes this reflection supports and consoles me.—I dwell upon it incessantly—I convince myself that Montalbert lives—I press his little Harry to my heavy heart, and feel it less agonized as I determine to attempt to live for them both.

"In the confidence that you, Montalbert, live for me, I tried, when I first recovered myself from terrors that almost deprived me of my reason, to give you some account of the letter I wrote at Naples to your mother, which was undoubtedly the cause of all that has since befallen me. It is now before me, incoherent and half-blotted with my tears; but it describes what I felt, and I will not alter it. It ends at the point of time when I was persuaded I should have an answer, and when my sanguine hopes flattered me that it would be favourable.

"I looked at our boy, and thought that, if once your mother saw him, his beauty, and his strong resemblance to you, would secure her kindness......I knew that I should tremble and falter; but yet I believed I could acquire courage enough to put him into her arms, with a few words which I mediated to speak. I persuaded myself, that infant loveliness and the voice of nature would do the rest. But the hours passed away, and no summons came for us, as I had fondly expected. I concluded that I should hear the next morning, and I endeavoured to compose myself for the night. "It passed, however, in restlessness and anxiety; but day came, and with it my spirits regained some degree of tranquility. I dressed my baby with more care than I had done the preceeding day, and again sat down to hopes, fears, and conjectures—the hours wore away as on ordinary days, and I received neither letter nor message. The Count Alozzi[1] paid me his daily visit, but it was shorter than usual, and he either did not observe or at least did not speak to me of that anxiety, which I thought, my looks and manner must have betrayed.

"Night came, and I now concluded that either Signora Belcastro would not condescend to notice me at all, or that her deliberating so long was a favourable circumstance; for, had she hastily and arrogantly determined to crush my hopes for ever, it was most probable, that, a temper so irritable and violent as hers, she would have done it at once, and with as much rage as her contempt would suffer her to show.

"In this persuasion then, which was calculated to calm my spirits as much as under such circumstances they would admit of being calmed, I again laid myself down by the side of my sleeping boy, and, notwithstanding the anxiety of my thoughts, fatigue overcame me, and I was lost in a dream that brought you, Montablert, to my view.....I imagined, that, reconciled to your mother, and in possesson of all our wishes, I was recounting to you the sad scenes which I had witnessed at Messina, when, suddenly awakened by a noise in my room, I saw a man, holding a small lantern, approach my bed, followed by one or two others. I shrieked in terror, and inquired, as well as I could, what they would have—and who they were?—One of them came near me, and, in a deep and solemn voice, told me that I must rise, dress myself, and follow them. I asked, why? and whither I was to go?—I implored their mercy—I earnestly entreated they would tell who had sent them, and on what pretence I was thus to be dragged from my bed?—To these questions, the men told me, they neither could nor would answer; and one of them, more savage than the rest, approached to take my child, telling me, that he supposed, if he took the little master, I should be pleased to follow. This cruel menace drove me to madness. I snatched my child to my bosom, protesting that I would die before he should be forced from me; but that, if I must follow them, and they would only send my woman to me, and retire while I put on my clothes, that I would endeavour to obey.

"As to a woman, they told me, none could be allowed me; that I must quit that house immediately; and that, if I would hasten, they would wait at the door till I was ready with the child. This last word gave me some degree of courage, for the dread of losing my boy had been more terrible than all the rest. I promised every thing required of me, and asked if I might not take some clothes? for I now concluded I was going to prison. They answered, that I might take what I would; but that I must be expeditious, and that silence would avail me more than remonstrance or complaint.

"The men then left the room, and I tried to acquire steadiness enough to dress myself. My infant needed little but a mantle in which I wrapped him, and our clothes were in two small trunks that stood near my bed. I had, therefore, nothing to pack, and was soon ready; but, expeditious as I had been, my conductors were become impatient, and I had hardly hurried on my things, and wrapped a large cloak around us both, before they entered, and, by the light of the same lantern, conducted me down the stairs, on which stood two or three other men; an equal number were in the passage, and two others, who stood at the door like sentinels, opened it, where I saw a coach, into which they lifted me; the man who seemed to have the most authority seated himself opposite to me, and drove it away.

"The night was extremely dark, yet I could not, even had it been otherwise, have formed the least idea whither they were carrying me......What a situation was mine!—Alone at such a time of night, with men whom I could consider not otherwise than as the banditti and assassins of whom I had often read in Italian stories. The strangeness and alarm of such a state alone enabled me to endure it, for I seemed petrified, and had no power to complain or to shed a tear. The man who was with me spoke not, and when I attempted to make any inquiries, which I once or twice collected enought courage to do, he gravely, but not uncivilly, told me, he could not answer them, and that it was merely fatiguing my spirits to ask any questions whatever. I know not how far we had travelled, when the coach stopped at a house where I was taken out by the attendants, who seemed as numerous as before, led into a dreary room, which I thought belonged to an inn, and left to myself for a few moments. Some refreshment was then brought, and the man who had attended me in the coach came in at the same time, and seated himself at the table: he bade me eat, and I obeyed him on account of my infant; he eat heartily himself, yet spoke very little, and wore his hat pulled over his face, which, by the glimmering light of a lamp that hung in the room, appeared, I thought, to be the face of an assassin, and not young in his profession; for the man was between fifty and sixty, tall, bony, and hard-featured, with hollow eyes and large eyebrows, under which he seemed sometimes to examine my countenance with a look that made my heart sink within me.

"When the most dismal meal I had ever made was over, he told me we must renew our journey. I obeyed in silence, and we travelled the rest of the night, stopping twice to change horses.

"When morning broke, I found we were in a mountainous coutry: between the high points of land, among which our road lay, I caught glimpses of the sea, and a faint and vague hope presented itself that I might be destined to some port remote from Naples to be sent to England. For none of the various conjectures, which, during this melancholy journey, passed through my mind, were so probable, as that the mother of Montalbert, enraged at what she had heard, and determined, at all events, to divide me from her son, had taken this method to conceal me from him while he was, perhaps, persuaded that I had perished in Sicilly. With this hope, therefore, I looked out anxiously for the element, which, I hoped, might restore me to my country, where I was sure the vigilant love of Montalbert would soon follow me......Ah! vain and flattering illusion!—I indulged it only to embitter the miserable moments which have since passed; and, as they passed, have told me that, though Montalbert lives, I shall see him no more.

"I must lay down my pen and try to conquer the tears which half efface the words I have written, and which will make my letter illegible.

"I have taken a few turns in the gallery—my little Harry in my arms.......Oh! would he could answer when I talk to him of his dear father—he smiles innocently as if he already understood me!—If he should be ill in this desolate place—what would become of me!—The idea freezes my heart; but, alas! why should I torment myself with possible miseries, when I have so many real ones. Heaven sure will spare me from a trial to which I feel my strength altogether unequal. I know that I ought to check these gloomy thoughts, and to preserve my own health, if I would avoid the distresses they represent to me.

"But this is, indeed, difficult, Montalbert!—The poor solitary Rosalie has no human being to listen to her complaints, or to strengthen her resolution. Day after day she wanders round the deserted apartments of this melancholy house; she sees the faces of two servants, mean, ignorant, and without pity, who perform, in silence, the common offices of life, but seem totally insensible of the state of mind of their wretched prisoner: even the beauty of my lovely child does not plead with these people for him, or for me!

"But I shall exhaust myself in lamenting my present situation, and become unable to pursue my narrative.

"I go back then to relate the sequel of my melancholy journey, which continued all that day and the next, with only short intervals of rest; one of these was at a lone inn, on the steep ascent of a mountain, where my conductors put up, rather, I believe, to avoid the violence of a storm that was likely to overtake them on the top of it, than to afford me and my child the repose we greatly needed.

"Imagine, Montalbert, your unhappy wife sitting in one of the most dismal places imagination can conceive; the walls were of brick, and concealed only by the dirt that in most places covered them; there were neither sashes nor shutters to the windows, through which the lightning flashed, and the rain drove with fearful violence: but I had lately beheld convulsions of nature so much more dreadful, that I saw this tempest without any additional terror. Had I been sure that such a destiny awaited me as I have since experienced, I should, perhaps, have been more than indifferent, and have implored some friendly stroke which might have ended mine and my child's life.....Alas! for what are we reserved?

"I looked at the group, which was assembled in the same room, with alarm infinitely greater than what I felt from the tempest without, violent as it was. I have seen paintings, Montalbert, representing such people; but in England we have no such faces, at least I never saw such!

"The men, however, seemed so well pleased with their quarters, that they were in no haste to depart, and I was afraid we should have passed the night in that hideous place; I could not imagine any thing that might await me at the end of my journey, for the people of the house seemed to be such as I remember reading a description of in one of Smollet's novels. Willingly, therefore, I obeyed the signal which my companion in the coach, at length, gave for us to proceed forward.

"The remaining part of our journey lasted until, at a late hour in the night, I was removed into one of the carriages of the country, and we again travelled in darkness, very slowly, through roads where a common coach or chaise could not pass, and which would have given me at another time great fears; but I was now so worn down with fatigue, and so bewildered in distracting conjectures of what was to come, that the present evil was less felt; nor should I, I think, have shrunk from death, could I have been assured that my infant would not survive me.

"At length, however, as nearly as I could conjecture, about three in the morning of the third night, we arrived at the place, where the man who was in the carriage told me, I was to remain.

"I was so enfeebled and dispirited, so cramped with a long and fatiguing journey, and so worn down with anguish of mind that I was unable to assist myself in getting out of the coach. The men, however, took me with as much ease as they did my little boy, and a coarse-looking man, who came out of the house, carried a light before us up a long and steep flight of steps. They led to a large hall, paved and lined with marble: it was so large, and so cold, that I fancied myself already in the catacombs; but, alas! I could not weep—I felt the blood forsaking my heart, which seemed to beat no longer. I sat down, however, as the people bade me, till the baggage was brought out of the coach.

"The few ideas, which fatigue and terror left me, pointed to imprisonment as what was certainly to be my lot, and I expected to be led to some dungeon beneath this immense apartment, and left to perish. After some moments, my conductor approached me: he told me, that here his commission ended; that he had orders to leave me in this house, where the necessaries of life would be provided for me, and from whence he needed scarce advise me not to attempt to escape, for escape was impossible, as I was far removed from all who had any knowledge of me, and the whole country was devoted to his employer.

'And who is your employer, Sir? (said I); tell me, at least, that—that I may know by what right, or on what account I am become a prisoner.'

'You may think yourself fortunate, (returned the man), that you are in the hands of those who do not use all the power they possess; your treatment will in some measure depend on yourself. The people here can do nothing to assist your flight, even if you should be weak enough to tempt them; but I advise you to content yourself with the assurance that every effort will be ineffectual; and, that if you give much trouble to the persons in whose care you remain, your confinement will be made more strict and severe.'

"To this I had nothing to reply, nor did the man stay to hear any farther remonstrance, but hastily left this gloomy apartment, and as dead a silence reigned as if I had been already buried alive.

"The immense hall, or rather cave of marble, was lighted only by a lamp that stood on a distant table, and it seemed to me to have been built for gigantic beings, so great were its dimensions and so heavy its construction.—'And is it here (said I to myself, as I surveyed the place) that I am left to die, unaided and unknown?—Or am I consigned to the mercy of the inhabitants of this place?'—Fatigue and fear, overcoming and depressing my mind, brought before it strange phantoms more horrible than any reality could be; and such an effect had this comfortless solitude on my exhausted spirits, that I thought my situation on the night of the dreadful concussion of earth, when I took shelter in the farm of Alozzi, was infinitely less dreadful. So much heavier do present evils appear than those of the past.

"I believe I had been more than half an hour alone, and began to think I might lie down unmolested on the pavement and die, when the door at the farther end of the hall opened slowly, and a figure, which I could hardly distinguish through the gloom, moved slowly towards me. When it came near me, I discerned that it was a woman in a kind of nun's dress; she spoke in a low and slow voice. There was someting in her language which I did not understand; but she seemed to invite me to remove from the place were I was. I arose, therefore, and followed her; she took up the lamp that was burning on the marble table, and proceeded through long and high passages, which appeared to terminate in utter darkness.

"At length we came to a very broad staircase, which my guide began to ascend, though very slowly, and like a person who was either unwilling or unable to arrive very soon at the place whither they were going. I looked up and round this great staircase. Never could a place be imagined more massive, or more impressing, fit to convey the idea of a habitation of goblins and spectres; almost every part was of dark marble, and, in places where ornament was admitted, old paintings, blackened and nearly effaced by time, and some faded gilding, served but to mark the long desertion of its owners.

"The top of the stairs led into a gallery, which, through a marble balustrade, looked down into the great hall I had left, where I saw, by a light they had with them, three or four of the men that had accompanied me, who appeared like assassins assembled to decide on the fate of their vicitm. Yet such were the terrors that had seized me, from the uncertainty and singularity of my situation, that I had more dread of supernatural beings, I knew not what, than of these men who had so lately been the objects of my apprehension.

"This surrounding gallery opened into another very large room, covered with some kind of mosaic painting, and that into another as big, but not in so good repair; at the bottom of which was a table with a crucifix upon it. The third door, that my silent conductress opened, discovered a bedchamber of nearly the same dimensions as the othe two; where a small low bed, that stood in one corner, was hardly discernable. All seemed cold and comfortless, and the air was damp and heavy, as if the room had been long without ventilation. My conductress led me up to the bed—'This (said she) is your room, Singora Inglese, and this is your bed.'

"I hastily asked, but in a manner the most conciliating that I could command, whether I might be allowed a light, a fire, and food?—and proceeded to say, how greatly I and my poor little boy were fatigued with a very long jouney of so many days and nights. The woman, whose face I now for the first time saw, looked at me and the innocent helpless creature for which I was pleading. Her countenance, which was sallow and sharp-featured, expressed rather distaste than pity or tenderness; she spoke low, and, as I understood, declined complying with my request; however, she lit an iron lamp that was fastened to the wall, and, without any more ceremony left me as I believed for the night.

"I heard her footsteps fainter and fainter, as she passed through the rooms we had before traversed; the doors shut after her, and again a death-like silence reigned. My child was restless, and I wished to undress him; but the comfort of a fire was denied me, and I surveyed my bed as if it had been my tomb, hardly daring to lie down upon it, yet feeling that I had no longer strength to sit up. I determined, therefore, to wrap myself and my boy in the cloak we had around us, and since I had no change of clothes for him, for my trunks remained in the hall, to attempt hushig him to repose on my breast—a breast torn, alas! with such variety of anguish, that now, though a fortnight has since elapsed, I look back upon those hours with a sensation of astonishment, and, recollecting the severity of my sufferings, am greatful for the power that was lent me to sustain them. "But I break off here, Montalbert, and must recall more perfectly the succeeding hours, before I can finish this narrative, which I intend as a sort of prelude to the melancholy register of my time which I have kept.

"I am supported, Montalbert, by the hope which in my calmer moments never entirely forsakes me, that we shall one day read this journal together, and that, while you suffer for the sorrows of your Rosalie, you will clasp her fondly to your heart, and rejoice that they are no more.

"If that moment ever comes, Montalbert, for what calamities will it not overpay us!"

CHAP.

Notes

↑ In her account of the reasons why she determined to write to his mother, Rosalie omitted those that related to Alozzi; she thought enought still remained to justify her taking such a step.

THE next letter from Rosalie to Montalbert thus described her subsequent situation......

"My jailers were, however, less severe than I expected. With a feeble step, and a heart overwhelmed with anguish, I was exploring, as well as I could, the room I was in, to see if it afforded me such security for the night as depended on bolts or locks: I opened a door on the farther side of it, which led into long and high passages, and from whence the wind rushed with a violence which obliged me to shut it hastily. I was endeavouring to fasten it withinside, by pushing the bolt that was too rusty for my strength to move, when I heard heavy steps as of several persons approaching through the great rooms adjoining. Alarmed, I returned nearer to the light; and, breathless and trembling, I waited for the entrance of these people. My fears, however, somewhat subsided, when I saw a man, who appeared to be a peasant, approach with wood, and another with the boxes that contained mine and my child's clothes, while the woman, whom I had seen before, stood at the door; one of the men made a fire, the other went away, and in a few moments returned with some provisions and wine. Every thing passed in profound silence, except when it was broken by my attempting to express to the woman, in whom all authority seemed to be vested, my gratitude for these indulgencies, and entreated her to allow that the door, to which I pointed across the room, might be fastened withinside. She ordered one of the men to do it, and having placed the supper before me, and left a small bundle of wood to feed the fire, they all departed, and I prepared to recruit my strength and refresh my poor baby by changing his clothes. He was soon in a sweet sleep, and now, for the first time for many hours, this melioration of my condition afforded me the relief of shedding tears. My destiny still appeared dreadful, but as there seemed to be no design to destroy my life, I trusted that whoever had taken so much trouble to remove me would at length relent, and that I should be one day restored to you, Montalbert.

"Determining then to arm myself with patience, and to resign myself wholly to that Providence which had hitherto protected me, I laid down on my little bed, after securing as well as I could the other door of the chamber; but, still prepossessed with an idea of its dampness, I dared not undress myself; fatigue, however, overcame all apprehensions, and I slept several hours, till the calls of my nursling awakened me to a sense of his sorrows and my own.

"I recollected instantly all that had happened to me, and turned my eyes toward the immense windows of my room, between the thick wooden shutters of which day appeared. I arose, and with some difficulty opened one of them, and beheld from it a diversified landscape of great extent, terminated on one side by the sea at the distance of hardly a mile; a river, which ran from the country on the left of the castle, fell into the ocean just beneath, where a few mean houses, intermingled with some ruined buildings, gave me the idea of an ancient port; between the place where I was and the sea the ground was marshy and cheerless, but on each side the land formed a mountainous curve, covered with woods, of which another window gave me a more distinct view. I opened the casement by the utmost exertion of my strength; and refreshed by the morning air and the cheering light of the sun, I took courage to examine the place where it seemed but too probable I was destined long to remain.

"I found that I was in an immense fortress, or castle, situated on an eminence, and covering for a considerable space its unequal summit. Great square towers, more ancient than the rest, projected over the declivity; but the spaces between these had more the appearance of old Italian houses, such as I had been used to see. On the side next the sea there was a deep fossé, beyond which the hill fell perpendicularly into a sort of marsh; but on the other side, on which the window I had opened looked, it appeared as if that part of it, immediately near the house, had once been cultivated as a garden or plantation, for amidst inequalitites, which seemed to have been made by human art for the purposes of defence, were a few groups of very old cypresses, and square enclosures bordered with evergreens, now wild and run into disorder. Among them I observed two or three colossal statues and pillars of marble, all of which seemed to have suffered from violence, for I could perceive that they were broken and mutilated: beyond this ground, which I ought, perhaps, to call a garden, the country rose into very high mountains on each side of the river, leaving on its banks a valley of about half a mile in extent, were a few straggling cottages surrounded with olive grounds such as I remember in Sicily, and there were some plantations of oranges about the houses, with vinyards on the hills where the wood was cleared away. Higher mountains closed the land prospect, and the course of the river was lost among them.

"Such appeared, on my first survey of it, the place where I was, perhaps, to pass my life; but, I saw the bright sun above me, I beheld variety of objects illuminated by his beams, I felt the balmy breath of Heaven on my face, which seemed to restore the enfeebled powers of life. My boy smiled on me, and appeared uninjured in his health by the faitgues he had gone through, and hope and peace in some measure returned.

"In examining, however, and reflecting on my situation, I began to be convinced, that what the man, who conducted me, had told me was true; that I was placed where there was no possible means of escape—I knew not in what part of Italy I was; the people I had seen, spoke, I thought, a language unlike the Italian I had learned, and I guessed from the manner of the woman, when I addressed myself to her, that she understood me with difficulty. I was entirely in the power of the person, whoever it was, to whom this castle or feudal residence belonged, and probably the whole country round was inhabitied by vassals and dependents who dared not assist me, even if I had possessed the means of speaking to or bribing them.

"It was impossible to assign any other cause for what had happened to me, than the rage and indignation of Signora Belcastro; and I now endeavoured to recollect, what I had heard you, my Montalbert, relate of your mother's property and power in a part of Italy at a considerable distance from Naples, and of a suit at law she had gained against your elder brother, which had confirmed her in the considerable estates he had disputed with her.—Careless as to what related to property which I considered only as a barrier to our happiness, I had given less attention to this detail than to almost any thing else, relative to your mother, on which we had ever conversed; but now endeavouring to recall that conversation to my mind, I thought it certain that I was her prisoner in one of those baronial houses that belonged to her; and as she might have condemned me, defenseless as I was, to a convent, or even to a dungeon, I felt somethig like gratitude towards her, for not having treated me so cruelly as she might have done.

"The very circumstances of her confining me at all counteracted part of the uneasiness it inflicted; for I refelcted, that had not my Montalbert lived, and still remained attached to his Rosalie, it could never have been an object to his mother to banish me thus from evey place where he was likely to inquire for me. It would have been easier for her, and more inimical to the pretensions which offended her to have sent me and my son to England, where, in the obscurity of poverty, perhaps of disgrace, (for you will observe that in my letter I have related the manner of our marriage), I should have been too much depressed ever to have troubled her more either with my child's claims or my own. But in England Montalbert might have sought me, and I was persuaded that it was her fear of that, which had shut me up in a fortress on a distant part of the Italian shore.

"There was, however, something soothing to my imagination in the sight of the sea, the only medium by which I could reach my native land, for thither my wishes were directed; thither

I believed Montalbert was gone in search of his Rosalie; and there, in my present disposition to sanguine hope, I flattered myself with believing we should meet again.

"The woman I had seen the evening before came into my room, and brought me dried fruit and biscuits for my breakfast; but she seemed to keep her resolution of being inexorably silent, and when I asked her to inform me what liberty would be granted me, she answered drily, that I might walk about the house. I then ventured to inquire where I was?—in what part of the country?

"The woman, fixing on me a look where pity seemed stifled by contempt and prejudice, answered, that I was in Calabria, and that, if my confinement had the happy effect of leading me from the heretical and bad opinions I had been brought up in, I ought to thank the blessed Saints who had permitted my escape from perdition. I cannot do justice to the strength of her language, for it was a dialect quite unlike common Italian; but the countenance and manner of the woman it would be still more difficult to paint. I received her admonition with an appearance of submission, and asked her if she belonged to a religious society?—She replied, that she was not a nun. This gave me no satisfaction; I wished to ask, to whom she belonged, if she was a domestic of the house?—and this question I endeavoured to make in the way least likely to alarm her integrity; but my art was all thrown away; neither then nor at any other time could I prevail on her to tell me whom she served, or by what prospect of advantage she was engaged to live a life more solitary than that of a convent. She was, in appearance and manners, a little, and but a little, superior to the peasantry of the domain whom I have since had occasion to see.

"I now took my little Harry in my arms, and began to survey my great and melancholy dwelling. I wandered from room to room—they appeared less gloomy, yet larger, than when I had seen them before; that next to mine seemed to have been used as an oratory, but, except a marble table, serving for an altar, and several seats covered with flowered velvet, of great antiquity, it was as destitute of furniture as the rest. Some, indeed, were quite empty, and others even without windows, in place of which pieces of board were nailed up, which rendered the apartments entirely dark. There seemed no end of these great gloomy rooms; the survey of them was little calculated to encourage that cheerful train of thought which I had indulged in the morning. As I looked over the bulastrades into the great hall, or cast my eyes along the extensive range of rooms and galleries, not even the brilliant light of an Italian sky could drive from my mind the idea of their being visited by nocturnal spectres.

"The remembrance of what my conductor had told me, that I could never escape, struck cold upon my heart. The lone and isolated situation of this mournful solitude seemed to confirm it but too strongly. I listened at a window to the sounds around the house, by which I thought I could judge whether there were many inhabitants; but I heard only the notes of birds, who were now in the season of song......No human voice was heard—no noise of mechanics, or labourers, about the offices; and towards evening, as the variety of birds without ceased their chorus, a silence so solemn pervaded the place, that I felt my terror return, as if my child and I were the only living creatures in this vast edifice.

"My silent keeper, however, regularly returned with food; and as I thought, on the second day, that she regarded me with less asperity, I again attempted to enter into conversation with her.

"I began by expressing my concern for the trouble I gave her, and asked, if she alone executed all the business of this large house?—She replied, that she had help when she wanted it.

'Alas! (then said I), how much happier you are than I am!—I should be content, methinks, if I had one female companion to speak to....Indeed I should be very much obliged to you, if you would now and then sit with me—it is extremely dreary never to hear the sound of a human voice.'

'Ahime, Signora! (replied the woman, who was called Cattina)—Ahime! you complain of want of company already!—and *I*, Signora, pray to the blessed Lady that we may not see at the castle any other persons than are here now, at least while I am its inhabitant; but perhaps, Signora, you might not hold in abhorrence such visitors as have been here in former times, and not so long ago, that is, not so very long ago neither.'

"I asked what visitors she could mean in a place like this, which seemed to me to be the very extremity of Europe.

'Yes, (replied she), it is a long long way off, to be sure, from any great town; but the visitors I mean are not Christians, as we are, of this country, but Pagans and Heretics like the wicked English. This castle has been plundered by the Algerines three or four times, and that is the reason that my———————(she suddenly recollected herself, paused, and then went on)—that the owners of it never have resided here for I don't know how many years; and nothing is now ever left in the house of any value.'

"My very soul failed within me as I heard this.—'O merciful Heaven! (exclaimed I), and these Algerines yet come occasionally to this coast!—and you think it not impossible but that they may return hither?——Tell me, Madam, I entreat you, how long it is since they were here?'

'Three or four years, perhaps, (answered Cattina, resuming her usual cold manner). I don't know, however, exactly as to that; perhaps they may not land on the coast again, not just here, for they know there is nothing of value for them to take: but then, indeed, we have no defense; formerly there was a guard kept at the castle, and those guns that you see there below were kept loaded to drive away the infidels, but all that is laid aside now. For my part I am not much afraid.'

"I now doubted whether Cattina had not told me this, to add to my punishment by all the aggravation of imaginary terrors. I had hardly courage to inquire farther; yet I ventured to make her some farther questions, and she took me to a window on the southern side of the house, where she showed me evident marks of the depredations made by the Barbarians, who had she said, about five and twenty years before landed to the number of fifty, and killed all the men who were then in the house, carrying off the women and children, not only from the castle, but the villages around it.—'And who (said I), then resided in the castle?—Were the owners themselves among those who suffered?'

"Cattina looked as if she would say—'And do you really think yourself cunning enough to engage me, by these questions, to betray my trust?'—She then, affecting not perfectly to understand my question, for we had already been once or twice puzzled in our dialogue, left me to brood alone over the additional dread she had impressed upon me. I went to the window and looked upon the sea, which I had formerly gazed at with so much pleasure: now, as the last rays of the setting sun illuminated its waves with glowing light, I fancied that they might guide some inhuman pirates towards these lonely and defenceless walls, and that the vengeance of your mother, your cruel mother had looked forward with malignant satisfaction to such a catastrophe, and had devoted me and my child to slavery—a fate infinitely worse than death.

"O Montalbert! what a night I passed after this discovery!—I forgot my real terrors only to be assaulted by all that fancy could collect: yet, I heard you, I saw you in my dreams, but it was contending with these lawless plunderers of the sea, for the safety of your wife and your boy......I saw you struggling with numbers; I shrieked, awoke, and listened in breathless terror to hear if this fearful vision was not realised, though you, Montalbert, I knew were not there. All, however, was still around me, and I heard only the soft breathing of my child as he lay sleeping on my arm, while my tears fell on his cheek. Thus passed the first eight and forty hours of my abode here."

END OF THE SECOND VOLUME.

IT appears as if the fears, which had distressed Rosalie, had in some degree subsided when she thus proceeded with her narrative, or rather journal:——

"April 11th, 1783.

"It is now above a fortnight since I have been here. Every day has appeared more melancholy than that which preceded it; for every day and every hour diminishes my hope that Montalbert is engaged in seeking me......Alas! could his vigilant love be deceived, or would not Signora Belcastro betray herself, had she been questioned?—Ah! fool that I am! I recollect that he could not question her; that he certainly could never know from her that Rosalie exists— Alozzi too is interested in deceiving him—perhaps we shall never meet again.....Montalbert! perhaps I am doomed to pass here, in this dreadful solitude, a long and wretched life. It is now four days since I prevailed on Cattina to let me wander over the deserted grounds that were once a garden; she finds I make no attempt to abuse this indulgence, and she does not now interdict the woods that surround the enclosure, or even the sea shore, though it is there only that I am likely to meet any of the few human beings who inhabit this depopulated region. I have been down to the sands, and on the wave-worn remains of a marble column, once, perhaps, the ornament of the port; I have been sitting to look at the sea. A very few days since I should not have ventured hither, for then my imagination was filled with the fears that Cattina had so recently taught me, of Corsairs and Turks. By habit, and from having assured myself, by subsequent conversations, that Cattina had exaggerated and misdated her accounts, I had appeased those apprehensions, or learned to think of them with more steadiness: nor, indeed, could my walks increase, whatever real danger there might be, since, during the day time, any vessel would be discerned from the coast long before it could land its crew. I saw today a group of peasant girls picking up the small fish along the sand; they were gay and sportive, and seemed to have no fear of such visits as Cattina has described to me as frequently happening. I wished to have spoken to them; but, perhaps, I ought to consider it as a part of my convention with Cattina, not to enter into conversation with any of the persons I may chance to meet.—Alas! these poor Calabrese could be of no use to me: they seemed to have no ideas beyond the little circle of their own necessities or pleasures; for though they must have known me to be a stranger, I excited no curiosity. Their happy indifference brought to my mind days when I was as thoughtless and as light-hearted as these simple peasants! That reflection was followed by the recollection of the circumstances that have happened to me with these last two years, and the chain of events, which, from one of the happiest, had reduced me to one of the most miserable of women. My waking dream lasted till the sun was set; the waves, as well as the whole horizon, assumed that rosy hue which mocks alike the pencil and the pen; I had heard that the exhalations from the marshes were unwholesome after a warm day, and I returned to my melancholy residence lest my child should suffer. Now, Montalbert, that he is sleeping by me, I relate on paper the sad employment of my solitary day—alas! how many more may pass in the same manner—what a prospect is mine!

"It is night.—I go to my window and look at the stars, which, in this clear atmosphere, are singularly brilliant. I seek the north star, because, Montalbert, I believe that you are in England—an idea that sometimes torments and sometimes sooths me; yet I encourage it even when I am most pained by it, for you have returned thither, perhaps, if not to seek your Rosalie, to weep with her mother for her supposed death.....That dear mother!—ah! how many tears have I already cost her—how many will she shed over my imaginary grave; while I, buried yet living, call on her name—on yours, Montalbert, in vain!

"Perhaps it is fit we should suffer thus—perhaps it is the proper punishment for our disobedience.....Oh! if it be so, may I alone be pursued by the vengeance of Heaven, and may that little innocent creature be spared and restored to the protection of his father. It is possibly to me, to my rash folly, that Montalbert owes much of his present uneasiness: his mother may have driven him from her with reproaches, with anger—he may, on my account, be loaded with a parent's curse!———Dreadful thought! I dare not dwell upon it.

"I cast my eyes round the high and gloomy room where I sit: all is silent and forlorn; cold and faint, my heart seems to sink within me, and I listen, with even a degree of eagerness, to hear the slow footsteps of Cattina, along the apartments, bringing me my evening meal.

"My keeper, for what else can I call her, is gone; she seems every day to soften in her manners towards me, and especially since she finds my child is to be brought up in the religion of his father. Poor, prejudiced woman; but she has not a bad heart, and there is something respectable even in her prejudices. I complained to her, this evening, of the languor I felt for want of some amusement when my child slept; and I asked if there were no books to be obtained here?—It was some time before I could make her understand my question. At length, however, she told me, that at the farther end of the castle, in a room which is never opened, there are a great many papers, and she believes books; she promises to show it me to-morrow. I may meet with some Italian poets, who may beguile those tedious minutes in which I am now tortured with my own thoughts. How well I remember, at Barlton Brooks, exploring the library of Mr. Lessington, and with as little success as I shall probably have tomorrow.

"But talking to this woman has a little relieved my spirits; for even the sound of a human voice is consoling to my ear!

"I will now endeavour to sleep.....Oh, come! thou image of my adored Montalbert—not as last night, in imaginary danger and contention, and risquing, for my defence, a life more precious than my own—but come to whisper peace and hope to the dreams of your devoted Rosalie!—Ah! would I could be assured that you will ever read my journal; that your eye will ever mark where the tears have blistered the paper as I write this, perhaps, fruitless wish!

"April 13th.

"I look back at my journal of yesterday, and of the preceding day, and am half-tempted to give up this monotonous account of lingering anguish. I have learned nothing by my research after books, but the great extent of this my prison, and that it is Formiscusa, a castle situated seventeen miles from Squilace, and was the seat of feudal government, when the Norman Barons possessed this country. A rude map or chart, hung up against the walls of the room I explored yesterday, has told me this; but not without my taking some pains to get at the intelligence, by clearing away the mould with which it was covered, and, like many others, I have fought only my own pain; for I now see that, from the situation of the place, there is but too much reason to believe it must be, at all times, exposed to hostile visits from Africa, or Turkey in Europe. I thought I had reasoned myself out of these fears, but they return in spite of me—so prone is the human mind, when under the pressure of actual evils, to aggravate them by anticipation of the future.

"You would chide me, Montalbert, for any tendency to indulge this disposition.—Ah! wretch that I am, if you were here, should I murmur?—should I dream of evil?—Ah!—no—with you, this solitary and frowning pile would be to me a Paradise! I should then enjoy the beauty of a country, which, in some parts, is really lovely, but over which my eyes now wander often half-blinded by tears.

"Since I have had permission to go out, however, and have walked about the garden, I am better; for there is a charm, in the contemplation of vegetable nature, that sooths my spirits beyond every thing but music.....When poor Rosalie Lessington was ill at ease, at Barlton Brooks, it was a seat on the turf of the downs, under the shade of an old thorn or a tufted beech, that she retired to sigh at liberty, though she then hardly knew why she sighed. Now the really unhappy Rosalie Montalbert, with her infant in her arms, and, ah! with sensations how different in her heart, finds a resting place on the plinth of a broken statue, or on a piece of granite rock, shaded with myrtle or embowered in arbutus, and surveys, with hopeless eyes, the sun sinking into the sea, from whence he will arise tomorrow to bring to her another day of tears and despair!

"Just as I had finished the last sentence, Cattina came to tell me, that a Turkish xebec, chased by a Maltese galley, was in sight; and that I might now be convinced how very near the Barbarians sometimes approached the shore. I trembled, and had hardly strength to follow her up to the western tower, which affords the most extensive view: I saw two vessels, one of which pursued the other, but they were too distant for me to distinguish with what nations they were manned. Soon afterwards, however, they were so near that I could distinguish the form of the Turkish vessel, and see the crescent she bore as an ensign; but fighting did not seem to be her purpose at that time; for, finding the Maltese gain upon her, set up more sail, and made every effort to get away. The enemy, however, pursued, and fired upon her; we heard the report, and soon after saw the flashes of the guns amid clouds of smoke; the Corsair returned the fire, but still made off, and, I suppose having some advantage as to lightness, soon got out of the reach of the firing. At length the xebec became like a doubtful spot in the horizon, and then entirely disappeared; while the Maltese vessel, to my great comfort, abandoned the chase, yet continued cruizing along the coast, as if to protect us against the invader, should he dare to return.

"My eyes are affected by gazing so long at the dazzling expanse of sea, and they and my heart still flutter with apprehension. I dread going to bed, for I shall fancy I hear hostile sounds in the adjoining rooms, and threatening tones in an unknown language: yet I know these pirates are gone, and unlikely now to molest us.

"I went down into the garden in hopes of calming my spirits before I attempted to sleep.—Already the heats have tarnished the lively verdure of spring, and the cicala has began to devour the leaves; while in England the trees are but just budding, and the earlier shrubs hardly in leaf. If I were a poet, I should be tempted, were my heart ever for a moment at ease, to add one to the number of those who have celebrated, or have attempted to celebrate, the nightingale; for here the note of that bird is infinitely more mellow and delicious than in England. I have been vainly trying to recollect some of the most beautiful addresses to this songstress of the night, but trouble and anxiety have driven from my memory the few images that, in my circumscribed reading, I had once collected......Montalbert! shall I ever again be restored to happiness and you?—If ever I am, shall I not feel myself so depressed, so undone, by this tedious course of suffering, as to have lost the few claims I had to your tenderness.—Ah! here is another source of pain opened—I become a self tormenter. But, conscious that it is weak, nay, perhaps wicked, I will try to check this continual inclination to repine—I will kneel by my sleeping infant, and recommend him and Montalbert to the protection of that merciful Being, who preserved me and my child among the crash of ruins, and the yawning gulphs that surrounded us in Sicily, and who can deliver us from this dreary prison, and restore us to the husband and the father."

The little narrative of Rosalie was now interrupted.

Wearied by the continual sameness of wandering about the fortress, where gloomy strength was not allied to safety, and where there was no alternative between the stagnation of cheerless solitude and the tremors of fear, (for whenever she conversed with Cattina these fears failed not to be renewed), Rosalie, on the day following that of which she has last given an account, took a walk hitherto untried, and went down to the village, if a small group of fishermen's huts could be called so.—These were built with pieces of marble, intermingled with clay, and among them lay scattered many remains of magnificent buildings, pieces of large statues, and broken pillars. The idea of the splendid works of man fallen to decay, and hastening to oblivion, yet having survived for ages the beings who toiled to raise them, has always something mournful in it to a reflecting mind; and Rosalie was imagining to herself how different the appearance of this port must have been seven hundred years ago, when it was crowded with vessels, and its streets displayed all that commerce then procured for the rich and luxurious. Now, strange reverse! a few half-naked children playing before the humble doors, where their sun-burnt mothers sat spinning coarse hemp, or a fisherman or two pushing off their barks with the evening tide, to fish during the night, on the success of which, their principal subsistence depended, were all the living beings visible in this obscure hamlet.

A high mound, rising in the midst of the village, had been formed by the fallen ruins of a temple. It was now covered with grass and low shrubs, but through them a marble capital, or an half-buried column, here and there were visible. On one of these last Rosalie sat down to rest a few moments before she returned home, and was sometimes indulging the reflections inspired by the place, sometimes talking to her child in a low and sweet voice, when she was startled by the footsteps of a person on the hollow ground near her; she looked suddenly up, and saw, not an Algerine pirate, but a gentleman, whom she immediately knew to be an Englishman.

Her amazement prevented her either moving or speaking; while the stranger, taking off his hat, said—"You must forgive me, Madam, if I cannot repress my curiosity—I believe you are English?—I fear I may appear impertinent; but it is impossible for me to restrain the eager wish I have to know by what extraordinary circumstance I here find a person so unlike the inhabitants—so unlike the objects I came hither to seek?"

However respectfully this address was made, there were places and occasions where Rosalie would have resented it as impertinent; but now, on the desert coast of Calabria, an Englishman seemed to her as a brother—and the accents of an English voice, as a voice from Heaven.

She tried, however, in vain to answer distinctly the unexpected question thus made, and, faltering and trembling, said, in a voice hardly articulate, "I do not wonder, Sir, you are surprised at seeing me here! I am, indeed, an English stranger, and brought hither by a series of events too long to relate."—At that moment she recollected, that, if she was seen speaking to any one, her walks would be put an end to, and her confusion increased. She took courage, however, to add—"I am detained here wholly against my inclinations, and despair ever to revisit my native country......I thank you, Sir, for the interest you seem to take in my misfortunes; but I dread being seen to converse with - - - - - -"

"Hasten then, I conjure you, (cried the Englishman), to tell me where you live, and how I can be of use to you....Good God! you are here against your inclinations!—But who dares to confine you?—I am a stranger to you, Madam, and a mere idle wanderer in this land; but, as a man of your country, you have a right to all my services—command, and be assured I will at least try to obey you."

A ray of hope now darted into the mind of Rosalie. Prepossessed with an idea that Montalbert was in England, the offers of this gentleman seemed to be directed by the interposition of Heaven to convey her to him. The tumult of her spirits were too great to allow her to reflect on the hazard she might incur by putting herself into the power of a stranger; the hopes of being conveyed to England, and Montalbert, by his means, absorbed at that moment every other consideration: but the more delightful the prospect was, the more she dreaded its vanishing, and this she know would happen if Cattina discovered her talking to any one.

Terrified, therefore, lest she should be observed, she said, in a hurried way—"I am so situated, that I dare not stay to explain who I am, or relate the causes that have made me a prisoner in the great castle you see above; but, if you are in the neighbourhood of this place to-morrow - - - - - - -"

"If I am? (cried the stranger eagerly), only tell me where I shall see you again, and I will wait your own time—I will attend you at the risk of my life."

"I hope, (interrupted Rosalie tremulously)—I hope there will be no risk.....If you will be, at five o'clock to-morrow evening, in a small wood, which is the boundary of a sort of garden on the other side of the castle, near a place where the remains of several statues surround a ruined fountain - - - - - - -; (she recollected that she was making an assignation with a man she had never seen before, and stopped, for she felt all the impropriety of it; yet, encouraged by her motives and the rectitude of her intentions, she proceeded)—I will be there, and explain to you who I am, and how - - - - you can oblige me, (she was going to say, but again checked herself, and only added)—but now it is impossible for me to stay." The stranger repeated her directions with earnestness, and assured her he would be there.—" And this lovely child too! (said he, still following her as she turned to go to the castle), is this too of my country?"—"It is mine, (answered Rosalie mournfully); but, indeed, you must now leave me, or your obliging offers of service will be frustrated."—The gentleman bowed, and suffered her to go, following her with his eyes till she reached the buildings adjoining the castle, which concealed her from his sight. He then slowly retired, while Rosalie, breathless and trembling, sought her guard, and so over-acted her part, by complaining of her solitary walks, and affecting her former languor, that a more accurate observer than Cattina would have guessed that some unusual circumstance had befallen her.

Cattina had, however, no suspicions, and Rosalie went to her room, and to her reflections on what had passed.

She endeavoured to recall the person, expressions, and manner of the stranger to whom she had spoken, that she might now, in a cooler moment, ask herself whether he appeared to be really a gentleman, and one in whom she ought to repose so much confidence as to put herself under this protection.——He was a young man, apparently not more than two or three and twenty; his countenance was less handsome than expressive, and there was something remarkable in it, which Rosalie could not define. He had the air and manners of a gentleman; but she knew that many have those advantages whom it would be extreme imprudence to trust. Perhaps too, notwithstanding the earnestness with which he offered her any services in his power, he might shrink from the trouble and expence of conducting her and her child to England; for young as she was, and little as she had yet seen of the world, she was not now to learn that those who most warmly profess friendship, are often those who fly from the performance of any kindness at all inconvenient to themselves. These and other reflections half discouraged Rosalie from the plan she had formed, in the first moments of meeting, with a man who seemed to have the power of releasing her. The disposition of Montalbert forcibly recurred to her; he might be rendered for ever suspicious of her conduct, if she thus rashly entrusted herself to a person of whom she could know nothing, and whose character might be such as would entirely ruin hers, in the opinion of the world, when it should be known that she had been conducted by him to England.—Yet, on the other hand, in losing the only opportunity to escape that might ever offer, she condemned herself and her little boy to perpetual imprisonment, and became accessary to her own misery and that of Montalbert......Ah! who could tell that he would not, in the persuasion of her death, yield to the importunities of his mother, and marry the Roman lady to whom she had so long wished to unite him. This idea was as insupportable as that of this death, and, compared with its being realized, every other evil became light, and every hazard disappeared.—Sometimes, however, the fear of her husband's having perished at Messina obtruded itself; but the pains his mother had taken to conceal her argued strongly against it. But, even if such calamity had really happened, it seemed to be the duty of his widow to claim the rights of his child, and how could this be done but by having recourse to her friends in England: for friends, she believed, she had, not only in her mother, who would protect and assist, though she could not own her, but in Charles Vyvian her real, and William Lessington her adopted, brother. Towards these she thought she might look for protection and kindness; and these hopes, added to her dread of remaining for life in the melancholy and even dangerous solitude of Formiscusa, determined her, if the stranger on their meeting still appeared willing to assist her, to endeavour, by his means, to reach England.

CHAP.

So various and contradictory were the thoughts which agitated Rosalie during the night, that she found it impossible to sleep; she arose with the earliest dawn, and, though so many hours were to intervene before that of her appointment, she could not forbear going to the place she had marked to her new friend for their meeting, that she might be sure she had described it accurately. She returned, however, almost immediately to the house, for, conscious of having something to hide, she now feared Cattina might suspect her.

From the windows towards the sea she now again saw the Maltese galley, which had been some days hovering on the coast. It cast anchor near the shore, a boat put off from it, and landed behind a small promontory, which formed one side of the port. It now occurred to Rosalie, that there was some connection between the arrival of this vessel and that of her new acquaintance. He came then from Malta, and was in all probability returning thither. If such was the case, how could he charge himself with her and her child?—or, admitting he would do so, how could she expose herself to the hazard of traversing the sea in a Maltese vessel, which, she knew, was liable to be continually engaged by Turkish and Algerine pirates. These doubts, added to these she had before, served to agitate her spirits so much, that, when the hour of the appointment came, she had hardly strength to go to the fountain in the wood, where her English friend had arrived before her.

Rosalie trembled, and looked so pale as she advanced towards him, that, alarmed, he said—"I hope, Madam, nothing has happened, since I had the honour of meeting you yesterday, to give you uneasiness?—I hope the favour you do me, by thus condescending to come hither - - - - - - - - -"

Rosalie, whose heart beat so violently that she was unable to speak, interrupted him by a deep sigh, and a faint attempt to articulate "No, Sir! nothing has happened—only I am so—so—unfortunate, and so uncertain what is to become of me, that - - - - - - - - -." She could not proceed, but leaned against a tree, and tried to recover herself, while the stranger, who was apprehensive she would faint, led her towards a piece of broken marble, and entreated her to sit down upon it; she did so, and, in a short time, assured him she was better, and begged his pardon for the weakness she had betrayed.

"I own, Madam, (said the stranger), that my curiosity is very strongly excited, and that I am impatient to know how I can be servicable to you? I might claim a sort of privilege to be admitted to your confidence, because I am of the same nation; but I rather rest my pleas on the earnest inclination I feel to be employed in your service: if, as I fear, you are unhappy, and suffering from the tyranny of some relation - - - - - - - - -." The stranger hesitated, as if uncertain how to proceed on a subject that might be of a very delicate nature, and, from his manner, it struck Rosalie as if he thought she was confined by her husband—an impression which might involve her in very disagreeable consequences. She, therefore, took courage to say—"It is true I am a prisoner at this place, and am most desirous of being released, in hopes of being restored to my husband, who would, I am sure, be very grateful to any one who undertook to assist me in regaining my liberty—if (added she) he still lives—as I will not suffer myself to doubt."

"Good God! (exclaimed the English stranger), by what accident, for it is impossible it should be from choice, could a man, happy enough to be your husband, allow himself to be torn from you; and who can have authority to confine you here?"

"My story is long and extraordinary, (answered Rosalie); I can only relate now, that I was separated from my husband in consequence of the earthquake which destroyed Messina, and that his mother, averse to his marriage with a woman of another religion and country, has taken occasion to divide us, as she hopes, for ever, by confining me here, and probably by persuading him that I am no more."

"He is an Italian then?" cried the stranger.

"Born of an Italian mother, (replied Rosalie), but his father was an Englishman, and of an ancient English family."—The recollection that Montalbert might at this moment believe her dead, and even be the husband of another, added to the fear that she was perhaps doing wrong, and putting herself into the power of a man who might take base advantages of her confidence, were sensations so uneasy, that, losing the little fortitude she had collected, she burst into tears.

The gentleman appeared to be really hurt at her distress; and, lowering his voice, said—"I thank you, Madam, for the confidence you have already placed in me; perhaps I ought not to expect you to trust me farther, till I tell you who it is that you so highly honour, and by what accident I am in a part of Italy so seldom visited by English travellers. But suffer me to ask, if you are now secure from the malicious observations of this Italian woman, who exercises over you tyranny so unjustifiable?"

"There are only servants in the castle, (replied Rosalie). My persecutors deemed them sufficient for the purpose of guarding me in a place so remote, that my escape seemed impossible.......I believe they will not molest me here, as I am accustomed to walk alone of an evening."

"Since you permit me then, (said the stranger), I will relate, in a few words, what you have a right, Madam, to know, before I can expect you will rely on my assurances, of being ready to render you any service you may honour me with; and yet I am sensible that a man is never more awkwardly circumstanced than when he is obliged to speak of himself, and, above all, to tell who he is. It is particularly difficult for me to do this, (added he, in a dejected tone), since I have not unfrequently forgotten myself, or, at least, been in a disposition of mind which made me very sincerely try at it."—

He paused, but Rosalie continuing silent and attentive to him, he went on—

"Perhaps, if your residence in England was in the west, you may have heard of the family of Walsingham—I am of that family.......It is not necessary to relate to you, Madam, the particular circumstances of a life which has had nothing uncommon in it, unless it be that I lost, at an early period, the person with whom I hoped to have passed it in as much happiness as mutual affection and a coincidence of disposition could promise.—From that time, the death of my elder brother having made the pursuit of the profession to which I was brought up unnecessary, I have wandered over the world, with the hope of finding, in change of place, a temporary relief for the wounds which no time can cure; and I have succeeded so far, as to take some interest in the objects which nature, or art, present to the traveller, particularly in Italy: as I had before visited almost every part of it, except Malta and Calabria ultra, and found that my spirits once more required change of place, I left England about two months since for Leghorn, from thence I got a passage to Malta, and having a curiosity to visit that part of Calabria immediately opposite the coast of Sicily, which had been so lately the scene of one of the most tremendous convulsions of Nature on record, I embarked in a Maltese galley, commanded by the Chevalier de Montagny, a French Knight of Malta, with whom I had been fortunate enough to make an acquaintance; and we designed to have extended our cruize to the Gulph of Manfredonia, but having seen an Algerine or Turkish xebec, which the Chevalier had reason to believe was hovering about the coast with piratical intentions, he determined to attempt taking it. We were in chase for many hours; after which, the Chevalier casting anchor about a mile from hence, I inquired, as I usually do, what there was worth landing to see?—and with some difficulty discovered, that we were near the ancient port of Formiscusa, where there were a few fine remnants of Roman buildings, and where I might very probably find coins, or small pieces of sculpture. My friend de Montagny, whose intention it was to watch the xebec, which, he believed, intended to return, assured me, that I might come on shore and satisfy my curiosity without any danger of his leaving me behind. I availed myself, therefore, of occasion, and had been purchasing some antiquities, of little value to them, among the peasants of the village, when, surveying that spot where there are evidently the ruins of a temple, I was surprised to observe a lady, whom I immediately saw was very unlike the inhabitants of the surrounding country, and who, on my nearer approach, I heard speak in accents which confirmed by first idea of her being an Englishwoman.......Ah! Madam, how happy shall I esteem myself, if, in the accidental indulgence of that curiosity, where the highest gratification it can afford, is but a very transient relief to a mind incurably hurt, I should prove the means of being essentially useful to a young lady—who—I am ill at expressing what I feel, and know that you are, that you must be, superior to common-place compliments: yet I cannot refrain from saying, that, as being of the same country, you have on that score a right to my best services, though, that were you of any other, one need only behold you to be convinced that you must command the most respectful homage of every man."

Rosalie, who had rather the latter part of this speech had been spared, now hesitated, blushed, and attempted to speak, but she failed; and Walsingham, who saw her embarrassment, and appeared perfectly to understand it, resumed his discourse.

"Unless I know more of your situation, than, on so short an acquaintance, you may think it proper to entrust me with, I cannot venture to advise; but I can, with great truth, assure you, that if you will venture to put yourself under my care, I shall think it the most fortunate circumstance of my life, to be allowed to conduct you from hence, in whatever manner you think consistent with safety or propriety, and to whatever place you shall point out. I will not leave you till you are secure in the protection of some of your friends, and I will attend you either to any part of the continent, or to England."

Rosalie, now confirmed in her resolution to depart, looked as it she would express her thanks, when Walsingham, who appeared already to have acquired the art of reading her thoughts, said, "And do not, I beseech you, Madam, imagine that, by my undertaking this, you will be under the least obligation to me: far otherwise, believe me—for you will confer the greatest to possible obligations on a man, to whom life has no longer any value, but what he can derive from being serviceable to others."

Rosalie now thought herself perfectly justified in accepting an offer which threatened no inconvenience to the stranger, while it promised to restore her to liberty, and, perhaps, to felicity. Dismissing then all the objections, which still attempted to obtrude themselves on her mind, she entered into a discussion of the best means of escaping from a place, where the few precautions, that were taken to secure her stay, arose merely from the supposed impracticability of her flight.

After a long conversation it was agreed, that however desirable it might be for her to go by land, yet she would incur great risk of being pursued, and in such roads must inevitably be overtaken.—Nothing therefore remained but for her to accept what Mr. Walsingham very earnestly offered, in the name of his friend the Chevalier de Montagny, a conveyance in the Maltese galley to any port from whence it was possible a passage to England could be the most quickly obtained; Walsingham assuring her that the vessel and its commander would be entirely at her orders.

This point being settled, it was next to be considered how and when she could leave her prison with the least probability of detection. This was not difficult; but aware, from past experience, of the many inconveniences which must be encountered at sea, it was necessary that what baggage she had should go with her, she reminded Walsingham that she could not convey this herself, nor could she even carry it from her room to the lower part of the house, without hazarding a discovery. After a moment's consideration he obviated this objection, by telling her, that as, from her description, the castle was very large, and that there were only two servants and a peasant who slept there, nothing was more easy than to introduce a sailor, or more, if more were requisite, who would probably be able to pass through the house unnoticed, and convey away whatever she wished to have with her. He added, "and I will come with them myself to prevent all accidents from rashness or blunders. There is a moon, about two o'clock, which will afford us light enough; it is an hour when your keepers will be asleep, and there can be no difficulty in your then leaving a house so slightly guarded."

Rosalie now recollected that there was a very material one—that of the doors being always shut of a night with great circumspection, at least so she imagined, because she had frequently heard Cattina, after she had left her of a night, go round all that part of the building adjoining the great staircase, up which the distant noise of shutting and barring the massive doors sounded in sullen echoes. She had often listened, after all had been still, for some moments, and believed that she heard the same precautions taken in the more remote parts of the edifice; parts, indeed, where she had never been.

When she communicated this to Mr. Walsingham, be became impatient.—"If the doors are not easily opened, (cried he), we will cut them down; any, rather batter them with three or four eight pounders, from our galley, than fail."—Rosalie turned pale at the very mention of any expedient of this kind.—Ah, no! (said she); if my escape cannot be effected without the hazard of shedding blood, I must resign myself to my deplorable destiny—for I had rather perish here than be the cause of one man's death.

Ah! Sir, you do not consider, that, by the least alarm given from the castle, the village below, as well as another higher up the country, would, in an instant, send forth their inhabitants; beside there are arms kept in a lower room, which Cattina once showed me, and a subterraneous communication with the cannon you see without."—Walsingham smiled at the formidable phalanx her fancy had thus embodied, well assured that a very few resolute men would put to flight not only the inhabitants of the castle, but all the peasantry around it who could be collected, and who could have little temptation to risk their lives in defending the mansion of a woman, whom they had, perhaps, never seen, and to whom they seemed to be very little obliged. Rosalie, however, after pausing a moment; said she recollected, that, on the day when Cattina undertook to show her where she might, perhaps, find some books, she had led her along a passage adjoining to her bedchamber, and from thence down several flights of narrow stairs to the bottom of the building, whence some places, that appeared like arched vaults, led into the room where the papers were deposited, and from thence there was a door opening into the fossé next the garden. She had particularly remarked this door, because Cattina had opened it to give more light to the apartment, which was extremely obscure, from part of it being under ground.— "Cattina (continued she) left me there alone for a considerable time, and when I came out of the room, the door still remained open; it is therefore probable, that there are no fastening to it, and that I might go from thence, as well as have my clothes conveyed thither, without alarming Cattina and the other servants, who inhabit quite another part of the house."—Walsingham eagerly seized on this idea, but started a difficulty that had not occurred to Rosalie.—"How (said he) shall we, who are strangers to the castle, find this door, unless we are first shown it?"-Rosalie had nothing to propose.—"Unless, (added her new friend, after a little recollection), unless I could, before it is dark, go round the castle, when I think I could easily discover the place; there we would wait for you, or, if we found the door open, make our way up, at the hour appointed, to your apartment."

To this scheme, though she had nothing better to offer, Rosalie objected, because she dreaded, lest the sight of a stranger should raise suspicions in the servants; and she knew that Cattina, whose head was filled with ideas of pirates, since the appearance of one of their xebecs on the coast, was become more then usually vigilant in watching, at the windows, if these objects of her terror again appeared.

"What is to be done then, dearest Madam? (cried Walsingham); we have no time to lose, and it is absolutely necessary that we determine on something.—Can you not, from some place where there is no danger of our being remarked, point out the side of the building where this door opens into the fossé?" ——This appeared the least perilous plan, but it was also the most uncertain. Rosalie then led the way, along the skirts of the wood, to a rising ground, affording a view of the whole building, and bade Mr. Walsingham remark three tall cypresses near its western extremity.——"If you pass them, (said she), and walk straight on, you will come to what was once a deep fossé immediately surrounding the castle; but now it is in many places nearly filled up, and the earth and wall are fallen in, insomuch that, when I looked out for a moment at the door in question, rather for air than from any curiosity, I perceived I could have got up into the garden by this way."——Walsingham fixed his eye steadily on the place, assured Rosalie he should not fail to find it; then again repeated, that he would be punctually at the place, with his own servant and a sailor, at two o'clock in the morning, an hour when he knew the moon would afford light to facilitate their getting on board the vessel, which would immediately sail. He inquired, if Rosalie had a watch; she had lost hers in leaving Sicily; and, therefore, that no mistake might happen as to the hour, he desired she would make use of one of his, which he set by the other.

It now became time to part, for the evening was closing in. Walsingham, after a renewal of every protestation which was likely to encourage the timid adventurer, whose fears and agitation he saw painted in her countenance, took a hasty leave, was presently lost among the trees, while Rosalie slowly returned to her gloomy prison, dreading lest any accident should prevent her leaving it; yet trembling at the hazard she must incur, and the difficulties she must encounter, to regain her liberty.

CHAP.

AFTER having given the usual attention to her little boy, Rosalie was at liberty to make the few arrangements that were necessary, and to recollect on the step she was about to take. However earnestly she had wished for such an opportunity as was offered her, she trembled now that the moment approached; yet all she had heard from Mr. Walsingham, and his zeal, which did not seem lessened by the knowledge of her being married, ought to give her strength of mind and courage. But the uncertainty of the time of when she should reach England; the comfortless circumstance of her being so long on board a vessel, which might be encountered by pirates, where she would be the only woman; the sickness and difficulties of such a voyage with a little infant; and the doubts how far her husband might approve of her thus putting herself wholly in the power of a stranger, were considerations, which, though they did not shake her resolution, gave dreadful agitation to her spirits as she was about to execute it.

Other fears too assailed her.—The door in the fossé might not be open; she was far from being sure she could find her way to it; and she shuddered at the thought of descending these long and intricate staircases, and traversing the vault-like passages leading to the room which she was not certain she should find. Cattina had told her a story of the former lord of this castle, she knew not his name, who, being jealous of his wife, had invited the Signeur, whom he suspected of being in her favour, to an entertainment, when he had killed him, and buried him in some of these rooms, and that lights had often been seen from the loops and windows, and strange noises heard in this end of the castle, and that nobody had lived in the lower apartments since that time. This was a story which had the less affected Rosalie when she heard it, because it was so common in all old houses in England to have such a legend. Holmwood had the ghost of a lady, in a ruff and farthingale, which always walked on Friday nights; and she was not at all surprised, that the old castle of Formiscusa was furnished with the spirit of a murdered knight: but now, that it was necessary for her to wander alone over the deserted caverns, which were the supposed scenes of such a tragic adventure, the same fears and feelings returned as had oppressed her mind on the first two or three days after her arrival in this desolate mansion.

While these thoughts passed in succession through her mind, the hour arrived for Cattina to bring her evening meal. Cattina came as usual, but was not in one of her best humours; she was sullen and gloomy, and, instead of such conversation as she sometimes held, she seemed disposed to mutter complaints, though in indirect and general terms. Rosalie, afraid of her staying, and too conscious of what was passing in her own mind, was not able to command resolution enough to sooth and flatter her into better temper, which she had not unfrequently done. Cattina, however, having fidgetted about the room in her odd way when her temper was discomposed, sat down, and a silence ensued, when Rosalie heard the watch in her pocket, and was struck with the fear that Cattina would hear it too, and knowing she had not one before, would inquire how she came by it; at this idea she felt the blood forsake her cheeks, and was so much discomposed, that, to a more accurate observer than Cattina, she would undoubtedly have betrayed herself.

Cattina, however, who had some grievances of her own, was fortunately less quick-sighted and intelligent than many who might have been chosen for the office of keeper, and after perplexing Rosalie by a longer stay than usual, while she talked and made as much noise as she could; the female warder of the castle departed, and, as she marched slowly through the adjoining rooms, Rosalie fervently prayed that she might never hear those sounds again.

She now debated with herself, whether it would be better to go down first and examine the door, or wait till the hour when she expected Mr. Walsingham to arrive at it, and, after some deliberation, she determined on the former plan, reflecting, that if they came, and found it fastened, the rashness of Mr. Walsingham, who seemed to despise every danger that could arise from within the castle, might either impede her flight, or stain it with some deed of violence.

It was necessary, however, to stay till she was sure that Cattina, and the two servants who belonged to the castle, were retired for the night; and indeed she dreaded the expedition too much to anticipate its execution. She endeavoured, by every argument she could draw from reason and religion, to fortify herself against the fears that assailed her, and, for a moment, thought she had conquered them. The appearance of such a man as Mr. Walsingham, at such a place as Formiscusa, seemed little less than a miracle, and she endeavoured to persuade her mind it was the particular interposition of Heaven in her favour; and that to neglect such an occasion of delivering herself from perpetual confinement, would be ingratitude to the Almighty, as well as contrary to the duty she owed her husband, her child, and herself. Innocent as she was of all offence towards God or Man, what had she to fear?

Fortifying her mind with these reflections, and endeavouring to look beyond present inconveniences, she thought upon the time when she should be restored to Montalbert, and should remember all that now perplexed and oppressed her only as a fearful dream.

Listening attentively to the well-known sounds of shutting the doors, in the in habited part of the building, she heard them closed for the night in the usual manner; she then went to the window to see what was the weather—there was more wind than common, and she saw the old cypresses wave in the blast. From the sea, on the other side, the moon that was to light her on her perilous way was just emerging. She addressed herself to Heaven, and implored its protection; and, conscious of the rectitude of her intentions, believed that she should go through the evening's task with resolution.

Her own and her child's clothes were collected in the trunks. She had dressed him ready for the journey before she put him to bed, and he slept undisturbed by the anxieties that agitated his mother's breast, who, having determined not to attempt to sleep, looked continually at the watch, and thought that time moved more than usually slow. It was, however, near midnight, and, once more collecting all her resolution, she determined on examining the door by which she hoped to escape. She opened, not without difficulty, that of her chamber, which led to the avenues of this lower room, and such was the violence of the wind that rushed along the passages, that had she had a candle in her hand it must have been extinguished; she trembled, and, retreating, shut the door hastily. Warned by this circumstance, she now considered what would be her situation should the light be extinguished while she was descending, and should she lose her way among the many winding passages which she remembered having seen when she followed Cattina. The apprehension was fearful, and again her resolution to go down the stairs failed her.

She returned to her child, whom she hoped would sleep till her departure, kissed him, and, imploring for him the protection of Heaven, tried to regain her courage; but as the dread of being left in utter darkness, which the rising wind gave her great reason to fear, was still the predominant idea, she endeavoured to take such precautions as occurred to her against it, and surrounded the candle, she was to carry, with a skreen of paper, lighting at the same time the lamp that hung in the room: then looking at the watch, and finding it past midnight, she once more summoned all her resolution, and softly opening the door that the force of the gust might be less suddenly felt, she advance along the passage that went from her room to the place where another branched from it, leading to the narrow winding stairs. She looked fearfully along these black and apparent endless avenues: the half-obscured light, lent by her shaded candle, served, indeed, to make "*darkness visible.*" She feared to look long on the dreary vacuity, lest her imagination should embody forms of its own creation; she reached the staircase, and a stronger blast of wind, gathering here as in a funnel, threatened to extinguish her light, which she even held with difficulty. She found herself, however on the next floor, in a sort of landing place, from whence other passages led off she knew not whither, and she stopped a moment to regain her breath, of which fear had nearly deprived her.

In this pause, however prone her fancy was to imaginary sounds as well as sights of horror, she heard nothing but the loud gusts of wind that collected beneath from various openings in the walls, and being confined among narrow-vaulted passages, groaned in loud gusts, then sunk into sullen murmurs. Still Rosalie knew it was but the wind, the same wind that would probably in a few hours lend its friendly assistance to waft her to the place from whence she might procure a passage to England. This thought animated her courage; she raised her eyes, and assured herself that she saw nothing which could give her the least alarm; bare and broken walls, and dark avenues, which she had no business to explore, surrounded her: she determined then to pursue her way slowly and cautiously, for the steps of the second flight of stairs were broken and decayed; she advanced, when she was suddenly stopped by a sound, which she thought was that of human voices speaking low—she listened with a beating heart. A gust of wind, more violent than she had yet heard, impeded for a moment her distinguishing any other noise; but, as it died away, she was convinced she heard talking, and that there were two or more voices.—What should this mean?—With a trembling hand she once more took the watch, Walsingham had given her, from her pocket. It was not yet half an hour after twelve, and the appointment was not till two. This noise then could not be occasioned by Walsingham and his people waiting for admittance.—What then should it be?—but that their project was by some accident discovered, and that the agents of Signora Belcastro were waiting to entrap those on whom she depended for her deliverance, and that they would afterwards punish her for attempting to escape; probably by tearing her child from her, and confining her to some dungeon beneath the castle. These terrific ideas deprived her, for a moment, of the power of moving from the place where she stood; but she had gained recollection enough to resolve on returning up stairs, and shutting her door, before these her cruel pursuers should arrive at it, when a loud and violent crush confirmed all her fears; she turned, and, as hastily as her trembling limbs would carry her, she ascended the stairs, treading lightly. Almost immediately she heard the footsteps of some person following her. Her resolution would now have failed entirely if the greater fear had not conquered the less; for she imagined, that while she was thus absent, her little infant, whom she had left sleeping in its bed, might be carried away; and that idea was so much more dreadful than any thing that could befal herself only, that she sprang forward with unusual swiftness—her candle was exstinguished, and she had no light to guide her, yet continued to make her way, where, at another time, she would have found it difficult even by day.—The steps behind were heard more near, and she thought the man that followed was but a very little way from her when she reached the top of the stairs; the door of her room, which she had left open, was so still, and the lamp that remained burning afforded her light to guide her to it. She ran forward to the bed; her boy was calmly sleeping as she had left him; she threw her arms round him, and sunk quite exhausted with fear, by his side—still sensible, but in terror too great to be supported.

The man who had so alarmed her, guided by the same light, followed her into the room, and approached her. Determined to die, rather than part with her child, she shrieked faintly, and implored inarticulately his mercy......But it was Walsingham himself that spoke to her, conjuring her, in the strongest, yet most respectful terms, to recollect herself, protesting that she had nothing to fear, unless from delay; since, from the noise he had been obliged to make, it was possible the people in the castle might be alarmed. He briefly accounted for coming so much before his time, by telling her, that the wind rising, the Chevalier de Montagny was afraid that the least increase might compel him to put out to sea; in which case she would have lost the chance of escaping, as he could not have returned while it blew from the same quarter, which it sometimes did for many weeks; and that they had, therefore, agreed that if would be better for them to force the door, in which they had found no difficulty, and rather to hazard alarming her for a moment, than not ensure her future safety.

Rosalie, restored to herself by this reasonable account, now exerted herself to fly for ever from this place of dread under the guidance of her generous protector, who told her two men were below that only waited his signal to fetch her baggage. This he immediately gave; and Rosalie, having only to wrap her little boy in the same coverings as had served them before, during their long journey, was instantly ready with him in her arms.

Walsingham conducted her carefully down with her sleeping charge, the two men following with the trunks. Some little difficulty occurred in her mounting the broken fossé on the other side; but she was light, and naturally alert, and though she still trembled from her late terror, the certainty of being released from her cruel confinement, of which there now seemed no doubt, lent her strength, with the assistance of Walsingham's servant, (for she would trust her child only to Walsingham himself), to conquer this impediment. Her deliverer then followed, and restored his charge to her, and offering her his arm, which she readily accepted, they hastened as much as her strength would admit, and, after about an hour's walking, found themselves on the shore, where the boat waited that was to carry them on board the Maltese galley.

CHAP.

THOUGH, on account of the tide, the embarkation was troublesome, and though the surge ran high, as the boat made its way to the ship, yet Rosalie, who now no longer doubted of her escape, was unconscious of inconveniences, which, at another time, would have alarmed her. The moment they were safely on board the Maltese vessel, Walsingham expressed his satisfaction in a manner that gave Rosalie the most favourable impressions of the goodness of his heart, and the sincerity of his professions; while the Chevalier de Montagny welcomed her with all the politeness and urbanity, for which military men of a certain age, and of his nation, were once so justly esteemed. He entreated her to consider herself as mistress of the ship, and assured her, that whatever merit there might be in the original purpose of his voyage, there was infinitely more in being instrumental to the deliverance of so fair a captive from imprisonment; and in answer to the mingled thanks and apologies which she attempted to utter, he said that he only did his duty when he lent what assistance he could to his English friend, for that he was bound, by his military and religious oath, to succour the injured and distressed in every part of the world. The Chevalier then led her into a small state cabin, extremely commodious for the size of the ship, and assured her it was hers till she was landed wherever Mr. Walsingham should direct, and about which they were then going to consult; that he would only direct some refreshment to be brought to her, and then leave her to repose.

 Rosalie, who, by the quick succession of fear and hope, had hardly had time to recollect her scattered senses during the last few hours, now looked round her, and saw herself in comparative security. Delivered from the power of the unrelenting Signora Belcastro, in the protection, as she believed, of men of honour, and in a way of returning to her country, where she assured herself she should meet her husband, she now offered up her acknowledgements to that Power who had miraculously interposed to save her; her full heart, relieved by prayer and tears, beat less tumultuously, and, notwithstanding the rolling of the ship, for the wind still continued high, she suffered less than she had ever done at sea before; and even slept many hours, awaking much refreshed in the morning, and able to go upon deck, where, as the sea was now calm, the sails only gently swelled with a summer breeze.

 Mr. Walsingham and the Chevalier de Montagny both attended her, and she very soon learned to consider the one as a father, the other as a brother; for the former was nearly fifty years of age. Walsingham no longer made those speeches expressive of admiration which had given her some pain on their first meeting; he seemed no more to consider her as a beautiful young woman, to whom such compliments might be acceptable, but as a wife, whom he was restoring to her husband; as a mother, whom he had preserved for her child. Since he knew she was married, she was to him but as a sister; and, indeed, he now repeated, that all his affections were buried with the amiable Leonora he had lost, and whose death he yet deplored in terms so pathetic, that, as she listened to him, the soft eyes of Rosalie were frequently filled with tears.

 The second day after they were on board, and as soon as Rosalie seemed quite recovered from the fright and fatigue that she had suffered the night she quitted Formiscusa, Walsingham took occasion to tell her, that he had consulted with the Chevalier de Montagny, who submitted to him at what port in the Mediterranean they would be landed; and that he had settled it should be at Marseilles, whither they were now making their way with a favourable wind. To this Rosalie had nothing to object. Wherever there seemed the greatest certainty of an immediate passage to England appeared to her the most eligible; and she heard with pleasure, such as she had long been stranger to, that, if the wind continued as favourable as it now seemed to promise, they should be at Marseilles in two or three days.

 In the mean time, though the dread of having been too sanguine as to the fate of

Montalbert, sometimes obtruded itself upon her mind, she endeavoured to appease these fears; and when she had once found courage to relate to her two new friends the circumstances under which they had been separated, she received consolation in hearing their opinions that Montalbert was safe; and when doubts and apprehensions, as to where he might be, tormented her, Walsingham bade her recollect how easily she might from Marseilles make inquiry at Naples, and, if he was in Italy, inform him of her health and residence. What was to become of her till all this could be done made now no part of her uneasiness; for she hoped and believed the dear mother she had left in England was ready, if not to acknowledge her as her daughter, to receive her as her niece, for her marriage with Montalbert could no longer be a secret. To Charles Vyvian also, and to William Lessington, she thought it might now be told; and to the former she believed the knowledge of it would render her as dear as if their nearer relationship was known.

  While these hopes soothed the solitary hours of Rosalie, her conversations with Walsingham impressed her every moment with greater respect for his character, and pity for the dejection he frequently seemed to feel. He seldom spoke of himself; but she found, from his general conversation, that, in the possession of an affluent fortune, he had no other satisfaction than as it afforded him the means of bestowing individual benefits on his friends, or assisting, with general benevolence, the unfortunate of every description. While he was thus engaged, the heavy pressure, which early disappointment had laid on his heart, seemed to be lightened. When neither of these objects happened to be immediately within his reach, his spirits were extremely unequal; sometimes he was apparently careless and gay, talked of the pursuits which usually occupy men of his age with indifference; threw some degree of ridicule on the importance so frequently affixed to them; and declared himself a philosopher, a citizen of the world, who never meant to fix himself to any country, or any plan of life; and Rosalie observed with concern, that, after these efforts, of what she could not but consider as forced and artificial spirits, he sometimes sunk into the deepest dejection; when silent, absent, and with a countenance where melancholy and regret were strongly expressed, he appeared rather to suffer life than to enjoy it. He had general and brilliant talents, a mind highly cultivate, and a taste elegant and correct. There was no science to which he was a stranger, and every European language was familiar to him. Young as he was, he had seen a great deal of the world; and he had not merely seen it as it appears to a man of fortune, for his devolved to him by the death of an uncle and an elder brother; but was perfectly qualified to judge of the different receptions given by that world to a young man who has his way to make in it, or one who possesses a large independent fortune. This knowledge had matured his judgment, without narrowing his heart. The variety of countries he had visited, and the characters he had studied, rendered his conversation extremely entertaining; for, when his spirits were really good, it was enlivened by flashes of wit, or by anecdotes well told. In his most melancholy hours he would seek the company of Rosalie, and engage her insensibly in conversation, which naturally turned on Montalbert. Of an evening, as they sat on the deck together, this sort of discourse sometimes continued till Rosalie melted into tears, and till, her fears awakened and encouraged by thus recounting them, she deplored Montalbert as if certain of his death, while Walsingham, instead of attempting, as he had often done, to dissipate her apprehensions, wept too. The tears slowly stealing down his cheeks, till suddenly starting, he would seem to recollect the weakness, and indeed cruelty, towards Rosalie, of indulging and encouraging such emotions, and hastily bidding her good night, would hurry to the cabin of De Montagny.

  This respectable man, who had conceived a sincere affection for his English friend, had, when Rosalie was first mentioned to him, imagined, that Walsingham had met with some fair adventurer, and was, according to the usual morality of his country, extremely willing to assist him in taking advantage of such a meeting; but when he saw Rosalie, and had conversed with her, he was convinced that he had formed a wrong opinion, and began to be apprehensive lest such an acquaintance should have serious consequences for his friend. When he did not make a third in their conversations, he judged of what had passed by the manner of Walsingham after them. The third or fourth day of their voyage, which, for want of wind, was lengthened beyond what he had expected, he took occasion to ask Walsingham, very seriously, what he meant to do with his fair countrywoman?

"What I mean to do with her? (replied Walsingham).....Nay, but, my dear Sir, what a question is that?—To restore her certainly to her friends in England!—to this happy Montalbert, if he be living!"

"If you do so, my friend, (said De Montagny), let your name be enrolled by the side of Scipio's, for assuredly your merit will be as great."

"Not at all!—Scipio was enchanted by the beauty of his captive, or there would have been no merit in restoring her to her lover. Now I am not enchanted with the beauty of Mrs. Montalbert, superior as I acknowledge it to be to that of most women I have seen; therefore I shall have no merit in acting by her, as I ought, indeed, to act, even if I *were* enamoured of her. But you know, Chevalier, that to me the most lovely women are become mere objects of admiration, like the pictures and statues of Italy."

"Indeed I do not know, nor can I believe any such thing, my friend.—For example, I know not how to imagine, that, if this lady had been an antiquity, such as you professed to search for among the ruins of Formiscusa, that you would have stormed the castle for her relief."

"It would not have been necessary; but in fact it is begging the question, for had not the lady been young and handsome, she would never have been imprisoned there. However, Chevalier, I trust that any woman in distress would have commanded my services, as I am sure she would yours, merely because she was a distressed woman."

"*My* services are dedicated, you know, to the distressed of every description; but to damsels in trouble I can be considered of little more importance than their confessors when once my service is ended, for I am but a kind of military monk: but you, my good friend, at the age of three or four and twenty, are, perhaps, a protector for a very young and very pretty woman, who might be less exceptionable in Italy, than among Messieurs les Anglais."

"You do not suppose then (said Walsingham) that Montalbert can be such a fool, or such a brute, as to be displeased that his wife has put herself under my protection to escape from the tyranny of his mother?"

"Oh, no!—(replied De Montagny); I suppose nothing......I only fear, that being continually with such a woman as Madame de Montalbert; hearing from those beautiful lips, professions of gratitude, and gazing on those charming eyes, filled with tears of tenderness, it may prove, at last, a very severe trial to my friend's fortitude, when the hour shall come in which he must give her back to this happy Montalbert."

"Would to Heaven that were to happen to-morrow, (answered Walsingham, clasping his hands, and speaking with warmth)—would to Heaven it might be to-morrow that I could see her happy!"

"I wish it were, (said De Montagny drily); but if, when the time is past, you can inform me that you really felt, as you now believe you shall *then* feel, I may then proclaim my friend the most extraordinary man of his age in the three kingdoms of his master."

"I verily believe I shall claim you eulogium, De Montagny, and I here promise honestly to relate to you what passes in my heart at that time.....Ah! (added he, with a deep-drawn sigh), you have no conception, my dear Chevalier, of the hold that such an attachment, as mine, to a lovely woman, who is now no more, has on the heart.—I say, *you* can have no idea of it, because, designed from your early youth for the Order of Malta, you never allowed yourself to form such attachments as were at all serious; but *I* feel it to be impossible ever to love another, and all my hopes of felicity are buried in the grave of my Leonora."

"All that is very well. I am sure you now think what you say; but—we have read, and even seen, certain events, that dispose me to believe much in the influence of time and despair, as remedies for these violent passions...........In short - - - - - - - - -"

"In short! (interrupted Walsingham); you don't believe the passion can exist when the object is no more?"

"I believe it is *transferable*, my friend, if not curable: I have seen—oh! I know not how many instances of it.......You have read perhaps, or, perhaps, you have seen a little after-piece, on the French stage, called Le Veus?"

"Oh! (exclaimed Walsingham impatiently), if we were to give up every sentiment as ridiculous, that your writers, or your dramatists, attempt to render so, there would not be left, in the human heart, one virtue to reconcile us to the misery of existence."

De Montagny, who meant not to hurt his friend, seeing that he took the matter more seriously than was intended, let the conversation drop, and Walsingham, whose spirits were much agitated, went upon deck, where the stars reflected in the clear expanse of a sea so perfectly calm, that the vessel did not perceptibly move; the stillness of the night, scarcely disturbed by its prow, and the mildness of the air, restored him to a more tranquil state. He bade the steersman and a boy, who was on the first watch, begin the evening hymn sung by the Maltese sailors. He sat down on the gunwale, and bore a part; the tumult of his spirits entirely subsided, and he began to wonder how they had been so disturbed!—"But it provokes me, (said he, as he reflected on the matter)—it provokes me, that a man of such good sense, and so excellent a heart, should adopt prejudices so entirely the result of the manners of his country, and his own particular mode of education....How *can* he, with sentiments so generally honourable, believe that I could suffer myself to feel, for this charming woman, any other degree of tenderness than might be inspired by an amiable sister?—No!—to suppose me capable of other views, is to destroy the pleasure I take in protecting and serving her; and why would he rob me of the only happiness I am now capable of tasting?—In love with Mrs. Montalbert, or in danger of becoming so!—Good God! how can he think so?—When I see her, I am calm and contented; when my heart throbs with recollected anguish, I hear her voice, and forget that I am miserable. She speaks of her husband, and I weep with her; she caresses her child, and I weep still more! If I loved her, the name of this husband would be hateful to me, and I should be jealous even of her maternal affection....Alas! I know I have severely learnt what love is, and I am sure the sensations I now feel have nothing to do with it."

As if, however, Walsingham, convinced of this himself, was conscious of the propriety there was in Rosalie's knowing it too, he now took every occasion when they were alone, and still more particularly when the Chevalier de Montagny was with them, to speak in stronger terms than ever of his widowed affections; and that he considered himself as wedded to the memory of his adored Leonora.—Rosalie seemed to hear him with mingled emotions of compassion and regard; she pitied the anguish he felt, and respected the constancy of his affection. He repeated one of the tenderest sonnets of Petrarch, and then an imitation of it, which he had written; and Rosalie, notwithstanding the advantage the Italian language gives to this species of composition, preferred Walsingham's imitation. De Montagny, an unprejudiced spectator of these scenes, saw that Rosalie's heart was at present secure; but he every day fancied he had more reason to tremble for that of his friend.

    At length, after being twice the time they had calculated on their passage, they landed at Marseilles. Walsingham secured a lodging for Rosalie in the most retired part of the town, where he hired a female servant to attend her, and he went himself to an hotel. Her heart thanked him for this delicacy; nor was she less sensible of the kindness of the Chevalier de Montagny, who, purely from motives of friendship to Walsingham, and of compassion to her, had taken a voyage of some length, and attended to her the whole time with as much good-nature and humanity as if he had been her nearest relation. It was, therefore, with infinite regret that she bade him farewell, when, three days after her arrival at Marseilles, he waited on her, with Walsingham, and told her his ship was then taking up its anchors, and that, in the evening, he should go on board, and get under weigh for Malta.

CHAP.

THE port of Marseilles was crowded with English vessels, for, after a war, trade suddenly revives. Walsingham, therefore, had his choice of conveyances by sea; but he doubted whether he ought not to propose to Rosalie making the journey by land to Calais. Long accustomed to travel, the method of going from place to place was indifferent to him, and his choice was usually determined by the opportunities offered of seeing some object worth notice that had not before fallen within his observation. As he had passed three times from the south of France to England, and every time by a different route, he had no curiosity to gratify, even if his attention to Rosalie had allowed him, in the present instance, to think of any other object in his way.

When, therefore, he bade adieu to his friend De Montagny, which lowered and depressed his spirits extremely, he walked to the lodgings of Rosalie, who had all day expected him, for De Montagny had taken leave of her the day before, and she imagined him gone. New alarms had possessed her, on the reasonableness of which she wished to have consulted Walsingham, but it was evening before he came, and then with so dejected an air, and a countenance so melancholy, that Rosalie fancied some new disaster, she knew not what, had overtaken them, and was afraid to ask. Walsingham, however, told her, that, believing it to be her wish to reach England as expeditiously as possible, he was come to hear her commands on that subject; the whole purpose of his present visit being to know how and when she would depart.

"Alas! Sir, (replied she, hurt, yet hardly conscious that she was so, at something in his manner which appeared unusual)——Alas! Sir—I know so little of travelling, or of the advantages or disadvantages of different roads, or different conveyances, that I must refer myself entirely to you. I only know, that the method which would be the least troublesome to you, would, on that account, be the most agreeable to me - - - - - -." Her voice faltered. "Yet there is one apprehension (added she) that I have to-day been taught to entertain, which has extremely alarmed me. I am told that the small-pox, of a malignant sort, is at Marseilles—if my child - - - - -."

Walsingham immediately comprehended what she would say. "I intended (said he) to have mentioned to you, what, I find, some person has anticipated; it will undoubtedly be a reason for you to hasten from hence. I have, I believe, often told you, dear Madam, (added he, lowering and softening his voice), that I have no use for the fortune I possess, but that of assisting my friends.....Alone upon this earth, with no very near relations, nor any distant ones who want my assistance, there are no claims on my property, to me a great part of it is useless—you would give it value by using it. After such a declaration you will not suppose that the difference of expence, between a journey by sea or land, ought to be a consideration. There would even be an indelicacy in my naming the subject, had you not once or twice talked of expence. There is then only to consider, whether you prefer going by sea to England, or travelling across France to Calais, or any other ports; consult your own ease and safety, and that of your dear little boy."

Rosalie, still unable to decide, and still more unable to express what she felt of obligation to him, was silent for some moments, and then referred herself again to him. At length, having weighed the fatigue of a very long journey by land, against the possible delays by sea, for there was hardly any *danger* to be named at such a season of the year, it was agreed that Walsingham should engage their passage in the most commodious ship he could find; and though Rosalie, who dreaded nothing so much as being troublesome to her benefactor, expressed but little of the anxiety she suffered about her child, Walsingham understood her, and, without saying he should do so, he took care to hire a vessel in which there was a surgeon and a stock of medicines. It had lately been engaged to bring over an English nobleman for the recovery of his health, and the accommodations and medical attendant, which had been engaged for him, seemed most fortunately at hand for Rosalie. The price demanded Walsingham gave at once, with a farther sum on condition that the captain should immediately depart, without waiting for any other passengers. Money is so forcible an advocate, that the captain was convinced it was his interest to comply with this request, and every thing was soon ready.

In little more than a week from her landing at Marseilles, Rosalie embarked for England, having written from thence to Naples, and enclose her letter to Montalbert to the English Minister.

During a very prosperous voyage Walsingham behaved to her with the affection of a brother; but as they had now lost the society of the Chevalier de Montagny, who used, with great propriety, to break their too-frequent tête-à-têtes, Walsingham lived more in his own cabin than he had done when they were on board the Maltese vessel, and was, or affected to be, engaged in the study of Arabic, in which language he had purchased some curious manuscripts at Marseilles. When these studies happened to be the subject of his conversation with Rosalie, he said he was making himself acquainted with Arabic, because, having already visited almost every part of Europe, he thought his next voyage would be to Asia. He frequently repeated this before the captain and the doctor, as they called, a surgeon's mate who was on board, and they, as well as the sailors, who heard the same thing from Walsingham's servant, could not but wonder that such a young man, who was happy enough to have so very pretty a woman belong to him, should be of so restless a disposition. That Rosalie was his mistress they none of them at all doubted, notwithstanding his reserved and respectful behaviour towards her; but he was too rich and too generous for them to make such remarks, as they would certainly have indulged themselves in, had their passengers been of inferior fortune.

Though to see England had been the first wish of Rosalie's heart ever since the miserable day that drove her from Sicily, though she knew all her friends she had on earth were to be found there, and though she had persuaded herself she should meet Montalbert there, yet, as she approached it, her anxiety became excessive; and when the man at the mast head cried Land! as they entered the Channel, her heart beat, as if, in a few moments, her destiny was to be decided. Now like clouds, doubtful and indistinct, the white cliffs rose above the horizon; and now they gradually become more visible, till, at length, from the deck were discerned those towering boundaries of the coast; which——
"Conspicuous many a league, the mariner
"Bound homeward, and, in hope already there,
"Greets with three cheers exulting!!!"

COWPER.

Rosalie gazed at them with eyes filled with tears, and silently demanded—"Is Montalbert there?—Ah! do the friends—the few friends that love me, yet exist?"—While Walsingham, though from different motives, seemed to be affected in the same manner, he, alas! knew, that England held only the ashes of her whom he had loved; but though tempted to say——
"Sento l'aura mia anlica; e i dolci colli
"Veggio apparir onde'l bel lume naeque
"Che tenne gli occhi miei, mentr'al ciel piaque
"Bramosi, e lieti; or Ii tien tristi, e molli
"O caduche speranze, or pensier folli!

"Vedove l'erbe, e torbido son l'acque: &c."

PETRARCH.

Yet, amidst this natural and just regret, which he had hitherto been proved to nourish, he was conscious that, if when they went on shore, he was to take leave of Rosalie, he should feel a new deprivation, which would make all his wounds bleed afresh.

This sentiment, however, he ventured not to communicate to her, nor had he ever yet found courage to ask her what were her intentions, or how she meant to dispose of herself after they landed at Falmouth, where he had engaged the ship to put them ashore?—When within an hour's sail, with trembling and hesitation, which he vainly endeavoured to conquer, he at last inquired to what part of England she meant to go?

Rosalie, though she had considered this before, had never steadily thought on what would be her best plan to pursue. Since, however, as it was now necessary to determine on something, she said she would wait wherever she landed, or in the nearest convenient town, till she could receive letters from Mrs. Vyvian, to whom she meant immediately to write, under cover to Mrs. Lessington, the only means by which she could be sure of a letter reaching her. The heart of Rosalie sunk when she recollected the state of health in which she had left her mother, and when her mind ran back to the many months of her absence, she trembled to reflect on what might, in such an interval, have been the consequence of that injured health, and of, perhaps, increasing anxiety. All her hopes were centered in her mother; from her only she could receive protection and comfort—from her only obtain information of Montalbert; till, therefore, she could hear of Mrs. Vyvian, she could herself form no settled plan.

She related as much to Walsingham as appeared necessary to account for her remaining in whatever part of England she landed, till she had answers to the letters she should write immediately on her arrival. He observed to her, that it would then be much better for her to be at an easier distance from London, and proposed that, instead of landing at Falmouth, he should engage the captain to go on to Portsmouth, for which the wind was extremely favourable. Rosalie readily assented; since she should in that country be very near the place which she once considered as her home. One of those, whom she had believed her sister, was an inhabitant of Chichester, another resided not far from thence; and though she felt no inclination to appear before these her relations, while her situation was liable to misinterpretations, yet there was something consoling in the reflection that she should be within reach of some persons she knew, and who could have no reason, when they were informed she was the wife of Mr. Montalbert, to be otherwise than proud of the connection.

The same fears that had disturbed Rosalie at Marseilles, for the health of her infant boy, assailed her when she landed with him at Portsmouth. There was no source for that evening but an inn; this and many other considerations induced her to wish to quit the town as soon as possible; and now she thought with confusion and anguish of mind, which had been less felt while they were both citizens of the world, that she was entirely dependent for subsistence on the friendship of Walsingham, to whom she was already but too much obliged. How could she reconcile this to pride, or to propriety? Yet there was no remedy; for till she could receive answers from Mrs. Vyvian, what resource had she?—The conduct of Mr. Walsingham had been delicate and generous; the more she was unavoidably in his power, the more reserved he became. But though she knew her own innocence, and was assured of his honour, she could not recollect, without apprehension, that she was now in her native country; that she had quitted it without daring to avow her marriage, and had since been lost to all her former connections; that she now must appear in a very equivocal character, and that few would listen to, and fewer still believe, an account of the extraordinary circumstances that had brought her into her present situation. Circumscribed, as was her knowledge of the world, she had seen enough of it to know that a very moderate share of beauty excited the envy of every woman who has less, and that there are crowds of gossipping people, to whom such a story, as her's appeared to be, would afford the highest gratification, and from whom it might excite the most cruel remarks.

To hide herself, therefore, from the eyes of curiosity and malevolence, till she could appear properly acknowledged and protected, ought certainly to be her determination; but whither should she go, and by whom should she be guided?—It was not possible for her to communicate to Walsingham the painful sensations these reflections brought with them; but he saw them in her eyes, in her manner, and he heard them in the tremulous accents of her voice—yet he knew almost as little as she did how to begin a conversation which every moment rendered more necessary. He sat looking at her, as she was writing to Mrs. Vyvian and Mrs. Lessington, considering what he ought to say, when, having finished her letters, Rosalie laid down the pen, and said, in a half-whisper, "And whither shall I tell my friends to direct their answers?"——This, though rather a soliloquy than an address to Walsingham, gave him occasion to say, "You will determine, dear Madam, whither you like to go......You will recollect, I hope, that I have only to obey you, and - - - - - - - -;" he hesitated—Rosalie, speaking faintly, interrupted him.

"If I knew (said she) any village near this place - - - - - - - - -."

"I mean not to dictate, (cried Walsingham, recovering himself). If you have no particular reasons for wishing to be near Portsmouth, I think any, indeed almost every, situation equally within reach of London, and of a daily post from thence, would be preferable. I have heard you speak of having once lived in the neighbourhood of Chichester; it is at an easy distance from hence, and - - - - - -."

"Oh! no—(said Rosalie), not Chichester—I cannot go thither.......I do not (continued she) wish to have it known there that I am in England till - - - - - - -."

Walsingham did not give her time to finish her sentence, but said, "Would you then like to go nearer London, or to some retired place on the sea coast, where, at this season, there will be very few people, and where you may meet with accommodations, in regard to lodgings, which country towns do not afford?"

"That would certainly be the most eligible, (replied Rosalie). I have no wish to approach London, (added she sighing), till I know what hope there is of my meeting there, or at least hearing there of, Mr. Montalbert."

"Have you ever visited any of these villages on the coast? (inquired Walsingham);—Is there one you prefer?"

"I was once at Eastbourne, (answered she, and it was at this time of the year. I remember thinking the country around it extremely pleasant, and there was then no company, or only one or two invalids."

"I know the place, (said Walsingham), and I believe you cannot fix better. It is necessary to determine, because you must give your friends your address before the post goes out."

"I will say then, that at the post-office at Eastbourne my letters are to be left.—But—I cannot help feeling uneasy that the wife of Mr. Montalbert should appear; perhaps I am wrong, Sir—but my situation is a very delicate one......I could wish my real name were not known till my family owns me - - - - -" she stopped; but Walsingham saw she meant more than she had courage to utter.——"My dear Madam, (said he), that is a matter on which I cannot even give my opinion; your own good sense must decide upon it. You will determine, (said he, getting up and leaving the room), and when you have done so, I will set out myself to secure your accommodations, as I conclude you will go from hence as early as you can."

Left then to decide for herself, and having very little time to do so, she hastily resolved to drop her own name till she heard from her mother, and requested that the answers she solicited might be enclosed to Mrs. Sheffield, (the first name that occurred to her), to be left at the post-office Eastbourne. Having sealed and sent out her letter, Walsingham returned. He heard what she had done, and then said, that as she might not travel in perfect security, attended only by a servant, he would, with her permission, go on first, bespeak post-horses on the road, and procure her lodgings at the place she had fixed upon—adding, "I will give proper directions to Waters, (his servant), so that you will have no trouble, and, I hope, not much fatigue......You will sleep on the road!"

"If you think it necessary, (answered Rosalie); but I do not recollect the distance, nor the stages, having never travelled along the coast. It will not be necessary, I suppose, to sleep at Chichester?"

Walsingham answered that he thought Brighthelmstone would be preferable, and then said, "I shall see you on Saturday at Eastbourne, I hope in health and safety; and afterwards (continued he, half-suppressing a sigh) I shall—that is, you know, I *must* take my leave, and once more, unless I can be of any farther use to you, become a dissipated wanderer, seeking for something that may supply the place of happiness."

Then, without staying to hear those thanks which Rosalie endeavoured to utter, he departed, and in about a quarter of an hour Waters came to her with a letter, which he told her his master, who was gone, had left for her. The man then desired to know at what hour the next morning she would be pleased to have the chaise ready, and, having received her orders, went away, leaving her to peruse her letter.

CHAP.

LETTER.

THERE are a thousand occasions in life, in which I feel that writing is better than speaking. When either the person I am speaking to, or the matter I am speaking upon, interests me greatly, I am the worst orator in the world; and, therefore, my fair fellow traveller, I write to you, for you must be convinced that I am deeply concerned for you and for your future happiness.

Though I have not the pleasure of being acquainted with Mr. Montalbert, yet I will flatter myself that, when we meet, I shall find in him another friend.

He must be generous, amiable, and candid, for he is beloved by Rosalie; but as we know not when he will return, and as I am, according to the opinion of the world, too young for a guardian, we must—ah! how cruel a necessity!—submit to the rigid ordinances of prudence; and, though I own to you that I shall relinquish the greatest pleasure of my life when I leave you, yet I mean to remain no longer at the village, whither you are going, than to see you settled. This, I know, is what I ought to do, since, however, disinterested my regard for you may be, the world is too uncandid, and too little refined, to give me credit for possessing such sentiments. You are infinitely amiable, and I am probably allowed no more virtue than other young men, thought I hope and I think I have never deserved the character of a libertine....All this, my dear Madam, you could not say to me, but I know you have thought it. Half my acquaintance would laugh at *me* for saying it, but I am accustomed to do what I know to be right, and to disregard every kind of censure which is not incurred by actions really bad.

With this turn of mind, and after what I have said, you will believe that I would not propose any scheme, merely to gratify myself, which should break in upon the regulations that seem necessary for your sake; nor will I, without your approbation, execute that I have in view. A friend of mine has a house at Hastings, whither he goes with his family for a month or two in the autumn, the only time when his engagements at the bar allows him to be absent from London. I once passed a few days with him there, and I am on that footing of intimacy which allows me to ask for the use of his house. He knows I am an unsettled itinerant, and will not be surprised at my sudden appearance in England, although he has lost sight of me for eighteen or twenty months, and believes me either in Spain, Portugal, or Italy; I shall tell him (what is true) that I am come home for a short time; that it is not convenient for me to be so far from London as at my own house in the west; and that this, united with a wish of being retired, are my reasons for borrowing his house at Hastings; I shall be within such a distance as to have continually the power of learning how and when I may be serviceable to you....Will you then give me your permission to remain there?—My visits to Eastbourne shall be regulated by your orders, and surely the most vigilant and censorious prudery cannot object to the friendly and unfrequent visits of a brother to a sister. Oh! would you were really my sister, with what delight should I then avow the interest I take in your happiness; suppose yourself to be so, I entreat you, and honour me by accepting the enclosed without ever mentioning the subject, lest I should doubt your honouring me with that esteem as to allow me to use that affectionate names of friend and brother, when I am permitted to assure you of the regard and esteem of,

Dear Madam,
Your most faithful
and obliged servant,

F. WALSINGHAM.

The enclosure was a bank note of a hundred and fifty pounds.

Rosalie, whose tears had fallen, she hardly knew why, while she read this letter, could not immediately determine how she ought to answer it. She had, it was true, time enough to consider it on her journey, but it hung upon her spirits, and drove sleep from her eyes. After placing, however, in every point of view, the intention which he so delicately asked her permission to execute, she thought there would be not only prudery and ingratitude in refusing her assent, but that it would show a mistrust, which she saw as degrading to herself and unjust towards him. The money which he sent her gave her more concern, yet she considered that it was less uneasy to her feelings to receive it in this manner, than to be laid under the painful necessity of applying to him for small sums, should she wait long for the letters she expected, and, till they arrived, what other resource had she?—The hope, ever alive in her heart, that Montalbert would soon return, and gratefully repay all the pecuniary favours she owed Walsingham, reconciled her to this temporary obligation, which she knew could be no inconvenience to him.

In the morning she arose, impatient to begin her journey, and sent for Waters to get the note changed in order to pay her expences; but he informed her, that it was already done, and that his master had given him directions for the journey in the same manner as when he travelled himself.

Rosalie, her Marseilloise maid Claudine, and the object of her constant solicitude, her child, were place in a chaise, which Waters had hired for the whole journey, to avoid the trouble and delay of changing baggage, and they were very soon at Chichester. As she passed through that town, and sat at the door of the inn, while the horses were putting to, a thousand recollections crowded upon her mind. The objects, formerly so familiar to her, brought back the days of Rosalie Lessington, and the strange vicissitudes that had happened since seemed rather like the fictions of romance than reality; she was then the daughter of a village curate, humbled by her supposed sisters, and shrinking with terror from paternal authority, which seemed likely to compel her to marry a man she disliked. Her present situation formed a strong contrast to that she was then in; but what was better?—She was now the daughter of parents who did not own her, a wife without a husband, and the mother of an infant who seemed to have been born to misfortunes. While she indulged these mournful thoughts she did not venture to show herself, lest she should be known; this precaution was fortunate, for just before the horses were put to her chaise, her former admirer, Hughson, mounted on an ungovernable horse, pranced up to the side of it. The beast was impatient to enter the stable; the chaise in which Rosalie sat was immediately before the gateway of the inn yard, and Hughson, ever solicitous to show his horsemanship, (though he now little thought to whom), spurred and irritated his horse; it began to rear and kick with a violence, which, for a moment, made her apprehend some mischief to the chaise that might compel her to get out. This fear, however, lasted but a moment; the contest between the horse and his rider, the latter of whom seemed much the least rational of the two, was ended, at least in that spot, for the former springing away with great swiftness was instantly out of sight, while the boys and people in the street, staring after him, exclaimed, "That Parson Hughson's horse had run'd clear away wi un."

Fortunately it was the contrary road to that which Rosalie was going; but the carriage had hardly proceeded ten paces farther before she saw Blagham walking with a gentleman of the neighbourhood whom she well remembered. She now rejoiced that she was going a distance from these her old acquaintance, whose notice and intrusion it was improbable she could have escaped had she remained at any place within their reach; a consideration which had confirmed her resolution of going into the eastern part of the country.

  The remainder of her journey passed without any particular occurrence or accident. She often amused herself by calculating the time when it was probable Montalbert would receive the letter which she had written to him from Marseilles; but this depended so much on circumstances, that there were no date on which her mind could rest with satisfaction.—The time when she might assure herself of an answer from her real, and her supposed, mother, was more easily ascertained, and to that she looked forward with the hope of having much of her present uncertainty and uneasiness alleviated. Just before the chaise mounted the high down immediately before the village, she saw Walsingham watching for her approach. He did not, however, stop the chaise, but gave Waters a direction to the house he had taken, that there might be no necessity for her to drive first to an inn. Rosalie was presently set down at the door of this house, which, though the most retired, was one of the most commodious lodgings in the village; when her baggage was taken out, and the chaise discharged, Walsingham made his appearance. He inquired eagerly how she found herself after her journey, and how her little boy was?—then asked, if she approved of her apartments?—He told her dinner was ready, and solicited leave to dine with her, adding that he had a chaise ready to carry him away as soon as dinner was over. All this passed with a rapidity which Rosalie easily saw was intended to prevent any conversation on the subject of his letter; and, indeed, she had neither courage or inclination to enter upon it at that moment. Dinner was served immediately; it passed in common conversation, Rosalie trying, but not very successfully, to bear her part. It was hardly over, and the servant withdrawn, when Waters came in to say that the chaise, his master her ordered, was ready at the inn. Walsingham directed to him to put his baggage into it, and wait there till he came; then, turning to Rosalie, he gravely said——

  "And now, dear Madam, it depends upon you to decide whither I shall go? If you think there is the least impropriety in my staying so near you at Hastings, I will direct my course to London....Alas! (added he), no place affords me happiness; and I have at this time no other purpose than to contribute what may be in my power to yours."

  Rosalie, pained and confused, knew not what to answer. A sense of all the obligations she owed to this excellent friend pressed heavily on her mind; she believed those obligations had been conferred with the most disinterested views, and, cautious as he seemed to be to avoid every other interpretation, she thought that to insist cause she resided in it, would be not only a needless and absurd piece of prudery, but imply a doubt of his motives; she was conscious too of her unprotected situation, and could not but be sensible that to have this friend within a short distance was a most desirable circumstance for her; neither did she imagine, as nothing was known of her, and but little of him in this country, that censure could find food for its malevolence in their residing, perhaps, for a short time only, within miles of each other. After some hesitation, therefore, she told him, that such was her opinion of his good sense, and such her conviction of the real friendship he bore her, that she was persuaded she might leave it entirely to him to act as was most agreeable or convenient to himself; at the same time she took from her pocket the bank note he had enclosed to her, entreating him to allow her to return it.

  The conclusion of Rosalie's speech seemed to hurt, as much as the beginning of it had gratified Walsingham.—"Ah! Mrs. Montalbert, (said he), can you talk of few services I have had the good fortune to render you, and yet mention such a trifle as that?—I beseech you do not mortify me, by suffering any obligation of this nature to dwell on your mind."

  Rosalie, however, insisted of giving him an acknowledgement of it in writing, to which he unwillingly consented. He then entreated her to let him know the moment she heard from her friends; asked if he might not ride over some morning about the time she expected her letters, as he had sent for his horses. Having received her assent, and tenderly caressed her little boy, he left her with visible reluctance, and, going to the inn, threw himself into the post-chaise that was to convey him to Hastings.

Rosalie, being now left alone, endeavoured to calm her spirits, so long the sport of incertitude and anxiety. Nothing could immediately occur to disturb her transient quiet, for it was yet some days before it was possible for her to receive the answers from Mrs. Lessington, which she had so earnestly solicited. It might even be prolonged, if, as was possible, Mrs. Vyvian was in the north.

Rosalie found that every thing had been settled in her new abode, where the people of the house were to attend her. The woman was very civil, and seemed to have no curiosity to learn more than she had been told of her new lodger, whom Walsingham had represented as a young lady, his distant relation, who was in expedition of her husband from Italy, and that her stay in Eastbourne was uncertain. It might be only a few weeks, or it might be much longer. An uncertainty that afforded a prospect of great advantage to this landlady, while the liberality, with which her terms had been agreed to, aided the favourable impression that could hardly fail to be given by the innocence, beauty, and sweetness of Rosalie's countenance and manner.

Claudine, carrying the infant boy, was the constant companion of her mistress's walks, which beguiled the greatest part of every day, and were varied between the green and shady lanes, open downs, or the immediate borders of the sea. On the sea itself Rosalie often fixed her eyes for hours, and her imagination went forth in conjectures about Montalbert, which became less and less pleasant as time stole on. From these pensive wanderings she constantly returned at the hours when letters were delivered, and impatiently inquired if there were any addressed to Mrs. Sheffield; but a week wore away, and none arrived; yet it was certain that she might have had an answer in that time; Walsingham too had reckoned the termination of a week as a period when intelligence was almost certain, and he, therefore, availed himself of the permission he had received to come over.—Rosalie rejoiced to see him, and sought not to conceal the satisfaction it gave her, while he appeared more dejected and melancholy than she had ever yet known. He had now no object in view on which to exercise his benevolence; nothing to rouse him from the despondence which so frequently obscured the faculties of his mind; and to this cause, Rosalie, who knew from observation that he required some generous motive for active exertion, attributed the gloom which hung over him.

This heavy depression of spirits seemed to break away after he had conversed with her an hour or two, and, in proportion as she appeared uneasy at the delay of Mrs. Lessington's answer, he found reasons to appease that fiend Inquietude. At length they began to converse on indifferent subjects, and, during their walk on the hill, attended by Claudine, who was always directed to follow them, Walsingham insensibly led the discourse to his own history and affairs. He talked of his family, and lamented that he was left an isolated being in the world. "I have now (said he) no nearer relation than a cousin of nearly my own age, who inherits a very large fortune from another branch of my family, and from his mother, who was an heiress; but our dispositions and our pursuits are so different, that we never associate, and have rarely met in England but on some family business.—Sommers Walsingham is one of the most gay and dissipated young men about town; plays a great deal, and has establishments and connections in a style of expence, where I have little inclination to rival him. He was abroad when I was there last; the French and Italians, among whom we occasionally met, were so dazzled by the superior splendour of this my magnificent cousin, that they distinguish him by the title of Milor Walsingham, while I was only

Le Chevalier. I have often thought it singularly unfortunate, that the only remaining relation I have should be a man with whom I cannot be on a footing of friendship, especially as when I die, for I shall now never marry, he will possess all my landed property, which is entailed on the next male heir."

"I hope (said Rosalie) that you will live very long to enjoy it yourself, and then transmit it to a family of your own."

"There *was* (answered Walsingham) a time when I thought I might be so happy—but that is now over!—For me, all prospect, all possibility, of happiness is vanished—never, alas! to return."——A long and mournful pause now ensued, which Rosalie had no courage to break, though she would fain have spoken words of consolation. Walsingham at last, speaking lower, and in a more dejected tone, went on——

"For every evil, but that which I have endured, there may be a remedy—but the death of what we love!——Do you think there can be any sorrow so deep, and so incurable?"

"Yes, (answered Rosalie, believing that he found a sort of melancholy relief in this conversation), I think the estrangement of those we love may be almost as dreadful as their death - - - - - - - - - -." She could not proceed—for she was sensible that should either of these calamities assail her, should Montalbert have deserted her, or should death have divided him from her for ever, she should totally fail in that fortitude which she wished to recommend to her friend; and finding her voice refuse to continue the argument with firmness, she was glad of the interruption now given by Claudine, who, coming near her, said, "Madame, Viola la belle Dame qui m'a si souvent loit depuis deux jours, et qui fait tant des caresses a notre petit."——Rosalie, who had hitherto avoided the very few strangers who were occasionally seen in the village, was now so near the person of whom Claudine spoke, that she could not escape her. But as she by no means desired to cultivate the acquaintance Claudine had thus begun, she hastily passed on, while the lady stopt the Frenchwoman, to whom she spoke in her own language with great ease and volubility. Her figure was very singular; she was not young, and her dress (then less common than now) was in that style which women affect who are above all prejudices, and look in a morning as if they passed the kennel; but though the habit and half boots might by symptoms of a masculine spirit, which some have believed to be the same thing as a masculine understanding, the pains which had evidently been taken about her face, which was very highly coloured, might convince the most superficial observer, that the toilet of this fair Amazonian was by no means neglected.

"Surely (said Walsingham) I have often seen that lady; it is, I think, a face familiar to me in public places; I cannot at this moment, recollect her name."

"I hope (said Rosalie) *I* shall not be under the necessity of making any acquaintance with her; do you think she is staying here?"

"Probably, (answered he); but you may easily avoid her.....Nothing is more common than for people, who are, what they fancy, retired for a few weeks to some of these places, to live in a constant exercise of the most impertinent curiosity. Oh! I believe I now recollect who that is."

"She has sometimes a friend with her, (said Rosalie), a younger woman, and of a less manlike appearance; but though they live, as Claudine tells me, in the same house, and the other scorns to be a sort of companion, I observe she is often sitting with a book in her hand, and frequently seems meditating or composing."

To this Walsingham did not answer, and, during the rest of their walk, which Walsingham sought purposely to lengthen by going about the woody environs of the nobleman's house[1] in the neighbourhood, he appeared to sink into more than his former dejection. It was now late in the month of June, and the sun was declining in all the radiance of that delicious month; Rosalie, to whose recollection it brought the evening sky, which she had so often, with a despairing heart, contemplated from Formiscusa, made some remark on the beauty of the scene; to which Walsingham, looking a moment earnestly and mournfully in her face, said sighing, yet with a kind of impatient quickness——

"Ah! do not talk to me of the splendour of the sun—of the beauty of nature! All—all is dead to me!—I enjoy nothing - - - - - -" then pausing, he added, in a low and plaintive voice——
"Mon Cœur n'a plus rien sur la terre
"Je ne peux plus aimer, je ne peux mourir
"Pune et fainte amitié, doux charme de la vie
"Je t'immolai l'amour; mais qu'il m'en couté
"Rends du moins le repos a mon ame fletrie
"On dit que tu suffis pour la felicité
"Loin de me soulager, tu comble ma misere
"Je remplis mon destin, je suis nés pour souffrir.
"Mon cœur n'a plus rien sur la terre
"Je ne peux plus aimer; je ne peux mourir."

Then pausing, he repeated the last lines with some little variation——
"Mon cœur n'a plus rien sur la terre
"Ah! je n'ose plus aimer, et ne peux mourir."

Rosalie, who understood perfectly the force of these pathetic lines, could not help being sensibly affected. She did not know they were a quotation[2]; and was at once surprised and pained by the particular manner in which the two last lines were a second time spoken. Equally unwilling and unable to make any remarks on what she had heard, and Walsingham appearing to be disinclined to converse, they both continued silent till they reached a place where one path led to the inn, and another to the habitation of Rosalie; Walsingham there wished her a good evening, and telling her he should be over again soon, to know if her letters were arrived, he departed.

CHAP.

Notes

↑ Lord George Cavendish's.
↑ From the Galatic of the Chevalier de Florian.

ANOTHER week passed, and no letters!—Rosalie, who became ever hour more uneasy, now wished to consult Walsingham whether she ought not to write again, and was even forming schemes to find Charles Vyvian, who might, perhaps, be in England, in which case her friend could greatly have assisted her, but Walsingham appeared not. In the mean time, in her walks, Rosalie continually met the lady who had made an acquaintance with her little boy, and, who often courtesying to her as they passed, engaged her almost unavoidably to return the civility. Her abode, indeed, was no longer so retired as it had been.

In proportion as the summer advanced, several families, who shunned the more gay and populous bathing places, arrived; and though none of them, except the lady in question, appeared at all disposed to make any acquaintance, Rosalie, who fancied herself the object of curiosity, was compelled to seek walks, more distant from the village, among the fields that arose behind it, or on a part of the sands farther from the general resort.

Every hour of her life was now embittered by increasing anxiety; for another, another, and another day passed without the answer she expected from Mrs. Lessington. At length she received, to her utter dismay and confusion, the letters she herself had written. That to Mrs. Lessington had been opened at the post-office and was now sealed with the office seal, while on the cover was written——"*No such person at Hampstead*;" and again "*Left Hampstead, no direction to be got whither gone.*"——The enclosure to Mrs. Vyvian was unopened.

The consternation and distress of Rosalie were now extreme, nor did she know what steps to take. After so many days of anxious suspense, she was farther than ever removed from the hopes of procuring that protection which she felt to be every day more necessary; farther than ever removed from the access to the only channel by which she might hope for intelligence of Montalbert, she now repented that she had felt so much reluctance to see or write to Mr. and Mrs. Blagham in her way from Portsmouth, and that she had not written, on her first arrival, to her other (some time) sister, Mrs. Grierson, either of whom could have informed her of Mrs. Lessington's having left Hampstead; a circumstance which had never occurred to her as possible, because not very probable.

To repair as immediately as she could an error, which she now suspected had arisen from false pride and false shame, she thought, although late, of making these applications; but having been so much accustomed to rely on the opinion of Walsingham, she hesitated whether she ought to take any measure without his participation. So many days had elapsed without his coming, that she thought he was, perhaps, gone to London, or had other engagements, and that his return might be uncertain. Indeed were he to be consulted, it would be impossible for him to give his opinion, since he neither knew the singular situation Rosalie was in as to her real mother, or the characters of the persons to whom she thought of applying. She recollected them, at least those of Blagham and his associates, with pain. If they appeared disgusting to her, when she had hardly been in societies of more elegance, they were likely to appear insupportable now that she had been accustomed to the intelligence and polished manners of Montalbert and Walsingham, to whom might be added Alozzi and De Montagny, who were men of fashion in their respective countries. But this contrast was not all that was likely to make Blagham appear disgusting to her; she dreaded his coarse raillery on her sudden departure from England, which she knew had been told in a manner very different from the truth, while the events she had to relate, as leading to her present circumstances, were so uncommon, and so little within the comprehension of people whose ideas had never travelled ten miles from their own homes, that she imagined she should inevitably expose herself to vulgar ridicule and malignant censure. The absence of Montalbert, and the presence of Walsingham, might be equally injurious to her reputation.

To the lingering suspense, therefore, in which she must remain, unless she adopted this expedient, any thing was preferable, and she determined to wait no more than one day, in which, if Walsingham did not appear, she would write to Mrs. Grierson and Mrs. Blagham, at the same time, and nearly in the same terms, that she might offend neither. The day passed, and Walsingham neither came nor sent. That evening, therefore, she sat down in a very dejected state of mind to compose these letters. Rosalie wrote with great ease and correctness; but, thought what she now wished to express required but few words, she never undertook a task which she found more difficult to perform.

To address two persons as her "dear sisters," who, she knew, were not related to her, was extremely irksome; that title, when they lived together under the same roof, and were called the children of the same parents, had obtained for her but little of their affection, and now, that she had been long estranged from them, she was afraid it would not procure her common civility. If she was considered by them as returning in an equivocal situation, they might repulse her as likely to need pecuniary assistance; if, on the contrary, she represented herself as the wife of Montalbert, a man whose fortune and rank in life was so much superior to those of the men they had married, she was sure of exciting their envy and indignation.——It was better, however, to be envied than pitied, and, knowing herself to be Montalbert's wife, she could not determine to appear in any other light, repenting that she had ever called herself by another name, for which she now thought her reasons were not sufficiently strong, and had been too hastily adopted.

At length she finished her two letters; in each of which she briefly stated her being returned to England without her husband, a circumstance which had arisen from events too tedious to relate; and she concluded with requesting to know where Mrs. Lessington was to be heard of, and whether her brother William, (the eldest Lessington, to whom she gave that name without reluctance), was still at Oxford. The uncertainty of this, as he was in expectation of a college living when she left England, was the only reason why she did not first apply to him.

Amid the extreme disquiet, which Rosalie was in about her mother, she could not but feel wonder and uneasiness at the long absence of Walsingham, who had now been more than a week without seeing her. The recollection of the melancholy state of mind, in which he last parted from her, added to her concern; for she fancied he might be ill, and she was too sure he was unhappy. Yet she saw the impropriety of communicating these fears to him, or even of expressing impatience at his not coming, when he might, perhaps, have other engagements; she knew, therefore, that she ought to wait, without impatience, his promised visit.

The little Montalbert was now between six and seven months old, and, from his strength and size, appeared to be more. Claudine was extremely fond and very careful of him, and was often entrusted with the care of him during a short walk, while Rosalie, who dreaded the observations that she had found were made upon her, confined herself more to the house.

Claudine, who was a lively Provinçale, was by no means so averse to society; and, though her mistress always directed her to go with the child into the most unfrequented walks, she generally contrived to find some admirable reason for choosing that where she was sure to meet "Des beaux Messieurs tres poli, ou quelques dames bein honnête; qui parloient un peu le Francois, et qui avoient tant, mais tant de bontis, pour elle, et tant de joli choses, a dire a son petit bon homme que c'etoit une charme."

Rosalie knew that her maid could tell nothing of her real situation, because she was ignorant of it, but she feared infinitely more what she might imagine, though the girl was always told that Mr. Walsingham was only a friend, who had taken care of her to England; and, though she had never seen any circumstance in his behaviour to contradict such an idea, yet Rosalie fancied she had, more than once, marked a sort of arch incredulity in the features of Claudine: but as she could not set about assuring her he was a mere friend, because that would rather confirm that avert suspicion, she contented herself with forbidding her to answer any questions that might be made by strangers, doubting, however, whether she would obey the injunction.

Rosalie, who saw new faces arrive at the place every day, occasionally formed wishes for a residence more secluded.—Yet when she considered that as soon as she could obtain intelligence of her mother, she should probably remove nearer to her; and when she adverted to the convenience of being in the house with very civil and quiet people, she thought herself hardly authorised to propose a change. She should undoubtedly have an answer very soon from one, or both her sisters, which might put an end at least in a great measure, to her present uncertainty.

Three days, however, passed before she found at the post-office the following letter——
"DEAR MADAM,

"THEY say that wondering makes one grow old, so my Kate and I will not wonder, but must confess ourselves a little surprised at hearing you were so near us, and had stolen a march upon us, when we thought you were among your Signors and Signoras, Italianos, and people quite out of our line; and my Kate is not so ready in the writing way as some ladies, (which I don't reckon among her faults I promise you), so you'll excuse my replying to your of 2d inst.— To be sure you must have dropped from the clouds, and have been quite in terra incognita, not to know that our good mother has quitted Hampstead these five or six months. I settled her affairs there for her when I went up on the matter of Poulcat versus Perriwinkle last Hilary; and she went to live with her son Francis, who, you know, was always a sort of favourite; but there was a rumpus at the house of Crab and Widgett, and he quitted and settled with his new-married wife at Carlisle. Sir Francis[1], when the King pleases, has picked up a pretty fortune I assure you, and is better off than our Episcopus, who has also married a wife, and so lost his fellowship; but he's got a living, though a small one, and I dare say will have a house full of sons and daughters. As to our olive branches, they flourish and increase, and my Kate has no chance of seeing much of the world this year, as we expect a third before its end; but as I must be at Grinstead, in a few days, for the summer assize, where I've three capital causes, I'll just peep upon you in my way. As to the Vyvians, you know, they are grand folks, much above our cut, so that we know nothing of them more than what every body knows. I heard that there *was* treaties going forward for the sale of Holmwood, but the entail made by *old* Montalbert could not be dock'd till the heir is of age; and they say he's not over and above willing to accommodate Papa and Mama: but more of this when we meet.—I am somewhat at a non plus how to direct, as my Kitty and I wonder why you should have an alias to your name; but I suppose you have good reasons.

I am, dear Madam,
Your humble servant,
JASPER BLAGHAM
Chichester
July 4, 1784."
The other letter ran thus:——
"MADAM,

"YOUR's we received.—My wife not being very well, this serves to inform you that Mrs. Lessington is at Carlisle, at Mr. Frank's, who is gone to live there, and she with him. I do not know that any other direction is required. My wife heard from her about six weeks ago; she was then in good health: wishing the same to you, with my wife's love and service,

  I am, Madam,
  Your very humble servant,
  DANIEL GRIERSON.
Brockhurst Upton Farm,
July 4, 1784.

     Though Rosalie had no reason to expect any other kind of letters than these from her two brothers-in-law, or rather those whom she had supposed such, her heart, naturally tender and affectionate, sunk in chill despondence when she reflected on the little regard there seemed to exist for her, among persons who had been accustomed to consider her as of their own blood; and who, she believed, had never been undeceived.—"Surely, (said she), had one of them been cast alone and unprotected into my neighbourhood, I should not have hesitated a moment in flying to their assistance."——Alas! had she known more of the world, she would have found this conduct of her supposed family too common to excite a moment's wonder; she would have seen that the man of law desired to reconnoitre her situation before he ventured even to profess kindness, lest he should find her in circumstances that might make such kindness expensive; while the gentleman farmer had no inclination to invite to his house a relation of his wife's, who was either humbled enough to give them some trouble, or in a style of life to mortify his wife by superior elegance, and give her occasion to make comparisons which might render her, who had been reckoned a great beauty, discontented with the inferior lot she had chosen. The coldness, however, of these letters, gave her only momentary pain; but she reflected with longer and more acute uneasiness, that the intelligence she had gained was not only unsatisfactory, but such as baffled the hopes she had entertained of being under the protection of Mrs. Vyvian. She now was almost determined to write immediately to her mother, but the caution she had received, and the dread lest her youngest daughter might be at the house, made her hesitate. It was possible too that Mrs. Vyvian might be removed from Hampstead, and to either of Mr. Vyvian's houses it was impossible for her to direct. One sentence in Blagham's letter was at once puzzling and alarming. It seemed to intimate not only a design on the part of Vyvian to sell Holmwood, which she thought would give infinite pain to his wife, but in intimated a dissention between the mother and the son, which appeared to Rosalie quite incomprehensible.

     All, however, that could now be done, was to write to Mrs. Lessington; but she knew it must be at least ten days before she could have an answer. Almost worn out by the cruel suspense she had so long been in, and feeling every hour an increasing distress about Montalbert, she looked forward with sensations of the deepest despondence, even to such an interval of solicitude and anxiety.

CHAP.

Notes

    ↑ By these names Mr. Blagham distinguished the two sons of Mr. Lessington.

THREE of these sad days were passed without any change in the situation of Rosalie; early on the morning of the fourth Walsingham appeared.

The moment he approached her she was struck with the expression of his countenance, where despair rather than dejection was marked; and, as intelligence relative to Montalbert was ever present to her mind, she was struck with the idea that Walsingham had learned, and was come to communicate, some evil that had befallen her husband. Without giving herself time to consider the probability of this, she advanced hastily towards him, and, with extreme emotion, inquired what sad tidings he brought her?——Walsingham, who perhaps rather expected a gentle reproach, for his long absence, than this sudden interrogatory, answered, dejectedly and somewhat coldly—"What have I to tell you, my dear Madam?—Alas! I have nothing *new* to tell you!"

Rosalie, checked and hurt by his manner and his answer, and not able immediately to recover herself from the emotion which she had felt, could only say faintly, "I beg your pardon; I thought—I fancied—I am so unhappy, (said she), that every thing alarms me."

She sat down, and Walsingham, moved by the sight of her distress, advanced towards her, and said, "If I had learnt any good news, my amiable friend, I should not have been absent so long, for I should have been eager to have communicated whatever might give you pleasure; if bad news that related to you, so unwilling am I to give you pain, that I fear, *at this time*, my spirits would shrink from so cruel, though, perhaps, so necessary an exertion of friendship."

"Have you *yourself* any new cause of uneasiness? (inquired Rosalie in a low and faltering voice)—I hope not!"

"Ah! Mrs. Montalbert, (replied Walsingham), does there then need any new cause?—Does, indeed, my unhappiness admit of addition?"

Rosalie, still doubting whether some calamity was not known to Walsingham which he had not the courage to tell her, related, in a few words, the circumstances that occurred since they last met; of her having the letter returned that she had sent to Mrs. Lessington, and the unsatisfactory answers she had received from Mr. Blagham and Mr. Grierson.—Walsingham read the two letters, and then said, "But what, my dear Madam, could you expect from these sort of people—I am sorry you applied to them."—Then thinking that he had spoken too contemptuously of Rosalie's relations, he added, "I only mean to say, that, from the slight sketches you have given me of these gentlemen in our desultory conversations on your affairs, it appears as if they were of an order of beings so different from her to whom I have the honour to speak, that nothing more than common civility could be expected of them."

"Their letters, I think, (said Rosalie, forcing a smile), hardly amount to that; but perceiving I had only to repair, as expeditiously as I could, the delay that has arisen, I have written to Mrs. Lessington according to the direction I obtained."

Walsingham then turned the conversation on indifferent subjects; but his thoughts appeared to be distracted, and his heart heavy. The morning was well calculated for exercise, for the sun, which was at that season too powerful at an early hour, was obscured by clouds, though without any immediate appearance of rain or storm—Rosalie, therefore, proposed to Walsingham a walk on the Downs, flattering herself that the gloom on his spirits might be dissipated by the pleasure he usually took in pointing out, with a degree of enthusiasm peculiar to himself, the various appearances of the sea, or the changing shadows of the landscape. Walsingham of course declared himself ready to wait on her, and they were just leaving the house, followed as usual by Claudine, when a smug pert figure came up to them, who looked as if he took great pains to appear like a gentleman, with very little success. To Walsingham he was unknown; but Rosalie immediately recognized Mr. Blagham, who, not at all abashed by seeing a stranger with her, pranced up to her, exclaiming, "Ah! my sweet sister-in-law, I have met you then at last! Long-parted friends, you know, (continued he, familiarly saluting her)—with this gentleman's leave, who, I suppose, is your spouse."—Rosalie, covered with blushes, answered coldly, "No, Sir—that is *not* Mr. Montalbert;" and then asking after Mrs. Blagham, she invited him in, though heartily wishing that he might not accept in the invitation.

"But you were going on a walk, (said he)—I beg I mayn't be any hindrance. I can't stay a moment—my head is full of business; a great number of causes I assure you....You know my way?——Vastly anxious always—eh!——and have hardly time to turn myself about. Well! but you look purely, my fair Rose!—I can't help remembering your former name, you see: you look charmingly—still as killing as ever—lilies and roses!—When shall we see Mr. Montalbert in England?"

"That is uncertain," replied Rosalie, who saw that, as Blagham was speaking, he turned his eyes inquisitively on Walsingham, with a look, as if to say—Ah! ah! Sir, who are you?"

Walsingham, suspecting that he might be the object of impertinent curiosity, and feeling already a decided aversion to Blagham, thought he should at once relieve Rosalie and himself by leaving her; he therefore said, that, as she was engaged, he would not now detain her, but would take his walk. Rosalie did not know, and yet dared not ask, whether she should see him again before he returned to Hastings, for she had yet many things to consult him upon. She saw him go without regret, and it was not without an effort that she concealed from Blagham what she suffered by this interruption.—Forcing, however, an appearance of tranquility she was far from feeling, and recollecting that she had now an opportunity of learning the particulars she so much wished to know in regard to the Vyvian family, she affected to listen with interest to the long detail Mr. Blagham gave her of his own affairs, which, he said, were very prosperous and flourishing; "and (then adding) you don't know all I have had to do with your poor quondam lover, little Hughson.......Egad! the poor fellow was over head in ears—in love—and, faith, in debt too. I had a fine time on't with Old Squaretoes his daddy, to make him down with the needful; but *at* last we got it all settled, and *I* patched up his pocket, poor rogue, though his heart was in a cruel plight for a long time!"

"If he had no other grievances, (said Rosalie), I think your friendship would have been put to no severe test; but pray tell me how and where are the Vyvians; I have been so circumstances since I have been abroad as to have had no opportunity of hearing of them."

"Why, I can give you as to those personages but little information: for since the young lady came down to Holmwood, they have never once been there, and it seems she took such a dislike to it, that, as the family were never likely to inhabit it, the Old Magnifico was trying to sell it."

"What young lady? (asked Rosalie); I don't comprehend who you mean?"

"Why, the fine lady that he married—Miss - - - - - - - Miss - - - - - - - - the Honourable Miss - - - - - - -;—Well! I have a vile memory for names. However, she was young enough to be his daughter, and belonged to a Lord's family, the lady he married."

"Who married?" cried Rosalie faintly.

"Why Old Vyvian....He married in less than half a year——faith, I think they said it was not above three months after the death of his wife."

"Gracious God! (exclaimed Rosalie, thrown quite off her guard by this shocking intelligence);——Dead!—my dear, dear benefactress—my best friend - - - - - -" Stunned, by a blow so cruel and unexpected, she became extremely giddy, a cold dew covered her face, and she leaned against the side of the window on the seat of which she was sitting. Blagham, who fancied she was going to be faint, began to call for help, and to ring the bell. Claudine was out with the child, Rosalie having sent her when she returned herself with Blagham; but Mrs. Hammond, the landlady, and her maid appeared, and the former, terrified at the pale countenance of her lodger, bestirred herself notably for salts, hartshorn, and water, exclaiming, at the same time, "Dear Madam, how ill you are!—Pray let me send for somebody.—Bless me I wish the gentleman was here—shall I send Jane to call him?"—"Oh!—no, no!"—was all Rosalie could say; but Jane, judging that nothing is so great a cordial as a friend, and having a very high opinion of Walsingham, from the liberality she had experienced from him, ran away without any farther orders, and Rosalie had not recovered from the first shock her senses had received, before Walsingham, who had not been far from the house, came in, and, agitated as much as the half-dead mourner before him, inquired, regardless of the presence of Blagham, what had been said to alarm her thus; then, turning in evident displeasure to Blagham, he cried, "Surely, Sir, this is very extraordinary!"

"I'm sure I think so, Sir, (answered the attorney, who did not half like the looks of Walsingham); for I had no notion that Mrs. Vyvian's death could have affected Miss Rose—— that is Mrs. - - - - -Mrs. Montalbert I mean, in such a manner, or I should have spoke on't more cautiously; but some people are so nervous.—Come, dear Ma'am, cheer up:—why have a little more philosophy—we must all die....The poor lady, you know, had been for a long time in a declining way!"

Rosalie, to whom every word was as a dagger, now arose, and saying she felt herself too ill to remain below, wished Blagham a good morning, and tried to add her love to his wife, with some other of these common-place sayings, that express much and mean nothing; but finding herself unable to articulate, she leaned on Mrs. Hammond's arm, and retired to her own room.

Blagham in the mean time had his curiosity awakened, which he was determined to justify. Many doubts arose as to the reality of Rosalie's marriage. He found her with a gentleman, whom she acknowledged not to be her husband: he saw that he took a deep interest in whatever concerned her....Who was he then, and in what situation was this young woman?—Why be directed to in one name, and yet acknowledge another?

Blagham now attempted to enter into conversation with Walsingham, who, disliking him too much to take the trouble of being civil at any rate, and now half-distracted by his fears for Rosalie, hardly gave himself the trouble to answer him, but walked out of the house, in hopes, that when he was gone, Blagham would quit it also.

But this was ill-judged, inasmuch, as under the pretence of inquiring after the health of *the lady*, Blagham now obtained an opportunity of making several questions to the maid as to the gentleman—who, he learned, came with her, took the lodgings for her, and often visited her; he heard too, that his name was Walsingham, and that he was, in the simple phrase of Jane, "A vastly rich gentleman, quite as rich as a nobleman, and prodigious fond of both Madam and little Master, though he wa'nt no near relation, only a cousin, or the like of that - - - - -."

Jane would have told more had she known it, but her intelligence went no farther beyond this, than that "Madam came from foreign parts;" for Waters, who was both sensible and faithful, had adhered punctiliously to his master's strict injunctions, and had never mentioned more of him than his name and his fortune.

Blagham, however, had gathered much for malignant conjecture, and, as the people, with whom he was travelling East Grinstead, were by this time ready for their early dinner, he now quitted the lodgings of Rosalie, leaving his compliments and a message, that he hoped to hear that she was better.

Poor Walsingham was in the mean time walking up and down a little sheltered lane near the house. He had never till this happened been so suddenly alarmed for Rosalie, and he now felt the full and painful conviction how much his affection for her had exceeded the bounds he had at first prescribed, and thought he should ever have prescribed to it in his bosom. The death of Mrs. Vyvian, on whom alone, he knew, she relied for protection, though he knew not all the claims she had to it, seemed to have thrown her more than ever into his power, and made her more than before the object of his solicitude and friendship; and he was shocked at being compelled to acknowledge to himself, that this friendship was no long disinterested. He had long been conscious, that, while he talked of his eternal attachment to the memory of another woman, he could have found consolation for every loss, if Rosalie had lived only for him; and this consciousness was the true reason why he had absented himself so long, in the hope that he might, by degrees, wean himself from the indulgence of a passion, which, if Montalbert still lived, was at once dishonourable and desperate. The ill success of this experiment had given him that look of melancholy, and of unusual depression, which had so much alarmed Rosalie when she first saw him in the morning.

Walsingham, from a rising ground, where he was not himself perceived, marked the departure of Blagham, and returned to the house.

Rosalie had, on the sight of her child, been relieved by a flood of tears, and her oppressed heart now sought still farther ease in the consoling voice of a friend, himself acquainted with sorrow: every prudish scruple vanished from the real distress of her mind; she wanted somebody to whom she might talk of her lost benefactress, and whose sympathy would sooth her still bursting heart.

Instead, however, of hearing from him such sentences of consolation as are usually administered, instead of being advised to have fortitude and patience, and recommended to submit to inevitable evils, Walsingham sat down and wept with her, and, without trying to check a sensibility, which most men would have blushed at as a weakness, he seemed to seize the opportunity of deploring anew his own misfortunes; though unconscious that Rosalie lamented the death of a mother, he thought the loss of the friend of her early youth was a calamity great enough to justify the sorrow she expressed. Violent paroxysms of grief are seldom mitigated by common-place arguments. Walsingham therefore acted, perhaps, more kindly, in yielding to, rather than in resisting, the first expressions of agonising sorrow. They subsided, and, though the tears stole slowly down her cheeks as she spoke, yet Rosalie was sufficiently composed to consult with Walsingham on the steps she had to take.

No possible channel of hearing from Montalbert occurred to her; she knew not whither to address herself to Charles Vyvian, or whether he was in England; and if the Abbê Hayward yet lived, he was also out of her reach: the changes that had taken place in the Vyvian family, since the new connection formed by its master, had probably dismissed all the old servants from Holmwood. Thither, however, Walsingham offered either to go himself, or send his servant; as nothing better occurred to him than to attempt gaining some intelligence of young Vyvian, while Rosalie, who still thought Mrs. Lessington her only sure means of information, determined to wait an answer to the letter, which, when she was able to write, he advised her sending to Carlisle.

A silent and melancholy dinner, to which Walsingham stayed without being invited, was soon over. He then asked Rosalie if air would not relieve the oppression, of which, though she did not complain of, it was easy to see hung over her.—"If you wish to be alone, (said he), I will go; but, if you will suffer me to walk with you, I will not intrude on your sorrows—I respect them too much."

"I believe (answered Rosalie) I should be better in the air; but I dread meeting any one—indeed I am quite unfit to be seen!"

"You need not be seen, (said he); for by a path about a mile off, with which I am well acquainted by my former rambles along this coast, we may go without any hazardous descent down the rock quite to the sea beach, and from thence along under the cliff called Beachy Head, where I think you may be assured we shall meet no one."——Rosalie faintly objected to this; for, as she never went out unattended by Claudine carrying the child, she thought the walk might, in his account, be rugged and dangerous. Walsingham, however, assured her that the path he spoke of led down to the shore by a descent of hardly ten yards, and that not steep; he added, with a forced and faint smile, "I undertake for the safe conduct of little Harry, and you may recollect that it is not the first time I have had the honour of being entrusted with your boy."——These few words brought instantly to the mind of Rosalie the scene of her departure from Formiscusa, and all her obligations to Walsingham; his active generosity the, his unwearied friendship since, arose sensibly to her recollection.—"Ah! when—(thought she)—when will Montalbert arrive to acknowledge our weight of obligation, and to repay as much as gratitude and attachment can repay this invaluable friend!....When will my husband assist me in the task I cannot execute alone, of soothing his incurable sorrows!—when, indeed!——Montalbert!—where are you?——what has happened to you?——why seek you not the unfortunate Rosalie?———She is now, alas! deprived of all succour but that of a stranger.......Oh! come then—console with her the generous friend she has found——mourn with her the mother she has lost!"

This melancholy soliloquy silently passed without Rosalie's answering, or seemed to attend to, what Walsingham had said, though she slowly followed the way which he led.

They hardly spoke during their walk, except that Rosalie, observing the heavy cloud that hung over the sun, now sinking westward, inquired of Walsingham, if he did not think there would be a thunder storm?—He answered, certainly not; and they proceeded still silently, for neither were disposed for conversation.

About half a mile to the eastward of their descent they reached that stupendous sea mark, the high cliff called Beachy Head, which is seen half channel over, and is the first land made in crossing from the opposite coast. On looking up towards its summit, Walsingham seemed to be struck with some painful recollection; he paused a moment, and said, sighing, "Ah! how long it is since the sight of this head-land made my heart bound with transport—since the cry of Beachy! Beachy! by the sailors, after a night passed in struggling against faint and contrary winds, announced the joyful appearance of an old friend—but now all local attachments are at an end!—England is still my country, but I am more wretched, I think, in it than ever, much more wretched than when I am wandering about."

Rosalie, by a deep sigh, showed that she sympathised in his unhappiness, and another long pause.

"In this cavern, (continued Walsingham, turning towards a deep excavation in the rock), Tradition says, a solitary being, of the name of Darby, took up his abode....There are times when I am disposed to try some such experiment myself. I think I should enjoy the horrors of a storm, in a cave under Beachy Head. I can imagine the raging of the elements; the swelling and foaming of the mountain billows dashing on the rock; and the isolated hermit patiently awaiting the surge that should overwhelm him....I could fancy, even now fancy, the sullen waves, which we actually hear breaking regularly and monotonously on the shore, to be the hollow murmur of the subsiding storm. The solitary man having escaped the tempest, ventures forth from his cave!—he heard, amid the whirlwinds of the night, the cries of the wretch driven on the inhospitable coast, then he could not save them!—but he now looks along the beach for their said remains; he tries with his feeble hands to bury them....He sees a drowned man, which, another wave will cast at his feet, he steps forward—-."

"In God's sake, Mr. Walsingham, (cried Rosalie shuddering), forbear to draw such images of horror!"—"I will forbear, (answered he), if they distress you, Mrs. Montalbert, but to me they present not images of horror........Ah! no—at this moment I envy those who are dead; I almost wish *I* were so!"

Rosalie had often heard him talk in a desponding style, but now there was in his manner dejection mixed with something of wildness, that made her tremble. Stunned as her mind was by its recent loss, every vague idea had force to torment her, and she now again apprehended that Walsingham might know something of Montalbert, which the agitation she expressed at their meeting in the morning, might have deprived him of courage to tell her; and that he was, by this unusual style of conversation, preparing her for it; but a moment's reflection served to dissipate this fear. Had it been necessary to inflict another wound on her heart, it was not to a scene so remote as that which they were now in, that he would have led her; for he had seen in the morning how ill she could bear such intelligence as Blagham had abruptly given her.

Walsingham then was unhappy, more than usually unhappy, and from some cause which did not personally concern Rosalie. The gratitude she owed him, and the friendship she felt for him, now called upon her to rouse herself and appear less depressed, in hopes that *he* might become more calm. She tried, therefore, but evidently with effort, to speak on common and uninteresting subjects. In their former conversations, Walsingham had frequently given her easy lessons on botany, which, with almost every other science, he understood, she now, with a view to detach his mind from the subjects that so painfully engaged it, gathered a branch of the sea poppy, and another of the eryngium, that grew among the stones of the beach, and began to talk of marine plants, and of those of structure more singular which lived under the waves; she remarked that these inhabiting the immediate margin of the sea, apparently formed the link between marine and terraqueous vegetables, and was proceeding thus, when, looking at her with an expression of countenance, which said, as plainly as if he had spoken it—"Ah! you would not now have found spirits to talk on such subjects, if you did not exert those spirits for me!"—he said——

"I am a miserable being to-night, and fit for nothing that belongs to science, or perhaps to reason. But as there are cold unfeeling mortals, who say, and perhaps truly, that poetry has nothing to do with either, I may possible be the better disposed to read to you what I once wrote, not many miles from this part of the coast of Suffex. It was soon after my return from the continent, when I thought all my fondest hopes of happiness would be realized, but when I found them vanished from my grasp for ever!—a friend, who loved me, would not suffer me to remain brooding over my sorrows, at a house I had taken, (ah! how fruitlessly taken), in London; but though it was late in the year, not far, indeed, from mid-winter, he was going to pass a month at Brighthelmstone, and he took me with him, careless of whither I went, and only in desiring not to be molested by condolence or inquiries........For some time (continued Walsingham sighing) the vigilant kindness of my friend would hardly suffer me out of his sight. At length convinced that *I had courage to live*, he allowed me to do as I would, and the use I made of my liberty was to wander of a night along the beach, or on the cliffs, on which the sea is continually encroaching. After a long succession of stormy weather, with heavy rains, great fragments of rock fell on the belt of stones beneath: the crash of their separation and fall echoed along the shore, like thunder intermingled with the incessant roar of the wintry waves....*My* gloomy disposition was gratified in describing the effect of this, and thus assimilating outward circumstances to my own sad sensations——

"The night flood *rakes* upon the stony shore,
"Along the rugged cliffs, and chalky caves,
"Mourns the hoarse Ocean, seeming to deplore
"All that lie buried in his restless waves.—
"Mined, by corrosive tides, the hollow rock
"Falls prone; and, rushing from its turfy height,
"Shakes the board beach, with long resounding shock
"Loud thundering on the ear of sullen night.—
"Above the desolate and stormy deep,
"Gleams the wan moon by floating mists oppress'd,
"Yet here, while youth, and health, and labour, sleep,
"Alone I wander;—calm untroubled rest,
'Nature's soft nurse,' deserts the sigh-swollen breast,
"And flies the wretch, who only 'wakes to weep!"

CHAP.

FROM the temper of mind which Rosalie was in, the lines she had just heard Walsingham recite in a full yet mournful voice, could hardly fail of affecting her; and, while he a second time repeated them at her request, the tears slowly fell from her eyes, and it might possibly have been some time before she was enough recovered from the mournful reverie into which she had fallen, had not she and Walsingham been equally startled by the sudden appearance of two females figures from behind a projection of the cliff, on a fragment of which they had been sitting. One of them suddenly advancing to Walsingham, said, "Upon my honour, my dear Sir, you must excuse me if I break through common rules:—but I do so doat on talents—I am such an enthusiast in regard to poetry!——Your name is Walsingham, I think—I have often had the happiness of hearing you, and once of seeing you, at dear Mrs. Paramount's.—I should be mortified—oh! mortified beyond measure, if I supposed it possible for you to forget it!"

Walsingham, very little delighted with this bold and abrupt address, and recollecting at once who the lady was, determined to give her this measureless mortification.—He, therefore, answered drily, "That he was sorry to say his memory refused him the pleasure of acknowledging, as his acquaintance, a lady who did him so much honour."——Turning from him with an air of pique, the admirer of talents then addressed herself to Rosalie, and, with confidence, not at all checked by the coldness of her reception, said, "I have been determined, my dear Madam, to make myself known to you ever since I first saw you, and your charming boy.....What a sweet creature!—a perfect angel!——I was told when first I saw you, that you were an Italian lady of rank, which only increased my violent inclination to be admitted among the number of your friends; but my acquaintance, Mademoiselle Claudine, undeceived me."

Rosalie, recognizing the lady who had so often spoken to Claudine, was never so little willing as now to make her acquaintance, and was, in truth, unable to answer all these fine speeches as the laws of common civility required; she, therefore, suffered the stranger to proceed, only muttering something which her new acquaintance deemed sufficient encouragement for her to go on talking.

While this passed, the other lady sidled up to Walsingham, and, in the softest whisper of affection, her head reclined and her eyes half shut, said, "Is it then indeed possible, that Mr. Walsingham can have suffered the remarkable traces Lady Llancarrick must leave on every heart, to be obliterated!—That wonderful being! whose talents, whose virtues, have been the admiration of the age in which we live—and whose person, worshipped as it has been and is, is the least of her astonishing perfections!"

Walsingham, however he abhorred ever kind of affectation, might, at another time, have found a momentary amusement in the fine sentimental phrases and ridiculous contorsions of this young woman. He recollected her to be a Miss Gillman, whom he had seen at parties in town, and who had acquired the name of "*The Muse*." But he was at this time so disgusted with her folly, and so impatient at being thus broke in upon, that nothing less than the consideration of her being a woman, and in inferior circumstances, (for she was a humble dependent on the scientific dames of better fortune), could have induced him to even the little show of civility with which he answered—"That it was his misfortune to have forgotten Lady Llancarrick, owing, perhaps, to his long residence in other countries."——"Oh! then (eagerly interrupted Miss Gillman) you have never, perhaps, seen any of her productions.—She writes the most divine things!—there is an originality or sublimity undescribable in her compositions—the effect of the strongest understanding guiding the amiable propensities of the softest heart!—She did me the very high honour to desire I would walk down to this singular scenery, where——

"The beetling rock frowns o'er the foaming tide."

For she is writing something wherein she thought the wonders of nature might assist her imagination.....We were sitting pensively together my friend invoking the muse!—and I waiting in silence the happy effusions of her fine fancy, when we were struck with pleasing surprise on hearing the beautiful lines you recited. They are, I am persuaded, from your own ingenious pen—I hope you will give them to the world."

As little more was necessary in answer to this rhapsody than a bow, Walsingham now turned a sorrowful look towards Rosalie, who was suffering even a severer penance than he had undergone, and was much less able to disengage herself.—They had risen on the first appearance of Lady Llancarrick and her poetical associate, and were now walking towards home; but this did not promise to afford them the means of escape, for the ladies declared they also were returning that way. Little more, however, was required during the remainder of their walk than to listen: for Lady Llancarrick having now got somebody to hear her, to whom she thought all the fine things she had collected were entirely new, and who could not doubt of exciting wonder and admiration, was soaring into the most elevated regions—and common life and common sense were left at an immeasurable distance. She mistook the silence of Walsingham (which arose from vexation and impatience) for profound attention and silent admiration. From the first time of meeting him, she thought him an object well worth trying to attract, and wished to find out the nature of his attachment to Rosalie; though, be it what it might, it impeded not her views, for it was one among her many real or affected singularities, that she pretended to have the most profound contempt for beauty, while her own figure and face betrayed the great pains she took to acquire or preserve in her own person the advantage she contemned.

She knew that Walsingham was reckoned a man of the first understanding and information, and was fully persuaded that Rosalie's youth and beauty would be weak attractions, when opposed to her charms, and those talents, which alone, she thought had power to fix a man of his genius.

Lady Llancarrick began life as a young woman whom accidental connections had raised into society much above her fortune, and who thought herself happy to be put on a level with them by marrying Sir Lodowick Llancarrick, a Welsh Baronet: but having unsuccessfully tried the charms of domestic felicity, she had, for some years, been one of those characters which the undistinguishing multitude have called—Veteran Women of Fashion—High Flyers—and other appellations which are doubtless quite undeserved.......The "universal passion," according to Dr. Young's description, was never more strongly exemplified—never did a female breast pant so vehemently for fame as that of Lady Llancarrick; and, after many struggles to raise herself to notoriety, she found every eminence pre-occupied that might have been obtained by singularity of dress or demeanour; she could not drive into the temple of Fame in a Phaeton, four in hand, without being incommoded by equal of superior skill—or ride thither without being crossed and jostled; neither could she leap a five-barred gate, or do many other feats to make people stare, without having innumerable rivals. One avenue to immortality, however, was less crowded, and Lady Llancarrick followed it: she became a poet and a politician—with a very moderate skill in her own language, she was certainly a singular, if not a successful, candidate for the Poetic Crown; but having neither the judgement that arises from natural good sense, or that which is acquired by study, her political opinions, and her poetical flights, were equally inconsistent and absurd. Together, however, they answered her purpose, for she became *wonderful*, if not admirable: some humble retainers of the *Tuneful Nine* were always ready to celebrate her genius;

and she furnished so many paragraphs for the newspapers, that the editors could hardly fail of being grateful.

But with so much genius could she escape being susceptible?—Alas!—no.—Many instances were given of the softness of her heart, and many men of the very first world had been supposed to wear her chains. In proportion as these became fragile through time, she had covered them with flowers, almost the last fortunate captive, who had escaped this charming bondage, was Sommers Walsingham; which, perhaps, from family partiality, inspired Lady Llancarrick with her present inclination to throw the same pleasing fetters over his cousin.

Perfectly unconscious, however, of her design, hardly hearing, and not at all attending to the excellent things she was saying, Walsingham walked by her side, accusing his destiny of cruelty in compelling him to part with Rosalie for some time, and to leave her in such a state of mind, without having an opportunity of saying to her much that he had postponed till he took leave, and which now appeared absolutely necessary to his own peace, if not for the guidance and consolation of his interesting unhappy friend. Yet, however, he wished to have a long conversation with Rosalie before he rode back to Hastings, he was persuaded that Lady Llancarrick and Miss Gillman had forced themselves thus into his notice, only to gratify impertinent curiosity, or find ground for malignant remark in regard to Rosalie, that he determined, whatever it might cost him, not to put it in their power. For a moment he thought of returning to her lodging, after they had shaken off their unwelcome companions; but, conscious that so unusual a visit much excite the invidious remarks of the woman of the house, and suspecting that Lady Llancarrick and her companion would watch his steps, he found himself compelled, on Rosalie's account, to relinquish the idea of seeing her again that evening; but rage and vexation seized him, and he no longer wore even the semblance of civility, though Lady Llancarrick did not, or would not, perceive it. Their way lay near the door of the inn where Walsingham's horses were put up. His groom was walking before it waiting his orders; he called to him impatiently, and bade him bring the horses out; they followed him in an instant, when, approaching Rosalie, he wished her a good night, and said, in a low voice, that he would see her in a very few days; then, coldly bowing to the other two ladies, he mounted his horse, and was out of sight in a moment.

Rosalie, trying to suppress a sigh that arise partly from regret at his going so suddenly, and partly from recollection of the state of mind in which she knew he was, was now very coldly and formally courtesying her good night to her two unwished-for companions; but they did not intend to let her off so easily, and Lady Llancarrick, bidding her dear Gillman take the arm of her sweet friend, said, "Oh! we will see her safe to her lodgings, you know!"

The distance was not far, but Rosalie thought it now lengthened on purpose: both the ladies besetting her with questions which she could not answer truly, and would very fain have been excused from answering at all. Indeed, during the former part of their walk, while Lady Llancarrick had engaged Walsingham, the gentle, sentimental Erminia Eliza Gillman had, albeit in the sweetest accents and with the most insinuating softness, put so many questions to poor Rosalie, that greater art and knowledge of the world, than she possessed, would have been necessary to prevent the sly sentimentalist from discovering that there was a great deal of mystery in her affairs, and that their obscurity arose from their being of a nature which she dared not reveal, yet knew not how artfully to hide.

When, at length, Rosalie was once more alone in her own parlour, all of the events of the day revived in painful confusion to her memory; but the death of her mother swallowed up every other sorrow, and, with a flood of tears, she accused herself of insensibility, for having, at such a time, suffered any other consideration to call off her thoughts a moment from that object of just and endless regret. Of the two ladies she had seen, she thought no more than to determine upon not continuing their acquaintance, and rather to quit the place than to associate frequently with people so utterly disagreeable.—Her heart heavy with regret, and her head aching from having wept so much during the day, she drank a glass of water and hastened to her bed, where the most tormenting reflections, on the cruel fate of her beloved mother, long prevented her tasting any repose. At length wearied nature gave her up to momentary forgetfulness; but she had hardly slept an hour, when she was awakened by one of the most violent storms of thunder, lightning, wind, and hail, that she had ever recollected to have heard. For herself she was unconscious of apprehension, but clasping to her palpitating heart its only certain possession, her lovely child, she shrunk from the slashing fires which made their way through her window shutters; she endeavoured, however, to appease the fears of Claudine, who crept into her room half dead with terror, but suddenly, as she was reasoning with her maid, she recollected that, from the time which had passed since Walsingham set out, it was impossible he could have reached Hastings. Her apprehensions, lest any evil might befall him, and the idea that she was the innocent cause of his being exposed, became extremely painful to her bosom; she yielded to those gloomy thoughts which too frequently aggravated sorrow—and exclaimed, "Alas! *I* am so unfortunate, that it seems as if I communicated calamity to all who are interested about me......Born the child of proscription, *I* destroyed the peace of my mother, and on my account it probably was, that my unhappy father was driven into exile!—Should *he* have survived long years of calamity, I shall never behold him, never have an opportunity of expressing for him the filial tenderness I should feel, or of weeping with him over the memory of my dear, dear mother. Again proscribed in my marriage, I have, perhaps, undone Montalbert, and loaded him with the malediction of his mother......Perhaps—oh! thought too terrible to be dwelt upon!——perhaps his tenderness for me may have cost him his life, and he may have perished amid the sulphurous gulphs and unwholesome exhalations at Messina.—No, I will not encourage such an idea. The precautions of his cruel mother counteracted it, and, by doing so, made my imprisonment and persecution favours.—Alas! I have present evil enough without dwelling on the past.—The noble-minded, the disinterested Walsingham, seems to be infected with my unhappiness; perhaps, even now, is the victim of his generous attention to me!—and you, dear little unconscious companion of my woes, sole sweetener of my sorrowful existence, may not you one day lament that you were ever born?"

This reflection was too distressing—and an ardent prayer to Heaven, that *she* alone might suffer, and that her boy might be as happy as she was miserable, ended the sad soliloquy.—The violence of the tempest abated, but not till morning broke.

Rosalie, after a short interval of rest, arose; she heard from her maid, as well as from her other servant and the people of the house, melancholy details of the mischief occasioned by the lightning; of which some particulars were true, but the greater part much exaggerated, or wholly groundless.

Rosalie, still depressed by the idea of Walsingham's possible danger, and by the effects of a sleepless night, tried to shake off both her mental and personal uneasiness by a walk. It was an hour when she hoped that she might venture to the sea side without meeting either of the ladies whom she so much desired to avoid. In this, however, she was disappointed:—they joined her as she returned home; talked over the circumstance of the storm—Lady Llancarrick declaring that she enjoyed its sublime horrors, and Miss Gillman tempering the same sentiment, with delicately expressing concern for the fate of those who might have suffered in it.

"Apropos, (said Lady Llancarrick)—my dear Mrs. Sheffield, do you know it came into our heads, as Gillman and I sat together looking at the lightning over the sea, that *our* agreeable acquaintance, Mr. Walsingham, could hardly have reached whatever place he was going to before the tempest came on:—he resides, I think, at some distance?"

As she said this, she fixed on Rosalie her fierce inquiring eyes. Rosalie, though no human being could be more void of offence, blushed deeply, and, before she could form a reply, Walsingham's groom came up to her, and delivered a packet with his master's compliments, and he had orders to wait for an answer.

Rosalie now saw, in the countenance of the two ladies, an expression which added, for a moment, to her pain and confusion. Relieved, however, from the uneasiness she had been in about Walsingham, she felt all the dignity of conscious innocence, and resolved to disregard censure, which, whatever appearances might say, she knew herself incapable of deserving; she recovered her composure, and telling the servant she would return home and write an answer, which he might call for in a quarter of an hour, she slightly wished the two ladies a good morning, and left them.

Their curiosity, which was strongly excited on many accounts, they scrupled not to attempt gratifying by questioning the servant; from whom, however, they obtained but little additional information. While these ladies were thus unworthily employed, Rosalie read the following letter from Walsingham——

LETTER.

"I was compelled to leave you, dear Madam, last night in an uneasy state of mind—for how could I be otherwise, when I saw you in such depressed spirits; and I fear your new acquaintances are not of that description of women, with whom, either in the hour of sadness or gaiety, you would wish to associate.—I hope, that if you find them too much disposed to trespass upon you, you will not suffer the fear of violating the common forms of society to force you into the most uneasy of all restrains, keeping up a show of regard to conceal dislike and disgust. I believe neither of them to be worthy of the friendship of Mrs. Montalbert. You know, I hope, that if this or any other circumstance renders your present abode less agreeable to you, my services shall be exerted to find one more eligible—but favour me with your commands immediately, as I shall go to-morrow to London, to plead with an old acquaintance of my father's on behalf of an unfortunate son, who, having two years ago married a young woman, whose only fault was her being a destitute fortune, and, having been brought up to no profession, is in a very distressed situation, with a wife and two sweet little children. I met him a few days before I had last the honour of seeing you, as he is here with his family; I bade him consider what I could do to serve him, and he has desired me to see his father on his behalf: persuaded that I should succeed in restoring him to comfort and his father. Without having very high ideas of my powers of persuasion, especially when the hard-cold heart of avarice is to be moved, I will, however, make the attempt, and, unless there is any thing in which I can first have the pleasure of being employed for you, Madam, I shall begin my journey to-morrow early. My friend's father lives in Nottinghamshire.

"May the bearer of this bring me as favourable an account of your health and spirits as can be expected after the just concern you have so recently felt:—I hope you were not terrified by the tempest of last night. It overtook me on a place so wild and dreary, that I cold have supposed it the scene where Shakespeare imagined the meeting between Macbeth and the Weird

Sisters. The spot I allude to is a wide down; in some places scattered over with short furze, in others barren even of turf, and the uncloathed chalk presenting the idea of cold desolation:—on the left is a ruined chapel, or small parish church, in which service is performed only once in six weeks; on the right are, in some places, marshes that extend to the sea—in others a broad spit of sand and stones, where nature seems to refuse sustenance even to the half-marine plants, which, in most places, are thinly sprinkled among the saltpetre of the beach.

"The hollow murmur of the distant sea, on which the lightning faintly flashed, foretold the coming storm some time before I reached this heath—there it overtook me; but as there are times when outward accidents make little or no impression on me, I quickened not my pace; and shall I own it without incurring the charge of affected eccentricity; that I found a melancholy species of pleasure of surveying the gloomy horrors of the scene——in fancying I was the only human being abroad, within the circuit of many miles—in cherishing the same spirit with which Young says in his Night Thoughts—-
"Throughout the vast glove's wide circumference
"No being wakes but me."

Yet I was more moderate, and more philosophical in my somber enjoyment; and, when I came to my lodgings, I wrote what follows, which I beg you will put into the fire when you have read——.

"Swift fleet the billowy clouds along the sky,
"Earth seems to shudder at the storm aghast;
"While only beings, as forlorn as I.
"Court the chill horrors of the howling blast.
"Even round yon crumbling walls, in search of food,
"The ravenous owl forgoes his evening flight;
"And in his cave, within the deepest wood,
"The fox eludes the tempest of the night:—
"But

"But, to my heart, congenial is the gloom
"Which hides me from a world I wish to shun—
"That scene, where ruin saps the moulding tomb,
"Suits with the sadness of a wretch undone;
"Nor is the darkest shade, the keenest air,
"Black as my fate—or cold as my despair."

"CHAP.

THE pensive, or rather gloomy disposition in which Walsingham wrote, was but too congenial to the feelings of his unhappy correspondent, who passed the rest of the day in her house, indulging melancholy reflections. She was glad, however, that he was gone an excursion likely to divert his thoughts, and knew that nothing so effectually won him from himself as such a generous service as he was now engaged in. The following day arose, and found her in the same dejected state of mind; left alone, without even the expectation of seeing Walsingham, or of hearing any intelligence, which, he assured her, he would not fail to attempt collecting as to Montalbert, or Charles Vyvian, she had nothing to look forward to but the answer she yet hoped to receive from Mrs. Lessington; and she reckoned daily when the course of the post might give her, at least, this melancholy satisfaction.

A mind, thus preying on itself, agitated by hopes and fears, and wearied by conjectures, could only be relieved, at last, for a few hours by books of amusement. She had sent to the only library in the place for two or three of these sort of books, but finding them only pages of inanity, which could not a moment arrest her attention, she determined, notwithstanding her fears of again meeting Lady Llancarrick and Miss Gillman, to go to the shop, and endeavour to please herself better. In doing so, she was under the necessity of passing through that part of the village most frequented. Congratulating herself, however, on not having met any body, she was returning, with her books in her hand, when her former persecutors, suddenly advancing from their lodgings, joined her, and, with their usual careless ease, entered into discourse with her, asking several questions, and, when to evade these, she turned the conversation on the books she had been in search of, the elder lady delivered her opinion of several celebrated and new productions, with a fluency which astonished Rosalie, so much did it resemble a dissertation learned by heart, and remind Rosalie of Jenkinson in the Vicar of Wakefield, who, whenever he met a stranger, began with—

"Sir, the cosmogony, or creation of the world," &c. &c.

Rosalie, however, better content to be a hearer than a speaker, listened, or appeared to listen, with perfect resignation, internally resolving, however, to take her leave as soon as she arrived at the turning which led to her own lodgings, whether the harangeu was finished or not; she walked, in the mean time, quietly along between the two ladies, (Miss Gillman having taken her arm), and gazing on the ground, as if she was counting the pepples, when two persons hastily approached, and in a voice exclaimed—"It is she!—it is my wife!——By Heaven it is herself!"——the voice was Montalbert's—Rosalie raised her eyes—it *was* Montalbert himself.

Almost unconscious of what she did, she sprang forward, and would have thrown herself into his arms, but he retired from her, with rage and resentment in his countenance, which suddenly changing into an expression of pity, he cried—"Lovely lost creature!—art thou, indeed, lost to me?——Yes—for ever lost!—and here—too well convinced that all I have heard is true—here we part for ever!"

Rosalie, who had advance towards him, heard all this with a surprise and terror that deprived her of the power of utterance. She tried, however, to say, "For mercy's sake, Montalbert, hear me!"—but seeing that he still retreated from her, and that seizing the arm of the person with him, he even walked hastily away; she made a vain attempt to quicken her pace and follow him, but her trembling limbs refused to second her will—her head grew giddy, her heart ceased for a moment to beat, and she would have fallen, had not Miss Gillman, who, with Lady Llancarrick, beheld this scene with wonder, stepped forward and supported her.

In another moment she recovered her senses, and, looking wildly round her, exclaimed, "Where is he?——Where is Montalbert?——Lead me, if you have pity—lead me to him!....Let me follow him—for God's sake let me!"——Miss Gillman, with the common phrase used on such occasions, besought her to be composed; Lady Llancarrick began to reason, and to prove very logically that nobody ought to give way to such violent emotions. Her eyes, however, had followed Montalbert till he disappeared;—though when Rosalie eagerly inquired which way he went, it was a piece of intelligence she did not choose to communicate.

Rosalie, when her sense and recollection returned, desired to go to her lodging, but, as it was evident she was incapable of walking thither without assistance, the two ladies of course attended her.—Miss Gillman, in the few intervals allowed her, spoke most sentimentally and pathetically, while the lady of superior talents affected to argue on the impropriety of yielding to extravagant expressions of grief or joy—not without some hints, that she could not comprehend how the gentleman they had seen could be the husband of Mrs. Sheffield, and yet be called Montalbert. Rosalie attended to neither of her new friends; she hardly knew who was with her; but, having formed a confused conjecture that Montalbert might be at her house, her eager eyes were inquiring for him the moment she came in sight of it. Claudine met her with the little boy; but Montalbert had not been there. In beholding her child, he recalled to her startled senses the conduct of his father, with his wild behaviour and strange expressions, and all the agitation of her spirits returned; but she was relieved by a flood of tears, and sobbed violently—while such comfort or remonstrance, as the ladies thought might either console or determine her to bear her distress with fortitude, were alternately administered.—Rosalie had nothing to answer. She wished, thought she could not propose it, that they would leave her as the only kindness they could do her; and at length, the one having exhausted all her sentiment, and the other all her reasoning, they went away, promising to call in the evening to see how she did. Rosalie assured them she should be very well, and begged they would not trouble themselves; she affected a momentary tranquility, to escape from a repetition of attentions, which, as they appeared to be well meant, she could not rudely refuse.

When they were gone, the astonished and stunned mind of Rosalie returned to a new contemplation of the scene that had passed; when she recalled the countenance, the words, and the attitude, of Montalbert, it appeared, but too certain, that her actions had been misrepresented, and that jealousy and anger possessed him. How could she find—how appease him?—Whither was he gone?—He had come in search of her; was he then so prejudiced against her, that he would not even hear her, that he would not even see the child whom he had so passionately loved?—These reflections, pressing with painful violence on her mind, deprived her for some time of the calmness that might have enabled her to determine what [must] be done. She sometimes thought [of going] out to inquire for Montalbert, then found herself unequal to the dread of meeting him, whom she had so long sough and so tenderly beloved, only to have her heart pierced by sounds of anger and reproach, from a voice in which she had been used to listen to the fondest language of adoring love.—She had no servant who either knew the person of Montalbert, or had sufficient steadiness and sense to perform so delicate a commission as that which she wished to have executed. The woman of the house, though older and graver than Claudine, was very ignorant, and to her it would be impossible to explain such a history as hers, and equally impossible to make her comprehend it. To her ever generous, considerate, and sensible friend, Walsingham, the thoughts of Rosalie naturally turned; but had he been still at Hastings, she could not have ventured to have asked his meditation. It was too evident, from the few incohe[rent w]ords Montalbert had uttered, that h[is col]dness and violence originated in jea[lousy,] and of whom, besides Walsingham, could he have conceived such injurious ideas?

Amidst these fluctuating thoughts one occurred to her, which compelled her to take some immediate resolution. If she could see Montalbert, when she was less under the influence of surprise, she thought she could talk to him calmly, and should be able to convince him that she had never, even in idea, swerved from the faithful tenderness she owed him: but to avail herself of this hope no time was to be lost. Montalbert might have left the village; and where was she then to seek him, that he might hear her justification. Impressed then with a conviction that she ought to find him instantly, she was hastening to leave the house, when the following note was delivered to her——

"THE father of the unfortunate child know by the name of Henry Montalbert, requires to have him immediately delivered to the two persons who attend for that purpose, and who will conduct him to

H. MONTALBERT."

Rosalie read this cruel order: she stood for a moment like the statue of despair—her blood circulated no longer; she was choaked by the convulsive struggles of her heart—but she could not weep, she could not even speak. The two persons, who were sent for her child, appeared at the door of the parlour into which she had returned, and, at the same moment, by another door, Claudine entered with the little boy. Rosalie started up, and eagerly seizing him in her arms, uttered a few incoherent words—"They shall not take you from me, my child (said she); let them rather kill me at once!"—Then, turning toward the man and woman, who approached without any apparent feeling for her inexpressible distress, she cried, her voice half stifled by sobs, "For mercy's sake, whoever you are, lead me to Montalbert!—Do not, oh! as you hope for Heaven—do not execute his cruel order, but let me find him—I will carry my child to him myself!"

The man, who had a countenance which seemed made on purpose to execute such a commissions, answered, with sullen coldness, "Madam, we can say nothing to all this—we must obey the order of our employer—we act legally, and cannot enter into any discussion....Come, Mrs. Jacklin, we have no time to lose."

So saying, he approached with his companion as if to take the child. Rosalie could only press her boy more closely to her breast, and, uttering a faint shriek, sunk with him upon her knees—"Have mercy!—oh! have pity on me!"——was all she could utter. The unfeeling man, regardless of her agonies, or of the tears and shrieks of Claudine, who wept, implored, and menaced, forced the child from the convulsive grasp of its apparently dying mother, and putting it into the arms of the woman, they hastened from the house.

Rosalie, who had sunk upon the floor, seemed, as if by a miracle, to recover herself. She rose, and, with wild looks and swift steps, pursued the cruel wretches who had thus torn her child from her; but they were already out of sight; her streaming eyes sought them in vain; her head became giddy; her senses forsook her, and she would have fallen had not Claudine caught her in her arms, and supported her till the woman of the house coming to her assistance, they carried her between them into the house, insensible and apparently dead.

She was now placed on her bed, and the remedies usual in such cases were administered; she opened her eyes, and, eagerly fixing them on the face of Claudine, inquired for her child. Claudine could answer only by her tears. The miserable mother then seized the hand of the woman of the house, conjuring her to go in search of him: but recollecting how little such a person could be interested, she attempted to rise herself, and again follow him. The woman refused to suffer her, and endeavoured to appease her by promises of going themselves; but her impatience became greater, and she raved, entreated, and wept, till the violence of her emotions exhausted her, and she sunk in total depression. A few moments sufficed to recover her to a sense of her misery, and then the same sad scene was renewed.

At length the woman of the house agreed to go out on inquiry, and something like hope suspended for a while the agonies Rosalie had suffered; but when the good woman came back, and related, though in the most cautious way she could, that the child had been carried away in a post chaise by the two persons who had fetched him from his mother—the unhappy Rosalie relapsed into all the horrors of despair. The whole night passed in incoherent ravings, in calling wildly for her child, or imploring the mercy of its father, while Claudine stood weeping on one side of the bed, and the landlady remonstrating and praying on the other. Before morning her senses seemed to have forsaken the wretched sufferer: yet her strength was so little impaired, that she again insisted on being suffered to follow her child. She directed Claudine to get her a post chaise; then attempted to rise and dress herself, till, giddy and sick, she sunk again on the bed. Thither the woman of the house had by this time summoned an apothecary, who began gravely to inquire into the cause of the agitation in which he saw his patient. Claudine could not explain it, and the good woman knew not how, so that, from what she said, the apothecary, concluding she had lost a child by death, commenced a grave harangue on submission and acquiescence, which served only to add to the tortures of the unfortunate young woman: nor was this gentleman, who really meant well, her only tormenter. Her landlady had sent for Lady Llancarrick and Miss Gillman, who, taking each their station on the opposite sides of her bed, began to administer consolation, such as is usually doled forth in set phrases, with some difference, however, arising from character; for the lady spoke like a philosopher; "*the Muse*" like a sentimentalist—while Rosalie, unable to answer either, repeated to herself in the anguish of her heart——

"She talks to me who never had a son." So totally unqualified were all these parties for the delicate office of comforting the afflicted, or so unfit was the mind of Rosalie for receiving consolation, that, before evening, her spirits were agitated to a fearful degree; her reason was evidently wavering; and, no longer conscious of the inutility of her exclamations, she called incessantly for her child; then implored her husband to pity her; and from thence her thoughts made a sudden transition to the scenes she had passed through Sicily and at Formiscusa; till, at length, all she said appeared so innocent, and was so little understood by those who heard her, that they became convinced her senses were totally deranged, and, that these wild and incoherent appeals to persons, as well as her descriptive ravings about places, were the effects of a disordered imagination.

Lady Llancarrick, who was writing for the stage, contemplated this sad spectacle with the sang froid of an amateur, who hoped to add some strong touches to her performance; while her more gentle friend with her attempts at showing sensibility, was considering how such an incident might weave into a novel; but neither felt any true sympathy for the unhappy object, who, in the early bloom of youth, was thus the prey of anguish, which was reducing her to insanity or death.

The woman of the house, however, and the apothecary of the village, began, after the third and fourth day, to be seriously alarmed for the unfortunate patient, instead of recovering her recollection, continued to fluctuate between violent ravings and fits of gloomy stupidity, while an alarming fever continually preyed upon her.—The ladies, who had at first appeared to attend her with patience and humanity, now slackened their good offices: Lady Llancarrick found that neither Walsingham nor Montalbert appeared; that she had no chance of making an interesting or profitable acquaintance by her affected humanity, and that she might, perhaps, be involved in trouble, and even in expence; to both of which, but particularly the latter, she had a decided aversion. As to Miss Gillman, she had no will of her own, but contented herself with gentle repetitions of the words, "Poor dear creature!—Sweet unfortunate!——alas! how pitiable!"—— While she occasionally addressed to her patroness eulogiums on her benevolence—"How good your ladyship is!—oh! what a heart, my dear friend, is yours!—what amiable sympathy for the distressed!"——These sentences were continually sighed forth from the delicate sensibilities of the sentimental Muse, and received by the lady as if she had really deserved them.

Ah! little could the consolations of such people avail towards healing the wounds of a broken heart. The unfortunate Rosalie every day became worse and worse. Claudine could not act for her; a stranger herself, and naturally helpless, she could only sit and weep by the bedside of her mistress; or, when she appeared to have an interval of sense, ask directions of her, which Rosalie was unable to give, or which, if given, were incoherent and impracticable.

The apothecary now consulted Lady Llancarrick on the propriety of sending for a physician. Uncertain how far the finances of the sufferer might answer such an expence, and fearful of being called upon herself to supply any deficiency, Lady Llancarrick would give no advice; the landlady doubted how far enough remained, in case her lodger died, to discharge the arrears that would be due, and to pay the expences which might be incurred; while Claudine, who had not the smallest idea of the mercenary principles on which these people acted, was continually imploring Lady Llancarrick to send for other advice, till, from this sort of importunity, she gradually withdrew; while Miss Gillman gravely held forth an opinion, that, perhaps, after all, this pretty young creature, for whom they had been interesting themselves, and whose adventures appeared to have something so extraordinary in them, might be merely a girl in inferior life, to whom some man of fashion had attached himself, and, finding her unworthy of any long or serious partiality, had taken his child from her for very proper reasons. While these two good ladies were thus prudently settling that they ought to decline any farther interference, the illness of the wretched Rosalie increased to such a degree, that the apothecary believed, and her female attendants were convinced, she had not many hours to live.

CHAP.

FIVE days had now passed, five melancholy days, since the sad victim of unjust suspicion had found no relief from anguish, but in her moments of insensibility. Her lovely face was quite faded and changed; her form emaciated and enfeebled, so that she could hardly support herself in her bed; sometimes she wildly started up, looked round her, and inquired for her child, until some degree of recollection sunk her again into the torpor of despair.

It was on the evening of the last of these days that three gentlemen, attended by servants, stopped in a post chaise at the door of the house, and inquired for Mrs. Montalbert. The landlady, who hoped that their arrival would put an end to her apprehensions of pecuniary loss, eagerly assured them that the lady was there; she was very ill to be sure—"But I will call Mam'selle, her maid, (added the good woman); and, for certain, Madam, will be glad to see her friends."

The three strangers, on this information, left their coach, and entered the parlour. One of them appeared to suffer from ill health; he was pale and sallow, and, though yet in the middle of life, seemed to have been the victim of sorrow or disease. The second had the habit and air of a clergyman; and the last was a young man, apparently of fashion, who might have been taken for the son of the one, and the pupil of the other.

Claudine, who, amidst all her solicitude for her mistress, never lost sight of little personal vanity, stayed to adjust her cap at the glass, to put a little powder in her hair, and a nicer fichu on her shoulders; and then expecting certainly to see Mr. Walsingham, whom she concluded, in some measure, as her master, she fluttered down into the room, where, in his place, she beheld three gentlemen who were entirely strangers to her.

The elder of them began to question her on the situation of her lady; but finding she understood little English, the younger, who spoke like a native of France, took up the inquiry, and heard, with great apparent concern, the sad account of Rosalie's health, which even the warmth and earnestness of Claudine's manner could but little exaggerate. Each of her auditors seemed almost equally affected, and each inquired whether she could conduct them to her mistress. Claudine, not knowing what to do, and having no idea of who these people could be, answered, in visible alarm, that she would go and inquire; forgetting, at that moment, that her poor mistress was probably incapable of attending to any question she might put to her, and certainly incapable of conversing with strangers.

It was in vain she spoke to Rosalie; she attended not to her. At length Claudine thought of a stratagem she had before used with some success, when it was necessary to rouse her unhappy mistress to temporary exertion—she spoke of her child; and Rosalie, who had appeared totally insensible for some moments, raised her languid head on her arm, and fixing her dim eyes on Claudine, faintly bad her repeat what she had been saying.

Claudine then told her, that three gentlemen were below, who, she was sure, were her friends, and who certainly came to tell her some good news about the dear little boy. Rosalie, catching eagerly at the hope these words offered, seemd to make an effort to recall her dissipated and confused senses to a point worthy her attention. Claudine saw that she had gained her notice, and repeated all she had said, enforcing, with her utmost power, the idea that the three gentlemen in question were certainly sent by Montalbert to treat of a reconciliation, and restore her child.

Rosalie by degrees acquired so much power over her scattered and enfeebled spirits, as to attempt recollecting what friends were most likely to be charged with such a commission; but her intellects were not equal to the research; bewildered and confused, she put her hand to her head, and sighing deeply, she appeared to give up the inquiry in despair. There were no friends of hers who answered the minute description Claudine had given of the strangers; nor did she know of any friends of Montalbert's, who were either acquainted with his marriage, or likely to be in his confidence. Hope, however, enabled her to re-assume her powers of reflection, and she became conscious, that, whoever the persons might be who thus interested themselves in her affairs, she ought to see them, if they were Montalbert's friends, on his account; if they were her friends, on their own.

But when it was necessary to make the exertion, which her returning reason told her was necessary, her strength so failed her, that it was more than an hour before she was seated, by the assistance of the landlady, in an arm chair, and half an hour longer before she had, by the aid of hawthorn and water, obtained resolution enough to let Claudine go down with a message, that any one of the gentlemen who were most disposed to take the trouble of visiting a sick room, was desired to walk up.

An interval of some moments passed before a foot was heard on the stairs; but Rosalie, so far from finding her courage strengthened by delay, had become almost senseless and breathless, when the door was opened by Claudine, and the figure which appeared at it she just distinguished to be Charles Vyvian, before her sight and consciousness totally forsook her, and she fell back in the chair, towards which he eagerly flew to support her.

"My sister! (cried he)—my dear, dear Rosalie!—But is it, indeed, my Rosalie!—Good God! how changed!—how altered!——Where is Montalbert?—what has happened?—and why are you reduced to this situation?"

Rosalie heard him not; but Claudine, amidst her efforts to recover her mistress, related all she knew. It appeared from the surprize Vyvian expressed, that, so far from knowing any reason for the conduct of Montalbert, he was not certain of his being in England, and that all the intelligence he had gained, as to the residence of Rosalie, came from Mrs. Lessington.

Claudine, who saw her mistress incapable of listening to this discourse, renewed her lamentations; while Vyvian, eager and impatient, and not considering the consequences, bade her call up the gentlemen below: an injunction which Claudine, as inconsiderate as himself, immediately obeyed.

Rosalie, therefore, hardly opened her eyes after so unexpected an appearance as that of Charles Vyvian, before they were struck with the figure of William Lessington, who, though greatly altered since she saw him last, she immediately knew: but the suddenness of his appearance, the distress visible in his countenance, and still more in that of the stranger who stood by him, with clasped hands, and an expression of mingled terror, pity, and affection, silently gazing on her, amazed her so much, that she was incapable of asking either who he was, or why he seemed to interested in her fate?—She was incapable, indeed, of speaking at all, but held out her hand to Mr. Lessington, in a manner which forcibly expressed—"Oh! friend and guide of my youth! why have you so long deserted your unhappy Rosalie?"

Lessington now spoke to her.—"My dearest friend! (said he), my sweet Rosalie, you are ill!—you are unhappy!"

"I am, indeed," she would have answered, but she could not articulate the words. Her attempt, however, had something so affecting in it, that the stranger could no longer restrain the emotions which arose in his breast; he burst into an agony of tears, and, turning from her, exclaimed—

"She too is destroyed—destroyed as her mother was, by the accursed house of Montalbert!——Yes!—the nephew resembles the uncle—he has murdered *my* daughter!"

These strange exclamations served entirely to overcome the feeble spirits of Rosalie; she no longer comprehended, and but indistinctly heard, what passed.—Lessington hung over her with the tenderest concern, while Vyvian walked about the room in great agitation; yet attempted to appease that of the stranger, and now and then spoke a broken sentence to Rosalie. It was evident, that far from relieving the sweet sufferer, for whom they were all interested, by a continuation of this scene, they did but increase her anguish, yet none of them had sufficient presence of mind to remark this; and there was no woman about her, who had sense or observation enough, to advise them to withdraw till she could acquire more composure.

The agitation of the stranger became more violent. It was Ormsby, the unfortunate father of Rosalie, who, having returned with an ample fortune from India, had been informed, on his first inquiries, that Mrs. Vyvian was dead. From Mrs. Lessington he had learned, that young Vyvian, her son, was, by a paper she wrote to him before her death, acquainted with the real relationship in which Rosalie stood to him, and with the circumstances that had rendered her marriage with his father a source of continual unhappiness.

Charles Vyvian, who had always loved his mother much better than his father, whose sole attachment to him originated in family pride, no sooner knew this history, than, with every attention that delicacy and duty required towards the character and memory of his mother, he sought, as soon has he returned to England, the family of Lessington. The eldest son, who was settled near Oxford, was more easily applied to than any other part of it. To him, therefore, Vyvian addressed himself, and thither also Mr. Ormsby was directed, when, on application to Mrs. Lessington, he found she was herself settled in the north. After an explanation between these gentlemen, they determined to seek Rosalie together; and set out for Eastbourne, without suspecting that she was suffering under any other unhappiness than that which arose from a temporary separation from her husband; they arrived at Eastbourne, and found her emaciated by illness, injured in intellects by grief, and incapable of feeling that portion of happiness and prosperity, which, they hoped, it would have been in their power to offer her.

Ormsby, from the moment he had learned that he had a daughter living, who was worthy, for her own sake, of the tenderness he was disposed to feel towards the representative of the woman he adored, he cherished the most flattering hopes of happiness with a lovely being, who would recall continually to his mind the hours of his early felicity, and gild the evening of his life. He now found all visionary bliss vanished at once, and the bitterness of his disappointment was aggravated, when he remembered that the blow, which had murdered his happiness a second time, came from the same family that had destroyed it before. The injuries, the deceptions, the tyranny, of Old Montalbert, which had driven him from the bosom of his first Rosalie to exile and to sorrow, now seemd to be revived in the nephew to rob him of all he had left; and, in the anguish of heart, which these thoughts gave him, he forgot, that, by his unguarded transports, he was deepening the wounds he deplored. Such, however, were the unhappy effects of his expressions on the bewildered mind of his daughter, who catching from them some vague ideas about her mother, (whose name he often repeated), though unable to follow the chain of circumstances to which these expressions alluded, that her spirits were entirely overcome; and, when he fondly called her his daughter, his only hope on earth, his poor unfortunate child! she was so far from understanding it was her father who spoke to her, that she wildly fancied it was the same person who had been sent by Montalbert to take her child from her. She shuddered, therefore, as he approached her; withdrew her hand from him, as he attempted to take it, and looking with wild and eager eyes towards Lessington, who engaged her notice more than Vyvian, she appeared silently to entreat that he would deliver her from the presence of a person, of whom, was evident from her manner, she had conceived some unfavourable impression.

Shocked by this conviction, and assured that her intellects were entirely gone, the unhappy father hastily left the room, and threw himself into a chair in the parlour below, where he gave way to the anguish of his soul.

The sight of Rosalie, though she resembled her mother more by her air and voice than by any positive likeness of features, had brought to his mind a thousand tender recollections; and, in believing her irreparable hurt both in her understanding and constitution, he felt as if the wounds that had been so long healing, after his separation from her mother, were now torn open afresh; and the happiness which he had fondly hoped might gild the evening of his life seemed now vanished for ever.—Why Montalbert had left Rosalie, or why he had so cruelly taken her child from her, he could not imagine. Vyvian had learned these particulars from Claudine, and had unguardedly communicated them to the rest; but as Claudine was herself ignorant of his motives, she could only relate the facts, and Mr. Ormsby, never disposed to think favourably of the family of Montalbert, could see nothing in such actions but an hereditary depravity and malignity, which he execrated. It was not long before Vyvian joined him in the parlour. Ormsby said little to him of the resolution he was silently forming, while Vyvian, who was extremely hurt at the situation of Rosalie, whom he had ever tenderly loved, believing it impossible that Montalbert could act, as he was represented to have done, without some very strange misunderstanding, determined to set out immediately in quest of him, and, representing the situation of his wife, endeavour to develope the cause of his having thrown her into it by his rash and unkind conduct.

Mr. Lessington, in the mean time, was attempting to sooth and appease the troubled mind of his ever-beloved Rosalie, in hopes of learning and alleviating her distress. He at length succeeded so far, as to procure from her the words "Yes!" or "No!" to some of the questions he put to her; but to others she remained silent, or answered only by a deep sigh. Finding he could gain, therefore, but little information, though he stayed with her near half an hour longer than the other two gentlemen, he left her, saying he would return to her immediately, and rejoined his distressed friends below.

Some conversation there passed between them, in which the calmness of Mr. Lessington was happily opposed to the agitation of the father oppressed with sorrow, and the natural vivacity of Vyvian, who now felt disposed to quarrel with his cousin, and now to account for conduct which seemed to him unpardonable, if some reason could not be given for it.

Lessington, whose attachment to Rosalie had grown up with him, listened to each of them with patience, but acquiesced in neither of their plans. That of Mr. Ormsby, though he did not openly avow it, was to seek Montalbert, demand an explanation of his conduct, and, if he could not give some very good reason for measures so harsh and violent as he had adopted, to demand of him the satisfaction due to the injured honour and peace of the unfortunate Rosalie. Lessington perfectly understood this by the half sentences and angry expressions of Ormsby, and he saw the necessity of preventing a measure which must involve the object of his solicitude in yet deeper calamity. It was not easy, in the present agitated state of his mind, to say any thing that would not rather irritate than sooth, and, therefore, Lessington affected to attend rather to the project of Vyvian, who proposed setting out immediately to find Montalbert, and endeavour to clear up whatever mistake had given rise to proceedings so unlike the usual tenor of his conduct.

Though Lessington was clearly of opinion that Vyvian was not the properest person to engage in this explanation, yet, as he hoped to obtain Ormsby's patience while he was about it, and that something might happen in the mean time to clear up the darkness in which they were involved, he seemed to agree to Vyvian's departure, still, however, with coldness and reluctance, and as if he meditated on some scheme which he thought more eligible. At this instant Lady Llancarrick and Miss Gillman appeared; the former having heard of the arrival of the strangers, introducing herself to them as the dear friend of Mrs. Sheffield, and, as such, it seemed probable that she could give them information as to the cause of the appearances which had so greatly distressed them. The change of name, which, though Mrs. Lessington had mentioned it, had been hardly attended before, now seemed to strike Mr. Ormsby as if it were entirely now to him—— Why should his daughter have changed her name?—An appearance of concealment is always injurious. It might, however, be at the desire of her husband, since their marriage was clandestine. This reflection satisfied his mind for a moment as to the circumstance, but, as Mr. Lessington and Mr. Vyvian continued to converse one with Lady Llancarrick and the other with Miss Gillman, Mr. Ormsby, who listened to them alternately, found so many obscure hints, or evasive answers in their conversation, and thought them women whose acquaintance seemed so little creditable to his daughter, that his uneasiness became unsupportable.

He dreaded lest in the conduct of Rosalie he should find but too strong a justification of that of Montalbert. This idea was infinitely more painful to him than to believe her innocent and suffering only from misapprehension or injustice, and unable to bear the distress of mind, which every moment increased, he started up, and, leaving the room, walked up a lane near the house, which he traversed with hasty and uncertain steps while the conference lasted, which had already given him so much uneasiness.

Before that conference ended, the conviction that both Lessington and Vyvian had entertained of the perfect and unimpeachable discretion of Rosalie was very cruelly shaken. They had learned from Lady Llancarrick, who either could not or would not conceal any thing she knew, that, under a feigned name herself, and under the protection of a young man of the name of Walsingham, she had appeared at the village, where she had lived since in a retired way, but frequently receiving him at her house, and, as it was generally understood, supported by him.

To two young men, who knew nothing of the extraordinary chain of events which had separated Rosalie from Montalbert, (for Vyvian had passed eighteen months in the German Courts, from whence he had come to England only three months before this period), these circumstances could not fail of having a very unfavorable appearance. Vyvian, as soon as the ladies from whom they had gathered this intelligence were gone, talked of seeking this Mr. Walsingham, and demanding an explanation of him; a scheme which appeared to Lessington to be more pregnant with mischief than even that proposed by Ormsby. They now went in search of the latter, and found him overwhelmed with sorrow and anxiety. The state in which his daughter was, gave him the most acute pain, which was infinitely increased by the dread he now entertained as to her conduct.—What Lessington and Vyvian had to say, though the former softened it all he could, was but ill calculated to appease these fears; and a conflict now arose in the breast of the unhappy father, between his wish to return to, and, if possible, comfort his afflicted child, and his reluctance even to see her, if it could be true that she had deserted her husband, and disgraced herself.

He determined, however, once more to see her, and to see her alone. He found, on entering her apartment, that all the symptoms that seemed to have a little subsided, while she had been flattered with hopes of hearing news of her child, had since returned with renewed violence; a deadly paleness overspread her countenance, and a fever seemed to devour her. If Claudine spoke to her, she answered only by a deep sigh, and when she became sensible that a stranger was in the room, and opening her eyes saw Ormsby, she cast a reproaching look towards Claudine, waved with her hand for him to leave her, and then, covering her face with her handkerchief, sunk into silence, from which not even the voice of Lessington could rouse her:— he, at the desire of Mr. Ormsby, went to her, spoke to her, and entreated her to attend to her own health, to the anxiety of her friends; he even named her father to her, but he could obtain no other answer, than a faint entreaty that he would leave to her destiny a creature born only to be miserable. At length, she said, "My father!—alas! *I* have no father!—Do not mock me! I never saw a father!—I had a husband—indeed I had a child, but now both are gone, and I am now a wretched outcast?"

"Have you no friends, Rosalie?—(Lessington then ventured to say)—Surely there are some in whom you place confidence and friendship, though you deny it to him whom you once loved to call by the tender name of brother?"

To this it seemed as if she was either unable or unwilling to answer directly; for again, with a deep-drawn sigh, and in a half-stifled voice, she said, "You—you *are* my brother still, William, if you do not disdain the title—and then I shall not be——as, indeed, I think myself now—quite—quite friendless!"

She was now again sensible, yet Lessington doubted whether it was a proper hour to speak to her of her father, since every time he had either spoken to her, or been named to her, her ideas seemed to have taken a confused flight, from whence it was not very easy to recall them; and though Mr. Ormsby earnestly wished she might be made to understand that he was her father, yet Lessington saw her mind so shaken by trying to impress on it what her mother had, he believed, never fully related to her, that he dreaded lest such an attempt now might be the worst of consequences.

All he judged prudent to do, therefore, was to sooth her mind as much as he could for that night, and persuade her father to leave her. This, though not without difficulty, he effected. Ormsby went again with him to the parlour, whither the landlady was now summoned to give information where the best physician in the neighbourhood was to be obtained.

A messenger was dispatched for one, but hardly was he gone, and Lessington entering into conversation with his two friends on what he thought was properest to be done, when a servant on horseback brought a letter, directed to Mrs. Sheffield, which, he said required an immediate answer.—On being questioned by Mr. Vyvian who it was from, the man answered insolently enough, "That he had no orders to tell that, unless to the lady herself; but that, for his part, he was never ashamed of his master's name—it came from Squire Walsingham."

Ormsby, who saw in the name of Walsingham, and in such a correspondence, a confirmation of all the fears that had assailed him for the reputation and peace of his daughter, determined to open the letter. Lessington at first doubted how far this might be justifiable; but yielding at length to the authority of a father, the letter was opened, and, to the astonishment and indignation of the parties, was found to contain these words——

"MADAM,:

"A gentleman of the name of Montalbert has taken the trouble to write to me, on a supposition of my being a much more fortunate man than I have ever suspected myself to be. He wishes me to meet him at my own time and place, to explain to him my pretensions to the very great favour which he assures me you have honoured me with, as well in a certain long voyage, which it seems we made together, as since our return to England, where he affirms you have remained under my protection.

"Having hinted to him that I am perfectly unconscious of all this, I have received a second letter, couched in terms which do not generally pass unnoticed between gentlemen. Now, Madam, if I must risk the penalty, it is but just that I should be made conscious of the happy trespass by which I have incurred it; when I am persuaded I shall meet with exultation whatever may happen; or if it hitherto exists only in the imagination of my correspondent, I am, nevertheless, ready to meet him as he desires, provided that before I become *his* adversary, you will permit me to assume the pleasing and honourable title of your champion.

"But, as no time is to be lost, I await your answer with extreme impatience, flattering myself it will bring permission to throw himself at your feet, one who is,

Dear Madam,
Your most devoted servant,

S. WALSINGHAM."

Vyvian had no sooner heard the contents of this extraordinary billet, than he flew out of the room to find the servant that had brought it, for it appeared as if the writer of it was waiting somewhere in the neighbourhood, and he was at all event resolved to find him.

Of Mr. Walsingham, neither Ormsby, Vyvian, nor Lessington knew any thing but the name; and this letter, of whatever nature might have been his acquaintance with Rosalie, having certainly the air of an insult, was not calculated to give them a favourable opinion of him. None of them could help seeing, that a meeting between him and Montalbert must be attended with fatal consequences, if not to the life of either, at least to the honour of the unfortunate young woman, who was the cause of their quarrel. Vyvian, breathing nothing but vengeance against a man capable of writing such a letter, would listen to nothing that Lessington could say; and Ormsby, lost in bewildering conjectures, but more uneasy than ever, determined at length to pursue his original plan of finding Montalbert; and, having learned the cause of his conduct, and of the present extraordinary letter, to take Rosalie and conceal her in some obscure retreat if she was guilty; or, if she was innocent, to vindicate that innocence in the face of the world. It was, however, necessary for him to await the arrival of the physician who was sent for, as it was certain the personal sufferings of his unhappy daughter became every hour more alarming. Lessington, with the most patient pity both for Ormsby and his child, remained with him; but his arguments had no longer any effect on the impetuosity of Vyvian, who having learned, from the servant he questioned, that Mr. Walsingham was at Brighthelmstone, set off thither in a post chaise, attended only by his servant, assuring his friends that he had no design of taking the resentment of Montalbert out of his hands; but that he was determined to clear up this extraordinary business in some way or other, and that they should hear of him in a very few hours.

With these assurances, since he would hear nothing Ormsby or Lessington could say to urge remaining with them, they were compelled to suffer him to depart.

CHAP.

IT was already late in the evening, and Ormsby and Lessington awaited in the most distressing suspence the arrival of the physician they expected; the messenger sent to him having returned, to say he would be with them as soon as possible. Rosalie, though still conscious of, and grateful for the attentions of Lessington, seemed too ill to enter into conversation or explanation of any kind. But at length in attempting to sooth and to reason with her, he prevailed upon her to say, that she should die contented, and even prefer death, if she could but see her child once more, and ask his father's protection for him. This was more than she had yet coherently said; and Lessington, who was now alone by her bed-side, made an effort to carry the conversation farther. "And why, my dear Rosalie," said he, "why do you doubt his protecting his son? Since he has taken from you, however unkind that step may have been, as far as it regards you, Mr. Montalbert had probably no other design than to take care of him, and give him a father's protection."—"Good God!" exclaimed Rosalie, "can you, my dear Sir, believe he could have been guilty of so very cruel an action, as tearing him from me, had he not determined to destroy me, and to erase all recollection of a marriage, which he probably repents, and is ashamed of?—His mother, his cruel mother, and his treacherous friend Alozzi"—she here paused a moment, unable to go on—"have prevailed on him to abandon me. Perhaps too, some newer attachment....for I can never think that *they* alone could influence him—some newer attachment." She could proceed no farther; the idea was too cruel to be supported; and her voice became inarticulate through the violence of her emotions.

Lessington had never heard her speak so much, and so consistently before, and greatly as he saw she was affected, he yet hoped that tears might rather relieve than injure her; he therefore ventured, after waiting a moment that she might recover herself, to go on.

"Perhaps, my dear Rosalie, neither of these causes may have occasioned the estrangement you deplore.—Perhaps,...forgive me if I seem to impute to you what you may be, and I believe are incapable of—but possible some *unintentional* indiscretion on your part may have been exaggerated and misrepresented.—Montalbert may have conceived himself injured by your conduct, and has rashly treated you as culpable, without hearing your justification."

Rosalie pausing a moment, as if to recollect her agitated spirits, raised herself on one arm, and with her other had taking the hand of Lessington, she said in a low, yet solemn voice, "My dear brother! as there is truth in Heaven, I was never guilty of the slightest deviation from my duty, even in idea:—Montalbert must know my heart too well to suppose it.—I long doubted of his existence; for you know how we were separated.—Yet never, Oh! no never did my heart wander from in faith and affection to him!"

"I do believe you, my poor Rosalie," said Lessington, "I sincerely believe you, though *how*, or even how long you were separated, I am totally ignorant."

"I have papers that will explain it to you, my William, but I feel that it must be when I am no more; then Claudine shall deliver you a small box, in which you will find a journal of my unhappy life, while I was able to keep a journal.—Yet a little, and I shall need no other justification to Montalbert.—When he finds that he has destroyed me, it is he, poor man, who will want consolation—who will be an object of pity."

Rosalie spoke slowly, and with difficulty, and in a weak, faint voice; yet her anxious father, who had glided into the room, heard her distinctly; and as she had never appeared to him so collected before, he was tremblingly solicitous for her to learn that he lived, and sought only to protect her:—Like one who sees his sole treasure half escaped from an abyss, yet knows it is not quite in safety, and dreads to see it again snatched from his uncertain grasp. So Ormsby seemed lost in the contrariety of emotions he felt: he softly approached Lessington, and in a whisper besought him to speak to Rosalie of her father. But, however carefully he uttered this, his daughter heard some words, which as every thing now hurried and alarmed her, made her hastily put aside the curtain.

The amazement, not unmingled with some degree of apprehension, which she expressed on seeing a stranger, was a proof of how little remembered of what had passed before: Ormsby, unable to command his emotion, sobbed aloud. As stooping over her, he took her pale and emaciated hands; "Rosalie!" cried he, "dear representative of the most beloved, and most injured of women—Speak to me—Speak to, and acknowledge your unhappy father!" The look with which she regarded him alarmed Lessington, who said, "My dear Rosalie, your mother has left with Vyvian papers, in which it is declared, that before your marriage she discovered to you the mystery of your birth, and why it was that you passed as the child of my parents, while your own were concealed.—Recollect, my sweet friend, all that your dear mother said to you; and then you will at once understand how it is that your father, who very lately arrived from the East Indies, now hastens to claim the only treasure his fate has left him." All the particulars indeed that her mother had related at that moment returned to her mind: her heart acknowledged the dear tie that was now offered to it; she raised her languid frame, and would have thrown herself into the arms of Ormsby, but her strength failed her—she was only able to pronounce, "My father," before she sunk down in the same state of weakness which had often appeared so alarming—but before Ormsby or Lessington could conjure how they should repair the imprudence they had thus been guilty of, the physician they expected arrived.

It was hardly possible that he could come at a more unfavourable time to judge of his patient: he found her indeed in a state, which, as the reason of her violent and extraordinary emotion could not be entirely explained, gave him an opinion of her danger, even beyond the truth; and when he retired with her father and Mr. Lessington, he expressed such fears as to the event of her illness, that Ormsby, half frantic, could hardly be prevented from setting out for London immediately, and bringing down, at any expence, the most eminent physician, who could be prevailed upon to take the journey. Lessington saw that this would answer no purpose, since if Rosalie was in so hazardous a state, as she was believed to be, it would be too late to expect relief from assistance that was to come so far. He thought it better to engage the gentleman now with them to remain all night, and to await the event of the morning; and this with some difficulty he accomplished.

The fever which preyed upon Rosalie, and which had originated solely in anguish of mind, increased during this miserable night; but it seemed no longer to affect her intellects: amid variety of pain, her senses were so clear, that she repeated to Claudine what she had said relative to the box which was to be given to her friends. She told her too, that it was her father who was below, and that she had never seen him before, but forbore any other explanation. Ormsby and Lessington, who could neither of them sleep, and who did not indeed attempt going to bed, had visited her room several times during the night, and flattered themselves from these symptoms that she was amending: but when Dr. G. saw her at an early hour of the morning, he thought the fever higher, and the whole house was in consternation and despair.

It was towards noon—the physician was gone, having promised to return in the evening. Ormsby and Lessington, as the suffering patient was apparently sleeping, had walked out to relive their fatigued and anxious spirits by the air, and having remained on about half an hour, they were met, just as they entered the house, by Claudine: who, with expressions of great joy in her countenance, told them, in her broken English, "That Mr. Walsingham was come; Le bon Walsingham, l'excellent Ami de sa chere Maitresse;" for all that, and more his generosity to her, had made him appear to Claudine. Claudine therefore was very much surprised and mortified to find, that the intelligence she was eager to communicate was so far from giving pleasure to either of the gentlemen, that they advanced towards the parlour, where she had told them Mr. Walsingham was, with evident marks of anger in their countenance and manner.

The letter they had seen addressed to Rosalie, impressed them with the most unfavourable idea of the person they were going to meet: Ormsby, shocked at his arrival, which seemed a confirmation of fears in regard to the conduct of his daughter, which had been a while suspended by fears for her health, was tempted to affront him even on the first moment of meeting him; and it was with difficulty he was diverted from this petulance by Lessington, who said, as they were entering the house, "I own I cannot see, my good Sir, what we shall gain by preventing an explanation from this young man, which he will certainly not give us, if we directly insult him: whereas, if there is any mistake in all this (as I cannot but believe there is), a little coolness may serve, if not to make us easy, at least to produce such an explanation as will direct our resentment. Above all things, it seems to me necessary to avoid every thing like violence in this small house, if you would not endanger yet more the life of your daughter."

Ormsby felt the reasonableness of this remonstrance, and checked his own feelings as much as possible, though his countenance and air expressed them but too forcibly. If these gentlemen were astonished at his appearance, after such a letter as he had written, they were still more so, to find him a young man of a very different appearance to what they had figured to themselves the writer of so impertinent a letter must be.

Walsingham, unconscious of any offence, and rather supporting he should be received as the friend and protector of Rosalie, (for Claudine had explained who these gentlemen were) was immediately repulsed by the angry countenance of the elder gentleman, and the cold and distant bow of the other. He advanced, however, and in that graceful manner which his habitual dejection rather made more interesting, he expressed the extreme concern he felt at hearing of the indisposition of Mrs. Montalbert. Yet how much satisfaction it gave him, (and he bowed to Ormsby as he spoke), to learn that she was happy in the tender attentions of a father. "If you *know* me, Sir," said Ormsby, "you ought to know and to feel, that your presence here is an insult which must deserve the deepest resentment of injured honour. Are you come, Sir, to overwhelm with shame my unfortunate daughter in her last hours? Are you come to triumph over a miserable family, whom you have ruined in their fame, and in their happiness?" All the passions of an injured father, combined in the bosom of Ormsby, who trembling, and for a moment deprived of breath, gave Walsingham (as he stood petrified by such an address), time to say—

"*Am* I come, Sir, with *this* design? am I come with *any* design injurious to the peace and honour of Mrs. Montalbert? Certainly not. You must greatly have mistaken me, if you suppose it." Ormsby, by a motion of his head and hand, expressed what he could not at the moment find words to utter: while Lessington, taking advantage of this involuntary silence, said, "After such a letter, Sir, as that with which you have affronted Mrs. Montalbert, and, though her, all her family, all her friends, you must suppose....."

"A letter, Sir," interrupted Walsingham, "a letter from me? and insulting Mrs. Montalbert? That is a charge which I own I am not prepared to answer. I have most certainly never written to Mrs. Montalbert since I had the honour of seeing her last."

Ormsby, naturally violent, yet subdued by time and trouble, was so overcome, that he had thrown himself half suffocated into a chair. Lessington, more master of himself, continued to speak for him.

"The letter, Sir, however, that we received, can admit of no excuse: you have seen or heard of Mr. Montalbert?"

"Pardon me, Sir, I have done neither—I did not even know he was in England."

The countenance of Walsingham underwent a visible change as he said this; Lessington failed not to remark it, but imputed it to emotions very different from those that Walsingham felt while he continued to speak.

"No, Sir, I did not even know Mr. Montalbert was come to England; but as it appears that he is, may I request the favour of a direction to him? You will also oblige me by showing me the letter, which I am supposed to have written to his wife, if she is, as I fear, too ill to admit of my applying to her for it personally."

The emotion of Walsingham increased; he turned very pale, and his lips trembled.

"I have not got the letter," said Ormsby, "nor has my daughter ever seen it; Mr. Vyvian has taken it with him to Brighthelmstone, where your servant told us you were to be found, in order to demand an explanation."

"*My servant!*" exclaimed Walsingham, more and more surprised; "there is certainly some strange mistake in all this. Pray, Sir, with what name was it signed?" Lessington then answering it was "S. Walsingham." Walsingham began immediately to suspect the truth; but when Lessington explained to him the contents of this letter, and that they evidently alluded to a demand of satisfaction, which the writer of it had received from Montalbert; and when he also said that Vyvian had left them the preceding evening in the full determination to have a meeting with Mr. Walsingham, all the mischief which might happen between Montalbert, Vyvian, and his gay, fashionable cousin (from whom he now easily understood the letter came), occurred in an instant to his mind. He saw that the death of one of them, perhaps of more, was likely to follow from the mere mistake of a name. He saw the extreme concern which Rosalie might feel, if any evil should happen even to a stranger, whose offence towards her was at least palliated by ignorance; but should Montalbert or Vyvian be wounded, or fall, the consequences to her must be still more dreadful.

All this no sooner struck Walsingham, than he explained as clearly as he could the nature of his apprehensions to Lessington, who saw at once they were too well grounded, for Walsingham described his relation as rash, haughty, and violent; one who could be much more likely to retort any affront with interest, than to enquire the ground on which it was given. Ormsby and Lessington were also well assured that Vyvian was irritable, proud, and impatient; and though neither of them were personally acquainted with Montalbert, they had no reason to believe, from all they had heard of him, that he was by any means of a calmer disposition. A collusion then between these three, or even any two of these fiery spirits, could hardly fail of producing some fatal event.

The generous mind and excellent heart of Walsingham were never more conspicuous than at this moment. Without seeming to advert to the challenge, which it was certain Montalbert had sent to his cousin, while intending it for him—without any menace, or even hint of his resentment, he expressed nothing but a wish to go immediately in pursuit of the parties, and endeavour to prevent a meeting, from which so much was to be dreaded. It was not till after a severe struggle, however, that he could determine to quit the house, not only without seeing Rosalie, but without enquiring after her health, or the circumstances which had deprived her of it so suddenly. Claudine had told him enough to convince him that Montalbert had been actuated by jealousy, and he supposed the object of that jealousy was himself.—A thousand painful thoughts crowded upon his heart—the husband of Rosalie was returned:—No doubt, therefore, remained of his existence; and it became more than ever prudent for the ill-starred Walsingham to stifle the growing affection which must now be utterly hopeless.—But so much did that affection partake of his noble spirit, that the happiness and the peace of Rosalie were infinitely dearer to him than his own, and he flew to save the husband, whose life was between him and those hopes which, in despite of reason, he had at times indulged.

If his talk was in this respect painful, it was hardly less so in what related to Mr. Ormsby; though the matter of the letter was cleared up, he saw, that the father of Rosalie regarded him as one who had been the cause of Montalbert's estrangement from her; that long and disagreeable explanations must take place, and that he could hardly hope to be received even as the friend of her to whom he felt such painful partiality.—Ormsby, while he anxiously hastened his departure, treated him with coolness, almost with incivility; but Lessington, with milder manners, was more ready to believe that no blame could attach to the conduct of Rosalie in regard to him. Walsingham saw enough to give him great fears on her account; and with a heart penetrated by sorrow, he set out post to overtake Vyvian, and, if possible, meet Montalbert, who, from the substance of his relation's letter which Lessington repeated to Walsingham, was, he concluded, either at Brighthelmstone, or in its neighbourhood, waiting the rendezvous which he had demanded.

The wild indiscretion of Claudine had communicated to her mistress the arrival of Walsingham; and though her regard for him was as pure and innocent as that which she felt for either of those whom she had learned to consider as her brothers, yet she suffered extremely when she found he was gone, and had not seen her: not only because she was sure it would give him pain, but because it convinced her that the generous protection he had offered her had been the cause of his becoming suspected by those who ought to have felt the greatest obligation towards him; and because she dreaded lest he should be involved in farther difficulties on her account.—She did not indeed know how near he already was to the dangers she apprehended for him.

Ill as Rosalie was, however, she was not so enervated in mind as in body; and after hearing from Claudine an account of Walsingham's departure, and all she had collected or fancied of the conversation while he stayed, she summoned resolution enough to determine upon putting into Lessington's hands the account she had kept of every event, from her arrival at Naples to the moment when she so unexpectedly met with a friend and protector in Walsingham, and was delivered almost by a miracle from her hopeless confinement. During her voyages she had also made memorandums of every occurrence, and since her residence at Eastbourne she had returned to her journal, and related the events of her life, monotonous as they were, in the flattering hope that Montalbert might one day go over them, and that they might bear testimony to her unceasing attachment to him, and to her duty.

In the effusions of an ingenuous and unadulterated mind there is always a simplicity of character, which at once evinces the truth of whatever relates. Though Rosalie though not of that, she yet felt, that if once Montalbert could be prevailed upon to read her narrative, all that had befallen her would be explained.—Shocked as she was at his cruel conduct towards her, and despairing ever to see him more, she had directed that these papers might not be delivered till after her death, which she believed to be nearly approaching; but as from what Mr. Lessington had said to her, from the sudden appearance of Walsingham, his departure without seeing her, and from all that Claudine had told her, of the manner and countenance of Mr. Ormsby, Rosalie had but too much reason to think the generous friendship of Walsingham towards her might endanger his life, she rallied her feeble and fainting spirits to consider how it was possible to avert the dreaded evil. She saw this could only by done by her putting into the hands of

Lessington these proofs of Walsingham's disinterested friendship, and leaving him to act as she knew his own prudence and sense would dictate.

CHAP.

CLAUDINE went down by the direction of her mistress, who requested to see Mr. Lessington. On his entering the room, he found her raised in the bed by pillars; her countenance was very much changed for the worse since he was with her last, and her pale hands trembled while she sorted some packets of paper tied with ribands, which she took out of two boxes that were before her.

She looked at him, but did not speak. It, therefore, immediately occurred to Lessington, that Claudine had informed her of Walsingham's arrival and departure; and he felt confused and distressed, not knowing how he could avoid giving the sorrowful information she would seek.—Rosalie, on her part, not only feared to ask any questions, but dreaded to hear what had passed—for she was now possessed of recollection enough to advert to all that Lessington had said, and knew that Walsingham was an object of suspicion to him and Mr. Ormsby: nor could she doubt but that the conduct of her husband had been occasioned by the same mistrust.—The appearance, therefore, of Walsingham, must undoubtedly have deepened all these ill impressions, and Rosalie could not think upon them without the most acute pain, since it was but too probable that the generous and disinterested friendship of Walsingham had brought upon him treatment he little deserved, and which she thought him very unlikely to bear patiently. If these fears and conjectures were almost insupportable, what would she have suffered, had she known how much of the evil she apprehended was already realized; while Walsingham, unweared in generosity, was more than ever entitled to her gratitude and regard.

Her sickened soul, where indeed rested the cause of all her complaints, so far affected her enfeebled frame, that, when she would have explained to Lessington the nature of the papers she put into his hands, by relating her situation at the various times on which they had been written, she could hardly finish even a sentence—but, putting the packets into his hands, she faintly bade him read them in the order in which they were tied.——"You, and my poor father, (said she, in a faint voice), will find that your unhappy Rosalie had done nothing which ought to make you ashamed of the affection you have felt for her.....Vindicate my honour, William!—rescue my memory from reproach!—and, for the sake of my dear, dear boy, convince his father that I die innocent of all reproach, and that even in death I bless and love him." - - - - - - - - She would have said more, but put her hand to her forehead, and signified that she could not.

Lessington, affected even to tears and sobs, could not command himself sufficiently to speak. The sight of his emotion added fresh pangs to what she endured, when, waving her hand, she seemed to entreat him to leave her, and he silently obeyed.

It was some time before he could recover himself enough to read aloud the melancholy narrative thus entrusted to him, to which Mr. Ormsby listened with anxious yet gloomy attention. When they had arrived at that part of the journal, written on board the ship which brought her to England, they saw far enough into her story to be convinced that the meeting of Rosalie with Walsingham was entirely accidental; that she could not have acted otherwise than she did, and that the conduct of Walsingham had been that of the most generous and disinterested of friends: little, therefore, remained necessary for the entire vindication of both parties, but to remove the false impressions given by Lady Llancarrick and her friend, that they had resided together at Eastbourne, which, though those amiable ladies had not asserted, they had spoken of in such a manner as to leave little doubt of the fact.

Jealous for the honour of his daughter, which her own artless narrative had nearly cleared, (so powerful is simple truth), Ormsby now pressed eagerly to have all remaining doubts satisfied. Though Claudine could not keep up a regular dialogue, she could make herself understood when plain questions only were put to her. Ormsby, with that trembling apprehension which is felt by those who dread the result of an inquiry which they are yet determined to make, called her into the room, and, with the assistance of Lessington, had already convinced himself, that Mr. Walsingham had acted with the utmost delicacy and propriety in regard to Rosalie, when a post chaise and four, the horses extremely fatigued, drove up to the door, and a gentleman, unknown to both Ormsby and Lessington, entered the room.

Pale, his hair in disorder, his eyes wild, and his whole person expressive of haste and distress, he uttered something, in a manner so incoherent, that neither of them understood him. He saw they did not; and, throwing himself into a chair, he said, "I suppose I speak to Mr. Ormsby and Mr. Lessington.....I imagine, Sir, (addressing himself to the former)—I imagine your daughter is here?"

Ormsby, alarmed and amazed, hesitated a moment, hardly knowing what to say. The stranger, without waiting for his answer, continued to speak——

"I known not whether you see before you the most injured, or the most guilty, of men——I only know that I am the most wretched!"

"It is Mr. Montalbert, I believe, to whom I speak! (said Lessington).—It is long, very long, since I saw you last, Sir—and I fear - - - - - - - -"

"You fear, and with but too much reason, (said Montalbert, interrupting him), that our meeting now can only be productive of pain........Vyvian has told me - - - - -"

"You have seen Vyvian then?" inquired Lessington.

"I saw him, but not till it was too late. He is gone in search of another man of the same name as him whom *I* most unfortunately met—and - - - - - - - -"

"Good God! (exclaimed Ormsby)—you have met then with that Walsingham, to whom Rosalie owes her safety, perhaps her life, and you have had the cruelty, the rashness - - - - - - -"

"To kill him!" cried Montalbert with fierceness, and in a tone that re-echoed through the house.

Claudine, on the first appearance of Montalbert, whom she had never seen before, had listened at the door of the room, which was left half open; she heard this terrible speech, and, shrieking aloud, ran up stairs, but before she reached the door of her lady's room, she fell down in a sort of fit, sobbing and screaming aloud. This was not wanting to terrify the unhappy Rosalie; for tremblingly alive to every alarm since her child had been torn from her, there was seldom any thing passed in the house to which she did not listen. She heard the stopping of a carriage, the entrance of a person into the parlour, and soon after the voice of Montalbert, uttering the dreadful sentence—"I have killed him!"—struck her ears; then the shrieks of Claudine, who seemed to be immediately at her door—desperation lent her strength.

She had on a loose dressing gown, when throwing herself out of the bed, and holding by the furniture, for she was unable to move without such help, she reached the door of her apartment. Claudine weak, and at that moment incapable of exercising the very little judgment she ever possessed, continued to intercept the way, having thrown herself down on the stairs. Rosalie, leaning against the door-case, attempted, but in vain, to obtain an answer; and her increasing terrors threatened every instant to deprive her of the little strength she had thus collected, when Lessington, aware of the sad effect that such a noise in the house must have, suddenly quitted Montalbert, without staying to hear all he had to relate, and hastened up stairs, in hopes of appeasing the foolish maid, and accounting to Rosalie for the alarm in some way which might not destroy her at once; to his utter astonishment he found her out of her bed, looking more dead than alive, and just sinking to the ground as he sprang forward, and caught her in his arms, then carrying her into her room, he placed her in a chair, and rang for assistance, for he believed her dying, and forgot, in that moment, every thing else.

The consequence of his violence, however, was that the father and husband of Rosalie rushed also into the room, where Lessington, supporting her head, and chafing her hands, continued to implore that assistance which none had the presence of mind to give. Some person, however, had by this time fetched the apothecary, and the usual remedies being administered, Rosalie seemed to be recovering. It was then, at the earnest entreaties of Lessington, that Montalbert and Ormsby were prevailed upon to go out of the room, and Lessington soon after followed them, declaring that his sister (for so he always called her) was much better, and, if left to the women for a little while, would soon be entirely recovered. It was, however, easy to see he did not think so; for, incapable of following advice he was so solicitous to give, he could not forbear listening at the door, going half-way up the stairs, and showing many symptoms of extreme inquietude. He dreaded, indeed, even the restoration of Rosalie's senses, when he was assured she would immediately ask questions; to which the folly of Claudine, or the matter of fact of the woman of the house, would give answers that might occasion the most dangerous relapse. These uneasy apprehensions were not appeased by the appearance of the apothecary, who expressed himself under the greatest alarm for the event, entreated that the lady might be kept quiet, and that the next visit of the physician might be hastened.—Montalbert heard all this in a state of mind it is impossible to describe. He knew, indeed, that Rosalie was ill from a report of Vyvian; but he knew not how ill, having seen him only for a moment.

Now all her dangers appeared to him with redoubled terrors. From the little explanation, which his passion would admit of during his short and unfortunate interview with Walsingham, he began to doubt whether he had not been guilty at once of ingratitude and cruelty, and whether he should not now be punished with eternal remorse, as well as by losing Rosalie for ever. Still ardent and impetuous, he inquired why he could not go or send for the physician instantly—then not listening to any reasons that were given him, why it would be ineffectual, he started up, demanded of Mr. Greenwood, the apothecary, his positive opinion as to the state of the lady above the stairs, and insisted upon being allowed himself to see her. Against this, however, Lessington remonstrated warmly, and Ormsby even angrily; while Mr. Greenwood protested to him, that, if she was subjected to any farther alarms, he would not answer for her life till morning. He said that he had already been compelled to quiet her harrassed spirits by a medicine for that purpose; and if its effects were countered, such was the weakness of her frame, and such the nature of the fever which continually seized her, that the most fatal effects would very probably follow: he then took his leave.

Montalbert threw himself into a chair; and gave himself up to the most dreadful apprehensions. Ormsby walked about the room in a state but little better, while Lessington, ever useful and composed, ascended softly to the chamber of the poor patient, whom he found sometimes uttering a few incoherent words in a low voice, then, with a deep sigh, sinking into silence. At length she seemed to become quite tranquil; and Lessington having insisted on Claudine's leaving the room, and engaged the woman of the house, with one of her maids, to remain there, returned himself to Ormsby and Montalbert, whom he was not very willing to leave long together.

The instant his immediate fears for Rosalie subsided, the idea that Montalbert had destroyed the unfortunate Walsingham recurred to the mind of Lessington. He shuddered, and, at once pitying and condemning him, recollected that his person was not safe; and if the event of his meeting with Walsingham had been as fatal as he represented it, he ought to hasten from a country where he was liable to be seized as a murderer.

Montalbert sat immovable; he seemed regardless of any danger that might threaten himself, but listened to every noise in the house; and if he fancied any one stirred in Rosalie's chamber, he started, and eagerly asked Lessington if he thought she was awake and sensible?

Ormsby, overcome with fatigue and anxiety, had now been persuaded to retire, and Lessington remained alone with Montalbert.

It appeared to the former to be absolutely necessary that Montalbert should be reminded of his danger, or at least that its extent might be known; taking occasion then when he made some sudden inquiry about his wife, Lessington said, "Allow me to remark to you, Mr. Montalbert, that your real tenderness for our poor unfortunate Rosalie, of whose innocence I am sure you will once day be perfectly convinced, cannot be so well shown as by your recovering your presence of mind in the present sad conjecture; and if the fatal event has happened, which you spoke of when you first arrived, you surely ought to think of your own safety, on which, I am sure, the life of Rosalie must depend."

"Walsingham was not dead when I left him, (answered he mournfully); but I fear his wounds are mortal!"

"Good God! (exclaimed Lessington); and you remain here regardless of the event?"

"Quite so, (replied he), as far as relates to myself.—What have I left, that should make me wish to preserve my life?"

"Pray, (interrupted Lessington, who feared from his manner that he might relapse into violence)—pray relate to me what has passed since you were separated from my sister?"

Montalbert pushed his hand to his head, as if almost unable to undertake the painful task; but Lessington, who had many reasons for wishing to engage him in it, urging him again, he said—

"I conclude you know the circumstances that so strangely divided me from Rosalie.—I was returning to rejoin her in Sicily; having left my mother so extremely displeased at my positive refusal to marry the lady she had chosen for me, that I intended merely to consult my wife before I declared our marriage, determining to return to England, and to live in the humble and obscure way our fortune demanded, till I became possessed of the property, however small, that must be mine after my mother's decease.

"There were reasons that rendered our residence in Sicily unpleasant to me, even when we were together; the frequent absences, which our fear of my mother's displeasure had obliged me to submit to, became daily more insupportable, and I was forming schemes of retired happiness when I had thrown off this cruel restraint, and dared to be poor and independent. Judge then how horrible were my feelings, when, awaking from this dream of felicity, I found Messina in ruins, and the country for many miles around it convulsed by an earthquake, which had, two days before we made the coast, buried half its inhabitants.

"I cannot tell you what were my sensations after I had with much difficulty landed, for I have never since been able to define them; nor do I know from whence sprang the resolution with which I explored the place where the villa of Alozzi had stood, of which no other vestige remained than some pieces of black and half-burnt ruins: yet I looked with tearless eyes into the dark chasms in which it was sunk, though I thought they but too surely contained all I had loved—my Rosalie and her child!

"The first evening that I arrived at this melancholy spot, where I had so lately left the lovely treasures of my heart in apparent safety, there was none near it—I was undisturbed in my gloomy contemplation, and remained lingering about the place, till my servant, who had followed me at a distance according to my direction, came to me at night fall, and led me to a cottage not far off, inhabited by a woman and her daughter, who had lost the rest of their family. Of these my servant made some inquiries, as they were tenants of Count Alozzi. He heard that the Count was seen after the first great shock, and had hired a vessel to take himself and some of his dependents to Naples; but whether he escaped the second, or whether he was drowned with many others on the sudden reflux of the sea, these women had no means of knowing.—Here then was a glimpse, and but a glimpse of hope, that my wife and child might exist; but, on farther inquiry the next evening, I thought even this faint hope vanished. I knew that when I left Sicily, Alozzi was gone to Agrigentum, and was to stay there some time longer than I proposed remaining at Naples. It was not now, however, a time to consider much the cause of his unexpected return. All my thoughts were bent on trying to recover from the ruins of his villa the sad remains of my lost family; and with this dreary sort of satisfaction I occupied my mind, repairing the next day to the place, where I found three or four stout peasants already at work.

"I inquired of them by whom they were employed?—they answered, in no very mild manner, by themselves, and for their own purposes and profit. I saw that they feared I was disposed, if not authorised, to impede their designs; but by the most infalliable of all arguments, (for I emptied my purse), and soon satisfied them that they should not be interrupted in the possession of whatever valuable effects they might recover, since my sole purpose was to search for the mangled relics of a wife and child. I offered them more money if they would procure farther assistance to expedite this search, and, explaining to them who I was, promised farther reward if they could procure any certain intelligence of Count Alozzi. They agreed that he had been seen after the first violent concussions of the earth; but all believed, or affected to believe, he perished in the second.

"It was now nine days, since the fatal catastrophe, three of which I stood by the yawning cavern that had swallowed the villa of Alozzi. Little was discovered by the men who went down among the ruins; they were, indeed, more intent on their own purposes than on mine. On the evening of the third day I went down myself, and I thought that by the remains of wainscoting, or furniture, I should be led to the ruins of that part of the house Rosalie inhabited. Desperate, I tore away, at some risk to myself, the door cases, broken or scorched pieces of building, and at length found the room where Rosalie usually sat. I could certainly distinguish that there were no remains of human bodies in it; two only had been found, and they were known to be servants; but though another day's search satisfied that no more persons were buried in the ruins, yet even this circumstance afforded no proof, that those my sickening soul inquired after were living.

"With an anxious and hopeless heart I left the peasants busily employed in labour, which had already amply repaid them, and now sat out to wander over the country, asking questions of the unhappy persons who were yet scattered about it, though their answers only irritated my misery, or confirmed my despair.

Most of them were too much occupied by the wants and woes of their own condition, to give much attention to me. After some days were thus vainly wasted, I crossed over to the other side of the island, and went among such relations and friends of Alozzi as had escaped any immediate share of the misfortune by being at a distance from that part where its violence had fallen. Among them I learned that Alozzi had quitted Agrigentum four or five days before the earthquake, and had gone, as they believed, to Messina, where they had no doubt of his having perished, as they had never heard of him since. There was hardly one of those families who had not some relation or friend of lament; and I only quitted one house of mourning to enter another.

To me, all appeared equally desolate and wretched; the image of my lost happiness continually haunted me, and I returned more unhappy than ever to the place where once stood the villa of Alozzi.

"By this time some peasants who had been dispersed, had come back to that neighbourhood also; among them I met two or three Sbirri, who were, I thought, likely persons to have seen Alozzi, if he had indeed escaped, for they were daring and active, and were probably busy wherever pay or plunder were likely to be had from the rich that survived the earthquake. I entered into conversation with them, and heard that they had passed the night, after the first violent shock, at a house belonging to the Count, where they had seen him with a lady and her child, and a Neapolitan servant. That they knew the lady was an Heretic from the woman of the house, who, as well as those to whom she had given shelter during the horrors of that night, had expressed their fears of remaining under the same roof with a person of that description, and that some of the women had actually left it, lest she should draw Divine vengeance on the house.

This ascertained, beyond a doubt, that it was my wife who accompanied Alozzi, I now endeavoured to trace her farther, with an eagerness which those only can imagine, who, amidst the darkest despair, are suddenly dazzled with a ray of hope. I inquired of every body—I offered money for the slightest information, and sometimes paid it for accounts which I knew to be false. At length a man was brought to me, who assured me that he had conversed with Zulietta, the Neapolitan girl, whom he exactly described, and who had told him that her mistress and Count Alozzi were gone to Naples, and she was only by accident left behind. He named the time when, and place where, he had seen Zulietta: I bade him lead me thither, but learned that this young woman was gone to Catanca, with a person who had promised to find a passage for her to her home. To Cantanca I followed her; she had left it a few days before with a family, who had taken her into their service, and was gone to Italy, but whether to Naples or not I could not learn. To Naples, however, I resolved to go, in order to pursue the clue, which I hoped would lead me to the recovery of all I held most dear upon earth.

"I had, however, lost above five weeks in Sicily, and on the voyage, which proved unusually tedious. At length I reached Naples, and, concealing myself with every possible precaution from all who were likely to know me, I hastened to the house of Alozzi.

"The porter knew and admitted me. He told me that the Count had escaped from Sicily, and had even remained a month afterwards at Naples, which he had left but a few days since at a moment's notice, and without saying whither he was gone, or when he should return. As this was not unusual with him, there appeared nothing extraordinary in it to the servant, who, when I questioned him as to any lady who had with her a child, and who accompanied his master, he assured me he knew of none, with such an air of simplicity, that I could not but believe he at least knew nothing of the arrival of my wife and his master. A thousand fears, and of various sorts, now assailed me. I trembled at once for my Rosalie's safety, and even for her fidelity, if she lived........All the symptoms which I thought I had formerly remarked of Alozzi's admiration, if not attachment, recurred to me: he had not brought her to his own house publicly as the wife of his friend, whom he had assisted to escape from destruction. This indeed might be accounted for my situation in regard to my mother; but why was she so carefully concealed from old and confidential servants? I closely questioned them all, and could not discover that one of them had the least knowledge of the Count's having rescued my wife and child. They all declared themselves equally ignorant whither he was gone; he had taken only his valet with him. On farther minute inquiry, however, I discovered that, for two or three days before his departure, he had appeared very uneasy and restless; was frequently shut up with his own man for a considerable time after he had been running about on business, which, though it was a profound secret, seemed by his manner to be of great importance. I passed a whole day in these examinations, and, in attempting to trace the road Alozzi had taken, determined to follow and overtake him. I found that he was gone towards Florence, and thither I impatiently hastened.

"I arrived at the house, whither I with difficulty had followed his track, the very moment he was stepping into his carriage, about which his baggage announced his being on a journey; when I advanced and spoke to him—he changed colour, hesitated, and trembled; I begged of him to go back with me for a moment, and, without farther preface, asked him what was become of my wife?

'What is become of her, Montalbert! (said he, still more agitated);—do *you* know nothing of her?'

'I know (said I) that she left Sicily with you—that you have since concealed her somewhere.'

'I hope (added he, in a hasty and faltering voice) that you also know, then, for which of your English friends she chose to quit such protection as I was able to offer her, and in which she might undoubtedly have remained safe till your return.' - - - - - - - -

'My English friends! (cried I)—what English friend?—How could she meet them?—and - - - - - - - - '

"But I should never conclude what I have to relate to you, Mr. Lessington, were I to repeat the long discourse that passed. Alozzi told me a very plausible story of his sudden return to Messina; of his having sought and saved Rosalie and her child; and of his having afterwards placed her in a retired lodging, where, after a stay of near a month, during which he had done every thing in his power to tranquillize and sooth her with the hopes of my return, she became extremely discontented; insisted on his trying to interest for her some Englishmen at Naples, with whom she might return to her own country; and, on my refusing to do so, (said Alozzi), she attempted, as I found afterwards, to bribe the servants I had placed about her, to deliver letters for her to any English gentlemen they could hear of. These people have protested to me, that they resisted every attempt she made to engage them in this research:—nor could I ever discover by what means Mrs. Montalbert contrived to find the person with whom she concerted her measures so well, as to escape during the night, and to leave no trace by which I have since been able to discover wither she is gone; though I have hardly slept since, my dear friend, so anxious have I been to recover, if possible, this lovely misguided wanderer, and to restore her to you, as a precious deposit of which I was not an unworthy guardian!'

"I then inquired of Alozzi, if he had come to Florence on any hope of finding her there. He told me he had, but that all his inquiries being baffled, he was departing for Rome, still on the same search. This was not enough for me; I insisted on his particularizing the reasons he had to believe my wife had gone to Florence; this he appeared ready to do, and I thought them so plausible, that I resolved to go among my countrymen, who were then numerous at Florence, in hopes of learning something of my poor fugitive. This inquiry, which detained me a great while, and which it was extremely painful to make on so delicate a subject, ended only in convincing me that she was not at Florence; and though, from repeated conversations with Alozzi, I was far from being satisfied that Rosalie had not very different reasons for withdrawing herself from his protection, that those he had given, yet her impatience to be in England, or among persons of her own country, if not a paritality to some individual of it, made me only waver between doubt and despair, and happiness seemed certainly fled for ever."

Montalbert appeared so exhausted, that Lessington intreated him to take some refreshment; after which, all remaining quiet in the house, he thus continued his narrative.

CHAP.

"WHITHER was I now to go in search of Rosalie? mistrusting as I did Alozzi, and doubting when he affected to be most busy in the pursuit, whether he had not himself concealed her. I determined, however, not to part with him—if his intentions were honest, he might assist me in my search; if not, I should at least have the chance of detecting him, by his endeavours to evade me, or by some of those oversights by which the most artful men often betray themselves.

"I therefore accompanied Alozzi to Rome, where we made acquaintance with every Englishman, and endeavoured to discover from them the names of their countrymen who had within a few weeks left Rome for England, or any part of Italy; and in short made such enquiries as might lead to the object of our painful research. We gained, however, no satisfaction till at the end of a fortnight, when Alozzi came to tell me, he had met a *valet de place*, who had been accustomed to live much with the English at Rome; Alozzi said, the man was remarkably intelligent; that he had entered into discourse with him, and found that about three weeks before he had served (though for a few days) an Englishman of the name of Walsingham, who came from Naples, attended by a young lady with whom this man believed he had eloped; for that his conduct while at Rome seemed calculated to baffle pursuit and enquiry, and that after a short time they departed very mysteriously, but he had good reasons to believe they went to Genoa, there to embark for England. Alozzi brought the man to me; I questioned him, and from his description I soon thought that Rosalie was the lady whom he had seen with Mr. Walsingham. I heard with anguish not to be expressed that she was gay in spirits, and accompanied this Walsingham evidently by her own consent. She had no child with her; but if she had so far forgotten the father, as to follow another, she would have found no difficulty in abandoning her child.—The longer I talked with this man, the more clearly the fatal conviction flashed upon me.—The time answered exactly to that on which Rosalie had left the house where Alozzi had placed her: the character of Walsingham was that of a man of boundless expence, and unrestrained libertinism; all served to persuade my senses that he had stolen from me the person and the affections of Rosalie.—Indignation and rage now animated a pursuit which had before been prompted by tenderness and hope. With whatever resentment I thought of the infidelity of my wife, my heart turned with fondness towards my child, thus abandoned, as I imagined, to the mercy of strangers, yet I knew not where to seek him; and the desire of vengeance was even stronger than parental affection. After some consultation with Alozzi, it was agreed that he should return to Naples, where, by offering rewards, he had no doubt but he should discover my son, of whom he protested he would take a father's care, and send him to me by some trusty person, whithersoever I should direct. Alozzi departed, and I made the best of my way to Genoa; thither I traced persons resembling those I pursued, and on searching the registers kept at the *Dogana*, of people departing from that port, I found that about a fortnight before my arrival, Mr. Walsingham, an Englishman, with his lady and two servants, had embarked for England.

"I had now no doubt remaining—Rosalie passed for the wife of Walsingham, and as such was proceeding to her native country.

"Stung even to temporary madness, I adopted the sudden resolution of writing to my mother, reproaching her with the misery she had been the cause of, by compelling me to take measures which had torn me from the woman I adored, and with her all the happiness of my life; I told her that to make me any amends was impossible; that I should never see her more; but that if she were not totally lost to every feeling of humanity, I implored her to receive and protect my child, whom, by a letter written at the same time to Alozzi, I desired him to send to her. I hoped that even her bitter and inveterate prejudies might give way to pity and concern, when I could no long offend her, and when she saw in a lovely and innocent infant the representative of a son whom she had driven to despair.

"Having done this, I gave myself up wholly to that thirst of vengeance which devoured me, and took my passage to England in the first ship I could meet with, but for which I had the mortification of waiting a considerable time.

"Every perverse accident, to which a traveller by sea is subject, conspired to retard my passage. The ship was old, and a bad sailer; the captain had not enough men to work it, and of the few he had, two were confined to their hammocks by an infectious fever. We were continually beaten back by contrary winds, and the mortality increased in our little crew so much, that when we came into the Strait, I insisted upon being put on shore at Gibraltar, where, having taken the fever, I became extremely ill, and, after a confinement of near a month, narrowly escaped with my life. This cruel delay over, I once more embarked in a sloop of war, and was at length landed at Plymouth. In London I could not fail to hear of Mr. Walsingham, for there a man of his fortune must be known. I obtained a direction to his house in Grosvenor Street, where I heard that he was just gone to Brighthelmstone. I could not longer entertain a single doubt of my being right as to the person, for on enquiry of his servants I heard, that he was, a few weeks since, returned from a tour to Italy.

"I hastened, therefore, to Brighthelmstone, and to a house taken for the season by this Mr. Walsingham; I heard he was gone on a sailing party to Portsmouth and the Isle of Wight, but was expected back in a few days: his character answered to all I had heard of him abroad. Afraid of missing if I attempted to follow him, I resolved to await his return; but sleep forsook my pillow, and I wandered about from the dawn of the day, till the latest hour of night, without any other purpose than to wear away the tedious time that prevented my doing myself justice. It happened that I was sitting at a very early hour of the morning in one of the public libraries, where two of those *bon vivans* were also sitting, who regularly make tours during the summer months round the coast, to repair the excesses of their winter. I sat pensively silent, thinking on subjects, how different; when these two good cits began a discourse on the various advantages or disadvantages of different bathing places: one related to the other, that he had lately left Eastbourne; where, said he, 'I got poultry pretty reasonable, and the wheat-ears were beginning to flock. There was not, indeed, much company; but then there were people that cared not what they gave for any thing; there was the famous Lady Llancarrick, and a Miss Something, one of your book-making ladies, with her. To be sure I thought it a little oddish to see her Ladyship quite hand and glove not only with that Miss What-d'y-call'um, but with another young creature, who goes, you must know, by the name of Sheffield, but as the people there say, is the mistress of one Mr. Walsingham, a man of great fortune, who brought her from abroad.—My son Jack, who came down to me from Friday to Tuesday, and is a mighty chap for a pretty face, fell downright in love with this fine madam—though, to do her justice, she looks very modest for one of that sort; and egad, Sir, it was as much as I could do to keep him from making up to her—Why, Jack, (says I), don't you see she is countenanced by Lady Llancarrick. He laughed, and said, the lady herself was no better than she should be, and he'd make love to them all three.'

"Imagine, Mr. Lessington, what I felt at hearing this conversation.—I knew not what I said to the man, but he told me, with many bows, and some gasping grimaces, all he knew; among other particulars, that the lady had a child with her; and then they both walked away, probably much amazed at my inquisitiveness and violence; while listening to nothing but my rage and indignation, I ordered a post-chaise, and taking a lawyer with me, and a person to attend on the child, I sat out for Eastbourne: as you have heard Rosalie's account, you know that I saw her but a for a moment: I could not indeed bear to look upon her—she was walking with the two women I had heard described:—I fled from her, and directing my son to be brought to me, I hastened back in a state of distraction, weeping over the innocent unhappy boy, now accusing his mother of cruelty, and now protesting I would never think of her more.

"I believe nothing saved me from attempting my own life, but my determined resolution to obtain satisfaction of Walsingham.—I waited a few days longer, and when he was returned, I sent to him a military friend, whom I met by accident, and who told me he was slightly acquainted with Walsingham. I stated my complaint, and this friend, Captain Wilmot, carried him a challenge from me, to meet at any hour he appointed the next day.

"When Wilmot came back, he assured me, that Walsingham was extremely willing to meet me, if I insisted on it; but that he protested he knew not for what, having never seen Mrs. Montalbert in his life, and being totally unconscious of having ever done me the least injury. This falsehood only irritated my impatience—But Wilmot advised me to recollect whether there might not be some mistake in all this? 'I do not,' said he, 'know much of Sommers Walsingham, but I am sure his courage is not to be doubted; and as to an affair of gallantry, he is much more likely to boast of, than to deny it. I am persuaded, that had he eloped with Mrs. Montalbert, he would very readily have given you the satisfaction you demand.'—More enraged than ever at what I could not but think a base and cowardly evasion, and almost ready to quarrel with Wilmot himself, I was determined to seek Walsingham instantly, and compel him to give an explanation—but Wilmot, who saw that some mischief must happen if I did, prevailed upon me to let him return once more to Walsingham.—He came back in about an hour, and declared to me that Walsingham had given him such a detail of the circumstances of his life for that last six months, that he was perfectly convinced he had never had the slightest acquaintance with Mrs. Montalbert.—'Good God!' exclaimed I; 'this is *too* much—did I not trace him from Rome to Genoa; do I not know that the woman who accompanied him must have been my wife?'

'My dear friend,' said Wilmot, 'Walsingham acknowledges that he had a lady with him, but declares it was not Mrs. Montalbert.—He has told me who it was, and, if you insist upon it, the lady who is not far from hence will satisfy you as to her identity. Can you suppose, Montalbert (added Wilmot, very gravely), that I have so little regard for you, or hold your honour of so little moment, that I would trifle with, or deceive you? If you insist of fighting, I am ready to attend you.—But I repeat, that in the grounds of this quarrel I do believe you are wrong.'—I knew Wilmot to be a man of unblemished honour, and of undoubted courage; and though it yet seemed impossible that I could be deceived, I hesitated. At that moment Charles Vyvian came to me.

'Not less rash, or less irritated than myself, for he had read Sommers Walsingham's letter, Wilmot (who was even more acquainted with him than with me), had the greatest difficulty imaginable to persuade him to hear what he had to say. At length it was settled, that as he knew the person of my wife, he should go with Wilmot to the lady; and if he was convinced that she had accompanied Walsingham from Italy, which he thought he should easily discover, it was agreed that I could have no quarrel with him.—This lady was at a small town, about twenty miles from Brighthelmstone, on the London road; and thither my friends repaired, with the consent of Sommers Walsingham. Towards evening I expected their return; I went out alone upon the hills, where I was accosted by a gentleman, whom my servant had, at his own request, accompanied in search of me. He told me, with very little preface, that his name was Walsingham; that on hearing I was in search of him, and that some disagreeable circumstances were likely to happen by my having mistaken for him a relation of the same name, he had come from Eastbourne on purpose to give me the explanation I demanded. I will not repeat to you the manner in which I treated Mr. Walsingham; my trembling servant, who dared not disobey me, brought the loaded pistols I sent him for; I absolutely refused to hear what Walsingham would have said.—The words, 'I came from Eastbourne;' and '*it WAS I—who accompanied Mrs. Montalbert from Italy*,' were enough for me.—When he found me deaf to his intended vindication, he took a pistol, and bade me fire mine.—I did so—with too good an air! the ball lodged in his side; he did not however fall: but firing his pistol in the air, he beckoned to my servant, whom I had driven with menaces to some distance; the poor fellow ran to him, and Walsingham, who had thrown away his pistol, leaning against him, said, 'I am wounded—I believe mortally: lay me on the ground; go call some persons to be witness that your master has acted like a man of honour, and that I acquit him of my death.'—I had in the mean time approached him; and guilty as I still believed him, I could not see the paleness of death on his face without anguish and remorse; he was lying on the ground, and seemed, amidst the pain which his countenance expressed, more solicitous for my safety than his own life.—Touched by his generosity, I bade my man fly for surgeons: and when he was gone, I knelt by the suffering Walsingham with sensations of mingled rage and regret, which cannot be described, while he thus spoke to me:

'Mr. Montalbert, it is probable I have but a few hours to live:—hear me, I conjure you, when I declare upon the honour of a dying man, that your wife is as innocent as an angel; that I have ever treated her as a beloved sister; and that you will be guilty of the most cruel injustice in throwing her from you. I have not breath to tell you what strange circumstance it happened that I was the instrument to release her from the power of your mother, who had her confined at Formiscusa. I feel very faint.—They tell me you have taken her child from her, and that she is reduced to the brink of the grave by sorrow.....Restore her child—restore to her you affections, and try to make her happy—she deserves all your tenderness; and—if it should happen, as I am persuaded it will, that you are convinced you have been too rash—let not any remorse for what has happened disturb your tranquility.—*I* am a being, who have long been weary of life—and for me Death has no horrors.—*You* may for many years constitute and share in the happiness of an amiable woman; and it is some satisfaction to me, to think you will one day know that I was incapable of injuring you.'

"He spoke slowly and with difficulty—*I* was incapable of answering!—but again he earnestly urged me to save myself by flight.—I incoherently told him, I hoped his wound was not mortal.—'I hope not, (said he)—but if it should, I intreat you, for the sake of Mrs. Montalbert, to take care of yourself.'—By this time my servant was come up with a surgeon; before he could decide whether the wound was likely to be fatal, or how he could attempt moving poor Walsingham, Sommers Walsingham, Wilmot, and Vyvian, arrived together with a chair, which they had the precaution to bring with them.

"I cannot relate what now passed.—Before the wounded man would consent to being moved, he insisted that the persons present should listen to the solemn declaration he made, that I had used him honourably, and was in no way to blame. I own this magnanimity, from a man whom I have perhaps injured, has deeply affected me. He bade my friends insist on my leaving the place, and Vyvian, I hardly knew how, forced me into a post chaise as soon as he had seen Walsingham's wound probed; for, till he had brought me some intelligence of him, I would not stir.—The surgeon had not yet attempted to extract the ball; nor could they pronounce with any certainty, but they entertained great fears for his life. Sommers Walsingham went off to London express, to bring down some very eminent man of the profession; and at the repeated intreaties of Walsingham I came hither, without, however, meaning to withdraw myself from any inquiry that may be made—if he dies! - - - - - -

'You will, I fear, have too much reason to reproach yourself, (interrupted Lessington).———You never received then a letter, which, from her journal, I see our poor Rosalie sent to you from Marseilles, under cover to the English Ambassador at Naples?'

'Never! (replied Montalbert).—But has my wife then kept a journal—and may I not see it?'

'If you will be calm, (said Lessington), I will put it into your hands.'———Montalbert, subdued as he was, was beginning to be conscious of his own rashness, promised all that was asked of him; and in this perusal passed the rest of the night; Lessington continually going to the door of Rosalie's chamber, where he found her much more quiet than he had ventured to expect.

At a very early hour of the morning, two post chaises stopped near the house. From one of them came Vyvian, with the little Montalbert and his maid; from the other, the physician who had attended Rosalie......Poor Montalbert saw them enter without having the power to speak. He questioned by looks the countenance of Vyvian, but found nothing that encouraged him to ask after Walsingham.—Vyvian, however, understood him, and said, "Walsingham is alive, and his case not desperate, though certainly dangerous."

"Thank God! (exclaimed Montalbert), I may yet then taste of satisfaction!"———"Be not too sanguine, (answered Vyvian); but I am all impatience to know the state of our poor Rosalie!"———Overcome by sensations so acute and various, Montalbert sat in breathless anxiety; his tears fell on the face of his child as he pressed him to his heart, and he cast an earnest look towards the door, as he heard the steps of the physician descending from Rosalie's room.

He gave, however, a better account of her than they had dared to promise themselves; and, as he had heard from Vyvian a sketch of her story in consequence of his attendance on Walsingham, he ventured to advise that Rosalie might, as soon as possible, have her child restored to her, and be told that her husband was returned.

"Mrs. Montalbert's illness, (said he), is so evidently occasioned by uneasiness and fear, that my art can do nothing while those causes exist; remove them, and she will soon, I believe, be restored to health."

Montalbert then ventured to say—"But, Sir, if this unfortunate Mr. Walsingham should die?"

"I hope, though I cannot say he will not!" answered Dr. F———.

"But at all events, (interrupted Ormsby, who having just heard what had passed, now joined them)—at all events let my daughter see her little boy; and you, Sir, (continued he, turning to Montalbert)—you, I hope, will now do her justice—you will."

"It is not yet time, dear Mr. Ormsby, (said Lessington), to discuss many points, which, I hope, we shall amicably talk over hereafter.....Mr. Montalbert allows that the conduct of my sister has been unexceptionable, and that of Mr. Walsingham most generous."

"It is I only, (said Montalbert, in a mournful and somewhat stern voice)—it is I alone who have been to blame."

Lessington, fearful of what might follow, cried hastily—"We can none of us think that.—Alas! which of us, situated as you were, might not have acted as you did!"

Dr. F——— now departed, promising to send a messenger from Brighthelmstone, with the opinion of the surgeons, as soon as the gentleman (Sommers Walsingham) expected was arrived; and Lessington went up to prepare Rosalie for the sight of her child.

She had no sooner in her arms this darling of affection, than she seemed to have obtained a new existence. Lessington thought he might then venture to tell her, at least part, of what had passed, concealing, however, the sad effects of Montalbert's passionate suspicions.

When he told her, her husband was in the house, she declared herself able to see him—for the slight view she had of him before seemed like a dream. She no sooner beheld him, than she attempted but vainly, to speak, while he, far from yielding to those transports of joy which he would have felt had not Walsingham been in danger, was wretched, though apparently restored to the bosom of happiness; and shuddered, as he thought, that Rosalie was perhaps embracing the murderer of her generous preserver, and one who might soon be an exile from her and from his country!

This painful suspence continued some days, for the situation of Walsingham was long doubtful after the arrival of his surgeon from London. Rosalie, though she did not yet leave her room, for she continued extremely weak, could not fail to remark the gloom that hung over her friends, and particularly Montalbert, who often fell into deep and melancholy reveries; then, suddenly starting, listened to any noise in the house, watched every one entering at the door, and seemed frequently so uneasy, that Rosalie, however, willing to impute his inquietude to the situation he was in with regard to his mother, which he had told her of, could not but discover that something of more immediate import pressed on his mind; she had never ventured since their reconciliation to name Walsingham.—Too well aware from the slight and half-stifled narrative she had received from her brother and her father, that Montalbert's jealousy had been the cause of the step he had taken as to her child, she feared to awaken it anew by naming him, while Montalbert, observing her caution, felt hurt that she did not speak to him openly and candidly—and these concealed sensations on both sides occasioned a sort of restraint that rendered them far from happy.

As Rosalie every day became better, and thought herself well enough to leave a place which reminded her of many days of suspence and uneasiness, she felt some surprise that neither her father nor Montalbert proposed her removal, for they had concealed from her their debates on this subject, which had not passed without some asperity on Montalbert's part. Conscious of high birth, and of his right to an ample property, he did not reflect, without bitterness of heart, on his reserve of fortune.—Instead of raising his wife to high affluence, he found himself and his son now almost entirely dependent on Mr. Ormsby, who, though related to him by blood, the notions he had acquired among foreign nobility taught him to consider as a merchant and an adventurer for gain. Ormsby, on the other hand, had been so long used to the most perfect obedience to his will from every body about him, that he was hurt at the little submission which Montalbert showed to his wishes, when he expressed an intention of making a considerable purchase, and placing Rosalie as mistress of his house and fortune. Montalbert fancied that Ormsby would not be sorry if the fatal termination of Walsingham's accident compelled him to go abroad; but secretly determined, if it did, that no considerations of interest should induce him to leave his wife and child in England.—Ormsby was not only conscious that he should have been happier to have found his daughter single, but fancied the sentiment justified by the pride and violence which he thought natural to Montalbert's character.

These heart-burnings between two persons, on whom the happiness of Rosalie so entirely depended, gave extreme concern to Lessington, and kept him from returning home, notwithstanding the repeated letters he received from his wife. Vyvian saw with equal concern that there was no cordiality between them; but the situation of Walsingham, whom he had twice visited, and whose character had impressed him with the highest esteem, was a source of still deeper regret.

How strange is the disposition of human events! Rosalie, who but a very few days back suffered every possible calamity, now saw her husband returned, her child restored, her father in safety, and master of an ample fortune (circumstances which even in her most sanguine moments she never ventured to flatter herself with); yet, with all these blessings united, Rosalie was not happy; and had she known the situation of Walsingham, would have been extremely miserable.

Convinced, however, that something very serious occasioned the restlessness and anxiety which seemed to increase on every face that approached her, from some unguarded expressions, as well as from the extreme solicitude with which they had been explained away, Rosalie caught some vague suspicions of the truth, she contrived to question Claudine so narrowly, that the poor girl, who had long been sadly overweighed with secret, burst into tears, and disclosed all she knew.

Disqualified as Rosalie was to bear such a shock, the necessity of supporting it with calmness immediately occurred to her. Claudine, already terrified at what she had done, besought her to say nothing to Mr. Ormsby, whom she heard upon the stairs—but her countenance betrayed her too evidently what had passed: hardly, however, had she time to attempt evading her father's questions, when Montalbert appeared, and the necessity of her artificial tranquility became more pressing. Vyvian and Lessington were walking; something like conversation was attempted between Ormsby and Montalbert, but it would have flagged, if Claudine, who dreaded their observations, had not opportunely brought the child, in whom the all took an equal interest. A packet, however, was brought into the room by the mistake of the servant, on which Montalbert had no sooner cast his eyes, then he changed countenance, and betrayed such violent emotion, that Rosalie, concluding Walsingham was dead, had only resolution enough left to avoid betraying, otherwise than by her features, the extreme pain this idea gave her. Montalbert, trembling with impatient dread, tore the letter half open: then recollecting himself, hastened out of the room, and Ormsby, who guessed that it brought some fatal intelligence, followed him.

The letter, however, instead of bringing to Montalbert the cruel intelligence he expected, was to this effect:

"DEAR SIR,:

"I have insisted on being allowed to write this letter, to satisfy those fears which the people about me have, I know, given you. My friend Bernard permits me to tell you myself, that he believe I shall in a few days be well enough to remove by slow journies to London, whither his business calls him so pressingly, that he can no longer attend me here; and as we have been friends from our childhood, I find myself so much happier in his than in other hands, whatever may be their skill, that I am resolved to accompany him. You will conclude from this, that all the dangerous symptoms which have hung about me are removed; and I trust that the pain this affair has given you will no longer interrupt your present happiness.—For you must be happy, Montalbert, with so amiable a woman!

"As soon as I am quite well I shall return to the Continent.—Consider whether I can do you any service with Signora Belcastro. It is not possible, that, from misrepresentations, her general prejudice may have been raised into particular dislike?—I own to you, that from Mrs. Montalbert's account, as well as from other circumstances, I fear Alozzi has been less sincerely your friend than you have believed. Perhaps I may be the fortunate means of undeceiving your mother; and you will really oblige me, by giving me an opportunity of being useful to you, either in this or in any other way.

"If Vyvian would come over to see me, before I go, it would give me pleasure.—I hope our friendship, however unpleasantly begun, will be permanent.—Permit me to offer to Mrs. Montalbert my most respectful good wishes; my dear little ward and fellow traveller, is not old enough to remember me, but I shall always recollect him with pleasure. Adieu, dear Sir, I have exceeded Bernard's permission, and must hastily assure you, that I am your most faithful servant,

"F. WALSINGHAM."

This letter, though evidently written in pain and languor, took from the heart of Montalbert such a weight, that he seemed suddenly restored to happiness and reason. He determined to go over himself with Vyvian to visit this generous man, who had suffered so much for his inestimable services, and unparalleled goodness, and, forgetting all his former precautions, he was hastening to show the letter to Rosalie, as soon as her father had read it, when the entrance of Lessington and Vyvian prevented him.

Montalbert and Vyvian agreed to set out immediately, and Lessington undertook to relate to Rosalie the truths which had been so long concealed from her.—He found her already informed of all but the late relief from their apprehensions. She could not hear of the sufferings of her benefactor, and of his unexampled generosity, without great emotion: Lessington bade her indulge it, but still fearing lest Montalbert should again feel suspicious, which had already cost him so much, she tried to check her tears when Montalbert appeared—but it was impossible. And he, by a thousand tender apologies, intreated her to forgive his rashness and injustice, and encouraged her to indulge those tears, which a little relieved her oppressed heart.

Montalbert, Lessington, and Vyvian, now set out on their visit, the two latter took leave of Rosalie: Lessington returning into Oxfordshire, and Vyvian having determined to accompany Walsingham to London.

During the short absence of her husband, Ormsby talked over with his daughter their future plans of life. It was probable that Montalbert, however his pride might be hurt, would not now oppose the wishes of Ormsby, who seemed to place all his satisfaction in bestowing on his daughter a degree of affluence, which should set her even above the daughters of Vyvian, who had despised and contemned her: but Rosalie represented to her father, that, beyond a certain point, fortune contributed nothing to real happiness; that whatever attracted towards her the eyes of the world, would quicken the envy and malignity with which her story would be related, and could not fail to reflect on the beloved memory of her mother. To this argument Ormsby was compelled to yield, and he found himself under the necessity, however painful, of continuing to conceal from the world the relationship in which he stood to Rosalie, wishing it to remain as much as secret as a circumstance could do already known to so many persons, and which, during Rosalie's illness, no pains had been taken to conceal.

Montalbert returned more deeply impressed than ever with the generosity of Walsingham. He had, however, paid all the pecuniary obligations Rosalie owed him, and they parted with mutual professions of friendship.

In a few days afterwards Mr. and Mrs. Montalbert, and their little boy, went round the coast into Kent, and took a house near Margate for the rest of the summer, while Ormsby made a tour through the western countries in search of a purchase for his daughter, where, at a small distance, he might find a residence for himself.

Montalbert, whose natural infirmities of temper had been chastised and corrected by the events which had so nearly deprived him of the felicity he enjoyed, seemed now to think that he could never make sufficient amends to his charming wife for the injury he had done her, by giving way to suspicions she so little deserved. About three months after his removal to London, Walsingham went to Italy, where, by means of some Italian friends of high rank, he procured an introduction to Signora Belcastro, and gradually contrived to inform her of the share he had had in delivering her daughter-in-law from her usurped power, while he undeceived her in regard to many representations made by Alozzi, who, finding himself baffled in designs, which the absence and probable death of Montalbert had occasioned him to form, had really been, in his turn, the dupe of Signora Belcastro, and had followed the scent she had artfully given, that Rosalie had eloped with an Englishman.——Walsingham acquired so much influence over the mind of this strange woman, that though he could not prevail upon her to forgive her son for having married as he did, she at length relented in favour of his children, and settled upon them what she had intended for their father, to whom, however, her pride and Walsingham's persuasions prevailed upon her to allow a handsome annual income.

Montalbert enjoyed, at a small but beautiful place on the coast of Dorsetshire, with which Ormsby had presented his wife, more happiness than usually falls to the lot of humanity. Rosalie passed her life in studying how to contribute to his felicity, and that of her father, and, by her sweetness and attention, she won them both from those little asperities and difference of temper which had once threatened to destroy their domestic comfort.

But notwithstanding the cheerful and even gay letters which Walsingham wrote to his friends, letters which greatly contributed to the happiness of Rosalie, who retained for him the most grateful regard, he was still an unhappy wanderer; and when he had done all he could to restore Montalbert to his mother's favour, and was no longer animated by the hope of serving Rosalie, he sunk again into that cold despondence, which a sensible heart feels when the world around is as a desert. The agonies with which he had wept over the grave of his Leonora had been suspended by the almost imperceptible attachment which had crept into his bosom for Rosalie, and which he had indulged but too much, after there appeared some probability that Montalbert was no more.

The last letters he wrote to England informed his friends that he was setting out on a tour through Spain and Portugal; and that finding himself more than ever disposed to wander, he thought it not improbable but that he might go from thence to the Cape, and so to the East Indies.——In the pursuit of science and knowledge he found consolation, when no benevolent action offered itself to satisfy his philanthropy; but so generally is misery diffused, that there were few places which did not offer objects for this indulgence—though none could interest him like the amiable Being whom he had released from the dreary confinement of Formiscusa, and restored to the possession of the happiness she now enjoyed—a happiness which alone could soften the sadness of his own destiny!!!

THE END.

CPSIA information can be obtained
at www.ICGtesting.com
Printed in the USA
LVHW101348061021
699701LV00009B/449